THE HUMMINGBIRD

The Hummingbird

ISBN print: 978-1-7324984-4-0
ISBN ebook: 978-1-7324984-5-7

Library of Congress Control Number: 2017946110

Cover Art by Kim G Design
https://www.kimg-design.com/

Second Edition: October 2018

THIS ONE'S FOR MY MOM, CIARA, AND FRED, AND TO ALL THE BELIEVERS. MAKE A WISH!

"As long as the hummingbird had not abandoned the land, somewhere there were still flowers, and they could all go on."

– Leslie Marmon Silko

CHAPTER ONE

THE OLD WORLD:
CASTLE RUINS / TRAINING GROUNDS

Enzo DiLegno could've summarized his new life in Florindale in two words.

"Think fast!"

Sometimes those two words meant Violet was coming and he had to put away his notes. Other days, it was just his father tossing an apple at him. Today the words preceded the twang of a bow, the swish of an arrow, and a pointed projectile sailing directly for his head. Enzo ducked, stumbled out of the way, and backed into a cool sharp object that poked his back.

Whipping around, he raised his sword and stared his opponent in the eyes, getting lost in the deep emerald pools. "Come on, Puppet Boy!" Rosana taunted. "I know I'm pretty, but if you get distracted again"—she pointed up in the rafters of the castle ruins, where Tahlia Rose stood with her bow in hand and a sly grin beneath her eyepatch—"Tahlia's really going to hit you next time."

Completely unfair, Enzo thought. "Why's Tahlia here? So it's two against one now?"

"Nope." Rosana shook her head, her dark hair spilling out beneath her helmet. "Three."

Enzo rolled out of the way in time for another arrow to spill from the opposite direction, where Augustine Rose took her post and reached into her quiver.

"Three?" Enzo cut another arrow from the sky and parried a blow from Rosana, who torpedoed through the area with swan-like grace. "C'mon, Zack never ganged up on me like this!" A small pang of sadness hit Enzo in the stomach. His best friends had been gone too long already, to the point that even Violet was starting to worry. They're okay, Enzo told himself. "I swear, when they come back from Neverland—"

"Your bro crush isn't going to save you, my dear." Rosana kicked out, and Enzo stepped backward and countered with an overhand cut that Rosana dodged with incredible ease. "This is a war, Enzo, you and I have got to push each other a little harder if we want to be prepared for what's coming!"

Smack! Their swords crossed in midair, and another arrow soared past Enzo's cheek.

"Then hit me for once," Enzo taunted. "Slowpoke."

Clang! Rosana whipped around and hit Enzo in the side. "You can hit me back, you know. I promise I won't break."

Enzo blocked another attack. "My dad would never approve of me hitting a lady."

Rosana used her blade to scoop Enzo's shoulder plate off his armor and knock it to the ground, exposing his skin. "Guess Avoria wins then, if Mr. DiLegno told you not to hit her."

Enzo drove his knee into Rosana's stomach plate. "Kicking, though . . ."

"That's more like it!" Rosana flew at Enzo with lightning speed, and the two danced with the swords clinging and clanging in midair, raising a film of sweat on his forehead. He knew he'd grown stronger since he arrived in Florindale because his armor no longer slowed him down. Sword training with Mulan, combat with Jacob, obstacle courses with the miners, and the general day-to-day life in Florindale had done him well. He'd put on some muscle since the day he left home with Pietro, and according to Rosana, the change looked good.

He especially appreciated Rosana pushing him to his limits. They always agreed to protect each other no matter what, and sometimes that meant training each other until their fingers bled.

"Somebody yield already!" Tahlia yelled, nocking an arrow. "You two are ridiculous!"

Augustine Rose sipped her tea and reloaded her quiver. "Patience, dear. You cannot rush these things, you know. Do you know how long it took me to catch the chameleon wolf?"

Another arrow hit the ground near Enzo's foot.

"Not as long as it's taking these two to stop making out and start hitting each other already."

"Tahlia Rose!"

"Sorry, Grandma. It's just true."

Twang!

A hot pain exploded in Enzo's shoulder, and he looked down to see an arrow protruding from his skin where Rosana exposed him. A rivulet of blood trickled into his armor. "Ouch! Dammit! Time out."

"Ooo, good shot, Tahlia!" Augustine cried, pumping a fist in the air.

Rosana threw her sword to the ground and studied Enzo's wound. "Let me see."

Enzo winced and sat down. This sort of injury wasn't uncommon for training. The Order of the Bell took precautions to make sure nobody fatally injured each other, but minor battle wounds weren't out of the question. This was Enzo's second arrow to the skin.

While Augustine and Tahlia climbed down from their towers, Violet, the fairy guardian of the realm, glided out from between two trees in the Woodlands, where she'd set up her new den to keep watch on the Order. She had agreed to take charge on any healing that needed to be done, as long as the group agreed they would train hard every day and promise not to hold back. However, her healing didn't usually come without some sort of lecture on the importance of training harder, better, and ensuring that "this doesn't happen again."

Violet stopped in front of the group, her one wing glistening in the moonlight. Enzo still wasn't used to the sight of the charred stump where her other wing should've been. She leaned over and inspected the arrow sticking out of Enzo's shoulder. "Which one of you hit him?"

Tahlia raised her hand. "That was me."

Violet stroked her chin. "Ladies, you are free to go."

While Augustine and Tahlia turned around and left, Rosana kissed Enzo on the cheek and said, "I promised my mom I'd have some dinner with her tonight, but I'll see you tomorrow?"

Enzo nodded. "Sure thing. Tell Ms. T I said hey."

Rosana flicked Enzo on the tip of the nose and turned around. "You can call her Alice you know. Puppet Boy."

As Rosana walked away, Violet took out her wand and tapped Enzo's shoulder, a tingling sensation spreading through his skin. Enzo couldn't bring himself to look right away. It made his stomach crawl to see pointed objects sticking out of other people's skin. He glanced at the ground instead, where he found Rosana's red cloak lying at his feet. He turned around to call out and let her know, but she was already out of sight.

"You need to hold still." Violet gripped Enzo's elbow with her free hand and continued to tap around his wound. "My point is proven, by the way. You are not ready to cross into the New World. Avoria and her shadows will eat you alive."

Enzo sighed. He'd asked her time and time again if he could go next and help join the fight, but her answer was always the same. "The New World is my world." He winced as the arrow pushed itself out of his shoulder and clattered to the ground. A minty tingle filled the hole, and he watched as bits of light crackled on his skin and fused the wound back together. "I know it better than anyone here, except for maybe Rosana."

"Don't you forget: I've been there, too, Crescenzo." Violet released his elbow.

"Yeah, hiding in the Hollywood Hills playing house." Enzo flexed his arm and rubbed his shoulder, amazed at how fast the magic worked along with the fact that Violet actually pronounced his true name correctly. His skin was good as new, though a little raw and pink where the wound was. "I grew up there. It's still my home. I want to go back and help."

Violet straightened her back and shook her head. "No, my dear. Your role was to bring us all together, not to march up to Avoria's doorstep and get yourself killed. We haven't heard from Jacob Isaac Holmes in days! Or James and the Volos! I cannot have that happen to you too, Enzo. Go back to your family, and be grateful for your life." She picked up the arrow and held it in front of Enzo's face. "Maybe you should keep this as a reminder that you're not invincible."

Sensing that the argument was pointless, Enzo gritted his teeth and turned on his heel. Why did Violet have to be so unreasonable? As much as Enzo recognized she was coming from a good place, her stubbornness made his blood churn. She's doing this all wrong. Days ago, she sent the Volos to Neverland with Captain Hook to recruit the Lost Boys. At the same time, she sent Jacob Isaac Holmes with a squad of five Hearts to gather intel in the New World. She's scattering us. We need to stand together. That's how we won the war in Wonderland.

Enzo shivered. Wonderland pushed him beyond physical, mental, and emotional limits he didn't know he could reach. Sometimes he'd wake up sweating, the mad King of Hearts's face burned into his mind. And here he was preparing for another war that would decide the fate of his home and everyone he loved.

She's not going to stand in my way. Enzo turned again and watched Violet retreat back into the Woodlands. I have to get past her somehow.

Over the hills, four more people appeared in the moonlight, each armored up in leather and fur and dark plates. They marched toward the Woodlands and carried small packs, quivers, and daggers, and they were the oddest-looking bunch Enzo could have imagined.

Jack Frost, the tallest, looked as pale as Enzo had ever seen him. Once upon a time, Jack had been the Lord of Winter—a conjurer of snow—and Avoria sapped that power from him. Cinderella was said to have been one of Florindale's sweetest, but she came back from Wonderland with fire in her eyes. Quasimodo had long resolved never to come down from Clocher de Pierre, but when Violet offered to induct him into the Order, he descended immediately and picked up a bow. Jinn stood no taller than his sword, but his will was bigger than anybody knew.

What are they doing? Enzo thought as they disappeared into the Woodlands.

Enzo picked up Rosana's cloak and threw it over his body. He looked down and saw nothing where his arms, torso, or legs should be. I'm not here, he thought. You can't see me.

He hurried into the forest, a place that always set him a little on edge. Laced with the beauty of the glistening leaves and the songs of the owls, there was always a pervasive feeling that something could be watching him. He'd heard legends of the chameleon wolves, the witch Hansel and Gretel defeated, and so many oddities that it was hard not to be on guard.

Enzo stopped and peered around a large oak, where the group of four stood with Violet and—Grandpa! Geppetto stood next to her with arms crossed and a smile on his face. Enzo steadied his breathing and tiptoed closer to hear what they were saying.

"Are the four of you ready?" Violet said. "Take these hand mirrors with you. I want to know about every corner of the Citadel, every shadow in the streets, and what Avoria has done to that realm. I'm sorry you'll miss the coronation in a couple days, but such is the nature of war."

Sweat coated Enzo's palms. No way. She's sending them to the New

World! Not to mention with a set of mirrors—the very objects that exposed them to Avoria in the first place years ago.

"You must maintain constant contact, and above all, you must remain safe. You may defend yourselves if attacked. You are not to engage any enemies without provocation. This is reconnaissance. It is important that we do not show our hand. Understood?"

The squad of four responded with a chorus of ayes, yeses, and huzzahs.

I've gotta get out there, Enzo thought. This is the chance I've been looking for.

"Geppetto, please carve the door open."

"Certo, Miss Violet."

Enzo watched in awe as his grandfather stepped forward, flicked out his ivory dagger, and approached the thickest tree in the forest. Carver magic can put us through? The idea seemed so simple that Enzo couldn't believe he'd never thought of it. After all, he and his grandfather carved their way out of Wonderland only weeks ago. Since then, Enzo had only been practicing on his figurines, training with Geppetto once a week. Could I really carve my way back home?

Geppetto placed a hand on the bark of the tree and shut his eyes. Enzo knew his grandfather was working to understand the energy of the tree. Carvers feel the living souls of the world around us, Geppetto once said. Then we set them free. Geppetto took his dagger and plunged it into the tree. A bright light burst from the bark and illuminated the forest. Enzo threw his hands over his eyes for a minute, and when he uncovered them, a white doorway stood in the tree.

There's no way I can miss my chance. If I don't go now . . . Enzo's heart thudded in his chest. He had to follow the group. And because Rosana left her cloak behind, this was his one and only chance to slip past Violet and his grandfather unseen.

Sorry, Rosana.

Violet curtseyed to her squad of four, and Geppetto saluted them with a reverent gaze.

"May the light be with you," Violet said. "Until we meet again!"

Jack Frost nodded once. "We won't let you down."

With that, the four formed a line headed by Cinderella, and she marched through the doorway with the other three at her heels. Their bodies turned to shadows in the light, and then they faded to nothing.

Enzo ran like he'd never run before, the autumn wind rushing at his cheeks and the crunch of boots on leaves filling the air.

Geppetto shivered. "Are we sure this is the right thing?"

"Yes. They've trained all they could. Now to seal up the door." Violet raised her wand and aimed it at the tree. She drew back her arm as if preparing to throw something, and then she stopped cold, a perplexed expression in her eyes. "Do you hear that?"

"Footsteps," Geppetto answered, staring right through Enzo and then at his feet. "Look at the leaves on the ground! Who goes there?"

With only a few more running steps, Enzo approached the doorway and jumped through.

Light swallowed him, only to be extinguished in a heartbeat with a swift cut to black as if somebody threw a light switch. His ears popped, and a biting cold set in on his bones. He opened his eyes and saw snow falling all around his feet, blanketing towers around him in a layer of frost.

This is New York City!

But not the New York I know.

He'd been here twice before, once with his parents and once with Pietro, where he first met Rosana and began this crazy journey. Enzo turned in a full circle. He'd emerged from a tree, where the faint outline of a door stared back from the frosted trunk. All around him, skyscrapers still scratched the heavens, but many of them either withered back to scaffolding, lost a few stories on top, or had simply become an abandoned shell. There was no indication that anybody still lived here. He couldn't even find the four warriors that arrived before him. He'd never felt so small.

Worst of all, far ahead of him, the most massive structure he'd ever seen sat in the middle of the city, an oppressive citadel of crystal, glass, and shadow. Enzo traced it from the ground—where a mass of people in black hooded cloaks stood at the gates—all the way to the sky, where he lost sight of the top.

That's where Avoria is. He'd never been surer about anything.

Enzo flexed his fingers, numb at the tips. He needed shelter. He needed to find out where Cinderella and the group went.

He dipped into the closest building, an abandoned movie theater rife with the tang of old popcorn, the sizzle of flickering neon and static fizzle of dying arcade screens, and the squelch of sticky, soda-encrusted tile. Theaters were among Enzo's favorite places to be, but he hoped he wouldn't have to stay in this one for long. He grabbed a pack of licorice from the concession stand and tore it open, his stomach churning. To his surprise, the sweet candy was still fresh enough to chew without much effort.

When the theater door burst open, Enzo ducked behind the counter and threw the cloak over himself again, his heart in overdrive when the door handle smacked against the wall. Had somebody seen him?

"I want him found immediately," an icy, feminine voice sounded. Two pairs of footsteps, booted and heavy, echoed on the sticky floor. "I can't have the Order of the Bell on my streets for even one minute. General, sweep this whole floor. I shall go upstairs. You may use force to bring him into submission."

"My Queen."

Enzo poked his head out, hardly daring to breathe. Standing in the lobby were a man in a long black hood, and a tall, bone-white woman with long fiery hair.

Queen Avoria herself.

Enzo ducked back down and squeezed his eyes shut. *How did she find me so fast?*

Regret burrowed in Enzo's brain. This was a terrible idea. All this time he'd been so bent on proving Violet wrong—on insisting that he was ready to fight for the New World—and here he was, alone with the soul-stealing queen of the three worlds. He thought about the arrow and rubbed his shoulder where Tahlia pierced him. *Definitely not invincible. I'm dead.* He wished more than anything that this were a nightmare, but the scent in the air was far too real.

Enzo looked around him for something he could use to defend himself. *I could take her by surprise,* he thought, eyeing the popcorn machine, the hot dog tongs, and the carving knife in his sheath. *I can end this whole thing right now.*

Avoria clicked up the stairs, leaving Enzo in the presence of the general.

The general took slow, careful steps, peeling back curtains and opening theater doors. He knocked over a velvet rope and checked the box office, dark and cobwebbed. When he finished his search in the ticket booth, he shut the door and started toward the concession stand, raising the hairs on Enzo's arms.

"I know you're here," the general said. "But you cannot hide forever. Why not make this easy, Beastie? Come out and surrender!"

Beastie?

As if on cue, a terrible, inhuman cry sounded from the second floor, rumbling the building.

Jacob! Enzo would know that roar anywhere, but he had never heard such pain from the largest and strongest original member of the Order of the Bell.

The general sprinted upstairs toward the source of the noise.

Enzo unsheathed his carving knife and crawled out from behind the concession stand. *I'm coming, Jacob.*

But before Enzo could even reach the stairs, Avoria and the hooded general emerged again with Jacob Isaac Holmes squirming and writhing in their arms. Four more hooded men and women rushed through the doors to meet them and distributed his weight among the group.

Enzo's spirits deflated. *Jacob . . . I can't take five of them plus Avoria all at once. But I can find out where you're going and make a plan to get you out.* He ducked behind an arcade game and tiptoed behind the group.

"You thought you'd get past me and my army, didn't you, Mr. Holmes?" Avoria crooned, stepping away from the group and letting the hooded figures hold her prisoner. She walked beside them with her hands folded behind her back and her chin held high. "Thought you'd save the world alone . . . save your lover? Oh, you'll see her again, Beast. Belladonna is in my tower now. But the Order of the Bell is about to fall. I'll let you be the example of what happens to Violet's slaves when they cross my boundaries."

The general let go of his hold on Jacob and said to Avoria, "My Queen. There is another in our midst. I detected him as soon as we walked in."

Enzo's heart dropped.

Avoria shook her head. "Then stay behind and deal with him, General. I haven't the time to dawdle. I finally captured one of the Order of the Bell's elite! We are only days away now, I suspect. Preparations—and *celebrations*—are to commence. When you return to the Citadel, we shall dine and discuss our final moves."

"My Queen." The general bowed as the Ivory Queen and her hooded men carried Jacob Isaac Holmes into the night and marched toward her Citadel.

Enzo closed his eyes and willed himself to be as still as a statue. *Go away,* he wished. *Get out so I can follow the group!* He squeezed the handle of his knife. *Maybe I can take this one head-on.*

The general raised his chin and scanned the room, sweeping his gaze from side to side.

Enzo took a careful step forward, preparing to strike, and—

Squelch!

His feet stuck in a dry puddle of soda and gave away his location.

Whoosh! The general closed the gap with a single, inhumanly quick step, and he whipped Rosana's cloak off Enzo's body, exposing him in the sizzling neon and the light of the moon that poured in from outside.

Enzo slashed out with his knife, but the general was too fast. He kicked the knife out of Enzo's hand, and the blade soared across the floor. With a quick move, the general shot his hand out, seized Enzo by the neck, and hoisted him in the air as simply as though toasting with a goblet.

"Boy." The moon lit up only the lower half of the general's face, pale and peppered with stubble, lips cracked and dry. "I don't know where you came from, but Queen Avoria knew she'd find good use for you. I know just what she has in mind."

"Put me . . . down," Enzo wheezed, kicking out with no avail. *It's over,* he thought. *He's going to take me to Avoria, and I'm never coming back.* "Who . . . are you?"

"That is of no concern to you, little Carver boy." The general's mouth was a graveyard, teeth cracked and gray like tombstones, and his breath cold like a winter night. "Here's your task. Go and tell your Order of the Bell they're too late. All will kneel and be part of the prime new world. Where you fit into that depends on you. Call off the Order, and you may rest at the feet of the Ivory Queen. If they do not leave us be, *Crescenzo*"—the general yanked Enzo within an inch of those terrible cracked lips—"your bones will fertilize her gardens. Do you understand?"

"Y-yes," Enzo whispered, saying anything to make the man release his throat.

"Good. In case you forget the message, why don't you tell them all what's already become of your world? Let me show you a few things." The man slapped the palm of his free hand against Enzo's forehead, and his vision tunneled into darkness. For a second, all he saw was black, and then a series of images flashed through his mind like a slideshow. A rainforest sparkled with lush greenery before disintegrating into ashes. A rich sunset painted the Grand Canyon in a palette of tangerine, ruby, and magenta. The Canyon imploded without warning, kicking colossal clouds of dust into the skies and swallowing the sun. Crystal rivers turned red. Stars blinked out of the sky. All the while, Enzo's heart lurched in his stomach. Screams accompanied the images of falling buildings, traffic jams, and natural disasters. He tried closing his eyes, but the gruesome montage filled his eyelids, flashing faster and faster until Enzo could barely stand it anymore. With an involuntary kick, he cried out and clawed at his eyelids.

With a wicked laugh, the general took his hand away and dropped Enzo to the ground. Pain exploded in Enzo's back. "Pathetic," the man said. "Buildings, forests, and towns are demolished every day, boy, always to make room for something better. Better is coming, but for the world. Avoria's world! The Ivory Queen will find Snow White and the eighth core soul any day now, and once she does, our real work begins. Until then"—the general drove his bootheel into Enzo's chest and then turned to escape into the New York night—"stay out of our way."

CHAPTER TWO

THE OLD WORLD: FLORINDALE SQUARE

Enzo told Rosana the whole story early the next morning. They met at the top of the bell tower, where they could see the world below and where their whispers couldn't reach the ground. With every word, he watched Rosana's eyes grow wider until they filled with moisture and she covered her mouth with both hands, blinking to keep the tears from spilling.

"Enzo," she whispered. "*Why* did you go through the door in the first place? What if Avoria saw you and took you and you didn't come back last night?" She made a fist and stamped her foot. "I can't believe how close I came to losing you!"

Enzo sighed and took Rosana's hands in his own. "First of all, I'm sorry, okay? I won't do it again—not without you. But can we focus on the part where our friend was kidnapped, our home is dying, and an evil queen is destroying the world as we speak? If we don't act soon, we won't have a place to go back to. And what's worse: I don't think we're safe here either. The guy kept talking about a 'New World Prime,' like she's going to wipe everything out and start over. This is huge."

Rosana took a deep breath, closed her eyes for a second, and when she opened them again, the tears were gone. "We *have* to tell everybody about how he threatened you."

"No." Enzo shook his head. "We can't tell anybody, Rosana. You can't tell your mom, or my parents, or Geppetto, or Violet. They'll drop everything to protect me, and all of this will just get worse. Violet's going about this all wrong as it is. She's expanding the Order, but she's sending us out there in little clusters and they're not coming back. We need *everyone* to stand together. The Hearts, Neverland, Florindale, me and you, Snow . . ." The hooded man's words played in Enzo's mind: *The Ivory Queen will find Snow White and the eighth core soul any day now.* "Snow. That guy told me they're going after Snow."

Rosana slipped an elastic band off her wrist and used it to pull her hair into a ponytail, eyes wide with thought. "Snow? Of all people? Didn't Avoria already get what she wanted when Hansel kidnapped everyone?"

Enzo used his finger to trace the jagged carvings in the brick ledges of Clocher de Pierre. His gaze fell somewhere beyond and rested on Snow White walking alongside Hansel, the man who tore down the walls between the worlds and thrust Enzo into this chaos. "I don't know, Rosana, it's something she did. She got her soul back somehow. And Avoria still needs it. We can't let her get it. We need to let him know."

"*Him?*" Rosana raised an eyebrow. "We've been through this before. We've tried! As much as you might want to believe, Enzo . . . Liam's not himself anymore. He's not the dashing prince or the jolly ol' chum we found back home. That man has demons now, and he's the only one who can fight them."

Enzo lowered his head and massaged his temples, hoping he could rub out whatever got in his brain and put a block on reality. Although the two had a slow start, Prince William Chandler Arrington became a close friend of Enzo's, one he looked to almost like an older brother. He came to know Liam as a man who would fight relentlessly for his loved ones and for the greater good, but after he accidentally killed the corrupt lord of the Woodlands, Liam lost his way. Nobody saw him leave his house for weeks, which posed multiple problems. The first:

Snow could barely stand to be around him anymore. And second . . .

"They're crowning him and Snow tomorrow," Enzo said. "He's going to be our king! Isn't it time he got off his ass and started fighting with us? If not for himself, then for Snow." He looked down and saw his hands were shaking. He clenched his fists. "I'm not taking no for an answer anymore, and I'm not asking anybody's permission. I'm getting Liam back, and after he puts that stupid crown on his head, he's coming to help me kill Avoria whether Violet likes it or not."

Enzo and Rosana made the walk to Liam's place as the city awoke, and Violet was already working her magic to splash decorations all over Florindale Square in preparation for tomorrow's ceremony. Despite the bells, frills, and velvet curtains all over the square, Enzo couldn't have been in less of a festive mood. Rosana hardly said a word to him on the way to Liam's place, except to demand that Enzo promise to never borrow her cloak without asking again. Violet made brief eye contact with Enzo as he passed through, and he imagined her raising a suspicious brow, but he supposed it might have been his guilty conscience getting the best of him.

Since Liam's castle recently fell to Lord Bellamy's forces, Liam and Snow had moved back into a little cottage in the woods, where Hansel previously lived, as well as Garon and the Florindale miners. The miners scattered to various locations on assignments for Violet, and the rumor was that Snow was hardly ever home anymore, that it was simply too hard for her to see her husband so haggard and depressed. It was difficult for Enzo too. In fact, it had been weeks since he even tried to talk to Liam.

Enzo took a deep breath and pounded on the door. "Liam! Open up!"

As he expected, there was no response, so Rosana pushed the door open, and the two stepped into the musty cottage together. The warm smell of cherry indicated that Snow must have been in here recently.

Enzo followed the smell into a bedroom where the sunlight streamed through the window, illuminating an empty mirror frame clinging to the walls, a whole cherry pie resting on a nightstand, a dusty pair of boots sitting in puddles of wilted leather, and a bearded man tucked into a bed. His once neat and handsome hair was a dark, shaggy mess, and his eyes looked hollow where they'd once been bright and filled with joy. "Liam?"

"I'm ready," Liam said, his voice rough. "If you've come to take me, Mr. Bellamy, make it fast."

Mr. Bellamy. The man Liam accidentally killed in battle while Enzo was in Wonderland. There was a time when Liam could calm another person's nerves just by being in the same room. Enzo remembered lying awake in the New World after he witnessed Pietro's abduction from Hollywood, and Liam promised he'd fight off Enzo's nightmares like a living dream catcher. Since then, everybody who had visited Liam spoke of his mumblings about Lord Bellamy coming back to get revenge. This was a haunted man, plagued by nightmares even while his eyes were open. If only Enzo could get the prince out of his home, where wraiths clung to the walls like nails.

Rosana knelt by the bed. "Liam, it's me and Enzo. It's Rosana. Remember?"

Liam turned his head and made eye contact with Enzo and then with Rosana. "I can't make him go away. The floor curses my toes, the wind screams my name, the walls keep whispering. He's coming back for me. I deserve my death."

"It's not your fault," Enzo said. "You did what you had to do for the greater good. You need to forgive yourself and come back to the resistance. Stand and fight the Ivory Queen with me. That's how we can make Mr. Bellamy go away."

"Enzo." Liam pushed himself onto his elbows, and Enzo was surprised to hear his name. So the prince really did have some shred of awareness left. "You should not be involved in this war. Poor, innocent lad. You, Rosana, and Zackary should never have been mixed up in this."

Rosana tried to grab Liam's hand, but he jerked it away as if she'd scalded him with her touch. "We didn't have a choice," she said. "But I know if you and Enzo never found each other, his family would be dead and so would my mom. So would Snow! That's just the beginning. Avoria's still out there."

Liam shut his eyes. "Every path before us ends in death. Don't you see that?"

"Then let's die standing on our feet," Enzo said. "There's almost nobody that I trust more than you. I don't know how long it's been since I was home. Maybe it's been a few weeks. Months. A year? It's all blurring together. But I can at least be grateful that I have my family back. I have you to thank, you know."

Enzo pulled a three-inch figurine out of his coat and then set it on the bed next to Liam's forehead. "That's you. My dad wanted me to find you because he knew you'd bring us back together. I'm not sure if I've even thanked you yet."

Liam poked his arm out of the covers and wrapped his fingers around the figurine. He spoke, his voice barely above a whisper. "Don't."

Enzo scrunched his eyebrows. "Sorry?"

"Don't thank me. *This* isn't me." Liam set the figurine on the floor and rolled it toward Enzo. "This is a good man—who I should've been. Who I was."

"No, Liam," Rosana said quietly.

"I don't believe that." Enzo shook his head. "You're a *great* man. I've been lucky to have found some great role models in my life: my father, Pietro, and *you*."

"It makes my heart sore to hear that, Enzo. I ask Lady Fortune that you will become nothing like me—that you'll grow up good."

"I know you think you're a horrible person because of Mr. Bellamy's death," Rosana said. "Yes, it's a hard reality, but what else could you have done? You were trying to protect everyone, like you always do."

Liam sat up. "No. No one sees it that way. If you'd seen the way

Pietro looked at me . . ." He blew a long breath and rubbed his face. "Those people have every right to be afraid of me. I'm a murderer."

"You're a defender," Enzo countered. "You defended Violet and Alice and Gretel and everyone else. Sorry, but I'm not afraid of you."

"Stop." Liam aimed a palm at Enzo. "I can't listen to an innocent boy justify my dark deeds. This is wrong. What have you come here to accomplish?"

"You and Snow are going to be crowned as the new king and queen of Florindale tomorrow. They are *already* decorating Florindale Square. We want you to lead us. The town needs morale. Can we count on you to fight with us?" Enzo picked up the figurine and pushed it back into Liam's bed. "I know I could've counted on this man."

"Tomorrow," Liam whispered. He gripped the sides of his bed as if he'd go flying into the wall if he let go. "That man is gone."

"It wasn't really a question," Enzo said. "We need your help. *I* need your help, and here's the thing: I went to the New World last night. And while I was there, I learned that Snow is the next target. I'm almost positive they're going to attack her at the cor—"

Liam leapt to his feet, ripped a black dagger off the nightstand, and grabbed Enzo's wrist. "You tell me it isn't true!"

Enzo took a deep breath. *It's just Liam,* he thought. *He's not going to hurt me.* "You think I'd lie to you?"

"Swear it!" Liam raised his dagger, stars flashing on the metal where the sun hit the blade. "*Swear it or I'll . . . I'll . . .*" He dropped the weapon and fell to his knees.

Rosana put a hand on Liam's shoulder. "Liam, please. You know us."

Tears filled the prince's eyes. "I'm sorry, Enzo. I've lost my way." He wiped his eyes. "I would never threaten you."

"Stand up, William."

Enzo turned to see Hua Mulan, the prince's tutor since childhood, tapping her foot in the doorway. With Enzo's help, Liam rose to his feet, the dagger still on the ground.

"Mulan!" Enzo said. "How much did you hear?"

"All of it. It appears we need to double down on security tomorrow and prepare to move in on the New World. Nobody *touches* Snow White, Liam, you kids, or my people!" She crossed the room with a brisk walk and tugged on Liam's arm. "Sit down, Liam. You will not be crowned looking like a chameleon wolf. You need a shave and a haircut. Then, we're going outside and brushing up on your swordsmanship. No more lying around feeling sorry for yourself. Are we clear?"

Liam nodded once, his gaze falling on the tiny figurine Enzo brought with him. "Aye." He made eye contact with Enzo, the hollow look finally fading away, and the determination crawling back to the surface. "Will you meet me at the bell tower when the sun sets? I should like to discuss one final thing with you in private . . . as your friend."

Friend. Enzo smiled involuntarily. No matter how dark things got, it was always good to hear that word. "Of course."

Mulan rounded on Enzo and Rosana and made wide sweeping motions with her arms. "You two, leave us be, and one more thing: Don't tell Snow White the extent of what you've learned."

Enzo looked down at his boots. He'd been debating whether or not this was a good idea. On one hand, it seemed unethical not to say anything. But Mulan confirmed everything that held him back.

"She probably already suspects, but that poor woman deserves to *enjoy* her coronation, and the people deserve but a few hours to forget about what's going on. I know Snow well. If you confirm her fears, she'll march straight to Avoria's doorstep and offer herself up to protect Liam and the people of Florindale. She's almost as reckless as *you* are." Mulan raised her eyebrows at Enzo and tilted her head toward the door, filling his conscience with guilt. "Now, go home. I'd keep that blade under your pillow tonight if I were you. I don't know what Lady Fortune has in store for tomorrow, but I can promise you this: It's going to be a *very* long day."

CHAPTER THREE

THE OLD WORLD: THE JORINDA SEA

The sails of The Hummingbird jittered in the night, and the sound gnawed at Zack's sanity. He wished more than anything that he could have flown the whole way, but flight was just one of the gifts Avoria had stolen from him and his friends. His greatest comfort during the voyage was having his parents with him. His greatest vexation was the captain. Zack's father, Pietro, had been sleeping with one eye open during the whole voyage, thoroughly upset he had to yield to the whims of James Hook, who kept the family busy fishing, cooking, and scrubbing the decks. *Come on, Pop*, Zack thought. *I know you hate this guy. Just toss the pirate overboard already!*

Neverland revealed itself after a few days on the Jorinda Sea, when the sails of Hook's ship announced the arrival of calmer winds. A massive crust of earth protruded from the water, and a smile erupted on Pietro's face. *Pietro's always smiling*, people said back in Florindale. But Zack knew his father better than anyone. This wasn't a happy smile. Zack could see the tension in his jaw. He was forcing it.

"What's wrong, Pop?" Zack slapped his father on the shoulder. "Aren't you happy to come home and see your old buddies again?"

Pietro narrowed his eyes. "Something doesn't feel quite right, Kid."

Zack studied the island. Red and gold specked the trees on the edge, and some were even barren of leaves. "Really? I think it's kinda pretty. It's like fall back home. This is right around the time you'd start drinking pumpkin spice, wandering the Halloween aisles at Target, planning your costume . . . what's wrong with it?"

"It's supposed to be, uh, how do I put this? *Greener*, I guess." Pietro's smile melted. "Leaves don't yellow here. Trees don't die. Seasons aren't supposed to exist here. Time ignores the island."

"Land ho!" Captain Hook cried, a hint of a question in his tone. "Prepare for docking. Destination Neverland in sight."

Zack's gaze remained on the clouds, tracing the path of a star blazing over the island, a fiery-blue dot with an electric tail. "Make a wish."

Pietro rubbed his forehead, sweat breaking out above his brows.

"Pops?" Zack queried.

"Sorry," Pietro said, turning back to Zack. "I never dreamed I would see this, you know. My son, my wife, and my childhood home, all in one view. I'm just surprised to see how much it's changed over the years, just like you have. You're growing *stubble*, and you look just like me and like your mom, and you just keep on getting taller like a freaking *moose*. It's a little overwhelming."

His mother Wendy reached up and swept a silky thumb across Pietro's temple. "You're worrying," she said. "Don't."

Captain Hook, smelling of beer and cheese and too much cologne, strode over to the group and wrapped his wrists behind his back, studying the Volo family. "Remember," he said. "This is not a pleasure cruise. You'll obey my every order, understood? If I say back to the ship, I expect that you run. If I—"

"Run?" Zack interrupted. "Pretty sure you're the only trouble in Neverland."

"You'll want to hold your tongue," Hook snarled. "I used to have an army here while you played hero in the New World. I am one of the five Elites of the Order. Violet won't be pleased if you smart off to me."

"We'll try to keep that in mind," Pietro said in a brisk tone that indicated he *wasn't* going to keep that in mind. "So who wants—"

Bam!

The Hummingbird's deck lurched underfoot and threw Zack on his shoulder. A sickening crunch roared in his ears. His shoulder bones remained blissfully intact, but the shredding of wood turned his stomach inside out. The ship rocked him back and forth with a force that nearly made him sick. He shut his eyes and waited for the motion to subside.

When he opened his eyes, half the ship was missing. A jagged hole unzipped the front of the boat off its center, as if a massive sea monster had burst from the surface of the water and bit half the structure away. Zack scrambled to his feet and called for his family. Luckily, everyone was accounted for, clutching the helm and the mast while Hook wrapped his arms around a barrel tied to the starboard. Their eyes were wide with shock and their faces pale.

Nothing in the ship's path suggested they had hit anything. No glaciers, no ship traffic, no rocks, and they hadn't scraped land quite yet.

"What just happened?" Zack asked.

"Is there something underneath us?" his mom asked.

Pietro rounded on Hook. "Did you leave a loose powder keg below deck or something? Our ship is ruined!"

Hook let go of the barrel and straightened his back, hot air driving out his nose. "My ship is ruined, Pan! How dare you accuse me of rigging it to blow when—"

"Stop fighting!" Zack wedged himself between Pietro and Hook and shoved them apart. "Can we worry about what just happened and how we're going to get on the island? And then home?"

Pietro massaged his temples. "We're probably going to have to swim. The bottom's probably already filling with water, and that means this thing's going down."

"You care to swim with the crocodiles?" Hook asked. "Not I."

Wendy pointed over Pietro's shoulder, her eyes sparkling with curiosity. Pietro whirled around, and a boy of about ten years old stood before him.

When'd he show up? How?

"State your business," the boy ordered.

Zack studied the boy's features. Baby teeth still intact. Pleasantly pudgy. A mop of dirty-blond hair.

"*Nibs!*" Pietro cried, throwing his arms over his head. "You haven't aged a day, buddy! Do you remember me? It's me, your old friend, Peter."

The boy called Nibs thought for a minute, rubbing his chin and eyeing Pietro with a calculated expression. The boy walked a circle around the family. Occasionally, he would poke Pietro in the elbow or grab his hand and then scratch his head and think some more. Finally, Nibs whipped out a dagger.

"No," he spoke. "You're not Peter Pan. You're a fake. Peter Pan knows we don't let grown-ups on this island. Ever. The island won't even let your ship dock. Neverland's magic shreds grown-up ships into tiny little pieces!"

Pietro frowned, backing away from the boy and his blade. "Dude, I swear on my life I'm Peter Pan. I even brought Wendy with me. Do you remember her? We came all this way just to see you guys again! We wanted to talk to you about something important."

"That's just what a grown-up would say!" Nibs growled. "Grown-ups can't be trusted. Either you're pretending to be Peter Pan, or worse! If you're the real Peter, then you're a traitor for growing up. Which one are you? A traitor or a liar?"

"A tr—I'm a good man!" Pietro protested. "Listen here. I came all this way to speak to you, and now you're gonna listen whether you like it or not. Can you just start by getting us off this thing?"

The ship tilted about thirty degrees, throwing Zack against the steering wheel.

Nibs lunged forward and jabbed the knife in Pietro's direction.

"Oops!"

Pietro held one hand in front of him, the other clutching the wheel. "Please?"

"You can't boss me around," Nibs declared. "I make the rules. And I say you're not welcome here! I should let you drown!"

"Wait." Zack aimed a palm at the boy, and he regarded Zack with wide-eyed wonder. "Time out. I'm not a grown-up! You can trust *me*, right?"

Nibs spun his knife through his fingers and studied Zack with the same calculated intensity used to walk circles around his father. Zack couldn't decipher the boy's ever-changing expression. Wonder? Confusion? Acceptance? Repulsion?

"You're not one of us." Nibs stopped and crossed his arms. "But you're not a grown-up either. You're something in between. And you look just like *him*. Your name!"

Zack closed his eyes and clung to the mast as it tilted another ten degrees. "Zack Volo. I'm the son of Peter Pan and Wendy Darling, and I've come to speak to the Lost Boys." Zack held out his hands as if to signal the end of his introduction. "Will you have me?"

Nibs put his hands on his hips and scowled for a bit. Finally, he said, "Yes. You may come and speak to our boys. The rest of you can't talk. We'll be tying your hands together and taping your mouths shut, because grown-ups aren't allowed to talk. Zack, if you try to untie them, we will feed all of you to the crocodiles! Do you understand?"

Sheesh. Zack couldn't believe his father was once the same age as this little brat in front of them. Zack forced a nod and made a circle with his thumb and index finger. "Yep. Crystal clear."

"Grown-up codfish, do you understand?"

Zack's father opened his mouth to protest. "But—"

"Without talking!" Nibs snapped. "Understand?"

Hook and Zack's parents nodded.

"Good!" Nibs produced a long coil of rope from his pack and a roll of duct tape. "Now hold still, or that guy's gonna eat you." When Nibs jerked his thumb behind him, a ten-foot reptile swam up to the broken boards of The Hummingbird and showed off its tonsils.

Zack watched his father shut his eyes and hold out his wrists to be bound.

Dad was right, Zack thought. *Everything about this is wrong.*

He didn't know Neverland firsthand, but there was a basic rule that made it different than any other place. People weren't supposed to grow up here. That meant time was completely irrelevant, and if time meant nothing, should the leaves be turning gold? Should the stars be falling? Should his father's old friends be threatening to feed him to a crocodile?

Zack thought about the shooting star, and how it had made his father sweat when he watched it fall. Every other day, he *loved* watching shooting stars, meteor showers, and the reddening of the trees. He'd camp out in the backyard with a thermos and a sleeping bag just to marvel at it all. Zack remembered being five years old, resting his head on his father's chest as he pointed out every star. *There! There goes another one! You want it? Man, it sure is beautiful. Ain't it somethin', buddy?*

The ripping of duct tape tore Zack out of his memory. His father reacted so differently to the comets here and the natural passing of seasons. When a second star blazed overhead, Hook drew his brows together and shook his head.

In a timeless place, stars and trees were dying.

What did this mean for the New World? Was Avoria growing stronger? Were the worlds growing weaker?

Zack never thought he'd worry so much about a meteor shower. He wondered if his father was scared that the new order of time meant Neverland was crumbling—withering under Avoria's thumb. In Avoria's quest for power, could it be that she plucked a star from the sky and cast it into the ocean? Whatever the star meant, time nudged the hour hand on the island's figurative clock.

The end of forever had begun.

CHAPTER FOUR

THE NEW WORLD: TIMES SQUARE

Jinn stared up at the Citadel and the boundless veil of snow that swallowed the land. Cinderella, Jack, and Quasimodo stood beside Jinn, rendered speechless by the state of the New World.

"It's not supposed to be like this!" Jinn stamped his feet and buried them in layers of fine white powder. "I've been here before. The New World shouldn't look like this. There should be *people*. Warmth! Light."

"That's b-because Avoria s-s-stole my gift," Frost growled. His icy-blue eyes were narrowed in anger, his lips were pale, and he kept his hands on his elbows. "She's cast the New World into infinite winter. Until we beat her, this isn't going away. It's only going to get w-w-worse."

"We can't stay out here," Cinderella declared. "We're not dressed for this. Jack, you're not used to actually *feeling* it, are you?"

Frost shook his head so violently Jinn worried the man would get a headache.

"Let's huddle and find a place to double our protection," Jinn suggested. "Seek an indoor space."

Quasimodo bit his lip, his breaths coming out in short, uneven bursts that clouded the air.

"What's wrong?" Cinderella asked.

"I feel her. Esmeralda." Quasimodo raised an arm and aimed it straight ahead, centering on the enormous tower piercing the sky. "She's in there. They must be using her gift for information." His voice quavered. "Gods, what if she's being *tortured*?"

"No, you mustn't think about that! We'll find her," Cinderella promised.

Jinn stroked his chin, forcing himself not to think of Esmeralda. Sadly, it was very likely Quasimodo's suspicions were correct. "Avoria is not a fool. She is always two steps ahead. We need to be *three*." He held up three fingers. "We would be dense to assume she doesn't know we're here, and that she's not up there planning her next move right this second. We must do the same."

The group huddled together, and a pinprick of warmth spread into a cocoon around Jinn's body. The four would keep each other warm until they migrated into the nearest building, but Jinn wasn't sure the shivers would ever subside. Too much tension blanketed the air, almost thick enough to chew on. What else hid in that horrible structure climbing the heavens? Where was Avoria at this exact moment? Was she watching them?

"Can we p-p-please g-get ins-side?"

Cinderella squeezed Frost's hand. "Let's move. Real quick and quiet, now."

As they shuffled through the trees and snow, Jinn wished he had taken Rosana's cloak with him. It had the power to render its wearer invisible, so long as the wielder possessed the proper focus and channeled their thoughts correctly. Maybe if Jinn had it with him, he wouldn't feel so exposed in this dark New World. On such empty streets, the four of them might as well have scuttled under a magnifying glass. They'd be caught and killed any minute.

At least I'll see my brother again, Jinn thought.

"In there!" Quasimodo hissed, pointing to an unlit neon sign that said *Petrelli's Pizza*. The four ducked into the shop together and let the door click shut behind them. They tracked gobs of snow onto the tiled floor and collapsed against the wall where they huddled for warmth.

"Do you think they evacuated?" Jinn looked around the parlor, a mosaic of abandoned, unfinished stories. The jukebox churned a bubbly melody into the dim room. An open wallet sat on a table by the door, while a meal receipt lay unsigned in the next seat over. Bugs scuttled over a crusty pizza tray covered in flour, and the door to the soda fridge hung lazily on its hinge. A newspaper announced the burning—and subsequent sinking—of Venice.

Cinderella got up and studied the oven before turning it on, leaving the door wide open.

"Did they all just get up and leave mid-bite?" Jack asked, blowing into his hands. "Or maybe they all had to run from something."

The door to the pizza parlor swung open again, and a black-cloaked figure entered. He took long, slow strides that echoed on the floor, stopped in front of the group, and wove his fingertips together. "Mind if I join?"

Jinn's muscles tensed. "Who are you?"

Without a word, the man lowered his hood, and Cinderella and Frost gasped. "Hua Jiahao!"

"Yes." He was an elderly man with silver hair, a pointed goatee, and angled eyes, and the heart shape of his face reminded Jinn of Mulan. She was close with her father once, and he was a leader for the army that combatted Avoria the first time.

"Where have you been?" Cinderella asked. "I've been thinking of you for a long time."

General Jiahao replaced the hood over his eyes. "Lady Fortune willed me to this realm. I cannot say how long I have been here. Roughly five hundred of us came. The other five hundred, I presume, ended up with *you*. One thousand men and women, once devoted to one cause we could not uphold." He knitted his gloved hands together. Jinn couldn't see the man's face but pictured a tight-lipped expression in the silence. "Jack. Cinderella. Why are you here?"

Frost scratched the back of his neck and shrugged. "We're here on reconnaissance for Violet. We're going to give it another try, General. We want to bring Avoria down."

Hua Jiahao's thumbs padded together and he straightened his back, staying silent for a while. The lack of speech made Jinn uneasy, and he fumbled around for something to occupy his hands, settling on a Parmesan shaker.

"Then we are not on the same side," General Jiahao said softly.

"*What?*" the group exclaimed.

"When I saw you here, I was content in assuming you had learned your lesson from our great battle years ago. We stood together at the Battle of the Thousand, foolishly believing we could dethrone the most powerful queen in history. We were, of course, mistaken. You mean to try again?"

"You mean *not* to?" Quasimodo mused. "Pardon me, General, but that's terrible! Surely you're not with her now?"

"I am fully devoted to Queen Avoria," Jiahao said. "I serve the hand of strength and reason. Of honor."

Jinn scoffed. "*Honor.*" He feigned a deep laugh. "Ho ho! That's rich. You can end the charade now. Come, tell us what you're doing."

The general cracked his back with a casual flick of the shoulders, and his hood swiveled about his neck with a fluid, ghost-like motion. Even though Jinn couldn't see the general's eyes, he wholeheartedly believed the man could see through bones. "Perhaps you might answer some questions of mine first," the general said. "Then, I will permit you *one* query."

"You're serious," Cinderella breathed.

"First question," General Jiahao proceeded. "What has become of my daughter?"

Jinn opened his mouth to speak. "She's—"

"Don't answer that," Frost interrupted. "He's gathering information for Avoria. We tell you nothing."

"I have been generous," the general said. "Consider the fact that I have orders to kill or abduct Princess Violet's warriors on sight. I am prepared to let you pass, given that we were comrades once. It is the greater honor. In return, you owe me just enough information to keep me alive. It is *the greater honor*."

"She lives," Cinderella whispered. "She's on *our* side. Fighting for *real* honor."

The general tapped his thumbs together again. "Such relief and yet such pity. Such shame on our blood to fight for separate causes."

"And what *is* your cause, exactly?"

"Prosperity. The glorious, wondrous new world Avoria can provide. We shall never hunger. We shall never war over our differences, because we will all be the same. The highest honor is to serve our leader. What, then, do *you* fight for?"

Quasimodo narrowed his eyes. "Love."

Jack rubbed his arms, pushing down the goosebumps. "Vitality."

"Freedom," Cinderella added.

Jinn cocked his head to the side. "Survival."

"These words mean nothing without a vision. Avoria can realize this vision. My final query: Where is the princess known as Snow White?"

Jinn swallowed. "She isn't here."

"I ask you where she *is*, not where she isn't."

"Why do you ask about her of all people?"

"You have exhausted your questions. Now answer mine."

Cinderella shook her head. "There's no way we're giving you that information."

Click. General Jiahao raised a hand and snapped his fingers in the air. A dark, wraithlike creature appeared in the air beside him—a disembodied shadow. It was loosely transparent and humanoid, but there was a large, circular hole in the center of its chest. The figure hovered in the air for a while, and then it lunged forward and revealed a set of razor-sharp silver teeth in the center of its face.

"*Ah!*" Jinn screamed, pressing his feet against the table to propel himself backwards.

General Jiahao clasped his hands again. "You will not cooperate?"

Frost stood and raised his bow. "No."

General Jiahao turned his head and addressed the shadow as if it were a waiter in the pizza parlor. "Study them. Trace their path to where they came from, and you should find the princess. Bring her back to the Citadel."

Quasimodo darted to his feet. "No!"

Jinn leaned back and nocked an arrow, trying to decide if he should aim it at General Jiahao or the creepy shadow creature. With an almost involuntary twitch, he sent the arrow flying toward the shadow. Had it been a solid target, Jinn would have caused some damage, but the arrow flew right through, and the shadow let out an ear-cracking scream.

"You would be foolish to waste your ammo on the shadows," the general said quietly.

The shadow jerked, and then it hovered inches away from Jinn, Cinderella, Frost, and Quasimodo. It twisted, expanded, and four ethereal hands reached out from its center. One of the hands seized the top of Jinn's head, while the others took hold of his comrades. A thunderous chill rocketed down Jinn's spine, and then pain surged through him like flames in his mind. His vision blackened, and the last weeks of his life played in front of him like a film.

Hansel and Liam facing off in Jinn's old cottage. The prince disappearing.

Snow White's castle. Bellamy's army galloping to the door and seizing Jinn's friends.

A cold, dark prison cell. Hunger. Fatigue. Aching, screaming joints.

Finn's final march from Florindale Prison.

The harrowing flight to Tower Nuprazel. Lord Bellamy's body falling from the top floor.

Training. Augustine Rose asking Jinn to concentrate as he leveled his bow and focused on a target in the Ginger Fields. Bo breaking into a slow clap when the arrow hit the target.

Stepping through the trees of the Old World and into the cold, desolate New World.

Jinn didn't realize he had been screaming until the shadow unhanded him and General Jiahao slammed the flat end of a sword against the table. "*I suggest you be silent!*"

Jinn looked around the table. Cinderella pressed her hand against her chest and took deep gulps of air. Quasimodo's eyes swam with redness, and Frost was drenched in sweat.

"What did you just do to us?" Cinderella breathed.

"The shadows sampled your memories." General Jiahao turned back to the shadow, which had regressed to its original shape. "Did you get what you needed?"

The shadow gnashed its teeth again. It passed through Jinn on its way out the door, sending another electric chill through his bones. He was too weak to react.

General Jiahao sheathed his sword again and stood. "I am not going to hurt you this time. You can thank our history for that. But consider this a warning. Go back to Florindale. The next time I see you, someone *will* die. On my honor." General Hua Jiahao slammed his chair into the table. "Should Lady Fortune compel you to switch sides, you have a spot in my army. But do not antagonize Queen Avoria."

In a trembling voice, Quasimodo said, "Your daughter would be ashamed of you."

General Jiahao scoffed and strode across the room. "Goodbye, old friends. May the mercy of our queen be with you."

CHAPTER FIVE

THE OLD WORLD: CLOCHER DE PIERRE

True to his word, Enzo met Liam after the sun went down. The prince had shaved and cut his hair as Mulan commanded, bringing youth back to his face. They shared a bit of bread from Midas's Pub, and Enzo asked Liam how he felt about the idea of being crowned.

"It's complicated," Liam said, staring down at the town. "I hardly expect a fifteen-year-old to understand."

"Hey, I might as well be your age," Enzo declared. "I've been through a ton of stuff most people won't experience before they're fifty."

"Or five hundred. It's true, you've lived a life beyond your years already, but my heart bleeds for you because the worst has yet to pass." Liam put his bread down. "It's almost hard to know you, to see you grow every day and know what you'll have endured by the end of this war."

"What do you think is coming?"

"Death," Liam said simply. "Not necessarily your own. You have my word that I am going to fight tirelessly for your protection—not only yours, but your parents. Miss Rosana and her mother. The Volos. My wife. We are all prepared to make great sacrifices. But I mourn for the cracks in our protection and what I cannot shield you from. If I had a thousand wishes, I would've liked to see you grow up the easy way. Books in hand, purely hypothetical sword lessons at the same time every day, two parents who never missed a birthday . . . It will be our honor to keep you alive, Enzo, but there's something I cannot protect you from—what dies within you when you end another life. May you never learn that horror."

"But what choice do I have? I don't see how this can end any other way."

"It's simple," Liam insisted. "Leave the battles to me. Stay off the frontlines until Avoria disappears. Don't go back to the New World unless you are the last man who can win. I want to task you with a higher honor than slaying the Ivory Queen."

"Aren't I supposed to be the battle leader, though? Violet always talks like it's me."

"No. All you had to do was bring us together," Liam said. "I am prepared to deal the killing blow, Enzo. I already know what it feels like to take a life."

"So then what do I do, if you're going after the Ivory Queen?"

Liam let Enzo stew in the silence for a second before answering. "Protect my queen."

Enzo turned the words over in his brain about a dozen times trying to figure out if he misheard Prince Liam. Protect my queen? "So, like . . ."

Liam clasped his hands under his chin, elbows on the table, and nodded. "I entrust you with the protection of Snow. I shall fight; she shall not. I won't allow it. I know she's strong. But I cannot physically stomach the possibility of losing her. It is my wish that you keep her safe in the event of my probable death. Keep her alive, humble—"

"Stop." Enzo turned his head and rubbed at his eye, hoping to hide the ghost of a tear and play it off as an itch. "I don't want you or anyone to talk like this with me. Don't you find this selfish at all? Doesn't Snow deserve the choice, or at least the knowledge of what you're talking about? What am I supposed to do if you leave to fight alone? This is my fight too!"

"Stars, it isn't my wish to burden you!" Liam pounded a fist on the table, his eyes more a portrait of hurt than anger. "It's imperative that you understand me here! I'm not ordering you to do anything for me, Enzo. I'm asking this of you as a growing man that I call my friend . . . my brother in arms."

When they first met, Enzo didn't like Liam at all. For a fleeting second, Enzo remembered why. The prince, despite his pure intentions, had a bit of a manipulative streak. But could Enzo really blame the man for wanting to do what was best? For wanting to protect his loved ones? He drummed his fingers on the bell tower's ledge. "If I do this, it'll be because it feels right to me. Violet keeps trying to hold me back, and I'm not letting you do the same. I might not be ready to face Avoria alone yet, but once I have some more people behind me to get into her Citadel, I'm going back to take her down. If you really care about my safety, then join me, because you aren't going to stop me."

Liam kneaded at his forehead with his knuckles. "You promise to keep Snow safe when I'm not around, and I'll agree to fight beside you when the time comes."

"I'll think about it."

"That's all I can ask."

Early the following morning, Enzo met with Snow, fighting his worry with a forced smile. Had Liam told her she was in danger? Was it right to try and keep it from her? *Maybe nothing will happen today,* he thought. *Florindale deserves* one *day of peace before this whole thing explodes. One day.* Regardless, he kept his knife with him and vowed to be ready to fight at a moment's notice.

"This is it," he said, marveling at the intricate labyrinth of streamers, balloons, cloths, and banners that bloomed and laced the city in a palette of silver and berry purple. At either side of him, Rosana, her mother, and Snow White sat with mugs of tea in hand. "You're going to become Queen today."

Snow smiled without turning her head. Her gaze seemed to fall softly on the horizon or somewhere beyond. Benjamin Baker, Enzo's mother, Hansel, and a task force of old Hearts had been up baking since midnight, and Violet filled Florindale Square with larger-than-life marble sculptures of Liam, Snow, and the Elite members of the Order. Carved, pocket-sized figurines topped the tables. Carved backdrops had turned Florindale into a festive wonderland.

"Yeah," Snow said. "I'm going to be Queen."

"And Liam the king," Enzo continued. "And I get to say I knew you both before everything changed. Before you forget us little people on the bottom." He didn't really mean to say it. The words sort of fell out of his mouth without a conscious thought, and he flushed when he realized he couldn't take them back.

Snow put a hand on Enzo's shoulder. Her palm radiated warmth from the heat of her mug. "Enzo," she said. "Nothing is going to change. You know why Merlin and Violet are so intent on crowning us, right?"

Rosana was the one to come to the revelation first. Enzo wasn't surprised. She was always the intuitive one. "For hope," she said. "To give the people somebody to look to and put their trust in."

"Yes." Snow nodded. "That's all it is. We're just friendly faces for the people. And I'm content with that. A monarch's purpose in Florindale is purely symbolic. What is there to rule right now? Liam and I wouldn't command an army. It's not our nature. That's what Violet and Mulan are here for. If we lose the war against Avoria, there will be nothing to rule. If we win, why have a ruler? Florindale in its purest form doesn't need one. It simply needs a heartbeat."

"But right now we need inspiration," Rosana's mom added. "And something worth celebrating. It's been ages since I saw a real Florindale celebration."

"It's been lifetimes since we've had one," Snow said. "Rosana, Enzo, what a time to be alive. You've never celebrated the Florindale way. This is going to be unforgettable!"

Yeah, Enzo thought. *Unforgettable.* "Just enjoy yourself today, okay, Your Majesty?"

Snow put her hands on her hips and chuckled with a shake of her head. "What did I tell you? It's still *Snow*, now and always."

CHAPTER SIX

THE OLD WORLD: NEVERLAND

Zack hardly said a word as Nibs and seven boys led the Volos, along with Captain Hook, through the crimson jungles of Neverland. Zack's parents and the pirate followed closely at Zack's heels, dragging their feet in chains and breathing heavily through their noses. Their lips were taped shut, and their wrists were bound behind their back, whereas the boys let Zack walk free.

Every twenty steps or so, he would turn around and flash his family an apologetic gaze. Both his parents and Captain Hook wore looks that could kill, their eyes burning with annoyance.

Zack imagined how the island probably used to be, fresh with emerald life and palm fronds opening into perfect fans. Now, the island glowed crimson, the way Zack suspected a Martian oasis might look. Trees gripped coconuts as round as bowling balls and just as black. The sand tugged at Zack's heels, and the ocean was like green mouthwash. The scent of salt mingled with weathered wood. Overhead, a rainbow of birds looked down on the passing troop. Zack suspected they were once beautiful and full of song, but many of them were missing feathers in odd, asymmetrical patches.

"Sorry, Ma. Sorry, Pop," Zack muttered, placing a gentle hand on his mom's shoulder. Hook widened his eyes as if to scream *what about me?* But Zack shrugged and didn't give him a word.

"No touching or talking to the grown-ups," Nibs warned.

"Sorry," Zack repeated. "Can I at least ask where we're going?"

"We have to do a judging," Nibs said.

Zack examined the words in his mind. *Judgment? Judge?* "A trial?"

"A judging!" Nibs insisted. "The thing where a Your Honor asks you stuff and then says if you're in trouble."

"Oh," Zack said. *So a trial.* He wondered what a Neverland trial might look like and what sorts of punishments a tribe of angry boys might dole out. "Won't you guys be bored? Grown-ups do these all the time, you know."

"They're for kids too," Nibs insisted. "Because *I'm* the Your Honor!"

Zack smirked. "You're the judge?"

"The Your Honor. That's what it's called."

"Oh. Okay."

Zack dabbed his forehead with the inside of his shirt. Despite the lack of green on the island, the air still managed to smother his skin with oppressive humidity. Even the stones at his feet seemed to hate it, because they sprouted crab legs and scuttled into little holes in the ground.

Nibs led the group into a strange hollow littered with—Zack couldn't believe it—*bones.* They weren't human, that much was clear by the feral shapes of the broken skulls and the oblong rib cages, but he hated the scene. He treaded carefully, doing his best not to step on the white mounds, but some were buried in the ground and snapped beneath his feet. Every time, he winced and willed himself not to be sick. "What happened here?" he blurted. "What are all these skeletons?"

Nibs cocked his head to a tall boy on his left. "Tell him, Curly."

"Tigers," the boy answered. "A grown-up hurt them."

Zack's stomach turned.

Nibs aimed a finger at an assortment of logs on the other side of the hollow, which were arranged before a chair that sat twice as high as his body. He marched the Volos to the logs, made them sit, and picked up a pearly pink shell by the chair.

"Hang in there, guys," Zack muttered. "I'll fix all this." He patted his dad's back and quickly let go when Nibs turned around again.

"Now we have to start the judging!" Nibs put the pink shell to his lips and blew. A low, long whine sounded from the makeshift horn, and the hollow filled with at least fifty more kids who emerged from behind—and above—the trees.

Zack looked around, more and more certain he didn't want kids of his own. Weren't they supposed to be sweet and innocent? These had unnatural fire in their eyes. If this was a trial, it wasn't going to be a fair one. These kids already hated him.

"Zack!" Nibs pointed at a tree stump next to his throne. "Come here! I have to ask you stuff."

Zack stood, folded his hands in front of him, and crossed the clearing. He avoided eye contact with the scary children who had filled the hollow in a broken circular formation. He stood atop the tree stump and nodded at Nibs.

The boy climbed the enormous chair and threw the shell back on the ground. Then, he scrunched his face and pointed at Zack. "Is it cereal that your dad is Peter Pan and Wendy is your mom?"

"Yes," Zack answered immediately. "They are my parents."

The hollow filled with the sound of gasps and excited chatter. The Lost Boys exchanged wide-eyed gazes and pointed at Zack's father.

"If that's your dad, why did he grow up?" Curly asked.

Zack bit his lip. He didn't know how to respond to this question. He riffled through his memory for clues about his father's past. Had there ever been any reason to suspect that Pietro Volo, the jaded office broker, was really Peter Pan? Zack accepted the fact with relative ease when he learned it, but no. Up until that day, Pietro Volo was just Pietro Volo. "I don't know," Zack answered honestly. He looked into his dad's eyes, their irises no longer pleading but sparkling with wonder, the way they usually did. "Knowing my dad the way I do though, I think he was looking for adventure. He doesn't like to do the same thing every day. He doesn't rewatch a lot of movies. He tries new foods all the time. He likes to do magic tricks and go skateboarding. I think maybe being a ten-year-old forever would have bored him. So he learned how to be ten and forty at the same time."

The tape on his dad's face shifted upward for a brief second, and his eyes gleamed with pride.

"I'm confused." Nibs thought for a minute, stroking his chubby chin. "Can your dad fly?"

Zack took a deep breath. "It's complicated. He's—"

"You have to say yes or no," Curly interrupted.

"Then yes," Zack said. "My dad can fly." Zack hadn't actually witnessed this yet, but he believed it in his heart.

"Why did you come here?" Nibs asked.

"There's an evil queen trying to take over the world," Zack said. "Her name is Avoria—the Ivory Queen—and we need your help to stop her."

"You need our help?"

"Yes. She's trying to fill the worlds with darkness and make people do whatever she wants. Like puppets. It's going to take a lot of people to stop her." Zack paused and raised an eyebrow at Nibs. "She's the most evil grown-up who ever existed. You could help us stop her."

Excited chatter broke out over the group again.

Zack's mom nodded back at him, as if telling him he was right and should keep going.

Nibs shushed the group, but when the chatter didn't die down, he picked up a rock and threw it near the boys' feet. "Shut up!" Nibs yelled, immediately silencing the Lost Boys. "I have another question. Why did Captain Hook come with you?"

A pause. "Captain Hook is our friend," Zack said slowly. "He wants to help. We're on the same team."

"But Captain Hook is a bad guy."

"Sometimes he does mean things," Zack said. "But Avoria is worse.

Even bad guys are joining us to stop the Ivory Queen."

"No," Nibs snapped. "Bad guys can't fight bad guys. I think you're lying."

Zack's heart sank. *This was going so well!* As much as he envied the simple, innocent, black-and-white logic of small children, it was not the ideal time to have it thrown in his face. "I'm not lying," he said. "Cross my heart, hope to die."

"Then prove it!" Nibs pointed at Zack's father. "I want you to show me you can fly."

Zack's father lowered his head.

The pit in Zack's stomach opened even wider. "Wait, no!" he blurted. "He can't right now because of the queen—"

"So you lied!"

"No, I didn't. He knows how. He just can't right now. The queen took his ability away."

"You lied," Nibs said simply. "If this is Peter Pan, he's not a good person anymore. His son tells lies." He hopped off his chair and jabbed his finger in the air. "Lost Boys! Take them to the Mermaid Lagoon! *Feed them to the crocodiles!*"

"No!"

But the mass sprung in an instant, and Zack had the crippling, humiliating sense that he was being carted off by ants as they hoisted him into the air and marched away, crushing tiger bones on the ground with every footfall. Zack silently mouthed a wish at the sky. *If anyone can hear me? If any of you are wishing stars . . . help.*

A few seconds later, the trees shook, and a shimmering golden bird—a hummingbird, perhaps?—darted out of the canopy, over the water, and far into the horizon. Zack laughed at his luck. *Even the birds don't want to stay here*, he thought. *Good for you, little bird. Go. Don't bother saving me or anything.*

CHAPTER
SEVEN

THE OLD WORLD:
VIOLET'S DEN

Violet felt the worry lines crease her forehead and the iron coat her lungs. Every other breath was a hefty sigh, one that anchored her to the ground. Her reflection sulked at her from a set of mirrors around the room.

"Come *on,*" she whispered. With every syllable, she grew louder. "One of you needs to *answer me!*"

Out of the corner of her eye, she swore one of her reflections sneered at her. Violet imagined the mirrors talking, telling her she was finally going insane.

And that's what you get for meddling, my dear.

Violet flinched. What would her father say if he were still alive? What grief would he give her if he knew that several members of the Order were lost in worlds apart? She hadn't heard from Pietro in days. All she wanted was the smallest confirmation that he and his family were okay . . . that they'd landed in Neverland, collected the Lost Boys, and begun their return back to Florindale. Violet hoped they would've been back before Liam and Snow's coronation, that all of the Order could celebrate together, and that with their newfound morale they could storm the New World and bring down Avoria's forces forever.

Maybe somehow, it would even be that simple.

"Miss Violet!"

The fairy blinked. Her thoughts had distracted her, but a deep voice pulled her back to the mirror. A gust of relief poured from her lungs when the bell ringer stared back at her.

"Quasimodo!" she cried. "What's your status?"

"The shadows are coming!" Quasimodo blurted, his face pasty and gaunt.

Violet's veins went cold. "What?"

"The shadows mean to reclaim Snow White's soul and harm the people of Florindale! Miss Violet, you *must* sound the bells and warn the people!"

"The bells . . ." Violet's heart crashed against her rib cage. "Yes, I will."

"Waste no time! You must *run!*" The mirror image changed and focused back on Violet's doe-eyed reflection.

As if on cue, a heavy rustle sounded from outside the den. Adrenaline poured into Violet's veins. She clutched the mirror against her chest, spinning on her heels. She called upon her wand and charged out of the tree, preparing to confront the shadows with all the magic and strength in her body.

But when Violet found the source of the noise, it wasn't the shadows that caused the rustling. It was a trio of men, one of which Violet recognized as one of her father's old guards at Florindale Prison. Silvery-blue armor framed his body and anchored him to a dark horse, and when he turned to face Violet, his eyes gleamed.

"Miss Violet," he said. "So we meet again, and on the eve of a rather momentous occasion, one would say. I daresay you remember me?"

Violet balled her hands into fists. She would never forget the hollow, sunken eyes of her father's sallow-faced guard, the man who dragged her out of Snow White's castle. "You mean trouble," Violet said, "and you would be wise to change your mind and turn back *right now*. We're stronger than before. We will never go back to Florindale Prison."

The main guard chuckled, and his partners joined in. "Oh, you endearing girl. Whatever gave you the impression we mean to take you back to Florindale Prison? That's *far* from my intention this day. I simply thought I'd go for a ride and congratulate William Chandler Arrington and his lovely lady on their coronation."

Violet narrowed her eyes. "I'll give them your regards."

"That won't be necessary."

The men drew their swords.

"Are you *threatening me?*" Violet pulled her wand out and held it in front of her, tip level with the bridge of her nose. "If so, may the light be with you, gentlemen. I am in no mood to be trifled with tonight, and my people are *off limits!*"

"You disgrace your father's memory," the soldier said simply. "He was a brilliant man with a genuine hope for the greater good. You are unraveling the safety of this world and marching your people to a fate no brighter. Prince Liam and Snow White are not fit to rule if they mean to do your bidding." He leapt off his horse and drew his sword behind his back. "Prepare for death, Miss Violet. It's time to ring in the *new age* of the Old World."

Violet raised her wand over her shoulder.

And before either of them could strike, the bark of a particular tree burst from its trunk, illuminating the white doorway to the New World.

From the door, the shadows emerged, a demon wave of amorphous silhouettes charging out of the trees with lightning speed, spooking the horses. The guards screamed and dropped their swords.

Violet closed her eyes, resounding herself to her fate. She was surrounded. Hopelessly outmatched. From the pocket of her dress, she clutched the handle of one of the mirrors. As the world went dark, she nodded at her reflection and decided she'd done the best she could. *I've fought for years. I've fought hard. Nobody can question that.*

May the light be with me.

CHAPTER EIGHT

THE OLD WORLD:
FLORINDALE SQUARE

The coronation ceremony had arrived, and Enzo's mind flip-flopped between states of constant anxiety and total awe at the way Florindale transformed to celebrate Liam and Snow.

"How do you put this into words?" Rosana asked. "Look at all this! I lived in New York, Enzo. I used to think New York was the capitol of holidays and parades. Nothing will ever compare to what we see right now. Ever."

Enzo shrugged, digging his fork into a warm cherry pie—one of countless desserts prepared specially for the coronation by Benjamin Baker. "I'll figure it out," Enzo said. "It's like the world's *best* prom night!"

"No," Rosana said. "Not epic enough." She pointed overhead, where a lavender unicorn trailed through the starry night air. In silver, shimmering letters, the words *Liam the Mighty and Snow the Wonderful! Hail Our Rising King and Queen!* appeared. "Look at the sky! What high school prom could possibly pull that off? And the real deal hasn't even happened yet!"

"Word is we're still waiting on Violet," Enzo said. "Kinda weird for her to be the last one to show up for something like this."

"It's her taste for the theatrical," Tahlia Rose chimed in. "Watch her fly in on an undiscovered moon made of ice cream just before the ceremony starts."

Enzo grinned and then shot a look at Liam, who calmly made rounds and mingled with guests in Florindale Square. "What do you think is going through his head right now?" Enzo wondered. "How do you think they feel, getting handed a whole world?"

"They deserve it," Rosana said. "I just hope Liam's emotionally ready for this. I'd be a puddle on the floor right now if I were either one of them."

"They can handle it," Enzo assured. "Look how happy everyone is." *Please. Let things stay this way. Just for another day.*

Rosana curled her arm under Enzo's, her fingers warm and soft. "You're worried, aren't you?" She narrowed her eyes and tapped his nose. "You're not thinking about doing something reckless, are you? Remember, you promised not to go back without me. We're supposed to protect each other, you know."

Enzo forced a smile, and an orchestra sprung into a beautiful, dynamic melody. "I have an idea. Think fast." Enzo grabbed Rosana's hand and leapt to his feet, determined to keep the ceremony's jovial momentum going. Faking an exaggerated, old-timey accent, he asked, "Fair lady, shall we dahnce?"

"Why suhtainly, kind suh!"

With a confidence that coursed through his muscles and a smile on his face, Enzo took Rosana in his arms and the two whipped around Florindale Square, spinning and sliding without a care in the world. For a brief moment, only Rosana existed, and she looked divine, her hair a vibrant cascade of silk, and her smile a portrait of all that was good in the world, or *worlds*. He decided he could travel to a hundred thousand possible worlds and he would never find another Rosana. Not one. He kissed her and caught the faint taste of cherry pie. When she pulled away, both of them stumbled slightly, and Enzo led her right back into the dance.

Soon, the rest of Florindale joined in and followed Enzo and Rosana's example. Every time Enzo whirled around, someone else was up and moving. His mom and dad had taken to the rhythm and fallen into a dance of their own. Tears sprang to Enzo's eyes without warning. His parents were together. Alive. Happy. Dancing right beside him. He caught his father's gaze for a brief second, and his dad winked.

"'Ey, my boy!" he called.

Meanwhile, his mom could barely get a word out through her laughter. "Pino!" she cried. "This is so much *fun!*"

Liam and Snow joined in next, the hem of Snow's dress fanning out like the petals of a moonflower every time she twirled. Geppetto fell in on his own, all hips and knees with sunlight in his eyes. Merlin danced with Augustine Rose, and Hansel carried Gretel on his shoulders as she clapped and nodded to the melody. Garon and the dwarves charged around in a sort of conga line, and before Enzo could identify the melodic transition, the music had picked up and the whole city seemed to be on its feet.

Colossal balloons, glittering stars, and vibrant rose petals rained from the heavens, making Enzo wonder just what magical being watched over Florindale from above.

They danced until their knees were weak, and then the music slowed and the people returned to their seats at the round crystal tables set up all around the square. It seemed that hours had gone by, and there was *still* no sign of Violet.

Mulan approached the stage, a silky red gown flowing down her body and her hair in a tight dark bun. Behind her, Snow and Liam sat in glistening silver thrones. Merlin appeared with two crowns on two velvet pillows, one on each hand. Far behind them, Clocher de Pierre and the palaces, cottages, and castles of Florindale rose against the horizon. Enzo wished he had a camera. He was determined to commit the scene to memory, to carve it forever into his mind.

Mulan clasped her hands in front of her and spoke quietly. "Well," she said, "against my better judgment, I feel it's time we begin the ceremony. We've enjoyed an evening of fun and the comfort of each other's company. But we've come together to crown our rightful leaders and the purest hearts of Florindale."

This is it, Enzo thought. *They're finally going to get their happy moment.*

"It is a new and exciting age for an old and weary world," Merlin continued. "We embrace that new age with this symb—"

A deafening explosion shook the air, the ground, and Enzo's bones. The crowns spilled from Merlin's fingers and rolled away, while a burning sea of crisp-orange light lit up the horizon, veiled by a mask of thin dark wisps.

A neighborhood in Grimm's Hollow had burst into flames.

Bricks crumbled, glass shattered, and metal screeched in the distance, only loosely audible over the sudden screams erupting from the crowd. It was all Enzo could do not to scream with them.

Thundering horses charged out of the flames and toward the group, wraith-like shadows hovering above them like hawks.

Mulan's eyes widened and her chest heaved before she faced the crowd and screamed, "Prepare for battle!"

Movement rippled through Florindale like a rogue wave. Hansel shielded Gretel with his body and rushed her in the opposite direction of the incoming army before scooping her into his arms and pushing through the crowd on his own.

Augustine Rose beckoned Tahlia to follow her into the Woodlands, resolve burning in the old woman's eyes.

The dwarves scrambled in different directions, though each seemed to make a deliberate beeline for a specific location.

As for Enzo, his fear and wonder rooted him to the ground as he watched the sea of darkness roll in on the horizon. *What in the world?*

When the army drew close enough for Enzo to hear their battle cries and clashing metal, his thoughts shifted. *What do I do?*

Time to fight.

He brandished his ivory dagger.

Enzo hadn't been holding it for more than a second when he realized the sheer impossibility of surviving against the sea of trained fighters barreling toward him. *One dagger versus hundreds of swords.*

If the army were a wave coming in from the ocean, what would he do? He turned on his heel and broke into a run, only to smack right into Liam's chest.

The rising king gripped Enzo right away and drilled him with a fiery gaze. "They're coming from the other side," Liam huffed. "The shadows. They're coming from the New World, and I know they're after Snow." He dug his fingertips into Enzo's shoulders and leaned forward so their eyes were inches apart. "This is it. You remember our agreement? My request, your word?"

Enzo's mind reeled. "Are some of those Bellamy's people? Some of them are *people!*"

"Don't worry about the people," Liam asserted. "Worry about the shadows. Enzo," he said more forcefully. "My request. Your word."

"Liam," Enzo said, "please don't try to do this alone."

"Our *agreement*," Liam repeated. "She's going to be heartbroken, as am I. Make sure she knows I'm doing this for her, aye?"

Enzo flinched and backed away in an attempt to shrug his shoulders from Liam's grip. Maybe if Enzo were adamant enough, Liam would change his mind.

Liam only squeezed Enzo tighter. "I know you don't like this, but this is a war. We *must* do things we don't like. There will be sacrifices. Goodbyes. You understand this?"

Enzo raised an eyebrow. "I do, but does *she* know you're doing this?" He paused to let his words sink in, and Liam's expression flattened. "You just got each other back, and now you're leaving her?"

With a bit of a scowl, Liam turned away. "You will not guilt me. Not you. This is our war." With that, the prince climbed onto his horse. "Look after her for me, brother, until we meet again in the next life."

Crack! Without even a wave goodbye, Liam whipped his reins and thundered toward the Woodlands, sword gleaming on his back.

Enzo turned around. *Okay,* he thought. *Bad things coming. Gotta get out. Where's Snow?*

The scream gave away her location a few seconds later, piercing the wind from the top of the stage where she was about to be crowned. Snow White stood at the edge, her toes pointed toward the Woodlands and her face a messy portrait of tears.

"*Liam!*" Snow screamed. "What is he doing? No! *No!*"

Enzo dashed for the stage, hoisted himself up, and took Snow's hands. It took her a second to acknowledge his presence as he talked over her screams, trying to calm her the way he would calm a scared child. "Snow, shh, it's me. It's Enzo. Look at me, please."

With a strobe-like breath and a series of sniffs, Snow quelled her sobs and looked back at Enzo through wet, pink eyes.

"He's gonna be okay," Enzo said quietly.

After another deep breath, Snow pulled Enzo into a tight embrace. Crying into his shoulder, she said, "He didn't even say goodbye."

"Liam will be fine," Enzo repeated. "You believe that, don't you?"

She nodded, forehead moving up and down against Enzo's chest. What surprised him was that she didn't immediately insist on running after her husband. Enzo was certain it would have been impossible to keep Snow in one place, but she just stood with her arms tightly around Enzo, who felt the weight of the world pressing down on his shoulders while he let the rising queen air her grievances. But they couldn't stand here forever. The shadows and the soldiers were about to tear Florindale apart brick by brick, and Enzo needed to get his friends to safety.

As Enzo surveyed the damage, panic crept into his throat. Where were his parents? Where was Rosana? Violet? He clapped a palm to his forehead, thinking of the days when he wished his life were more exciting. This was not the excitement he had in mind.

"Look," Enzo said to Snow. "I need to make sure you're safe. Where's a good place for us to hide? Somewhere underground? Somebody's house? Maybe a ship or the bell tower?"

The bell tower.

Enzo cast his gaze to the massive structure on the horizon. A cloud of gray circled its base and wound its way up the building, coloring the brick with an ashy iron hue. *Okay, not the bell tower.* "We'll head toward water, okay? I promise we'll go find Liam when this clears up."

Snow followed Enzo out of Florindale Square, charging through cobblestone alleys and around crystal fountains that he feared would turn red by the time the wars were over.

When Enzo bolted past Midas's Pub, a trio of armed horsemen peeled into view and drew their swords. Only one—a blond, lurchy sort of man with a bulbous nose—took notice of Snow and Enzo. The second rode past and into Florindale Square. The third dismounted and kicked down the pub door.

Enzo ran for the unattended horse.

"Jump on," he told Snow. "Right behind me." He grabbed a fistful of mane and swung himself into the saddle. The other soldier's legs were considerably longer, but Enzo didn't have time to worry about adjusting the stirrups. He took Snow's hand and pulled her into the empty space behind him.

Snow used Enzo's shoulder to steady her balance. "You know how to ride?"

"I might have a little experience," Enzo confirmed. "Courtesy of one Peter Pan and his family." He whipped the reins and dug his heels into the horse's sides, clucking his tongue twice. Wind rushed against his face as the horse sped away from Midas's Pub.

Behind him, a faint voice cried, "Hey, stop! Come back with my—"

"Fat chance, stupid!" Enzo yelled. "In *my* world, you don't leave your car keys in the ignition." A smile took him by surprise. *I just stole an enemy soldier's horse.* He felt young, rebellious, and free.

"Enzo," Snow said, "make it go faster. There's a large man riding after us."

"I'll lose him." Enzo dropped his smile and cracked the reins again.

"Stop the horse, boy!" the soldier barked.

Enzo guided the horse through a series of wild turns and changes in his path with a little help from Snow. She pointed out shortcuts and turns, leading him into a winding street that branched out into at least seven different side roads. Enzo made a wild turn to the right, clipping through the garden in front of a rustic cobblestone house and kicking up clumps of soil.

The turn threw the soldier off the trail, but after a couple more twists, three more soldiers emerged on the road. Enzo swore under his breath.

"And I thought only my husband was haunted by Mr. Bellamy," Snow muttered.

"I don't know what to do," Enzo confessed. "You're not armed, are you?"

"No. Just keep trying to lose them." Snow's tone acquired a sad wilt. She was losing hope.

When Enzo turned and thundered down another row of houses, a gold spark flashed before him in the distance, like a ray of sunlight bouncing off a sheet of bronze suspended in midair. He thought he imagined it and blinked a couple times, but after each time, the glint only grew brighter.

"You see that?" he asked Snow.

"Is that a bird?"

Only after Snow's words did Enzo notice the object flapping a thin set of pearly wings like a translucent butterfly. The way it moved almost reminded him of a hummingbird, but he'd never seen a bird with such shimmering wings. The visual effect mesmerized him, almost completely submerging any care in the world.

"Turn here!" Snow advised, but Enzo kept straight and followed the bird.

In fact, when Enzo really focused, he was positive the bird *called* to him. It required his presence.

Come toward me!

The voice chimed like a series of warm bells, rich and soothing with a feminine timbre.

"*Stop!*" the men roared behind Enzo. Reins crackled and hooves thundered. *Pop!* A blunderbuss went off, and Enzo's blood turned cold.

"They're firing at us!" Snow cried.

"Dammit!" Enzo steered the horse into a hard left, losing sight of the bird.

Pop crash! A window shattered near Enzo's ear.

When Enzo put his heels to the horse's withers again, the beast finally had enough. It slowed to a stop and, with a long whinny, threw Snow and Enzo off its back. His head hit the ground with dizzying impact, and the horse thundered away without them.

"I'm all out!" one of the riders cried, his firearm clicking.

The trouble was the three other beasts charging toward him. His comfort was that Snow managed to crawl out of their way and slide her back against the alley wall, wincing with every inch she moved. She picked up a potted plant from the window above her and lobbed it at one of the riders. While the rider sagged and toppled to the ground, the horse raged on.

The head rider sneered as his horse drew closer to Enzo. "Goodbye, boy!"

With his adrenaline doing all the thinking for him, Enzo leapt into the air, seized a pole from which a Florindale flag hung, and swung his legs out in front of him, a fire glowing in both his arms and his thighs. His bootheel connected with the rider's nose, and to Enzo's satisfaction, the momentum propelled the soldier off the horse and onto the ground. Enzo couldn't help but wince when the next horse trampled the soldier's stomach and he cried out with fiery agony.

The third rider looked to be in no mood to be outsmarted by a teenager. With a cold gleam in his eye, the soldier stood in his saddle. When the horse flew past, the man grabbed on the other side of the ladder's rung and propelled himself out of the stirrups so the two faced each other nearly an inch apart on the flagpole. The rider flashed a wicked grin, popped his heels together, and Enzo heard the *shhhing* of a blade popping out of the toe of the soldier's boot. The man raised a knee and prepared to deliver a kick Enzo would never forget.

"*Nnno!*"

The next thing Enzo knew, Snow was behind the rider, and she ripped him off the ladder with her bare hands. Though they barely hung a couple feet off the ground, an awkward twist of the ankle caused the man to crumble onto his back. He winced, put his hands above his head, and regarded Snow with wide-eyed fear.

She stood over him with one hand on her hip and the other pointing a dagger-nailed finger in his face. "Stay down!"

The soldier huffed, laid his head down, and shut his eyes. "All right. I . . . I give up."

Enzo shook his head and dropped down from the ladder. That was when the golden bird descended in front of him again.

"You're some fighter," the bird said. "Did the Order teach you that jump and kick thing?"

Enzo blinked and rubbed his eyes, wondering if he dared believe that a talking bird was communicating with him. "Whoa."

"Are you Enzo DiLegno? The son of Pinocchio?"

After a closer look, Enzo realized he and Snow had been wrong. The creature wasn't a bird at all. She was a tiny golden fairy with angled honey-colored eyes and bow-shaped lips. Her hair was an iron sheet of thick, silky hair, and her lashes fanned out into perfect arcs. After meeting Violet, Enzo assumed all fairies were fully grown like she was.

"Well?" the fairy continued.

"Yeah," Enzo answered. "I *am* Enzo DiLegno. Are you a friend of Violet?"

Snow drew her brows together. Noting the expression on her face, Enzo wondered if she didn't understand the fairy's speech.

"Enzo," the fairy said, "I'm Tinker Bell, the fairy guardian of Neverland. We have mutual friends, but if you don't come with me this instant, they will surely die."

On reflex, Enzo's hand found his stomach, which churned within him. *Pietro. Zack, and Wendy.* Enzo swallowed, willing himself not to be sick. "You can't tell me these things right now. It's—"

"Horrible timing, I know," Tinker Bell answered. "I understand you don't want to leave this place in the middle of a battle, but you were the only one I could come to. If you don't come now—"

"Wait," Enzo said. "Can you give me ten minutes to find my friends? To warn my parents?"

"No," Tinker Bell said. "If the light is with us, you'll see them all again and can explain everything. But if you wait ten more minutes, you'll lose much more."

Enzo dropped his chin, and he buried his hands in his hair. *Why do these things always seem to happen to me?* He lifted his head, scanning his surroundings one more time for Rosana or his family. *Maybe this will be a quick turnaround. I'm sorry, guys. I'll be right back.*

He pointed at Snow, thinking of Liam's request, and told the fairy, "She comes, too."

"Naturally," Tinker Bell said. "Come on, then. We need to get you two in the air."

CHAPTER
NINE

THE OLD WORLD:
FLORINDALE SQUARE

When the buildings erupted in flames, Rosana's first thought was that Violet had gone above and beyond on the theatrics for the coronation. The fire had a strangely hypnotic quality, and Rosana caught herself staring until she registered the screams, shadows, and soldiers. Her heart sped up to a gallop, and she took a step back, hands clasped over her mouth. She remembered Enzo's warning. *This wasn't part of the act.*

After the terror settled in, her first instinct was to take Enzo's hand and run. Rosana spun around, finding herself lost in the panicked crowd. She saw hundreds of civilians rushing about the square in an orange-tinted blur, pushing past each other and clamoring for safety. Her first priority was a single person. "Enzo?" Sweat beaded down her forehead. "*Enzo!*"

Hansel clawed his way out of the crowd and dug his fingertips into Rosana's wrist. "Rosana, where's Gretel?"

Rosana buried her hands in her hair. "I . . . I don't know. I'm looking for Enzo. What's happening right now? Where's Snow or Liam or—"

"A thousand curses!" Hansel turned and swatted one of the columns near the bell tower. "You should maybe grab a sword or something.

This is war." Without waiting for an answer, Hansel disappeared into the crowd again, calling for his sister with throat-shattering screams.

Rosana forced her feet to move, completely numb from the terror of the attack. She moved without a destination in mind, calling for Enzo and her mother and Violet.

Augustine bustled out of a nearby shop with her arms filled with guns, ammo, spears, and a stone mug she balanced perfectly on her elbow. "Tahlia! You're with me!"

Tahlia took a knee and started dipping the spears and arrows into the mug. They came out dripping with a dark solution that burned the ground when the droplets spilled.

A sea of catapults, stones, and cannons crossed Florindale Square, wheeled by dwarves and old Heart soldiers from Wonderland.

Pino DiLegno patted Garon on the back as he rushed by him. "Don't hold back, Garon."

Rosana hurried to catch up with Pino and planted a hand on his shoulder. "Mr. DiLegno!" Rosana breathed. "Where's your son?"

Pino turned and regarded Rosana with wide, gleaming eyes. "Enzo isn't with you?"

As if to answer, a man in a long crimson coat with Dominick Bellamy's old insignia emerged behind Pino and raised a sword over his head, posed for attack.

Rosana grabbed Pino's arm and leapt back, pulling him with her. "*Look out!*"

The sword came down with a hard *whoosh*, narrowly missing Pino's jacket. He spun around and drew his carving knife, facing his attacker. Pino's blade met the assailant's longer blade with an ear-splitting screech. "You picked the wrong day, my friend," Pino said.

With a cocky smirk and a simple swipe, the attacker swatted Pino's dagger out of his hand and raised the sword again. "This is for the king."

Crash!

A gleaming white vase came down on the attacker's head,

leaving twenty jagged pieces on the ground and a pound of potting soil spilling down his neck. His irises retreated behind his eyelids, and he fell to his knees, revealing Carla DiLegno standing behind him. *"Liam's* our king now."

Pino pulled his wife into a quick embrace. "Good hit, babe!"

But the third and youngest DiLegno was still nowhere to be seen, and Rosana found herself baffled by the additional enemies. Not only was Avoria against them; Lord Bellamy's old forces had returned to avenge him. Rosana had learned all about how his army captured Violet, the DiLegnos, and the Order with embarrassing ease and efficiency, cleaning out Snow White's castle in a matter of minutes.

You won't hurt my friends again, Rosana decided.

Not too far off, a horse whinnied and raced into the Woodlands, and Rosana swore she caught a glimpse of Liam on the animal's back.

The pieces snapped into place. Wherever Liam went, Snow was sure to be close by, and given that she was in the most danger out of everyone in Florindale, Enzo was sure to play hero. *He's in the Woodlands.* Rosana didn't know whether she felt more proud, exasperated, or downright terrified. She threw her hood over her head and sprinted into the Woodlands, willing herself to disappear and to find the galloping horse. She pulled herself into the treetops and moved along the edge of the forest, dropping beehives and throwing pinecones at the enemies below, and she watched her town come together.

Benjamin Baker emerged from the bakery with knives and torches. Garon and Chann operated catapults, accepting boulders that their comrades pushed into the field from the riverbanks. Boulders flew over Florindale Square and into the mob of invaders, while some of the old Hearts from Wonderland charged directly into the action with blades and shields at their sides.

While the action unfolded, fire spread. Tangerine flames danced across rooftops, engulfing neighborhoods, taverns, marketplaces, Benjamin's bakery, and ultimately the destruction seeped into the periphery of the Woodlands themselves, forcing Rosana out of the treetops. On the forest bed, she couldn't see much of the action beyond the pines, but the screams, cries, and crunches were enough to paint terrifying images in her imagination, each with a burnt-orange tint.

Rosana picked up speed on her way to Violet's tree, wanting to focus on the song of a bird or the rustling of squirrels to drown out the sounds of pain, but the Woodlands had never looked barer. Rosana would have been lucky to spot a caterpillar.

She collided with someone and fell to the ground, part of her hood slipping off her head. Without looking, her assailant drew a sword and prepared to strike.

"*Wait!*" Rosana threw up her hands. "Mulan! It's just me!"

Mulan breathed a sigh of relief and sheathed the sword again. She extended her hands and helped Rosana to her feet. "Rosana, you should not be out here alone! What are you doing?"

"Looking for Enzo," Rosana panted. "I can't find him!"

"You shouldn't be alone," Mulan repeated. "No excuses. Stay close to me."

Instead of following Mulan's order, Rosana ran ahead. "I'm sorry!"

"Impossible girl," Mulan growled, sprinting in the other direction.

Not far from where Rosana had fallen, a flat, shining object glinted on the ground. Compelled by its radiance, she picked it up.

No way, she thought, staring into her reflection. The mirror on the ground painted cracks on her face and shattered the image of Florindale behind her. Rosana instantly recognized the mirror as one of a few Violet had been using to communicate beyond Florindale. The Order had expressed disapproval of the measure many times.

It might've even been a clue to where Violet was, or rather, where she wasn't. Rosana became more and more convinced in her heart that Violet was no longer in Florindale. Rosana bit her lip, simultaneously relieved, angry, and terrified for the fairy guardian.

The explosion in the distance jarred Rosana back to reality.

She dropped the mirror, ran out of the woods, and confronted the most horrifying image she'd seen in a while.

Clocher de Pierre drowned in flames, a phantasmic blanket of smoke shrouding the town square in darkness.

Rosana's heart assaulted her bones, and she fell to her knees. *No.*

The Order of the Bell's meeting place, stronghold, and very symbol collapsed into a pile of disintegrated brick, molten metal, and lost history.

The silence in the square signaled that the fall of the bell tower ended the battle. While Lord Bellamy's remaining loyal followers were mighty, they were also few and far between. Many of them fell to the shadows that attacked both sides without mercy. Remarkably, those same shadows were extinguished by the arson that left a great portion of Florindale in ruins.

From Rosana's stilted vantage point on the edge of the Woodlands, she had trouble making out the identities of the fallen warriors, but one confirmation left her numb: Mulan, Tahlia, Merlin, and several dwarves and Heart soldiers marched into the Woodlands covered in soot, cuts, and tears as they carried the limp body of Augustine Rose. Rosana's heart burst into pieces for Tahlia, Augustine's comrades, and for herself.

"We shall tend to our wounded and honor the dead," Mulan spoke, her voice shaky and cold. "Comfort your young, and love your families. Then . . . sharpen your blades. The door to the New World is wide open, and the Ivory Queen will no longer hide behind her shadows! Tomorrow, we take the fight to her doorstep!"

Not if Enzo's already there. Rosana's gaze trailed to the ground, where she made out a relatively fresh set of horse tracks leading to the thickest tree in the woods and a bright light that radiated from within. She approached the door and tightened her cloak. *Avoria must die.*

CHAPTER TEN

THE OLD WORLD: THE WOODLANDS

Liam wasn't sure if the autumn night air had taken on a wintery bite or if it was the fear that chilled his blood, but as he galloped away from his own coronation, the air whipped his face like an iron rod. He gritted his teeth and flexed his fingers in his gloves, snapping the reins and driving his bootheels into the horse's sides.

"*Faster!*" he roared. He clicked his tongue against the roof of his mouth to drive his command.

Liam hoped Enzo had done as asked and taken Snow White to safety.

Numerous evils rose in Avoria's shadow. Lord Bellamy. The dark wraiths Avoria made. The army that wanted to avenge Mr. Bellamy.

Am I a better man than they? Liam wondered.

He shook his head and put the thought out of his mind. He couldn't afford self-deprecating behavior anymore. All he could think about going forward was the Ivory Queen and how he intended to snuff the evils from Florindale. Liam reached over his shoulder to be sure the sword followed him. It felt weightless on his back, like a razor-sharp feather. *I'm coming for you, Avoria,* he thought. *Before this night is through, I will bury this blade in your venomous heart.* Weeks ago, he didn't think he could kill the queen, but now, he knew he could—he must—finish the deed. The proof lay six feet under the perimeter of Tower Nuprazel.

When Liam charged into the Woodlands, the flames of the outside world disappeared and the darkness obscured everything. He slowed his horse and let his vision adjust to the dark. The forest chattered with unearthly screeches, spooking Liam's horse and causing it to buck several times. The prince tightened his grip on the reins and stroked the creature's mane. "Shh, shh. Steady, girl! *Easy.*"

But Liam's heart was anything but steady.

He was alone. He was at evil's doorstep. There was no sign of light. His internal compass used to point to Snow's cottage, where he slept after the castle burned down. Now, Liam didn't know east from west, and he certainly didn't know where home was.

The breath of the wind called to him, barely a whisper. "*William.*"

Liam spun his horse around and hunted for the source of the voice. "Who's there?"

"*William. Come.*" The crinkled leaves above him shook with every syllable. As if he were in a fever dream, a path in the Woodlands stretched in front of him and compressed into a gnarled, earthy tunnel of dry ground and dead wood. "*Come.*"

The horse whinnied, tossing its mane despite Liam's attempts to be soothing. Finally, he dismounted and started down the path alone, leaving the beast to gallop away.

Before his eyes, the tree branches knitted together and a shadow materialized at the end of the lane. It swirled like a black veil, though a finger protruded and beckoned him to follow.

Liam's heart dropped into a cage in his stomach when the shadow contorted, sprouting a pair of slender-booted legs and a mane of ragged silver hair. A dark robe enveloped the shadow's new form, and its eyes sunk into its newly wrinkled face, turning a deep shade of crimson.

"*No,*" Liam breathed. "Get out of my head!"

The ghostly figure of Lord Bellamy strode up to Liam and seized his neck, hoisting the prince a few inches in the air. "Would you kill me *twice*, boy? Do you have the guts and the gumption to do what is necessary?"

"Yes." Liam thrust the blade through the center of the ghost, and the shadow dropped him and gruesomely reverted to its true form. Bellamy's face shriveled, sunk, and stretched across an imaginary skull, disintegrated into ashes, and his fingers and legs retracted into stubs before the dark, translucent form reemerged. The shadow squirmed on the blade's end, and with two swift motions, Liam withdrew the sword and cleaved it through the silhouette in a straight cut from top to bottom. A thick white light swallowed Liam's vision for a second, but he didn't know if it had emanated from the shadow or the blade. All he knew was that when the light disappeared, the shadow burst into a material like charred paper and drifted into the wind, softer than snow.

Liam rested his palm against a nearby tree—a tree thicker than all the rest, surrounded by lanterns and deep footprints—and vomited. *He'll never go away,* Liam thought. He cupped his other hand over his forehead and pulled at his hair, feeling like he'd just run a marathon with his arms. He doubted he'd have the strength to hold an umbrella, a set of keys, or even a pencil for a few hours. But he knew he needed to press on and find the Ivory Queen.

When air came back to his lungs, Liam sheathed his sword, his legs on fire. He took one look at the threshold, swallowed the fear and bile in his throat, and leapt.

He went through the tree without blinking.

Liam burst through, a shower of cold air blasting him, and he watched everything change between two heartbeats.

Thump. Foliage. The crisp breath of autumn.

Thump. Iron, steel, and concrete. The harsh bite of winter.

Liam scanned the area for civilians, or any signs of movement within the ice. No matter where he looked, his eyes kept straying back to the massive structure towering ahead, probably twice as tall as Clocher de Pierre and three times taller than the Empire State Building. Liam couldn't really tell because it penetrated the clouds. Where did it end?

She's in there. Liam knew it innately. Avoria was in the fortress.

"We shouldn't go in there yet," a female voice declared from somewhere behind Liam. "We should wait to see whoever makes it through and make a plan."

Liam swiveled, his heart dropping when he identified the young girl behind him in her crimson jacket and her thick white gloves. A ghostly cloud of air escaped his lips. The next sentence came out with an angrier bite than he intended, and he had the sudden urge to grab the girl and shake her. "So foolish, Miss Rosana, *what ever are you doing here?*"

THE CITADEL

"General," Avoria said. "You owe me a report. Where is Snow White?"

"She has not yet arrived, My Queen. The shadows have hit a small snag."

Avoria rounded on her servant with a single turn of the ankle. She drew in a deep, cold breath, hands clasped neatly at her waist and a casual smile on her lips. "Excuse me? Surely I haven't misheard you?"

The general stood stone still, calm as the breeze. "You have not, My Queen."

In a swift movement, Avoria shot her arm out, reached inside the general's hood, and seized his throat. Her fingers on his prickly neck, she hoisted him in the air and slammed him against the wall. A crack spidered through the marble behind him, and the lights flickered and swayed. "Explain yourself!"

"*Cannot—breathe.*" The general's feet writhed beneath him.

"Fool." Avoria spun around, threw General Jiahao to the floor, and watched him pull himself into a sitting position. "Explain," she repeated.

"The prince entrusted his wife to the boy of all people. The Carver," General Jiahao wheezed. "And at the opportune moment, something whisked them *both* away. Snow White and the boy are no longer in Florindale Square. Nor are they within our realm. The shadows track them as we speak."

Avoria swooped over to the general, dug her fingernails into his wrist, and yanked him back to his feet. "Tell me where they're going."

"Neverland, My Queen. So it would appear." General Jiahao dusted his knees and returned to his stiff, straight posture.

"Neverland," Avoria whispered. "Where The Flying Man came from."

General Jiahao bowed. "My Queen, I—"

"I must go there," Avoria continued.

"I cannot recommend—"

"Silence." Avoria held up a hand. "I grow tired of watching Snow White fall through the cracks. I must go to Neverland myself and claim my prize. In my absence, I require you to hold down this Citadel. By the time I come back, I expect that all intruders will have been dealt with, the gypsy will have talked, and my dominion will stand taller than ever. Can I count on you for this, at least?"

"Your Majesty, before you make this decision, might I direct your attention to a more immediate, pressing matter?"

General Jiahao raised his arm and pointed out the window, where a speck of a man stood in a coat that gleamed on the horizon, and he appeared to be reprimanding a young girl who wore a blinding shade of red. The general beckoned Avoria to come closer, and the queen peered out the window with her hands clasped behind her back. Her expression teetered and flickered between a knowing smile and a hateful sneer.

"The prince and the girl," she said. "They come here and dare to stand in the open and conspire against me. I want nothing more than for that hateful man to see his wife's lifeless body when I rise to the crux of my power." Avoria made a grand gesture with both arms, spreading them in front of her. "However, sacrifices must be made. William Chandler Arrington and the daughter of Alice are too dangerous to keep alive. I will gladly trade the satisfaction of watching them suffer for the satisfaction of snuffing out the spark of life within them, and watching how their comrades fall like straw houses without the morale of their charismatic prince or their innocent golden girl." Avoria opened her eyes and spun around. "General, will you please open the window on the hundred sixty-seventh floor?"

"Might I suggest we wait?" General Jiahao answered. "Perhaps you will need one of them when Esme talks. Consider that one of them may be the eighth core soul. Once you reclaim Snow . . . who remains?"

For a moment, Avoria considered the general's words and advice, biting her lip until a thin layer of skin cracked between her teeth. "Very well. I want them within an inch of their lives, but see to it that nobody is killed *until* Esmeralda talks. She has until midnight." She swept an immaculate white cloak around her back and fastened it at her throat. "I trust that by the time I return, you will have identified my sacrifice and purged the weeds. That prince and the girl? When I come back, either they're both dead, or one is in your captivity mourning the other. If you cannot keep the Order of the Bell off my streets, then you *paint the streets red!*"

The general bowed. "Naturally."

"Open the window."

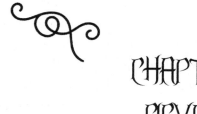

CHAPTER ELEVEN

THE OLD WORLD: THE JORINDA SEA

Enzo wasn't sure he would ever get used to the sensation of flight. He always imagined it would bring the same daring thrills of a roller coaster, but when the comfort of a lap bar or a seatbelt fell away, all that remained was a rush of milk-curdling stress. He had been unconscious when Pietro flew him through the streets of New York, but Enzo would never forget hitching a ride with Zack's shadow to smash the mirror in Violet's den. They'd gone over stormy waters, the world still brand new to him and Rosana, and the Ivory Queen was only minutes away from returning to power.

I really hope this doesn't become a regular thing. Not only was Enzo being asked to fly *again*, but this time, he had to rely on a tiny fairy to support both his own weight and Snow White's. He wanted to give up his quest entirely when Tinker Bell cried, "Take my hand!" and hoisted both him and Snow off the ground while the shadows followed. It was a bit like being carried by a Barbie, and the clouds overhead did nothing for Enzo's hopes.

The dust jumped from Tinker Bell's wings and drifted onto Enzo's head and shoulders. Beside him, an equally heavy dose splashed Snow in the face, and her eyes suddenly looked brighter and wider. Enzo felt lighter, like a helium balloon, sure if Tinker Bell let go of him that he'd rocket over the clouds.

A cold snarl sounded from below, and against Enzo's better judgment, he looked down. A grotesque, vaguely humanoid shadow unfurled at his feet, launching itself upward and wrapping its fingers around his ankle. Snow's screams did nothing to warm the chill in his spine. The shadow had seized her ankle, too. The grip was like a tight shackle on his leg, and a minute later, Tinker Bell engaged the shadow in a midair tug-o-war.

"Let *go* of me!" Enzo growled, jerking his knee and attempting to stomp on the shadow's face. Snow did the same, but their feet passed straight through the creature's forehead.

"Can you hover?" Tinker Bell asked. Without waiting for an answer, she said, "I'm going to let you go for a second. Think of something happy! It should keep you in the air."

"*Should?*" Enzo answered. "So there's a chance we'll—"

Tinker Bell pried her fingers free from Enzo's grasp, and he felt himself fall—the awkward, heart-searing sensation of missing the last step on a staircase or stepping off a curb, followed by the sensation of being pulled to the surface from underwater. Enzo looked down again, filled with both awe and horror. *I'm flying.*

Finally came the feeling of falling through a trap door, and the fairy dust's gentle hold disintegrated. Enzo and Snow plummeted several feet, the shadow climbing their legs and clawing into Enzo's shirt.

Tinker Bell zoomed around, a toothpick-sized wand in her fist. "Happy thoughts, happy thoughts!" she cried.

Enzo squeezed his eyes shut, and Rosana's face filled the inside of his eyelids. *Ice cream. Ice cream with Rosana. Balloons. Zack. Sparring with Pietro. Being at home with my parents! Bringing Rosana to visit my home!*

Enzo stopped falling, feeling as though an invisible iron hook caught him by the collar and anchored him to a cloud. Snow, however, fell a bit farther before Enzo reached down and caught her by her wrist. "Happy thoughts!" he urged. "Liam! You and Liam are going to be reunited when this is all over and live happily ever after!"

The shadow transferred its weight onto Snow White, scuttling up her back and wrapping its lanky arms around her shoulders.

"Get off her!" Enzo yelled.

The shadow responded without opening its mouth. *We reclaim the soul of the fairest. She is mine.*

"Oh, no she isn't!" A jet of gold light flew from Tinker Bell's tiny wand and hit the creature's forehead. "Be gone! Don't follow us!"

The clouds opened, and a barrage of raindrops fell from the sky.

The shadow hissed and turned its head, squirming in anger, but its arms remained locked around Snow White, rainwater dripping off her hair.

"*Let go!*" The fairy fired another ray of light at the shadow creature. This burst had a much greater impact, causing the shadow to let go and fall a few feet before grasping at Snow's ankle again. Tinker Bell did a full spin in the air, using the momentum of her elbow to shoot one more stream of light at the shadow. A crack like snapping wood echoed through the air, and the shadow fell a greater distance, but then it simply resumed its ascension with greater speed. It was a show unlike Enzo had ever seen—streams of light and darkness colliding in midair and crackling like lightning bolts, all magnified into prisms of color against the raindrops.

"The best I can do is hold them back," Tinker Bell said. "I can buy us time, but they will always come back now that they've found their target."

Struggling to maintain his flight, Enzo bit his lip. "What can we do?"

"Leave it to me. But you might want to close your eyes."

Enzo did as instructed, but he might as well have been facing the sun. From what he could tell through the veil of his eyelids, Tinker Bell grew brighter than a star, like she'd been wrapped in gold and dipped in sunlight. A swirling pattern zipped across Enzo's eyelids, and when he opened them again, a sort of sphere had formed around the shadow. It looked as though somebody had spilled a canister of glitter in a bottle of soap and used a huge wand to blow a bubble around the creature. Silver mist clouded the air around them. Tinker Bell made a thrusting motion with her arms as if pushing a large boulder, and the sphere whisked the shadow far away at a hundred miles an hour.

Enzo pretended to swing a baseball bat. "Homerun."

"It will find us again," Tinker Bell promised. "Be on your guard."

"It's after Snow," Enzo said. "Somehow, she took her soul back from the Ivory Queen, and Avoria's not happy." Enzo faced the rising queen and realized in horror that her eyelids were drooping and her arms hung limp at her sides. "*Snow!*"

Snow let out an exhausted moan and fell five more feet.

Enzo tried to fly down, but realized he didn't know how to control his direction in midair. He imagined it would have been a lot like swimming, but when he kicked his legs, it didn't seem to propel him anywhere. He reached desperately for Snow.

Tinker Bell zoomed after the queen, caught her by a finger, and hoisted her back in the air. Enzo marveled at the tiny fairy's strength.

"She's not used to being exposed to this much fairy dust," Tinker Bell noted. "Poor thing. She may be out for a while. Can you carry her?"

"Is that gonna happen to me?" Enzo worried. "I've never been exposed to fairy dust in my life."

"Oh, poor thing!" Tinker Bell cried, flying in a slow circle around Enzo. "You're so new to magic, you don't even understand your own blood! Boy, your heart *thunders* with dust. I shouldn't say I'm surprised. I've heard legends about your father. He was made from oak by a famous Carver. The oak could move and the puppet could breathe, but he wanted to be a real, living person. That can be arranged when a nice thick dose of fairy dust soaks into the wood and all the little tree rings, which eventually turn to human veins. This stuff"—Tinker Bell fired a playful stream of dust from her wand—"is a river in your veins. I can *hear* it. You're made of it."

Enzo held his arm in front of him, studying the veins on the back of his hand. "There's fairy dust inside me?"

"Yes. And we've just given it a jolt. Now, if you would please help me carry the fair woman, I'll teach you to fly, and we'll head straight for Neverland. Ready?"

Tinker Bell transferred Snow's dazed body onto Enzo's arms and modeled the proper method of flying without wings. The trick, she explained, wasn't so much in the bodily muscles as it was in the brain. "Think *up*," she insisted. "Uplifting thoughts. And then you just put a little thrust in it. A lean."

"Like a rocket," Enzo said. "Or a paper airplane."

"Or a hummingbird."

The act wasn't entirely easy. In fact, it worked Enzo's mind in the same way that it taxed him to do a lot of math homework. Tinker Bell's idea of being like a hummingbird turned out to be an accurate representation of the labor it required to stay airborne, fight the rain, and keep up with the fairy as she soared into the night. Enzo knew he had a million questions drifting beneath the surface of his mind, but he was so exhausted he could only call on them after long pauses.

"What kind of trouble are my friends in?" he asked.

"The deep kind," Tinker Bell said cryptically. Every time Enzo brought up the subject, Tinker Bell scrunched her face in resolve and flew even faster.

"You've *got* to be more specific."

"Lost Boys." Thunder followed Tinker Bell's response. "They're angry. Inconsolable. Almost *savage*."

"But Violet asked Pietro and Hook to recruit them for our war," Enzo said. "Is that why they're mad?"

"They're mad because they feel *betrayed*. Heartbroken."

Enzo noted the acute angles of Tinker Bell's eyebrows. Her lips were in a hard pout. "You say that like you—"

"Know firsthand? You're right. I do."

Enzo thought about the fairy's words for a moment. Peter Pan was said to be the boy who would never grow up, forever dwelling on the enchanted island called Neverland with all the Lost Boys and the magical fairy that helped them fly. Of course, Pietro's existence was proof that the boy known as Peter changed his mind. He left the island. He might have retained some of the temperaments of a boy, but Pietro was a full-fledged man with a family, a job, and voting rights. Enzo deduced that in Pietro's quest to grow up, he never said goodbye to Tinker Bell or the boys.

They must feel exactly how I felt when I thought Mom left, Enzo thought. *That she got up and walked away without even saying goodbye to Dad and me.*

It wasn't much easier to find out that his mom had been kidnapped, but there was something sad about imagining Pietro getting up and leaving his first home without a word.

Enzo didn't say a word to Tinker Bell for the rest of the long flight. Not until the island appeared through the rainy veil, a decaying mountain protruding from choppy waters. The whole island glowed a Martian shade of red except for a patch of palm trees at the eastern tip, which turned unhealthy, putrid hues of yellow before Enzo's eyes. Then the trees burned black, fell to the ground, and burst into a thick cloud of ashes.

CHAPTER TWELVE

THE NEW WORLD: NEW YORK CITY

"Rosana," Liam scolded, his thumbs digging into Rosana's shoulders. "You should *not* have followed me here! What ever were you thinking?" He released the girl and pressed his fingers against his temples. "*Are you trying to get yourself killed?*"

He shouted so loudly that Rosana took a step back, eyes wide. She swallowed, planted her foot, and raised a finger. "Don't scream at me like that again."

Liam lowered his head, heart filled with shame. When did he become somebody people feared? "I'm sorry," he breathed. More gently, he said, "Why are you here?"

"Looking for Enzo." The fear melted off Rosana's face, and she rubbed her arms, white puffs of air bursting from her lips. "I *know* he would've followed you here."

Liam tilted his head back, shut his eyes, and breathed out. "Of course that's what you're up to. You're looking for him." He pressed his palm to Rosana's back. "Come. We're not safe in the open. Stars, you must be *freezing*."

Rosana followed Liam through the snow and into the darkened alleys of the New World. With every step, a sad gaze deepened in her eyes. "I barely recognize home anymore," she said. "So where is he?"

These foolish children. "Rosana," Liam said. "Enzo's not here. I forbade him from following me. I should've known *you'd* come after me too."

Rosana stopped, posture wilting. Liam could tell that it required all the girl's strength not to let the tears come. Instead, she bit her lip, nodded twice, and said, "Then I'm staying to help you. We can stop Avoria together, you and I. That's why you came here, right?"

Liam spun on his heel, blew into his hands, and then rubbed them together. He unsheathed his sword and made a diagonal slash in front of him, admiring the arcs of light that the metal tossed into the air. "Yes," he said. "But *you* should go back to the Old World."

Rosana scoffed and rolled her eyes. "Because it's so much safer there right now? Come on."

"Because you have family there. You deserve every remaining minute with your mother. And with Enzo. Your blood will not be on my hands. This is not a joust meant to entertain, Miss Rosana, or a trip across the country. This is a fight to the death."

"Good thing I'm prepared, then." Rosana reached behind her back and shook a bow and quiver. "I've *been* prepared. You didn't see us fight the King of Hearts in Wonderland. You haven't been around for my training. While you lay around these past few weeks, I've been fighting like hell so I could be ready to come back and save my home. I'm ready. Are you gonna deny me the chance to prove it?"

"Yes," Liam said shortly. "Turn around and go back to Florindale."

"No." Rosana shook her head, arms crossed over her chest. "I've come too far. I'm not sitting on the sidelines while you—"

"That was an order," Liam interrupted, holding up a finger. "As your king."

Rosana did a double take. "Well I refuse your order! You weren't even *crowned*. And even if you were, we're standing in a free country right now."

"I would hardly call this free."

"Well, it's *supposed* to be," Rosana protested. "You want me out of your hair? Fine, I'll leave you alone, but I'm not going back through the door until Avoria's gone. Either way, I'm fighting. At least if we stick together, you can helicopter over me and be sure I'm safe. Or you can walk away and wonder. Your pick."

"Stars, you are *impossible!*" Liam exclaimed. He lowered his voice again. "Impossible. All right, Miss Rosana. We're in this together, then, but you stay close and follow my orders. I sympathize with your impulsive teenage rebellions, but I won't tolerate them here. Have you understood me?"

"Yes," Rosana muttered.

"Good." Deep down, Liam wasn't convinced yet, but he nodded, sheathed his sword, and made a fist. "Let's do what Enzo always likes to do."

With a soft grin, Rosana made a fist of her own and bumped her knuckles against Liam's. *The poor girl.* Her knuckles were frigid and dry.

"So what's our plan?" Rosana asked, looking around the city.

"I'm thinking," Liam said. "It isn't wise to go charging into that structure all alone without knowing what's in there. Stars, there could be anything! Aquamantulas, chameleon wolves, undead . . . I haven't got a clue where to start. But it's best we keep moving."

Rosana forked her fingers through her hair. "Didn't Violet send others here before? Cinderella? Jack? Do you think they're okay?"

"I should hope," Liam said. "Avoria would make a show out of capturing them. She'd want us to know if she had them already. If she even knows *we're* here." There wasn't a doubt in Liam's mind that she did, but more than anything, he wanted to believe he might catch her by surprise. *Straight through the back*, he thought, eyeing his sword.

As if the building read his thoughts, a window opened in the Citadel, making a horrible screeching sound that made Liam press his palms to his ears. Rosana doubled over with her ears covered as well, gritting her teeth and squeezing her eyes shut. Liam stared up at the balcony and understood that the windows weren't the lone source of the screeching. Something else roamed up there—something inhuman—and it was either terribly pained or incredibly angry, if not both.

Liam drew his sword again. A shadow appeared in the open window, this one more human and wrapped in a cloak.

"What is it?" Rosana took her hands off her ears and rubbed her elbows.

Liam watched in horror as the cloaked figure marched out onto the balcony, pushing what appeared to be a gray leather ball in front of him. The ball must've been about fifty feet in diameter, and a series of thick rusted chains circled it in tight arcs.

The cloaked figure waved at Liam, which jittered his nerves with an intensity he couldn't explain. The person turned around and unfastened the first chain, keeping an obscured arm on the leather ball. The metal binds fell away at once and then spilled off the balcony. Liam followed the chains to the ground with the tip of his nose, listened to them clang together, and then his gaze shot back up to the balcony.

A leathery wing uncurled from the ball like an ashy rose petal blooming from a gray bud.

Stars.

The cloaked figure moved to the other side and undid the second chain. The clanging of the metal links reminded Liam of Clocher de Pierre. If those bells had lost their musicality, they'd have the same eerie ring as those chains.

"Run, Rosana," Liam ordered.

"Where do I go?"

Liam turned and pressed his fingertips against Rosana's shoulder. "Anywhere." With a little more force, he turned Rosana in a circle and broke into a brisk walk, steering her forward. Behind him, the second set of chains smacked together in the snow. Another horrible screech pierced the air above. "Come on!"

Rosana's pulse thundered against Liam's fingertips. "Is that a—"

"Don't say it. Just keep moving!"

"O-okay!" Rosana trembled.

Liam picked up speed, blazing a frantic path through the snow. He swept an arm around Rosana's shoulders and steered her to the right. "Down that alley!"

Against his better judgment, Liam turned his head and looked behind. A second wing unfurled from the ball, and a long scaly head rose from the center. Crimson, bulbous eyes, a snake-like nose, a tongue of fire . . . before Liam could face forward again, the shadow shoved the creature off the balcony. The tail and feet appeared, the wings stretched from building to building, and Liam's worst fears burst forth as the fully formed dragon cleaved a beeline through the air, rocketing toward his head and taking out several dead trees in its path.

"*Get down!*" Liam wrapped himself around Rosana and tackled her to the ground, tasting iron and blood when he chomped down on his tongue. Unwittingly, he drove his elbows into Rosana's back. He tucked his chin against his chest, and a gust of cold wind ruffled his hair. His neck went numb as the massive shape passed over the ground, but a sharp pain in his back made him grit his teeth and let out a soft groan. One of the dragon's talons had skimmed his back.

The dragon swooped upward again, and Liam took the opportunity to spring to his feet and help Rosana up. "Take cover!" he shouted. "It's going to turn around!"

Rosana sprinted into the alley, but Liam didn't follow. His expression contorted into a hard glare. *It's time for me to kill my first dragon.* He reached behind his back, grasped for his sword, and felt nothing but the thin line of lightly perforated skin on his back.

What in the stars?

He looked over his shoulder. Small streaks of blood smeared his shoulder blades, but there was no sword.

Liam looked up and saw it clutched in the dragon's talons, a mass of silver and rubies in a knot of grimy spikes and leathery scales.

"No," he breathed.

He needed that sword back.

When the dragon circled back around and shot a rope of fire into the air, Liam closed his eyes. *I despise myself,* he thought. He glanced at Rosana, noting the horror written in her eyes. With a deep breath, he put up his arms, grasped the dragon's leg, and let the monster snatch him from the ground.

Blood rushed to his ears as he pressed his cheek to the dragon's leg and attempted to steady himself. A myriad of sounds rang through his body. His heartbeat. Rosana's screams below. The low gurgle in the dragon's veins. The rushing of wind against his torn cape. The crackling of fire that almost licked his elbow. Liam dug his toes into the dragon's skin, turned his head, and centered his gaze on his sword, which the dragon clutched in its other leg. It would take skilled maneuvering to get from one leg to the other. For a minute, Liam closed his eyes. He must've been a hundred feet in the air, clinging to death itself.

The dragon screeched again and swerved in a violent zig-zag, shifting Liam's balance from bone to bone. The monster dipped back toward the ground, and then next thing Liam knew, Rosana clung to the dragon's tail.

"Rosana!" Liam cried. "Are you daft?"

The dragon swooped up again, leaving Liam's stomach on the floor, and the creature flicked its tail around and swerved in agitated patterns.

Rosana's face was nearly a blur with the dragon's speed, but Liam watched her cling to the beast with admirable ferocity, hands red and teeth gritted. "Liam!" she screamed. "Let's steer it back into the building! We need to get up there!"

"No we don't!" Liam called. "You promised to obey my orders, Rosana! We don't need to fly it into the building; we need to kill it! And then I should hurt *you* for your recklessness!"

"I'm coming over to you!" Rosana replied, wiggling and clawing her way up the dragon's tail. "Hang on!"

Liam bashed his forehead into the dragon's leg, catching a whiff of its putrid scent. "If you're going to climb this beast, at least throw me my sword!"

"I will!"

Liam shook his head, trying to determine if he had been joking with Rosana. He reached up and around the dragon's leg and dug his fingertips into the monster's skin. Feeling like a koala on a tree trunk, he pulled himself up, knowing he had barely moved an inch or two. The muscles in his shoulders and back didn't protest as much as Liam expected they would. It wasn't long ago that he had scaled Tower Nuprazel and suffered the biggest workout of his life, one that burned a long-lasting memory into his muscles.

When Liam reached the top of the dragon's leg, he grasped the protruding mass of skin and muscle that jutted from the back of creature's bone and used it to maneuver around and up to its thigh, sinking his fingertips into its leathery exterior until he could get his foot up. He felt like he was performing at Ye Olde Renaissance Faire again, where he used to ascend the rock-climbing wall to amuse the guests. Only now, nobody was amused, and the wall had wings and the intention to kill.

"I almost have it!" Rosana shouted.

Liam couldn't tell where she shouted from, but she had moved quite a bit. He craned his neck and tried to find her. "You almost have the sword? How did you get to it so—"

Graaah!

It was all Liam could do not to let go and plummet to his death. The dragon veered and flipped sideways, wings nearly scraping Liam off the side of its body. It also twisted its neck so its eye was inches away from Liam's ear. He closed his eyes and swallowed, feeling his Adams apple moving. *This is where I die.*

A sharp thud sounded above Liam's head, and when he opened

his eyes, he hardly dared to believe them. A silver spear protruded from the dragon's skin, exposing a modest rivulet of dark blood. The creature screamed and rolled again.

Spears?

"Attack!" somebody bellowed below.

Fantastic. If the dragon doesn't kill me, somebody on the ground will.

Liam summoned the strength to look down. A circle of familiar faces converged under the dragon with weapons in hand and fingers jammed into the sky as if daring the beast to fly back down. Liam and Rosana weren't being attacked after all.

Cinderella, Bo, Frost, and Quasimodo.

They were being aided.

One by one, and sometimes in little groups of three or four, the spears and bolts flew up from the ground, some narrowly missing Liam's ear or ruffling his hair. And every time a new weapon pierced the dragon's thick skin, the monster roared and careened into a greater fury. It no longer had a straight flight pattern or dipped up or down, but jolted and bucked in sharp angles.

Liam had a horrifying thought. If they killed the dragon and it plummeted from the sky, he and Rosana were not going to have an easy time with the landing. His only hope was that they could manage to injure the beast enough that it would land on its own volition and crawl away.

But the agony didn't taper down. With every wound, the dragon only grew more violent. Liam realized with a sinking feeling that he couldn't hear Rosana anymore. Did she fall off? Did a javelin hit her?

The creature flicked its tail, and a deafening boom sounded behind Liam. Tiny particles of glass and pebble-sized bits of concrete rained on his back. The dragon had smashed a building. A crater dripped open from the skyscraper's walls, and Liam realized in horror that everything above it was going to fall.

No. No, no, no!

The dragon rolled in midair, driving its wing through another window. Vertigo spun Liam into oblivion as his side hammered against something rock hard and rough. Everything went dark while deafening crashes continued to surround him. Stabbing pain shot through his body, and then his consciousness fell away with a swift cut to black.

INSIDE THE CITADEL – THIRD FLOOR FROM THE TOP

When General Jiahao exited the elevator, the usual sound of defiantly jovial humming burned his ears. It sounded through a barred cell on the right side of the room. Four more cells flanked the marble corridor that led up to the white pedestal in the front of the room. A thick wall etched with the words *Avoria is watching* divided each cage. General Jiahao clasped his hands behind his back and stalked down the corridor, passing the sleeping Beast on the left, the empty cage on the right, and stopping between the two women at either side.

The humming ceased and yielded to the echoes of the general's bootheels.

"Are you ready to talk yet?"

The woman on the right, frizzy-haired and gaunt, shook her head. She wore gray robes that were at least two sizes too baggy, falling below her fingertips and shielding her feet. "Must you make the same mistake every day, Hua Jiahao? Madame Esme will never answer your questions. She will never serve your queen."

General Jiahao leaned forward and gripped the cage bars. "She's *our* queen. If you do not start to respect her, people you love will get hurt."

"People will hurt either way," Madame Esme said. She sat down, letting the robes pool around her, and stared at the wall. "Madame Esme will not be the instrument that ends this world. She will die with it if she must. If it is the will of the cosmos, so be it."

"Is it the fate of Quasimodo, who is outside this very tower looking for you?"

Madame Esme turned her head.

A grin crept across the general's face. "I have your attention?"

"You lie!" Madame Esme cried, darting back to her feet and running to the bars. "He would *never* come here. He never comes down from Clocher de Pierre. If you were still half a human, you'd remember."

"Clocher de Pierre has fallen," General Jiahao said coldly, eliciting a wide-eyed expression from Esmeralda. "But your bell ringer didn't fall with it. It would seem he came down of his own volition to join in some sort of rebellion against our queen. He thought it *that* important. How important is *he* to *you*?"

"You lie," Madame Esme repeated, though the confidence had deflated from her voice.

"Aren't you all-knowing? Would you like to see him for yourself?" Without waiting for a reply, the man took a key from inside his coat and unlocked Madame Esme's cage. He wasn't worried about her fighting him. She had grown too thin, too dreary, and ultimately too weak to overpower him.

She must have sensed it too, because when the cage opened, she stepped out with slow, uneven steps, and let General Jiahao guide her to the window. He pointed to the ground below, where a series of dots carved a trail out of the blanket of snow. Madame Esme put her hands and forehead to the window, her lips curling into the most pathetic pout the general had ever seen.

"Why," she whispered. "Why have you done this?"

General Jiahao stood behind Madame Esme and folded his hands. "This was not my call, Esmeralda. I acknowledge that I am merely a pawn."

"Madame Esme wasn't talking to you," the woman whispered back. She turned around and looked at the feral man in the cage, almost pleading for help with her expression. And the Beast looked back with his thumbs pressed together and his scaly knees against his chest.

They held eye contact for only a few seconds before he turned away and stared at the girl across from him.

"How do you feel about him?" General Jiahao asked.

Madame Esme shook her head and leaned on the window again. Her breath fogged up the glass, and she scrubbed a vertical line down the center with her finger as if tracing a tear. "You don't care."

General Jiahao scooped Madame Esme's elbow into his hand again. "But I do, Esmeralda. I care about *you*. You have until the sun goes down before I break the bell ringer's spine." He leaned in. "I implore you to speak before Avoria returns. Tell me who the final soul is, and I'll spare you *both* on the edge of time. I am much more merciful than she."

"Return?" Madame Esme breathed. "The queen isn't here?"

"No. She's gone to Neverland, where Peter Pan once resided. And you can be sure she will come back with the shadows on her side. I suggest you speak up before they swallow you forever."

CHAPTER THIRTEEN

THE NEW WORLD

When Rosana opened her eyes, a storm of dusty debris trickled through hot, orange light. She couldn't tell where the dust ended and the ash began, or where the snow fit in. Her head throbbed. Her shins felt like she'd driven knives through them. She could barely wiggle her toes.

She blinked a few times, trying to assess her position and her location. She lay on a floor, flat on her back, but she wasn't quite horizontal. The carpeted ground bobbed beneath her, tilting and bouncing like a ship. A ceiling fan hung at an acute angle above her. Rosana turned her head and scanned the area. Ashy cubicles leaned like the Tower of Pisa. Cord phones dangled off their hooks. An office chair rocketed past her ear and slammed into something ahead. She propped herself on her elbows, lifted her head, and screamed.

She didn't know how many stories up she was, but she stared at the world through a gaping hole on the inside of a skyscraper. Part of the ground was missing, and the rest tilted at such an angle that if she slid too far, she'd roll out of the building like a log.

"Miss Rosana."

Rosana would know that voice anywhere. Her heart sank when she perceived Liam's pain. His throat sounded raw, and his words came out in feeble croaks somewhere just ahead.

"Liam!" Rosana cried. "Are you hurt?"

"I can't see anything," the prince answered, his voice a bit clearer this time. "I think my legs are trapped."

"Liam." Rosana swallowed, mouth dry and lips cracked, and she forced herself to sit straight up. "We're gonna get out of here, okay? Stay right where you are."

"Where are we?"

"I think we're"—Rosana winced as the sensation of needles shot through her shins again—"in an office space. I think we crashed the dragon."

"The dragon," Liam repeated. "Right. Stars, all of this is wrong! I couldn't even kill the dragon. Do you see it?"

Rosana shifted onto her knees, clenching her teeth to keep from crying out again. "I don't see it," she said. "Why can't you see anything?"

She could almost hear him thinking between heavy breaths. "I don't know," he confessed. "I think I hit my head. I think I may have gone *blind.*"

"I'm coming, Liam." With nothing to brace her balance, Rosana pushed herself to her feet. Her toes throbbed, and she worried that her knees would betray her at any minute. She surveyed the room again and saw Liam inching bit by bit to the broken edge of the floor. Blood framed his face, and his chest rose up and down with a frantic pulse. She couldn't see his legs beneath the mountain of file cabinets and the desk that hammered into them. *Oh no.*

As quickly, softly, and carefully as she could, Rosana padded across the floor and maneuvered her way around the maze of tilting cubicles and crushed computer monitors, at one point stubbing her broken toe on the leg of a desk and causing a hot tear to spill down her cheek.

"Hold on, hold on," she recited. "Liam, can you sit up for me?"

Liam grunted a few times, moaning through clenched teeth, and finally affirmed, "Aye."

"I'm almost there." When Rosana finished her sentence, the floor shifted another ten degrees, pulling on Rosana's heels. Pulse accelerating, she shifted into a sort of surfer stance and took a deep breath. "I can do this." She crept up behind Liam, leaned over him, and breathed deep again. With one hand, she grabbed Liam's palm. She put her other hand on the file cabinet that had crushed his leg. "Can you see me?"

Liam blinked, eyes filled with tears. He seemed to be looking past her face. "I can only see shapes and shadows. I can't see your eyes."

The floor tilted again, and Liam slid forward an inch.

"I'm going to count to three, Liam, and then I'm going to push this file drawer off your legs. If you can move them, I'll need your help getting you out of here. If you can't . . ." Rosana closed her eyes. "Then we'll figure it out, okay? One . . ." She let go of Liam's hand and grabbed the file drawers.

"Two."

Liam squeezed his eyes shut.

"Three!" Rosana shoved with all her might. The file drawers, each seeming to weigh a hundred pounds, scraped against each other, resisted, and finally rolled off Liam's shins. The cabinets slid away and sped toward the edge of the building. It only took them five seconds to go over the edge, breaking off a small piece of the floor as they tumbled. Liam cried out in pain, brought his arm up, and bit his sleeve.

"Can you stand?" Sweat ran into the corners of Rosana's eyes. Without waiting for an answer, she shoveled her shoulder underneath Liam's armpit and attempted to heave him into a standing position. To her great relief, he managed to do a lot of the work himself. With a few grunts, Liam steadied himself, wrapped an arm around Rosana's neck, and took a shaky step forward. Rosana took the next, fighting the incline as hard as she could. *Where's the door?*

Rosana wanted to fall down and cry. Fear and pain overwhelmed her. She was scared for Liam. But she had come way too far to lose. If it were the last thing she'd ever do, she would get out of this building before she or the prince could fall out the window.

"Grab here!" a woman called from the far side of the room. "Take the rope!"

Rosana looked ahead, wondering if she had imagined the voice, but sure enough, Cinderella herself stood in the doorway with Jack, Jinn, and Quasimodo. A length of thick rope snaked through their hands and wound its way to Rosana's feet. *It's a miracle.*

"Take it," Cinderella insisted. "We tied it to a doorknob out here, and we have it as well. We won't let you fall, but you need to hurry."

"Stars," Liam breathed. "Cinderella, is that you speaking?"

"Hurry!"

Rosana scooped the rope into her hands and wrapped it around Liam's waist. She continued to follow its trail and pulled her way to the door, where Jinn immediately put a hand on her back and steered her and Liam into a crooked hallway.

"You're okay now," Jinn said. He did a two-finger point straight ahead. "Down the hallway, turn the corner, and follow it to the stairwell at the exit sign. It's more stable over there. You need to get back to the ground floor as soon as possible."

"Thank you so much." Rosana nodded and then narrowed her eyes when the four warriors headed back into the tilting office, rope in hand. "Wait, why are you going back in there?"

"You may have left your sword behind," Jack said simply.

"My sword!" Liam gasped.

"We'll see you at the bottom," Quasimodo insisted.

"Right." Rosana looped her elbow around Liam again and steered them down the hallway, energy fading with every step. "Just a little more. We'll be on the ground soon. We'll try to figure out why you can't see. We'll fix everything. We'll fix all of this."

The journey down the stairwell defied space. She couldn't count the floors. They seemed to be infinite. Every step taxed her feet. Knowing that Liam couldn't see, she took every step as slowly and carefully as possible, and it bothered her that Cinderella and the others didn't catch up in the middle. Every few floors, a rumble vibrated through the building, and Rosana swore she could hear a piece of the skyscraper breaking off and plummeting to the ground.

When they finally reached the ground floor, they ran out of the building and back into the snow, where Rosana assessed her surroundings for a safe space to wait for Cinderella and the other members of the Order. What was taking them so long?

Straight ahead, the dragon lay in a crumbled pile, half-buried in the snow, and Rosana almost felt sorry for the beast. Who knew what kind of creature it really was before Avoria enslaved it? Perhaps Zid could have done some good with it. Perhaps it would never have been so dangerous if it had just been left alone.

Rosana and Liam trudged through the snow to the other side of the street and took shelter in a hotel lobby. In fact, after rubbing her eyes, taking a seat, and catching her breath, Rosana realized she had been to this hotel before. She stayed here with Enzo and Pietro the night they first met.

"Rest your head, Liam," Rosana insisted. "I'll see if I can find some covers anywhere."

Rosana rubbed her elbows and poked through various doors on the first floor until she found a bundle of thick, fresh comforters, an unopened case of water bottles, and even a modest supply of basic medical materials. She draped two comforters over her shoulders, cradled some water bottles and rubbing alcohol in the crook of her elbow, and stuffed a wad of gauze, bandages, and ibuprofen into her pockets. She carried them out to Liam, who had curled up on the lobby couch already, and threw a comforter over him. Then she unscrewed the cap of her water bottle, took a deep swig that partially missed her mouth, and knelt beside Liam.

"I'm going to clean you up." Rosana opened the bottle of alcohol and spread the gauze and bandages in a fan beside her. "You hit your head somewhere. I don't see blood anywhere else. Do you feel like you might be bleeding anywhere besides your head?"

Liam moved his head back and forth, wincing the whole time.

Rosana tipped a small portion of the alcohol onto a bit of gauze and applied it to Liam's left temple. "Does that burn?"

"No."

"Tell me if it starts to hurt, okay?" Rosana rested her free hand on Liam's shoulder and scrubbed away at the blood on his face, which congealed and turned the rusty color of copper.

"Rosana," Liam said, his tone soft and warm, "are you frightened?"

"I've *never* been this scared in my life." Tears sprang to Rosana's eyes, and she paused her scrubbing for a second. "We don't stand a chance. I know that now. We don't stand one chance of beating Avoria. We've been stupid and ridiculously underprepared. What can we do?"

"We could hope," Liam suggested, but his voice didn't match the confidence of his words. "We could do that much."

"No we can't." Rosana shook her head. "We're powerless. Enzo isn't here. The Order isn't here. It's me and you, and we just let a dragon fly us into a building. We're weak." She moved her hand to the left side of Liam's forehead and continued to scrub and dab.

"The dragon's dead," Liam pointed out. "Is that not a victory?"

"Did killing it accomplish anything?"

"We still have our lives." Liam sighed. "This is why I worried about you coming to fight with me. At a certain point, it starts to feel disturbingly easy to justify taking a life to save others. I'm not sure we're going to have much more to fight for when this is all over. We fight for our lives, and I suppose we hope to have done some good in the end. But we're not done with the pain, and we're unlikely to be done causing harm. Do you understand this? Do you understand what you're at risk of losing?"

"Yeah," Rosana said under her breath. "I suppose I didn't really understand before. I just thought I was going to pluck my mom out of some fairy tale world and go back to our normal lives. I didn't think I'd be a part of an actual war, but it's bigger than me and my mom. I understand why it has to happen, even if I don't like it."

For the first time in a while, a faint smile spread across Liam's lips. "You're strong," he said. "You should be proud to be you, Rosana. I'm proud to know you, to fight with you, and call you a friend."

Rosana smiled through a fresh stream of tears. Each word had been like a hug on such a cold night, and yet something about Liam's tone stung her. The heartache. The burn. The thought that he might never be the joyful, carefree prince from Ye Olde Renaissance Faire.

"What happens if we do win?" she asked. "If we beat Avoria, I mean?"

"I imagine we'll have to break down every door between our worlds," Liam guessed. "Every mirror, every portal, and every bridge that exposes your world to dangers like Avoria. That may be the only way to stop this from ever happening again."

Rosana frowned, but the expression didn't stick. "Someone will find another." The thought made her smile. "There's always another way between the worlds. Can you lift your head, please? I need to clean back there."

About a half hour later, she fell asleep curled up on the other lobby couch. She knew she'd need her rest in the hours to come. Though her mind was full, her dreams were empty, and time passed by in a void. But she'd never been happier to wake up to a familiar voice.

"Woe betide you, William Chandler Arrington!"

Rosana sat up and found Cinderella tapping Liam's shoulder with the blunt end of her bow. "Things were quiet here! Then you come riding in, and all hell breaks loose! Did Hua Mulan teach you nothing? Are you happy you ruined our recon mission?"

"Aye," Liam said, his voice throaty and weak. He must have taken a nap as well. "Avoria is one dragon short of an army now. Good to hear your voice, Cinderella."

"But now she knows we're here! We've lost the element of surprise!"

Rosana counted the people in the lobby. There was herself, Liam, Cinderella, Jack leaning against the wall, and Jinn stamping the snow off his boots by the door. The group was one short. "Where's Quasimodo?"

The group fell somber, and Jinn took off his hat and looked around, as if waiting for one of his comrades to say something.

Jack cleared his throat. "He's been taken," he said with a quaver in his breath. "When we retrieved the sword, a shadow flew into the building and carried him into the Citadel."

"*What?*" Liam sat straight up on the couch. "Why did this happen?"

Rosana put her hand to her chest, lungs fighting for breath.

"My guess is they're using him to provoke Esmeralda. He said he could feel her in the building. If she's there, they're using her for information."

Liam bowed his head and buried his fingers in his hair and then moved them down and massaged his temples. "We've got to end this soon."

"If you have any ideas on how," Cinderella said, "I'm glad to listen. We just don't have the manpower right now. We have arrows and a sword."

Jinn moved to the center of the lobby and placed the sword by the fireplace. "Be careful that you don't lose this again, Mister Liam."

"I hardly feel like I'm fit to wield it." Liam pointed to his eyes. "I may have lost my sight."

"Liam hit the back of his head," Rosana added. "He told me all he can see are shapes and shadows."

Cinderella groaned. "Great. Our king has lost his vision."

"It could come back," Jack said. "Knocks on the head can mess with you temporarily. I've seen people lose their sight for a short spell. Be patient with yourself. If only Violet were here to help. Has anyone seen her yet?"

"No," a new voice sounded from behind.

Rosana spun around and looked into the face of Hua Mulan, followed by a crowd of people who looked like they'd just been through hell, including Merlin, Geppetto, and Hansel.

"*Mulan!*"

"Nobody's seen Violet," Mulan said. "We have to assume the worst has happened and fight without her." She let out the longest sigh, as if letting go of a truth that had burdened her for hours. "Let us set up headquarters, heal, and devise our battle plan."

CHAPTER FOURTEEN

THE OLD WORLD: NEVERLAND

"What's happening to this place?" Enzo asked.

"It's dying," Tinker Bell replied, voice low and sad. "It was never supposed to be this way. In a sea of worlds governed by time, Neverland was the haven of youth, a small island of eternity and stability. Nobody was to age. Nothing was to die. Not even so much as a single rose petal."

The idea pulled at Enzo's heartstrings. He had already come to accept death as an absolute in the world. Nobody was immortal. Even the sun couldn't last forever. But after a moment of reflection, Enzo realized that subconsciously, learning about his family and Pietro and all the people of Florindale had tricked him into believing that some things *could* last forever. He wasn't sure when the idea really sank in, but he knew that watching Neverland crumble broke his heart. Before he realized how much the sight had affected him, a tear spilled from the corner of his eye, catching him by surprise. He swallowed and blinked hard, trying to prevent any more tears from escaping. "But why is this happening?"

"Because the guardian of youth lost half his soul. Now, if we don't hurry, he's going to lose his life."

"Right," Enzo said, "take me to him."

Without another word, Tinker Bell descended and sped toward the island, leading Enzo toward the trees and lush sands that seemed to sizzle under the songs of hummingbirds, many of which rocketed from tree to tree and chattered with increasing excitement as Enzo drew closer. He let his feet dip into the waters and skim their surface like a jet ski, savoring the cool mist on his face until a mountainous splash erupted behind him and Tinker Bell shouted, *"Look out!"*

Enzo turned around and stared into the bulbous eyes of a massive crocodile, who had leapt into the air like a shark, and with his heart in his throat, Enzo jerked upward and narrowly escaped the reptile's iron jaw. The crocodile's teeth snapped together, and it flopped back into the water with another thunderous splash.

"I should have warned you about the crocodiles," Tinker Bell said. "Be careful in the water. Come now."

Wiping the sweat off his forehead and steadying his heart again, Enzo let his feet touch the soft sands of Neverland. He didn't have much time to commit the step to memory before Tinker Bell darted into the rainforest and beckoned him to follow.

"Please!" she said. "We need to hurry!"

Enzo zoomed after the fairy, weaving between trees and vines and rock formations. At one point, he swore one of the stone tikis laughed at him. Hummingbirds swept across his path, and parrots squawked their commentary from overhead. *"Brack! Long live The Carver boy! Brack!"*

It was strange how the island seemed to be communicating with him. It gave his spirit a boost, and he soared as fast as he could. Tinker Bell led him over a rickety bridge suspended over a roaring river. They flew through a waterfall, which had drops of water that seemed to soothe every pore of Enzo's body. Scabs and scrapes he'd earned over the last few weeks receded into his skin, and when he flew out through the other side of a small mountain, he looked brand new. To his surprise, Snow White also awoke with a startled cry.

"Enzo! Where are we?"

"Neverland," Enzo answered. "Do you think you can fly yourself now?"

Snow, who seemed to glow with a new vitality, assessed her surroundings, nodded, and gently levitated off Enzo's shoulders. "Yes," she said confidently. "We're coming, Peter!"

"*Brack! Long live Snow White! Brack!*"

The rainforest swam with color and life. The sounds of drums synced with Enzo's heartbeat, though he couldn't tell where the beat came from. It seemed to pulse from the trees themselves, and it followed him across the whole island. He wished he would've had time to stop and admire all the beautiful elements of his surroundings. Several species of monkey swung in his path, some of which even pounded their chests when he passed. He saw his first wild lion, which roared with pride and solidarity from its cozy little den on the ground. With every creature he passed, Enzo felt something awaken inside him. He felt like he could do anything.

"This place is amazing," Snow marveled.

Enzo nodded, keeping his eyes forward. "It is."

Soon the animals in the trees became scarcer, replaced by intricate webbings of rope and vine and several tree houses that would have put Enzo's own house to shame. They were castles in the sky, and Enzo hoped they would still be standing when all of this ended.

Signs dotted the trees, painted in berry juice or scratched in with burnt pieces of wood. *No grone-ups! Lost Boys own lee. Top see crit! Pirits tern back!* A chill scuttled down Enzo's spine. He was pretty certain he'd just rocketed into Pietro's past.

"Just ahead!" Tinker Bell cried, and a hole opened up in the forest. The ocean bloomed into view again, but it didn't quite match the side Enzo originally landed on. A rocky, jagged cliff barred him from the water, murkier and grayer than the crystal seas he'd flown over. Ash streaked the ground in imperfect spirals, and when Enzo skidded to a stop, a group of trees fell into a pile behind him.

"Pietro! Zack! Wendy!" Enzo cried.

The three, along with Captain Hook, stood with their backs to the water, each with their feet tied together and their hands wrapped behind their backs.

"Enzo!" Pietro said. "Kid, am I ever glad to see you again!"

"Enzo, what the hell, man? You shouldn't have come here!" Zack exclaimed.

"Enzo," Wendy said, quieter than the rest, "please be careful."

A group of boys lined the cliff with slingshots and wooden swords in hand, and when Enzo landed, they turned their attention to him.

"What's going on here?" Enzo asked. "Are you the Lost Boys?"

"Yes. We are the protectors of youth. Who are *you*?"

Tinker Bell hovered between the two groups, tiny arms folded across her chest. "This is Enzo, the son of Pinocchio, and Princess Snow of Florindale."

When Tinker Bell spoke, Pietro's eyes lit up as though he were seeing an old friend for the first time in years. Enzo wondered if he had even interacted with her since the day he grew up. "Tink?"

"Hi," the fairy snapped.

"A princess?" one of the boys repeated.

"Yes," Snow answered. "And I'm very pleased to meet you all. However, I'm a little disappointed to see that you've tied these innocent people up today."

"What are you doing tying Peter Pan up like this?" Enzo interjected. "Is this any way to treat your friends?"

"He traded us to be a grown-up and hang out with pirates instead," the boy answered. "He doesn't want to be our friend anymore. And we don't want to be *his*!" At the same moment the boy finished his words, the Lost Boys drew their swords and aimed them at Pietro, Wendy, Zack, and Captain Hook. "We send them to the crocodiles! Doom on them for betraying the Lost Boys! Doom on the betrayers!"

"Put those down!" Enzo roared. "Drop the swords right now."

"Enzo, be gentle," Snow said softly. "Children respond more kindly to warmth."

"They're about to jab our friends off a hundred-foot cliff!" Enzo whispered. "How am I supposed to be warm?"

"Children," Snow said, "I understand that you're angry with Peter. You feel betrayed because you missed him. But doesn't it make you feel good that he came back to see you? He kept you in his heart all this time because he cared about your friendship. Doesn't that make you feel warm and happy if you think about it like that?"

"Doesn't it?" Pietro added, his voice cracking like an adolescent teen's. "That I cared enough to visit out of the kindness of my heart? I even wanted you to meet my son!"

"You're trying to save yourself!" the boy leader hissed, tipping Pietro's chin up with the edge of a wooden sword. "Stop talking."

"We'd like to be friends with you," Snow offered. "We really would. Can we put down the swords and listen to each other for a few minutes?"

"You're talking to them like a grown-up talks to them," Enzo whispered. "They don't like that."

"No!" the boy snapped. "No, no, no! Grab the newbies! Kick them to the crocodiles!"

The words echoed in the air, and on cue, the kids divided in two equal groups. Half of them turned to Pietro, Zack, Wendy, and Hook and shoved and kicked. The other half sprang away from the edge of the cliff and charged toward Snow and Enzo, all screaming guttural battle cries.

"Never having kids," Enzo muttered. He leapt, focused on the current of the wind, and let it carry him high over the crowd. Snow followed suit, and the Lost Boys reached up and jumped with the intent to pull the two back to the ground.

"Get 'em!" the Lost Boys cried, and for a moment, Enzo feared for his own safety, but then he saw Pietro and Zack tumble back first over the edge of the cliff.

"No!" Enzo shouted, channeling all of his energy into flying over the cliff. "Snow, come on! Tinker Bell! Go, we need to catch them!"

Enzo thrust himself forward and sped over the Lost Boys, suddenly conscious of a chill in the air that wasn't there when he first arrived in Neverland. It sliced at his cheeks and stung his eyeballs, and when he soared over the choppy water, his arms prickled. Several green shapes poked out of the water and opened into oblong, dark holes with jagged teeth, while Pietro and Zack fell like logs, unable to reach up or kick or do anything else but scream.

"*Enzo!*" Pietro yelled. It sounded like a cry of terror, but then he followed up with, "You're flying!"

"I've got him," Enzo said.

"I'll get Zack," Snow said, already speeding along the cliff's rocky sides.

Enzo followed, and Tinker Bell circled his head as if marking a ringed path for him to fly through. His heart hammered against his chest, and his fingertips went numb. He wasn't sure if he could fly faster than a man could fall.

Push, he thought to himself. *Push!*

He imagined himself as a rocket, fire blowing out the soles of his shoes. He imagined all the times he'd sit and watch *Iron Man* with Zack, flipping an imaginary thruster in his mind. "I'm coming, Pietro!" Enzo shot downward and stretched his arm out, feeling the pull in every little muscle in his fingers and shoulders. "I've got you!"

Icy cold ocean mist sprayed Enzo's face, trying to force his eyelids shut, but he kept them wide open. He zoomed in on Pietro, close enough to see his eyes, and then the scuffs on his Nikes, and then—

Whoosh!

Enzo plunged a bit deeper, spread his arms out, and caught Pietro in the crooks of his elbows. To his great relief, Snow managed to catch Zack at the exact same time. The weight of their friends and the momentum of their fall brought Snow and Enzo down another couple feet, but they managed to stop their flight with a bit of space between their toes and the tips of the crocodiles' mouths.

Pietro brushed his arm across his brow. "You know," he heaved, "there was a time when I would have thought that was fun. I don't think I ever want to do that again."

Enzo closed his eyes and exhaled, burying his forehead in Pietro's shoulder for a second. "Pietro," he said, "don't talk for a minute, please."

"Missed ya too, buddy."

Enzo undid the rope around Pietro's hands. The knots were tight and more complex than anything he'd ever learned, but when he managed to work them out, he let the rope fall to the carnivorous beasts below.

Pietro massaged his wrists where the hard, red rope indentations bit into his skin. He threw a hand around Enzo's neck in a sort of one-armed hug that smashed their faces together, pricking Enzo's cheek with facial stubble. "Anyone ever tell you you're a damn hero, Kid?"

Enzo rubbed his cheek. "Anyone ever tell you your face feels like sandpaper?"

Pietro squirmed and reached for his ankles to untie the rope binding his feet together. He tossed the ropes into the water and then rubbed his chin. "Really? Wendy says I'm silky smooth."

"She's lying," Zack chimed in. "She says your kisses are like knives, but she likes your face, so she won't tell you to shave."

Pietro narrowed his eyes. "Huh."

Above, one of the boys cried, "Push!" and then two shadows draped across the water.

"Pietrooo!"

Enzo looked up. Wendy and Captain Hook were plummeting head first toward the water.

"Look out!" Snow cried. She hovered to the side, and Zack put out his arms. Enzo and Pietro followed suit.

"Wendy, love!" Pietro yelled. "We've got you!"

"Mom!" Zack shouted.

"Oh no, oh no, oh my *god!*" Wendy almost dropped past them, but Pietro managed to reach out and catch her. The weight doubled in Enzo's arms, bringing him down again.

"Wendy," Pietro breathed. "I've got you right here." With a bit of difficulty, he worked on the ropes around her wrists.

"Isn't anybody going to catch—oof!" Captain Hook narrowly escaped the crocodiles, saved by his jacket. Zack had managed to catch him underneath the collar, and now the pirate dangled from the weight of a few fingertips. "Thank you . . . thank you. *Please* don't drop me."

"I can't hold you all forever," Enzo said. "We need to fly up. Hang on, okay? Snow, are you good?"

Snow let out a long breath. "I think so. I'm ready."

Enzo and Snow White ascended slowly and carefully, while Tinker Bell hovered between the two as if to offer moral support. Pietro finally looked at her and beamed. "Hiya, Tink."

"So you married her, huh?" Tinker Bell asked, a note of bitterness in her voice.

"Oh, it's like that? No *hey, how are you, I missed you*? You jump right into that?"

"You understand her?" Snow asked.

"You don't?" Zack asked.

"I do," Enzo said.

"I never did," Wendy admitted.

"Please don't drop me," Hook repeated.

Pietro waved an arm. "I'd like to remind you all that those kids up there have slingshots. What are we going to do about those?"

"Is your hollow still here?" Wendy asked. "The little burrow you made on the other side of the island?"

"The Lost Boys know about that," Pietro answered. "If it's still here, it's not safe right now."

"The skull rock," Hook said. "We head to the skull rock. Your boys were always too afraid. We'll be alone there."

Pietro frowned. "I really hate it when you're right."

"I can't fly you much farther," Enzo said. "I'm dying here."

"Hey!" Pietro scolded. "Be polite. We aren't that heavy."

"We can fly back into the rainforest and run from there," Snow suggested. "To your skull rock."

"Done," Enzo said. They were approaching the top of the cliff. "Everyone get ready to run."

"Still tied at the ankles here!" Hook cried.

"We're coming up to the top," Enzo said. "One . . . two . . . three!"

Enzo launched into full speed flight again, every muscle protesting with Pietro's and Wendy's weight in his arms, as he soared over the top of the cliff and past the Lost Boys, who had done exactly as Pietro predicted. They drew their slingshots, and acorns flew into the air from all sorts of angles.

"Get 'em!" the boys yelled.

The acorns caused more annoyance than pain, but one thumped Enzo just below the eye, and hot anger bubbled within his blood. *I won't punch a kid*, he told himself.

"A thousand curses to all of you!" Hook shouted, his feet flailing underneath him. "Knock it off! Curse you all!"

Enzo and Snow flew them into the rainforest and let their feet hit the ground again. The relief was heaven for Enzo when Pietro and Wendy finally leapt out of his arms and shared a brief embrace.

Pietro turned to Wendy and cupped her face in his hands. "How 'bout a kiss?"

Enzo saw Wendy smirk at Zack, but she leaned in and pecked her husband.

"Right," Enzo said, taking the blade from his pocket to saw through the ropes around Captain Hook's boots. "We gotta run! Hook, lead the way."

CHAPTER
FIFTEEN

THE OLD WORLD:
NEVERLAND

Zack lay on his back, peering at the stars through a hole in the ceiling and rubbing his arms for warmth. His breath came out in little white wisps. He turned to Enzo, who had given up trying to sleep and started to whittle away at a stone he picked up by the water. "Dude," Zack said. "We're in an actual skull rock. In Neverland. Do you understand that?"

Enzo chuckled and blew a layer of dust off his rock. "Makes you wonder when we'll finally see *everything*, huh?"

"Yeah," Zack said. "It really does. Because you know what's funny? We've seen all this epic stuff together, but we haven't even seen point zero one percent of our own world."

Enzo looked up. "Point zero one?"

"Like I don't even think I've seen point zero one percent of America. We've never been to an In-N-Out together, huh?"

"No. We should go though."

"I know, right?" Zack grinned, but the smile dwindled like a snowflake in the sun. "This whole trip has been a dud. Violet wanted us to recruit the Lost Boys. They pelted us with acorns and tried to feed us to a bunch of dinosaurs."

"We've gotta try again," Enzo replied. "Violet had to have had a good reason. I mean, she doesn't always make sense, but I agree with her. Numbers can't hurt."

"True. But you tell me Florindale got attacked, a bunch of people already went to the New World, and you don't even know where Rosana is, do you?"

Enzo put down his knife and let his stone roll onto the floor. "No," he confessed. "I don't know if she stayed behind or if she followed Liam to the New World. I don't like either option for her. This is what sucks about feelings and love and stuff like that. The weight of the world's already on our shoulders, and every other thought I have is Rosana."

"Rough, man," Zack said. "I'm not so sad I haven't found my Rosana yet, now that you put it that way. Come to think of it, I'm not really sure what I'm looking for."

After a yawn, Enzo answered, "Well, whenever it hits you, it hits you, and it's pretty wonderful when it does. I'll be the first to tell you you don't have to go looking for it. Just don't fight it when it comes."

"You're a good friend, Enzo. I don't think I've said that enough over the years."

Enzo shut his eyes and smiled. "You'll never need to."

The boys were quiet for the rest of the night, and Enzo turned his attention to the breath of the ocean and the incoming tides.

Meanwhile, Snow White sat on the far end of the beach, throwing stones into the ocean. After each rock skipped away, she'd stare into the water and wait for the ripples to clear. Then she'd pick up another rock, throw it, and repeat. Enzo wondered if she was doing some sort of meditation exercise. No matter how much she disturbed the water, she'd sit patiently and wait. It always calmed down again.

Tinker Bell flew in slow circles around the skull rock, as if on patrol. Every now and then, she'd stop and change direction, bobbing up and down and flittering gracefully with her tiny hands behind her back.

The rhythm of the night calmed Enzo until he nearly drifted off to sleep, but then somebody tapped him on the shoulder from behind and startled him into full alertness again. He turned around and stared into the abyss of a black hood and a cloak that almost swept the ground. Enzo guessed that its owner was probably male by its hulking stature.

Enzo sat up on one knee, bracing himself to run if need be. "Hello?"

In the blink of an eye, the man disappeared.

Enzo ground his thumb knuckles into his eyelids. *I must have hallucinated him.* The dark tended to supercharge Enzo's imagination, even more so since he discovered the existence of magic and worlds beyond his own. Anything could be lurking in the dark—or even the light, for that matter. He stood and rubbed his elbows, pacing a few steps in each direction just in case the figure was still around, but he found nothing.

But that night, Enzo's imagination churned with the vivid, active intensity of a three-dimensional movie. Seconds after he shut his eyes, his dreams took him around an untarnished version of Neverland, where he followed two men around that were a little younger than his father.

The first man had all the looks of a black-and-white movie star, tall and clean-shaven with a toothpick tucked between his lips. He wore clean overalls and kept his hands tucked in the pockets. The second man walked close beside him, equally handsome despite his opposite features. Where the dark-haired man was a portrait of joyous youth, the second man had more of a hard confidence, a sunburned nose, and a chiseled jaw framed by a five o'clock shadow. In spite of the fact that they couldn't have looked more different, their proximity and their casual pace suggested their bond was iron. In the dream, Enzo followed from a bird's eye view. They started on the shoreline.

"So I was commissioned," the first man said in a voice Enzo recognized right away. "The king himself wants me to restore the gargoyles on the bell tower!"

The second man's heavy blond eyebrows shot up, though his chin remained pointed at the ground. "Is that so?" He paused and nodded, his smile waning while his friend's brightened. "That's quite the good news, Geppetto. I'm proud of you. This calls for a drink later."

"P'shaw," Geppetto answered. "I still owe you a brandy for showing me that new finishing technique. It really enhanced my craft." The young man looked up at the sky. "What are *you* working on lately?"

Enzo could hardly believe these two young men were Geppetto and Master Cherry. *Grandpa, you looked so different,* Enzo thought. He'd never seen the other man before, but his identity was apparent from his relationship to Geppetto.

The two men continued to converse as they entered the jungle, saturated in humidity and lush greenery. This version of the jungle was much more lively than the one Enzo arrived in earlier in the day.

The most notable addition was the tigers. A bright warm shade of orange with electric white stripes, they reminded Enzo of orange creamsicles. But the most distinctive feature wasn't their stripes; it was their *horns*. Each tiger had three positioned symmetrically about its head, like a triceratops. Enzo thought they must have been the strangest and most beautiful animals he'd ever seen. They padded along the jungle floor without batting an eye or baring a tooth at the two men in their territory.

Enzo's attention returned to the men. Geppetto strolled as casually as though he were walking through a mall instead of a wild jungle, hands never coming out of his pockets and his gaze always sharply forward. "*Allora,* I wonder if we'd find any oak trees on the island?"

"For?" Cherry prodded.

"Our friendly competition!" Geppetto said. "I have some ideas in mind about what I'd like to carve. I won't share them now, of course. I know I can find oak in Florindale, but I have a feeling about this place. What's your material, chum?"

Master Cherry didn't say a word. Instead, he stopped to pet one of the tigers, his hand resting between its bright sunny eyes.

"You know that gypsy girl who dances in Florindale Square sometimes?" Geppetto continued with a playful smirk. "She doesn't think we should do this competition. Thinks we'll end up destroying the world or something."

"Esmeralda?" Cherry finally answered. He let go of the tiger and circled his ears with his fingers. "She's always been a little balmy. I should tell you some of the daffy predictions she's made for me. She said"—suddenly, the dream went fuzzy, and Enzo's vision became shrouded in mist. Master Cherry looked up at Enzo, and in a deep, distorted voice, he said—"*Enzo. Wake up. Avoria is coming.*"

A black shadow eclipsed the sun, throwing Neverland into darkness, and cold air penetrated Enzo's bones.

The sudden shift in the dream space was so jarring that Enzo's eyes immediately snapped open, and Pietro stood beside him shaking Enzo's shoulder.

"Kid? Kid!"

Enzo caught his breath and processed his surroundings.

"What happened?" Pietro said. "You were freaking out, man! I thought you were having a seizure or something."

"No," Enzo said. "Bad dream. More like a vision."

"Vision? What do you mean?"

"Avoria," Enzo said. "Pietro, we have to warn the Lost Boys and get everyone off the island. Avoria is coming here. She's on her way right now."

CHAPTER SIXTEEN

THE OLD WORLD: NEVERLAND

"She can't be on her way," Wendy breathed. "Avoria's in the New World, right? Why come here?"

Snow, Pietro thought. "We have to warn the kids. I have this cold feeling inside me, like there's a big metal clamp on my spine or something."

"Wait, wait, wait," Captain Hook interjected. "You say the Ivory Queen herself is on her way to Neverland, and your first plan is to warn the Lost Boys? The rats that kicked me off a cliff today?"

Pietro made a chopping motion with one hand, beating it into his other palm. "James, it's the right thing—"

"No," Hook shot back. "We leave. If the boy is right about this, we can't afford to waste time reasoning with those lunatic children. It's suicide! They won't listen. She'll kill us all! I say leave them to her as an offering. Maybe she'll leave us all alone after that."

"That's wrong," Enzo argued. "They need us, and who knows? Maybe they can help us like Violet predicted."

"*Miss Violet* led us on a wild goose chase, boy. As usual, she made assumptions without understanding what she was meddling with. There's nothing here for us."

"Isn't it worth another try if they can help us beat Avoria?"

Hook narrowed his eyes, leaned forward, and pointed his good hand in Enzo's face. "I question your fitness to lead, little swine! You still know nothing of these worlds! I overrule you. I'm Captain, and I say we're leaving."

"*Stop*," Snow said, using a tone that reminded Enzo of his mother. "We're not going to accomplish any more standing here arguing than we will if we start *moving*. I'm with Enzo, by the way. It's the right thing to do."

"Yeah it is!" Zack exclaimed, throwing his arm around Enzo's shoulder. "Let's go, man. Let's go be heroes."

Shhhing!

Captain Hook pulled his blade and aimed it at Enzo's throat. His eyes were a storm of fire and fear. "Take. Us. Off. This. Island."

Enzo rolled his eyes. "You really wanna fight right now? Of all times? We don't have time, man. Put your sword away and come with us. If you're afraid, why even join the Order in the first place? What's your plan for the final battle if you're trying to run right now? Leave the New World at Avoria's fingertips?"

"That's different," Hook spat. "We can't battle the queen on this island. If we die here, we doom our friends. They need us, and we need them."

"The *boys* need us," Pietro argued. "If we leave now, our goodness dies. Or maybe you don't care about being good."

"I care about *survival*." Hook thrust the sword until its tip scratched Enzo's neck. "Will you take me off this island, or will you doom us all?"

"I'm not leaving yet," Enzo asserted. "Swim away if you want. That or help us. I have no use for cowards."

Hook's chest puffed in and out, his eyes flaring with glints of red. Seeing that he was outnumbered in his endeavor, he slowly lowered the scabbard back to his waist and calmed his breaths. "If they resist us," he said, "I leave. Forget the Order. At a certain point, it's every man for himself."

"Just move." Pietro tapped on Hook's shoulder blade.

"Pietro," Enzo said, "will you lead the way?"

"Thought you'd never ask, Kid." Pietro winked. "Stick close, and let's hurry."

A snowflake descended from the heavens and landed on Pietro's nose. By the time the group found the Lost Boys playing on the beach, a light, careful flurry peppered the air, a true Neverland first that jittered Pietro's nerves.

"Look who's come back," Nibs sneered. "Somebody's feeling real brave! What are you doing here, Peter Pan?"

Pietro took a breath, holding his hands up to show that he intended no harm. "Nibs. We've come back to warn you guys. The Ivory Queen is on her way to this island. We want you to be safe. We want you on our side, Nibs."

"Tell me why I would believe you. I pushed you off a cliff. Why should we trust each other?"

"Because we were friends, weren't we? *Aren't* we?" Pietro took a step forward. "There are things that I've learned as a grown-up that made me come back for you. You pushed me off a cliff, and I'm back trying to shake your hand. That's called *trust*. I'm trying to save your life because I care about you. That's called friendship. Some people call it love. Brotherhood. Politeness. Call it what you want, Kid, but instead of flying away to let you die, I came back because I *care* about you. So it's up to you. Stand and fight with us, children and adults side by side, or we can all die together. What do you say, big guy?"

Pietro could almost see Nibs's brain whirring to life, his eyes narrowing and his lips twisting in odd patterns. The boy stayed silent for a while, and then he held up a hand and said, "We need to discuss this. Turn around."

Pietro obeyed, and Enzo, Wendy, Snow, Zack, and Hook followed suit. It was a hilarious command, as Pietro could still hear every word Nibs and the boys exchanged. Their harsh whispers might as well have been screams.

"What do you think?" Nibs asked. "I think he might actually be cereal."

"Me too! But he's still friends with that stupid pirate!"

"The pirate might be nice now. Plus he has that hook instead of a hand. If the queen lady comes, he can cut her and protect us!"

"I like the man-boys. I think they wanna help. Plus there's that nice lady."

"Okay! Do we agree? Will we be Peter's friends again?"

"Yes!"

"Okay! We're gonna tell him. Ready? One, two, three." Nibs raised his voice to a yell. "Hey Peter! Turn around again!"

Trying not to smile, Pietro spun on his heels. "So what did you decide?"

Curly folded his arms and exchanged a knowing gaze with the rest of the boys. "We're friends again."

"Oh, boy!" Pietro clapped his hands and pretended to be surprised. "I'm so happy! Does this mean you'll leave Neverland with us? Will you come to the New World and fight the queen?"

"Yes," Nibs affirmed. "But first we need to get stuff. We need coconuts to throw at the queen. We need pixie dust. And then we'll leave with you. But we're *not* gonna grow up no matter what you say. We wanna come back to Neverland, and we want you to come too."

Pietro's heart sank. Of course the boys were going to have conditions of their own. Of course they were going to want him back on the island for good. How could he break their hopes when it took so long for them to agree? He forced himself to nod, removing his hands from his pockets and stepping into a handshake with Nibs. "Okay. Done."

"Yes!" Enzo pumped a fist in the air. "Then let's move. Let's get off this island and join our friends. Avoria's coming for Snow White, so I think we should all leave in waves. If Snow leaves first, we can distract the Ivory Queen and give Snow enough time to get back to Florindale, so I think the priority should be to get her off the island first. Nibs, will you and the boys fly her away? I promise, when this is all over, you'll have our full support to come straight back here."

Nibs tapped his chin, looking deep in thought. Finally, he nodded. "Okay. I'll choose ten boys to fly Snow out of here right away. The rest of us will stay and protect you, and we'll all fly together."

Pietro smiled. *That's the friend I know.*

"Good," Enzo said. "Who's leaving with Snow?"

Nibs pointed out ten different boys, all of whom stepped forward and saluted.

"Thank you," Enzo said. "Take Snow and get out of Neverland before Avoria comes. Head toward Florindale. We need to send a message to Princess Violet. If you can't find Violet, find Hua Mulan or Prince Liam. Tell them we're on our way. Can you do that for me, buddy? Can you remember those names and protect Snow White?"

"Yes!" the boys affirmed.

Snow bit her lip.

Pietro raised an eyebrow. "Uh-oh. Princess isn't happy." He patted Snow's shoulder and nodded reassuringly. "Hey, you okay? You don't want to do things this way, do you?"

"No," Snow admitted. "I don't like leaving you all behind. We're supposed to be in this together. Protecting *me* is *not* the trial. Protecting Florindale and the New World is the priority."

"But we can't do that if Avoria takes your soul again," Enzo argued. "We need to keep her as far away from you as possible, if only to buy us some time. I don't think she'll hurt me." He looked down and kicked a rock into the water. "She thinks she needs me for something. She told me so in Wonderland."

"Yeah?" Snow's voice took on a sarcastic bite. "What if it's the same reason she thinks she needs me? It would make a lot of sense, wouldn't it? Take the boy hero's soul, complete her rituals, rule the worlds? You need to be just as careful as I do, Enzo. Don't forget this."

"If that's true, then so be it. You know this is smart. If she wants both of us and we're standing in the same place, she wins. It makes sense to separate for a bit. I need to *act*," Enzo insisted. "I'll be fine with my friends here. *Please* go? I promised Liam you would be safe. If you don't go, I'll feel like I'm breaking a promise, and I don't want to feel that way."

Snow turned away and pressed a hand against her chest. "Of course you don't," she said softly. "I stand with you, Enzo. But know that I don't like this."

"None of us do. But I'm with our man on this one." Pietro tapped Enzo's back.

"Okay." Snow took a look at the group and nodded. "I'm ready then. I expect I'll see you all soon. You'll be right behind me, right?"

"*Right* behind you," Enzo affirmed. He snapped his fingers and summoned the golden fairy.

Tinker Bell took one look at Snow, and the next minute the fairy zipped around the air, showering the group with her dust. Silver snowflakes mingled with the shimmering powder, casting a beautiful effect through the air, but Pietro couldn't shake the feeling of foreboding, especially after Snow and her group burst into the air and soared toward the horizon without a word.

Pietro picked a snowflake off his nose and watched the ice dissolve on his finger. It was never supposed to snow in Neverland. They were running out of time. The fairy dust hit him in the forehead and washed over him like warm sunlight, but something felt *empty*. He didn't get that feeling of levity he used to have, like all his problems would drift into the sky. He looked at Enzo, whose toes were already off the ground. "Kid, this won't work for me."

"Yes it will. It has to," Enzo protested.

"I can't. I can't fly anymore." Pietro looked at his son, who seemed to be feeling the same. His feet stuck firmly to the ground, and he kept staring at his toes as if waiting for something to happen.

"I can't either," Zack said.

"Yes you can!" Enzo argued. "I saw you do it in Wonderland. You can fly, Zack."

"That was different. That was the power of darkness. The king got me to fly. It didn't count. I don't have my soul, Enzo." Zack gestured at Pietro and Wendy. "None of us do."

"I refuse to believe that," Enzo said. "Yes, Avoria took your souls. But if the power of darkness can make you fly, then so can the light! Stop resisting it! Pietro, stop fighting it and believe. Like you asked me to do in Maryland. Remember? *Focus.*"

"*Focusss,*" the wind hissed back.

The chill that lurched through Pietro's spine had little to do with the snow.

Enzo did a twist in the air, his chin to the sky and his eyes wide with alarm, before he drifted toward the Volos. "Pietro?"

The skies opened up, and a wall of ice rose from the choppy waters, reaching the clouds and circling the island.

Even after childhood, the icy voice never released its iron grip on Pietro's memory. He pulled Wendy and Zack close to him and gritted his teeth.

"*You're not going anywhere, loves. The Ivory Queen has come to play.*"

CHAPTER SEVENTEEN

THE OLD WORLD: NEVERLAND

As the Ivory Queen descended from the sky, Enzo's mind and heart whirred into overdrive. She came from the clouds as if she were a feather, falling with a sort of calculated grace. Her rust-colored hair billowed in a fiery star behind her, and her eyes were cold, dark marbles. Her cheekbones were like daggers and her lips were a blood-red bow, extremely prominent against her pale skin.

I'm truly going to die right now.

Avoria landed about ten feet from Enzo and addressed him directly. "Hello, Carver. At last we meet in the flesh, boy and queen." She took a long step forward and held her hand in front of her. "To see you standing before me at last! The boy the mirrors warned me about!"

At any other moment, Enzo would have backed away, but he descended from his flight and planted his feet on the ground. He could almost feel the frosty roots of his fear sprouting from his heart and curling around every nerve of his body. Numbness took hold of his temples, and he couldn't bring himself to react when Avoria took another step.

"You're a bit shorter than I expected you to be, but there's much to be admired," Avoria continued. "I've learned all about what you went through to get to me, Enzo, and I must say I'm proud to see you come this far. You were once such a simple boy. Dispassionate. Unappreciative. Selfish. There's no way I would've *wanted* your bland, tasteless soul in its original state."

Enzo couldn't bring his mouth to move.

"But now," Avoria said, "now look at you. To see you standing here in front of me and to know *everything* you must have gone through to get here and all the ways you must have grown in the process . . . You're quite a specimen, Enzo. You're nearly ready."

Enzo made a fist, and he stood tall. "I'm ready now! Why don't we finish this?"

"No, boy. I admire your bravery. But you still have some growing to do before you'll suit my tastes. Once you've had more time to stew in your fear, your loneliness, I'm certain your bitter soul will be *just* what I'm looking for."

A little flame of anger seared through the cold roots of Enzo's fear, and he summoned the strength to reply. "I'm sorry to disappoint you."

"He won't be alone," Pietro said, stepping in front of Enzo as if to shield him. "This boy will *never* be alone!"

"He never has been," Wendy added, taking Pietro's hand.

Avoria turned her lips up in a cold smile. Her eyes didn't move. "Your love is endearing. But he *will* be alone before all of this is through, as I was when the people of Florindale turned their backs on me." She pushed Pietro aside, tossing him to the ground like a piece of trash. The sand scraped his elbow and he winced, his eyes filling up with a fire Enzo hadn't seen from him before. Meanwhile, Avoria made a beeline for Enzo and used one fingernail to tip his chin up forty-five degrees. Her other hand clamped on Enzo's wrist and shot an icy shiver through his body. "Don't worry, boy. It's not terrible to be alone. Nobody will have to listen to you scream, for instance. Uncle Pietro and dear old Dad won't have to watch you die. Mother won't have to mop you from the stairway to my throne. It's an event of kindness, really, being alone."

"*You shut up, hag!*" Zack shouted. He dove at Avoria from the side and tackled her, effectively releasing her grip from Enzo's wrist and chin.

For a split second, the surprise petrified Enzo. Zack managed to attack Avoria? All this time, Enzo imagined that she was untouchable. Did the element of surprise tip the scales?

Avoria and Zack entangled themselves in a sloppy arm-in-arm combat. Enzo seized his chance to help his friend and rushed to her from behind, wrapping his arm around her throat in an attempt to pull her off Zack. "Let go of him!"

Avoria brought her heel down on Enzo's big toe, elbowed him in the stomach, and tossed Zack to the ground with a flick of her wrist. Then she spun on Enzo and threw him backward with the palm of her hand. He suspected a bullet to the chest would have felt similar. His nerves screamed and his anger flared, but it wasn't enough to pull him back to his feet. Avoria must have been doing some sort of telekinetic trick, because her palms were out and her gaze locked onto Enzo's face. Her eyeballs had taken on a dark, shadowy quality, as if the sockets had been emptied, and suddenly it felt like a thousand pro wrestlers were holding Enzo to the ground. He could barely wiggle a toe.

"I'm not here for you today, Carver, or your band of flying monkeys," the Ivory Queen droned. "But I see potential in you. How do I bring you to your full potency? What would help you stew a little bit more? Do you need to get *angrier?* Do you need to lose something precious for *good* this time? Do you need a thirst for vengeance?" She swiveled her palm toward Zack. "Do you need to watch a loved one die? You know, nothing forges a man like losing someone he's known since boyhood."

Enzo gritted his teeth, wishing he could resist Avoria's hold and make her feel his anger. "I swear," he grunted, "if you hurt Zack, you're going to get what's coming—"

"Oh bless your heart, you poor, stupid boy!" Avoria interrupted. "Fool! Without even finishing a sentence, you made two dire assumptions. Shall I enlighten you?"

Enzo didn't answer. He pressed his lips shut and forced a hot breath through his nostrils. It was the most he could move.

"I'm not talking about Zackary Volo," Avoria explained. "Though he *is* quite useless to me now, I want him to burn a bit more before I snap his strings. In fact, I wasn't even talking to you when I spoke of claiming a boyhood acquaintance."

She wasn't?

Avoria rounded on Pietro and smirked. "I was talking to *you*, fallen hummingbird. And I was talking about *him*."

Avoria shifted her palms again, and Wendy screamed. The sound chilled Enzo to the bone.

When Avoria moved her hands, the gravity shifted enough to let Enzo roll onto his elbows. But when he sat up, his blood ran cold. Captain Hook hovered in the air with his arms and legs spread apart, as if he were modeling Da Vinci's Vetruvian Man. His eyes were wide and pleading, and his throat looked tight as though an invisible serpent had wrapped its body around his neck.

"I wonder what else I can make your pirate prince do." Avoria tapped her foot. "What other poses shall I put him in?"

"Let him go, Avoria," Pietro warned. "You have an island full of people who are *not* going to be happy if you hurt that man. And that's only *this* island. Who knows what you're doing to Manhattan right now?"

"Oh, it's quite beautiful," Avoria assured. "Not all of you will see it, of course, but perhaps I'll let Mr. Hook come along under the right conditions. I know you're not a stupid bunch. I didn't come here to babble with you all day. I came for a *special* soul that keeps slipping through the cracks—lucky number seven—and quite frankly, I'm fed up. My wellspring of patience is dry right now, so I'll make this simple. Tell me where Snow White is hiding, and I'll release your pirate.

Dawdle, and you'll watch him peel his own throat open." Avoria flicked her wrist, and Captain Hook's arm bent so the tip of his hook pressed against the tender skin of his neck.

Hook winced and squeezed his eyes shut, a thin rivulet of liquid running from the corner of his eye and mixing with the dirt on his cheek. Enzo couldn't tell whether the man was sweating or crying.

Avoria held the pose, her expression cold and her body stiff. "Your move."

The pain in Pietro's eyes would haunt Enzo forever. For a moment, he had returned to his helpless, jaded form that lived next door to Enzo for a couple years, refusing to take a step or speak a word. Something inside Pietro had broken, fractured under the pressure of Avoria's choice.

"Dad, don't tell her!" Zack blurted. "Don't say a word! Keep your mouth shut for a minute."

"What's that you said, child?" Avoria asked. "Kill the pirate? You're not old enough to have such murder in your heart. Wait a few more minutes or so, when you've acquired more *life experience.*"

Surprised by Zack's outburst, Enzo gave him the evil eye. *Shut up!* Enzo mouthed.

Zack mouthed *sorry,* but the subtle flicker in his eyes told Enzo that his friend meant *look over there.* Years of friendship had trained them to have intricate conversations with their facial expressions alone, and it tended to drive their families up the wall.

What did I miss? What is he looking at? Enzo thought, shifting his gaze back to the rainforest.

"I throw the question back to *you,* Pan," Avoria said. "Where is Snow White?"

A slight flicker of movement disturbed a bush in the jungle, and that was when Enzo understood what Zack had been looking at. Spears, pointing straight up at the sky. There were eleven of them, made mostly of wood with carved stone protruding from the tips.

Enzo immediately knew who carried them, even though their faces were smeared with mud and the head with the darkest hair was laced with vines.

No! Enzo thought. *Why did they come back? She swore she would listen to me!*

Enzo made a mental note that if they all escaped the island together, he would have a word with Snow. His fists curled at his sides. He looked at Zack and wondered if he'd understand the facial expression for *Snow White is my least favorite person right now.*

"We sent her away," Wendy blurted. "Snow isn't here. She's on her way back to Florindale. We're one step ahead of you, witch!"

"I believe I asked *your husband*," Avoria sneered. "But since you're zealous to open your mouth—"

"It's true!" Pietro confirmed. "Snow isn't here. You want her? Go get her. But good luck finding her without us."

"You *lie*," Avoria whispered. "I have her scent, and it is ever present on this infernal island. You think I'd forget the taste of fruit and sugar? The tarty warmth of her soul? You're trying to hide her right underneath my nose, and hiding from the Ivory Queen is most unwise." She flashed a venomous smile at Hook and added, "How are you feeling, handsome? Is your arm getting tired? Are you afraid it might *slip?*" Avoria finished her sentence by making a swatting motion with her arm, and Captain Hook's elbow bent away from his neck, leaving a thin trail of blood on the side of his neck as though he'd nicked himself shaving.

"No! Stop!" Pietro put up his arms.

Avoria's nostrils flared, and she hovered a few feet in the air. "I'm *done* being charitable to your people. I am *done* with mercy and patience. Now, it's time you understood the meaning of pain! Say goodbye to your captain, darlings." She raised her arm again and aimed. "Looks like his cruise is *over!*"

"Charge!" Several screams poured from the beach as Avoria

prepared to execute her threat, but the loudest yells shook the jungle when Snow White and the Lost Boys thundered out of the rainforest with spears, rocks, slingshots, and arrows in hand.

A thick arc of rocks and arrows curled overhead, causing Avoria to turn. For a second, Enzo thought a glint of horror flickered over her face, bringing her jaw down and raising her brows. The terror quickly melted into an angry scowl, and Avoria shifted her palms to form a wall in front of her chest.

When the shift happened, Captain Hook dropped onto the beach and let out a startled cry, whereas the arrows and rocks froze in time and space, hovering in their arcs nearly ten feet from Avoria's body.

"Hook!" Pietro cried, scrambling to check on the pirate.

"You mean to do battle here of all places?" Avoria snarled. "In the heart of worlds? You would have been wise to save your energy until you could die with your precious Order beside you. You cannot hope to defeat me with a handful of sand?"

"How 'bout a dagger?" Enzo darted to his feet and swiped at Avoria, nicking her shoulder and opening a wound as wide as his thumb. The sound of her skin tearing made Enzo want to vomit, and he was surprised the blade had any reaction at all. He half expected the wound to heal up and close with the next second, and by the look on Avoria's face, she expected the same thing. Nobody made a sound.

She stared down at her shoulder, hands still up in front of her and her eyes in wide formations as the blood trickled into her sleeve. She swiveled her head and turned her anger to Enzo, who was ready to strike again.

"How *dare* you?" Avoria blocked Enzo's attack and swatted his face with the back of her right hand.

Enzo went flying along with the rocks on Avoria's right side. Some reversed direction, whereas others changed course and sought out new targets.

"Kid, be careful!" Pietro threw himself in front of Wendy and made an X with his arms, blocking an assault of smaller pebbles from hitting his face. He managed to catch a few, and he grabbed a slingshot out of one of the Lost Boys' hands, setting out to retaliate.

Zack dove for the ground, narrowly avoiding having his head clocked by a blunt rock the size of his shoe. With less than a second to catch his breath, he sprang back up and ran for Avoria. "I've got you, Enzo!"

"Get Snow!" Enzo snapped, still reeling from the bone deep sting of Avoria's slap.

Avoria waved her other hand and sent the rest of the rocks and arrows soaring through the air with twice the speed of the first batch. With both hands free, she dropped back to the ground and made a beeline for Snow. Avoria walked slowly, a devious smile spreading across her face. "Hello again, fairest one," she said. "I've spent many an hour wondering what you did to reclaim your soul from me. Your reputation doesn't do you justice. Sure, you're beautiful, kind, and fair, but few have spoken of your wile and your fighting spirit. I still don't know how you did it, but this time I'm going to take you myself, and your days shall come to an end. 'Tis a shame, really, but you've earned your pride. After all the measures that have been taken to keep you from interfering with my dominion, you fought hard right up until we met face to face. Your prince hardly deserves you."

"You have no right to talk about Liam," Snow spat, every word a dagger. "No right at all. After all you've done to keep us apart, I swore I would end you or watch you burn." She spread her arms apart and took a bold step forward. "So take me away, Your Royal *Highness*. At least I'll be that much closer to snuffing you out!"

"No! Snow, what are you doing?" Enzo sprinted through the sand and met Snow face to face. "We had a plan! You're walking right into her arms!" He spun around and shielded her with his body, meeting Avoria's gaze with a fire of his own. "I'm not letting you take her!"

Avoria threw her head back and cackled. "Oh, how endearing! You would continue to defy me, risking your own bones to save this woman. Why do you toy with me, Carver? You got your family back. You even got yourself a *lady friend*. Go play house with them, and stay out of my hair until I come for you!"

"This is *bigger* than family!" Enzo gestured to Snow and to the people around him. "They're my family, too. And they're not going anywhere."

"You have a mouth." Avoria placed her hands on her hips and nodded as if to express a modicum of respect for him. "Listen up, Carver. You and I shall have a duel of blades. Show me you're more than your words. This is your chance to act. You have a minute to land a single blow, after which I leave Neverland with empty hands. You can even choose a *partner* to aid you. So what do you say, hero? Save the worlds from me?"

Three iron swords appeared in the ground, two crossed in an X with the third dividing it in half. Enzo thought about Avoria's deal. Could he actually beat her? The Order had prepared him well. He practiced enough with Mulan, Pietro, Liam, and even Geppetto, and every one of them remarked at how he improved over time.

"You have my iron-clad word, if that's why you're dawdling," Avoria added. "Had you grown up in Florindale, you'd know the value of one's word. Even I am not so heartless as to break an ironbound promise. So are you feeling brave, Carver?"

"Don't do it, lad!" Hook shouted.

"You've got this, Enzo!" Zack said. "I'll help!"

"Enzo," Snow whispered. "Do what your heart tells you. I support you."

Says the woman who turned around and went against our plan, Enzo thought. He was too bitter to respond kindly, but he nodded once and turned back to Avoria. "You have a deal." He took the middle sword out of the ground and inspected its weight and angles. "Zack, you're my partner."

Wendy went ghost white, and Pietro sank onto the ground, face in his hands.

Zack jogged over and took a second sword. Enzo gave him a meaningful look, and Zack muttered, "Stay defensive, Enzo. Don't get cocky."

The corners of Avoria's lips went up and all her teeth showed, their whiteness a stark contrast to the darkness in her eyes. "Good. Now one final detail. A simple precaution that I will lift when our minute is up, regardless of the outcome." She waved her hands once, and time stopped around them. Pietro, Hook, Wendy, Snow, and the Lost Boys froze like mannequins. Even the ocean tide stopped breathing. "This tips the scales in *your* favor, of course. You hardly need the added distractions."

"You just don't want them to interfere," Zack said.

Avoria ignored Zack, picked up the third sword, and spun it with a flourish. "Now, remember the conditions: One minute, and I leave Neverland empty-handed. Any questions?"

"Yeah, what should we put on your headstone?" Enzo asked.

"*Enzo*," Zack scolded. "Focus!"

"Fools." Avoria laughed through her nose and contorted into a battle stance. "Let's see how much you've *really* learned from the Order of the Bell."

Enzo leveled his sword in front of him, and Zack mirrored.

Avoria raised the blade above her head. "Begin."

CHAPTER EIGHTEEN

THE OLD WORLD: NEVERLAND

Zack, Avoria, and Enzo smacked blades with a deafening ring, and Zack knew that surviving for a minute wasn't going to be easy. *This could be our last minute alive.*

Avoria pushed back with the force of a bull, throwing Enzo and Zack aside with heavy grunts. Without wasting any time, she ran for Zack and hacked, slashed, and jabbed at the air, trying to poke holes in his courage. He wasn't proud to say that it was working. *I'm in much more danger than Enzo is.* Of course the Ivory Queen didn't want to kill Enzo. She was still terrified that he might be the final soul she needed. Zack was expendable. She *had* his soul. He would have to distract her and keep her busy so that Enzo might have a chance at beating Avoria.

"Come on!" he taunted, beckoning the queen. "Take your best shot! I'm standing right here!"

Avoria kicked Enzo's chest and drove him to the ground, and then she spun and lunged for Zack. Zack gritted his teeth, thrust his own sword horizontally above him, and the blades connected. The second they met, Zack's shoulders turned to jelly. The metal vibrated in his fingers, and the jolt surged through the bones in his arms.

What surprised Zack the most was the sound. The blades didn't ring. They thundered with a ground-shaking rumble, and the earth lurched beneath his feet. The sand turned jet black with a ripple of wind. Trees toppled in his peripheral vision. And Avoria sneered behind her sword, hair in a static-filled web behind her. "You resisted the shadows," she said. As if on cue, the clouds darkened overhead. The waters churned and slapped against the wall of ice Avoria built around the island. "Love won't always save you, boy. It couldn't save your parents, and it certainly won't save your friend!"

Enzo climbed to his feet and stumbled behind Avoria with his sword drawn.

Zack smirked, blade still locked against Avoria's. "What will save *you?*" he asked.

With a harsh *whoosh!* Enzo swung his weapon, and Avoria whirled around to counter, leaving Zack free to strike her from behind. He smacked her side with the tip of his blade, and the ice walls exploded around the island, crumbling back into the ocean as another wave of trees fell around him. This time, part of the ground crumbled, too.

Avoria shrieked as the freeze on time melted away, and Zack's parents, Hook, and the Lost Boys stirred back into motion like wind-up toys.

"Commendable, Son of Pan," Avoria said. "I shall uphold my bargain."

The sword dissolved into air in Zack's fingers, and Avoria's and Enzo's disappeared as well. Only when Zack looked around him, something was wrong—not just with the island, but with the group. They were short one person.

"Where's Snow?" Enzo bellowed. "No! What did you do with her?"

Zack marched up to Avoria and jabbed her with his finger. "You promised!" he roared. "You promised you would leave this island without her! Where is she, you lying, cheating—"

"Silence!" Avoria boomed, every one of her teeth showing as

she pronounced the word. She lowered her hands, and her devious grin returned. "Fools. I *never* break my ironclad word. You fail to understand it for what it is. I told you I'd leave Neverland empty-handed, and I shall." She showed her empty palms as if she were a magician trying to earn an audience's trust before a magic trick. "See? Nothing in my hands. As for *them,* however . . ." Avoria gestured to a particular point in space, and Zack and Enzo traced the path of her finger. "*They're* entitled to whatever they please."

Zack's heart dropped.

The shadows.

There were three of them, zipping through the air with a disturbingly silent Snow White in their arms.

Cries of anger and fear erupted all over the beach.

Dark visions and memories scuttled into Zack's mind. A floating island in the sky. Attacking Rosana. Being locked in combat against Enzo. Breaking the mirror in Wonderland and releasing the shadow that filled Zack's veins with cold, unfiltered darkness. He flinched, his adrenaline coursing through him like a river.

"You witch!" Enzo cried, tears flowing from the corners of his eyes. "Why are you the way you are? She's done nothing to you! Why are you so evil?"

"Because"—Avoria took a step forward and tilted Enzo's chin up— "I was *made* this way." With a dirty sleeve, she wiped her mouth and flashed a wicked grin. "Dry your tears, Carver. Accept your defeat. Not even your simple *grandfather* had the gall to *cry* in front of me."

Enzo let out a feral sound and became a flurry of fists and kicks that bounced off Avoria like tennis balls.

Avoria laughed with her hands on her hips. Over the next few seconds, she ascended slowly and gracefully into the air like a helicopter, cackling the whole time without pausing for a single breath. Once she was high off the ground to where nobody could touch her, she rocketed backward and away from the island. She waved her hand in front of her as she soared, and a horrible lurching noise sounded from the center of the island.

The ground shook. Zack spread his feet to keep his balance, staring Avoria down until she became a speck in the sky.

Enzo's knees hit the ground while Zack's heart flushed ice cold.

His father rushed between them and put his hands on their backs, making soft shushing noises and pulling the boys onto his shoulders. "Kid, take it easy, please. I'm as angry as you are, but this is *not* the way this ends. Do you hear me?"

"Why didn't Snow follow the plan?" Enzo sobbed. "She could've gone free, and now Avoria's one step ahead again. One more step and this is all over. All of it."

Hook took a seat on a dark boulder next to Enzo and buried his fingers in his hair, resting his eyes and taking deep, meditative breaths.

Zack's father sighed, worry lines appearing in his forehead. "I don't know. She's a fighter. She's probably going to try to take Avoria down from within, or weaken her a bit before we move in. That's how she is, Enzo. Nothing we do can ever change her spirit. She's set."

Enzo stood, wiped his face, and paced back and forth with his arms crossed. "Let's go, please. I'm done here."

Zack knew his friend better than anybody. Enzo had reached his wit's end. He would make Avoria pay *soon*, or he would die fighting, and Zack would be standing right beside him.

CHAPTER NINETEEN

THE OLD WORLD: NEVERLAND

"We need to get off quickly and fly in pairs," Enzo said. "Zack, you're with me." He took his knife from his pocket and held it out to Zack. "I'm trusting you with this. Slash anything that tries to knock us out of the sky."

Zack wrapped his fingers around the knife with a cautious expression in his eyes. "Really?"

"You'll be fine," Enzo said. "Just keep me in the air. And don't drop it. Pietro, who is carrying you? I'd like you to lead the way. I'm pretty sure only you know the way back to Florindale."

"I've got you, Pete," Nibs assured him.

After all the non-flyers confirmed they had somebody to carry them, it was time to leave, and not a moment too soon, for the ground had dissolved into a soupy mess at Enzo's feet. Water soaked his boots and penetrated the space between his toes. Behind him, trees crumbled and sank into the island. At the rate the island sank, there would be nothing left to stand on in a matter of minutes. Enzo worried more about Zack than anyone else. He couldn't swim.

Zack climbed on Enzo's back, found a center of balance, and held the knife in a ready position. Despite the fact that Zack was taller and heavier than Enzo, Enzo adjusted quickly and took it as a sign that he'd gained some muscle.

"Tinker Bell," Enzo said, "get us going."

The golden fairy returned and poured her magic over the group, warming Enzo to the bone again. As he rose, the ground beneath receded into the ocean until the water had swallowed the castles in the trees.

Sadness pooled in Pietro's eyes. His voice was heavy when he breathed, "Goodbye, Neverland."

The words were blades to Enzo's heart, almost paradoxical. Neverland was a place nobody should ever have to say goodbye to. If people never grew up here, time shouldn't change it. It should exist forever. He looked at the hovering crew around him. "Everybody ready?"

The group nodded their affirmations and responded by hovering a foot or two off the surface of the water.

Pietro jammed a finger in front of him. "Straight ahead," he said. "Where Avoria went. That's the way back to Florindale."

Without another word, Enzo sped away, his feet dipping into the water and creating a jetstream. His friends either flanked him or hovered right behind, and they all fell into a neat formation that looked a lot like a flock of birds. As he flew, Enzo silently pleaded. *Don't let her hurt Snow White. Let us catch up, please.*

And do what? How are we going to beat her? The thought nearly weighed Enzo down. He caught himself sinking, and his toes dipped into the water again.

Behind him, a wet, desperate sputtering noise sounded, followed by the gruff voice of Captain Hook. "Watch where you're splashin', lad!"

Enzo hovered and smirked. "Sorry."

"Don't you fall," Zack warned. "I'm trusting you with my life here, bro!"

Caw!

A seagull dipped through the sky, narrowly missing Enzo's ear before it veered away and flapped backward toward Neverland.

"I'm trusting *you*," Enzo said. "Still got my knife?"

Zack let out a rich, full laugh, rattling the bones in Enzo's back.

"You're joking, right?" Zack asked. "You really don't expect me to cut an innocent bird out of the sky, do you?"

Enzo grinned. "I don't know. Is your aim that terrible?"

Zack thumped Enzo's ear, filling it with a light stinging pain. "*You're* terrible!"

"Ow!" Enzo massaged his earlobe. "I was only kidding! Of course I don't want you to kill the birds. Just shoo them away or something."

"Bird killer." Zack started to pocket the knife.

Pietro's voice rang out beside them. "Don't put it away."

"Why?" Enzo resisted the urge to turn his head. The slightest movement could steer him off course. "Pietro, what did you see?"

Boom!

A black humanoid shape rocketed out of the water in front of Enzo, screaming and wailing like a banshee. Though it was only above the surface for about two seconds before it arced back into the water, Enzo immediately noticed the shimmering tail that split into two flaps and met a rough, dark human torso made of shadows. And in its hand, a coal-black pitchfork burned with electric blue fire at each of the three tips.

"Whoa!" Enzo veered up and over before the dark figure pierced the water again. He could feel Zack's heightened pulse hammering down and into Enzo's bones.

"What the hell was that?" Zack asked.

"That was a merman," Pietro said. "I recognized him. He used to be a nice, non-shadowy dude once upon a time. The shadows must be in the water now."

"Let's fly higher," Enzo said. "I don't want that thing popping out again and dragging me un—"

The water's surface exploded again, and a grimy, slippery hand yanked on Enzo's wrist.

"Kid!" Pietro shouted.

Enzo looked into the dark merman's face, eyes filled with shadows, and attempted to fight his pull with basic mastery of flight. Somebody accelerated behind him, grabbed his feet, and ascended, tilting Enzo at a forty-five-degree angle. "Nibs and I have you, Enzo!" Pietro yelled. "Don't let him pull you under!"

Enzo reached up with his free hand. "Knife!"

Zack hooked his ankles together underneath Enzo's stomach and attempted to slash the merman beneath them. The effort was fruitless, cutting right through the shadow as if Zack had poked a hologram. He pressed the handle into his friend's palm. "It's all you, buddy!"

When Enzo took the knife, however, his soul hummed with the blade's power as if the handle had become one with his hand.

The merman sneered, snapped his teeth at Enzo, and tugged harder, bringing him a full two feet closer to the water. Zack waved his arms and dug his ankles into Enzo's chest, struggling to balance on his shoulders.

"Let me go!" Enzo swiped the knife in front of him, once again yielding no effect except to agitate the shadow and tighten its icy grip on his arm. He sank another foot, and his wrist went underwater. A cold burn plunged through his fingertips.

"Enzo!" Zack cried.

Nibs and Pietro pulled hard on Enzo's feet.

"Hang on!" Enzo shouted back. He squeezed the knife and imagined Rosana's face. He had to get back to her. He had to get back to Liam and Snow and the rest of the family. The thought of their faces filled Enzo's heart with light, the kind that radiated from the chest out and melted through his joints. He raised his knife again and slashed.

Whoosh!

A jet of water arced out of the ocean, its trajectory a perfect mirror of the path Enzo traced through the air with his knife.

"What did you do?" Zack asked, his voice soft with wonder.

Enzo could barely believe the sight himself. "I don't know." He carved another path through the shadow and the air. Another stream of water burst in front of him. He drew a squiggle in the air, and the water mirrored it. "I think my knife is controlling the water!"

The shadow merman jerked on Enzo's arm, and a second later he took in a cold mouthful of water. His eyes stung. His lungs burned. Zack tumbled into the ocean and off Enzo's back.

Enzo forced his eyes open, processing a blurred outline of the dark creature that dragged him into the water. The next thing he knew, there were five outlines of equal size and similar shape rising from the ocean's depths, and they were all making a beeline for Enzo.

Then a memory bloomed in his mind. A rich, deep voice cut through the murk and eerie bubbling of the water, and Enzo thought of his grandfather.

Yes, boy, a true Carver can work with anything! Wood, marble, stone, diamonds, even the earth itself.

Enzo thought for a minute. *Water?*

He flicked the knife, and it ripped open a path in front of him, parting the water with a sudden force that divided the group of mermen in half. The opposing currents pushed the shadow creatures apart, and Enzo watched them struggle to regain control of their own tails. Determined not to let them do so, he made two more slashes, one in a horizontal line and one straight down the original merman's line of symmetry.

Shrill screams and wails blasted through the water, and Enzo watched as three of the mermen dissolved into miniscule bubbles of dark smoke that swam up toward the surface, burst, and evaporated into clean air.

A thick hand plunged into the water and seized Enzo by the collar of his shirt. He struggled, slashing wildly at the water until he rose to the surface and saw that he was in Nibs's grasp. Pietro pulled Zack out of the water and gripped his hand.

Enzo coughed and sputtered until he could gain control of his flight again. "Thanks, Nibs," he breathed.

"Don't thank me yet. Keep fighting!"

Five more dark creatures leapt out of the water in calculated arcs, and Enzo growled to himself. He took Zack from Pietro and let him steady himself on Enzo's back. He looked at his knife. *If you can do anything else, now's the time to help me out.*

Enzo flicked his wrist. A geyser spurted from the water and swallowed one of the mermen. A dull ache pulsed in Enzo's arm muscles as if he'd moved the water on his own.

"Watch out!" Zack cried, and a merman hurdled toward Enzo with the pitchfork aimed straight for his forehead.

Enzo countered the pitchfork with his knife, satisfied by the sound of metals ringing together, and then he moved the blade in an arc above his head like a rainbow. An arc of seawater cascaded from the ocean and ripped through the shadow, leaving only damp salted air spraying Enzo's lips.

The remaining shadows dipped back into the water. For a solid minute or so, nothing came back out of the surface, and Enzo and the Lost Boys continued to fly with no interruptions or siege.

Dad, Geppetto, I can't wait to show you what I did, Enzo thought. He smiled, but he kept his guard up. As long as those things were still in the water, they would continue to attack. Enzo took the opportunity to pull up, motioning for the boys to follow suit until it seemed they were a safe distance from the shadows' reach. Then again, he had no idea how high those mermen could jump.

"Pietro," Enzo said. "How much farther, do you think?"

"We're probably about halfway. Man, it goes *so* much faster when you fly than when you take a ship."

"Faster doesn't make it better. You miss the beauty of the journey," Hook argued.

"Beauty? Since when are you the sentimental type?"

"I think he means *booty*," Zack joked.

"Now you're stereotyping," Hook growled. "I don't appreciate it much."

Enzo rolled his eyes. "You're a pirate. By definition, you attack people and steal their stuff."

Hook grunted. "Hm. I suppose that's fair."

"Heads up," Pietro warned. The sounds of heavy splashes cut through his words. "Fish out of water again. Pissed-off mermaids straight ahead. Got your knife ready, Enzo?"

"Always."

Ten mermen leapt out of the water at the same time, but strangely, they didn't reach for Enzo or anybody else in the group. All ten of the shadows were swimming and jumping *away* from him, as if they were only trying to get ahead. It wouldn't have been hard, because they were all considerably faster. Somehow, Enzo found it more foreboding that they were swimming away, though he wanted to believe they started to fear him and decided to flee.

The group followed for a while, Enzo's fingers on the blade handle the whole time in case the mermen turned around and decided to attack again. Ultimately, it turned out they had a worse plan in mind.

When the shadows were a few football fields away, barely visible against the dark horizon, Enzo watched as the mermen peeled high out of the water, did a full turn, and converged upon a single point in the sea. All ten of them landed in the same spot at the same time, and when they hit, all the water within a fifty-foot radius turned black and bubbled like a pot of soup.

"Oh no," Zack muttered, echoing Enzo's own thoughts. "I don't like that."

"We should stop," Wendy suggested.

"We should *hurry*," Enzo said. He zoomed forward, determined to make it back to Florindale before any other attacks could come up, but things weren't looking good. The bubbles grew bigger, each so massive that Pietro could have stood inside one and still had room to wave his arms over his head. Enzo wasn't in a hurry to find out what lurked underwater and what the mermen had done.

But then a mighty silhouette rose from the center of the black spot, and Enzo was certain his life was over. The ten shadows had knitted themselves together and formed a colossal super-merman, his protruding torso about as tall as a skyscraper, with a flaming trident to match his height. His long, wet beard and tangled hair dripped with shadows, and the darkness in his eyes could have swallowed Enzo whole. The merman's mouth could have done the same. One simple gulp, and the world would end.

"Go around him!" Enzo yelled.

The group broke formation, with roughly half swerving to the left while Enzo and the other half curved to the right. He quickly learned that fleeing wasn't an option. The merman laughed, a terrible noise like an avalanche, and raised his pitchfork. Blue fireballs the size of Pietro's truck hurtled from each prong and aimed for different members of the group. One of them made a beeline for Enzo.

"*Zack, hang on!*" Enzo screamed. Shutting his eyes and gritting his teeth, he rolled over in midair and dodged the fireball.

Zack lost his balance and cried out in the roll but managed to hold on. "Hey buddy, how 'bout a *little* more notice next time?"

"I told you to hang on!"

A fireball collided with something on the merman's other side, and Enzo watched in horror as somebody in the group plummeted into the water.

"*Curly!*" Pietro shouted, his voice raw and broken.

"You'll pay for that one, you overgrown jerk!" Nibs declared.

Another set of fireballs rocketed from the trident, and Enzo shot upward to avoid one.

Enzo's heart twisted into knots. He knew he would have been foolish to believe they could actually complete this journey without casualties, and yet he actually had a glimmer of hope that it might happen.

"Enzo," Zack said, "you've gotta make some waves, man. You're the only one who can stop this thing."

Enzo bit his lip. He raised a stream of water with his knife, but as he suspected, it was barely a couple drops compared to the massive size of the merman. "I can't." He swiped three more times, each slash a little harder and wider than the last. "I can't make a splash big enough to do any damage."

Zack clamped his hand on Enzo's shoulder and gave it a brotherly squeeze. "Maybe don't make a splash. Make something else."

Enzo scoffed. "What are you talking about? Start making some sen—" An idea flew into his mind, and he grinned. "You're a genius, man. Hang on."

With that, Enzo dipped into the water one more time and submerged his knife. He closed his eyes, the way his father and grandfather advised when they taught him their craft. And all the sounds and vibrations of the water flowed into Enzo's fingertips. The sensation overwhelmed him in the most hauntingly beautiful way. He saw baby clownfish hatching from their eggs. Starfish clung to the ocean floor and quietly observed the world above them. Anemones danced in the waves, and jellyfish pulsed and flexed with the heartbeat of the ocean. And in a pocket of water that had yet to be disturbed by the dark, a mermaid sang a song in a language Enzo had never heard before.

The water has a soul.

The blade guided Enzo's hand in a deliberate pattern through the water, making circles, lines, and squiggles before it let him stop. He opened his eyes in time to dodge another blue fireball and rocket out of the water again.

"Kid, I hope you're doing something!" Pietro called out.

"What *did* you do?" Zack asked.

"Wait," Enzo answered.

Not a second later, Tinker Bell soared into view and dipped her feet in the water where Enzo had touched it. A bright light pulsed beneath her feet, and to Enzo's wonder and amazement, the head of a serpent emerged from the surface, followed by the rest of its enormous body. It was made entirely of water, but the detail was mesmerizing. Every individual scale sparkled in the moonlight, and each of its teeth was at least as big as the merman's head. The sea serpent winked at Enzo and flicked its tongue, releasing drops of water into the air. Enzo grinned.

"*Snake!*" Pietro cried. "I think I'll take death by fire, thanks."

"No!" Enzo said. "This is a good guy! He's gonna help us!"

"You made that?" Zack asked.

"I did. Here, we need to get on its back. He'll take us back to Florindale. Right?"

The snake winked again.

"We're trusting you," Zack said.

Enzo drifted down onto the snake's head, and the rest of the group followed suit. Immediately, Enzo felt a wave of fatigue crash over him. Sometimes that happened when he finished an elaborate carving, especially when he worked with something other than traditional wood or marble. Until now, he never even fathomed working with water, and it sapped the energy in his bones, paining his knuckles. Nonetheless, he was proud when everybody fit snugly onto the serpent's back, and the water held the group's weight as easily as a chair or a floor would.

Enzo reached forward, muscles screaming, and patted the snake between the eyes. "We need your help, okay? We need you to get rid of that shadow guy and take us to the shores of Florindale."

The snake nodded, and the next thing Enzo knew, they rocketed toward the shadow merman with frightening speed. At the same time, three more fireballs shot out of the trident and converged on a single point. Sitting on the head of the snake put Enzo directly in their trajectory. But the serpent opened its mouth, swallowed the fireballs as easily as though they were candle flames, and rolled along like a vicious tsunami.

The merman's face grew closer every second, its eye almost as big as Enzo himself. He shut his eyes and braced for impact, friends screaming behind him as his serpent met the shadow head on.

CHAPTER TWENTY

The next time Enzo woke up, the gentlest touch on his sore shin jolted his eyes open. His breaths were heavy and short, his mind still filled with images of dark shadows, fireballs, and infinite waters. It relieved him to wake up in an actual bed, bundled up to his collarbone with warm blankets and thick, fluffy pillows. He blinked, steadied his breath, and his mother's voice completed his transition from sleep to lucidity.

"Good morning, my son," she said. "Mr. Baker and I made breakfast. Do you wanna eat something?"

Enzo rubbed his forehead, heart full. No matter how much his world changed, he could count on one consistent factor to stay the same. He could fail an exam, break a bone, or ride home on a tidal wave shaped like an enormous sea monster, and the next morning, his mom would always start his day by asking if he wanted breakfast.

"Hi, Mom," he breathed. "I'd love some breakfast, thanks." He removed his blanket and started to roll out of bed, only for his father to lean into view and put a firm hand on Enzo's chest. Enzo jumped. He hadn't even seen his father sitting there.

"Better stay in bed a bit longer," he said. "You have a few bruises and burns. One of Ben's muffins and some homemade cooking should fix you up."

"Nice of you to come back to us, by the way," his mom added.

The tone in her voice made Enzo's heart twist inside his chest, especially during that last sentence. It wasn't like his mother to lecture or scold, but the hurt in her voice could freeze water.

Enzo threw his head back against the pillow, hoping to jog his memory. What happened, anyway? The last thing he remembered was summoning the serpent from the water? Where were the others?

Where's Avoria? He took it as a good sign that he woke up near his family and they didn't mention the Ivory Queen right away. Perhaps she never reached Florindale. Maybe the merman dragged her underwater? But if that were the case, where was Snow White?

"Mom, look—"

"I was just worried about you, that's all," his mother interrupted. "I understand your role in this, son, but when the fires died down and they started identifying the casualties, and you still hadn't popped up anywhere . . . I only wish you'd understand how worried you made me. In fact, one day you probably will, and that will be your punishment for scaring me. I'm *not* discussing this any further with you." She dipped out of the room and followed the steam drifting in from the next room, which smelled of crisp bacon, fresh fruit, and rising bread.

Enzo rolled his eyes and stared at the ceiling. Without looking at his father, he asked, "Are *you* mad at me, too?"

"She's not angry, Enzo," his dad said. "Neither am I. Sure, I worried. That's only natural. But any worry that *I* feel for you in this world, your mother feels tenfold. She's still a little bit fragile trying to adjust to everything. Me? I've *lived* this before. I know how dangerous it is, but I also believe in the light, my boy." He paused and drew a breath. "That being said, yes. I *do* wish you would have informed us before you took off like that. We *just* got you back."

Enzo winced. There it was.

"Do you know that half the town was destroyed in the time that you were gone? Bellamy's forces *ravaged* the place. The bell tower? Gone. Ben's bakery? Gone. Houses belonging to people who weren't even supposed to be a *part* of all this . . . obliterated. I feel obligated not to put this lightly for you. There were casualties, Enzo. We buried some of our own. I thought you might have been among the dead. Then this tide comes in over by Grimm's Hollow, and Pietro and Hook and a handful of kids who call themselves the Lost Boys carry your unconscious body into town, right along with your buddy"—his father pointed across the room, where Zack lay sleeping in an identical bed— "and his mother, who needed immediate medical attention because her lungs were filled with water. Hook and Peter, carrying a body together. That's how I know things have gone wrong. I tell you all of this because yes, I did worry for you, and on an equal yet opposite level, I am so *proud* of you! You carved a beast made of *water* to take down that shadow. Unbelievable!"

Enzo scratched his head, unsure of whether he should apologize or say thank you first. He looked down and opted for the second option. "Sorry about everything, Dad."

"Oh, I don't need your apologies, son. But you might want to apologize to your mother, if for no other reason than to acknowledge the validity of her concern. You know how hard it was for you and me when *she* was missing."

Enzo's first instinct was to state that on some level they would have to get used to him disappearing and that his obligation to stop Avoria trumped any responsibilities to inform his parents about every move he made. Plus, he was a teenager. If his life ever went back to normal, it would bloom in new directions. He'd be driving a car soon. Then, he'd be able to get into R-rated movies with Zack and Rosana without sneaking. Enzo wondered if there were any age-related rites of passage in the Old World.

Eager to end the discussion and relieve some of the guilt, Enzo changed the subject. "What else has happened around here?" He looked down and picked at his cuticles. "You said we lost some people." His heart skipped a beat. "*Where's Rosana?*"

His mother reentered the room, along with Benjamin Baker, and they lowered trays of muffins, eggs, and bacon by Enzo's bed. Ben nodded, uttered a soft, "Mister Enzo, sir, enjoy," and left the room.

Enzo's mother frowned and shook her head. "I was afraid you were going to ask that first. Maybe you should eat, and then we'll talk."

His father twisted his lips to the side and spoke in a quiet, soothing tone. "We need to tell him, Carla. He needs to know."

"Pino!"

"How about this? Eat your breakfast so you can heal up, and then we'll go for a walk, okay? We'll catch you up on everything that happened, but it's better if we *show* you. Hopefully Mr. Zack over there will wake up soon as well."

Enzo's shoulders tensed, and his hunger fell away. "Why are you being coy? Just tell me, is she alive? Tell me that and I'll eat."

"Yes, she's alive," his mom answered.

"She's alive *and* . . . is she hurt?"

"She's *fine*, Enzo," his dad answered. "But you should know she's not here right now. She went looking for you, and she thought you might have gone over to—"

"The New World," Enzo finished. "Dammit, Rosana! Why did she do that? We were supposed to go together!"

His dad rested his hand on Enzo's chest. "I promise you, she's okay. There are others with her, you know—Liam, Mulan, Hansel, people who can keep her safe until you arrive. Most of those boys who came back from Neverland with you are out there too. The movement has begun. We're going to get you ready to join them, but you need to let us help you first."

"Now *please* eat your breakfast. I worked hard on it for you." Enzo's mom's lip quivered, and she drew a shaky breath. "It's all I know how to do for you here, Enzo."

"Mom," Enzo breathed, feeling all the little fibers of his heart unspool. He beckoned her to lean closer, and he hugged her with everything he had.

He ate his breakfast with a bit of a lump in his throat, overcome with emotions he found impossible to contain. He didn't like seeing his mother sad or claiming that she felt useless. The silence beyond the house's walls also disturbed him. No birds chirping, tree leaves dancing, or dwarves humming a merry tune. No Gretel playing outside and filling the air with laughter. No knowledge of where Rosana might be. He wolfed down his muffin, eager to get out of bed and look for her. With every bite, the burns on his chest smoothed over and healed, and his bruises faded from a stark purple to his natural peachy-colored skin, flipping a switch in his veins. Lethargy turned to energy, and Enzo sprang out of bed.

Zack awoke shortly thereafter, and after a few remarks about the previous night's journey, he and Pietro accompanied the DiLegnos on the hike they had promised Enzo.

While they trekked, Enzo's dad used a walking stick and led the group into the Woodlands. "Nobody has seen Violet since before the coronation," he explained. "We all know she's strong and she can hold her own, but for the time being, we must prepare as though the worst has occurred." He raised his stick and rapped on a knot in the thickest tree of the Woodlands. "That's why Carla and I have taken over Violet's den until further notice."

The tree trunk opened like a curtain, revealing an enormous room containing Violet's elaborate set-up of mirrors, books, and fancy trinkets for which Enzo had no idea the purpose.

"Come in," his mother said, and the group followed. Once they were all inside, the tree knitted itself back together and sealed everybody in. Enzo walked around, studying the various mirrors adorning the walls and surfaces in the den. At first glance, they all looked like picture frames, each a different shape and size containing a unique image. But soon Enzo noticed the glimmers of movement in the frames: a bird gliding off a telephone pole in one image, a flash of lightning in another, a boy about his age smoothing his hair and winking at himself, and the scenes went on and on.

"This is moderately terrifying," Pietro said. "All these mirrors. This feels wrong."

"We needed to gather all the information we could. You see, when you were in Neverland, most of the Order moved to the New World. Some were chased, some followed Liam, and many of them went through after the battle." Enzo's dad put his hands on Enzo's shoulders. "And Rosana is among them."

"We almost went too. But then we found an easier way." Carla gestured to a long, rectangular mirror on the far side of the room. "We saw Rosana in that frame over there with Liam. Merlin helped us collect these all over Florindale. It turns out we can see almost anything happening in the New World if we have enough resources. Violet left some notes to rig them and show us reflections in mirrors, puddles, treated windows back home, you name it. So we looked for you, but we found almost everyone else instead."

Enzo dragged his heel across the ground. So Rosana was okay, but was she truly safe?

"And what's happening over there?" Zack asked, his arms folded as he swiveled his head and studied each mirror one by one.

Enzo's dad beckoned the group to follow him to another frame, which showed the bottom of an enormous white structure. "That's where Avoria lives right now. We can't see anything on the inside, but *outside*, there's a lot going on. See these little black dots here?"

Enzo squinted. The mirror was small to begin with, but the dots around the building were so tiny Enzo could barely see them. "Ants?"

"People," his father corrected, "or about as close as one can come to personhood without being human. They're a lot like the Hearts you pulled out of Wonderland, or like Cinderella or Jack, but they're on Avoria's side. They're protecting her building from anybody who wishes to enter. Nobody's getting in there until all of those things are gone, so you can probably guess what *our* people are working on over there."

"Whoa!" Zack breathed, pointing to another mirror with a fractured image. "Is that a dragon?"

Even with its cracks and lines, the image was unmistakable. The leathery wings of a dragon were folded into the rubble of a building with a gaping hole in the side. *A dragon in New York*, Enzo thought. "Now I've seen everything."

"Whoa," Pietro breathed. "Hey, Pin, remember when I asked for a dragon at a pet shop and they looked at me like I was an idiot? Man, I really hope that guy sees this somehow."

Zack shook his head. "Pops, please don't try to take that one home. What happened to it?"

"We don't know," Enzo's mom answered. "All we know is that right now our people are coming together over there. Those boys from Neverland just went into one of the subways, for example. Everyone moves around a lot, so it's hard to track their movements, but they're getting ready to storm that army outside the building. They're clearing a path for someone to get in."

"For you, son," his father finished. He pointed to a mirror in which Garon hammered away at an unseen object with a large metal mallet. "He's been building weapons, armor, and all kinds of strange little gadgets on that side. Zid's over here doing the same for you. Those are some of the craftiest men I've ever met."

Pietro shook his head. "Pin, it's really great of you to keep an eye on all this, but now what? What happens now? You say they're about to go storm that dark army and clear the path for us?" When Enzo turned his head to open his mouth, Pietro held up a hand. "Don't even try to interrupt, Kid, you already know I'm going in there with you. But are we ready? Hell, are *they* ready?"

"Can we talk to them?" Enzo asked. "I need to find Rosana. I need to talk her out of this! This is insane!"

"Son." His father laid his hands on Enzo's shoulders again,

squeezing harder this time. "I don't like this any more than you do. In fact, I can't tell you how much sleep I lose thinking of you on the front lines. But this is our reality. And if Rosana's out there getting ready to fight, it's her choice. You can't stop her any more than I can stop you. Can I stop you?"

"No."

"Then there you have it. The most I can do is *prepare* you. I set this up so I could get a full view of what's going on out there. Zid says he's about done with his little invention over here. It's supposed to make sure I can talk to you from this side. Your mom and I will stay in the den and keep an eye on everything. If we see another dragon swoop out of the sky, you'll know. You'll hear it from me before you can even see it. Finally, my boy, I'd like you to hold on to a bit of hope. We were vastly outnumbered by Bellamy's army, and we won. We overpowered them by sticking together, and now they're not a threat anymore. Some might have said that was impossible, but it happened. Why shouldn't we have hope that the Order is going to triumph over those shadows? We can beat Avoria, Enzo! I know it!"

"Who were the casualties?" Enzo asked, his voice a bit rougher and louder than intended.

"Son, please refocus. I'm trying to offer you some encouragement—"

"*Who's dead?* You told me we ended up burying some of our own when I was in Neverland. Who, Dad? Who did we lose?"

His father sniffled, took his hands off Enzo, and turned around. "Several Hearts and an original member of the Order. Augustine Rose."

No. Enzo wished he had spent much more time getting to know the old woman who would bring him tea and tell him stories of her time in the Order, fighting giants and hunting dark witches like it was a simple hobby. She was easily one of the kindest and most interesting people he had ever met, and yet he didn't know her as well as he wished.

There were so many people Enzo wanted to know better and on

deeper levels. Tahlia. Merlin. Snow White. Even Hansel. Enzo hoped he would have the chance to see them at all.

Mom brushed her fingers over his cheek. "Tell me what you're thinking."

Enzo's gaze flickered from mirror to mirror, and he shook his head. "I need to walk it off and think for a minute. Then, I'm going to leave. I'll come say goodbye first."

Enzo's mom put her hand to her chest as if she were clutching a brooch or a necklace. "Okay, then. Make sure you keep your word on that."

"You're not leaving without me," Zack said.

"Or me," Pietro said. "Let us know when you're about to go. We'll get the Lost Boys together."

Enzo pushed on the walls a few times, trying to decipher how to get out of the tree.

His father watched for a second, a half smile on his face when he said, "You have to give it a little tickle. A soft brush with your fingertips."

Enzo rolled his eyes, feeling ridiculous when he stroked the tree, but sure enough, the little fibers parted and invited him to step out into the Woodlands. His mind, heart, and adrenaline raced as his foot hit the forest floor again. He wasn't quite sure where he was going, but he needed to let all the little strands of worry and fear unspool. He needed to catch his breath before Avoria and her army snuffed it out forever. He needed to get one last look at the realm of magic and say his goodbyes.

With that thought in mind, Enzo followed the path he believed would take him to the highest possible ground. He kept his hands in his pockets and his head up, drinking in the sounds and sights of the Old World. He wondered if feeling close to death made everybody appreciate the tiny details around them, from individual blades of grass and their perfect shades of green to the mystical beauty of a dark sky. During his journey, Enzo had come to loathe the darkness, but walking around in it right now, a bud of appreciation unfurled in his heart. *If it weren't for the dark, we wouldn't have bats, owls, or fireflies. We'd never see the stars.*

Enzo turned a corner and wove around a tree, but a shape in the distance made him stop mid-step. He blinked and rubbed his eyes. A tall figure in a dark cloak stood with its back against a thick tree, and if Enzo could see its eyes, he'd swear they'd be aimed straight at him. *There's that man again. I saw him in Neverland!*

Curling his fingers into a fist and trying to sound brave, Enzo shouted, "Hey! Who are you? Why are you following me around?"

To Enzo's annoyance, the hooded person didn't reply or move.

"Come on! I asked you a question!"

When Enzo took a step, the man in the hood bolted into a run, arced around his tree, and by the time Enzo could reach it, the man in the hood disappeared.

CHAPTER TWENTY-ONE

THE OLD WORLD: VIOLET'S DEN

When Zid walked into the den, rusty metal armor coated his body and made him look like a tiny scuba diver. He carried a pair of boots in his hands and stopped in front of Pietro and Zack, who had been discussing the events of Neverland.

"Your boots, Mr. Volo," Zid said.

"Which Mr. Volo?" Zack asked.

Zid jerked his thumb in Pietro's direction. "That Mr. Volo. I assume you have the bigger feet, man-boy?"

"That's probably me, actually," Zack said. "Size twelve."

"Thirteen!" Pietro boasted. "Got you beat, son."

Zid attempted to stroke his chin, forgetting that he had sealed his head in a big copper helmet. Pietro chuckled to himself every time Zid walked by with it, but he claimed it helped him in the forges when he worked on new gear. He pointed to Zack and beckoned him to follow. "This way, Son of Pan. I don't understand your feet numberings, but I'll straighten you out to be spry and heroic. Follow!"

"Aye aye," Zack said and followed Zid out of the tree.

"Be careful," Pietro warned, stepping into his new footwear, a concoction of leathers and metals that matched the rest of the armor Zid prepared. Taking a few steps in every direction, Pietro found his new footwear surprisingly more comfortable than his worn-down Nikes. He stopped to admire himself in the one mirror that didn't show any images from the New World.

Wendy appeared in the reflection, wearing a suit of her own, and patted Pietro's back. "You look handsome."

Pietro spun around and pulled his wife in for a kiss. "Thanks, love. How are you feeling?"

"Invincible," Wendy said, a playful smile on her lips.

Her eyes twinkled, and for a minute, Pietro felt like a boy again, soaring weightlessly through an open window to be with her. People always said eyes were windows to the soul. Maybe that was why Pietro had that same weightless feeling when he looked into Wendy's.

"We're about to storm a castle together. The biggest castle there ever was. It's like when we were young, isn't it, Pete? On a *grand adventure.*"

"And what an adventure it's been," Pietro breathed, rubbing his thumbs along Wendy's palms. "Couldn't ever ask for a better one. But I wouldn't have complained if it were easier." He winked.

"None of us would have," Wendy answered. "But look at us. Whatever happens, history will remember that I got you to grow old with me."

"Hey now, *easy,*" Pietro scolded. "We aren't *that* old. I think we can still pass for thirty-five in the New World. Going on thirty, right?"

Wendy moved her hands up Pietro's arms, grazing his shoulders and neck before she cupped his face, her thumbs silky smooth behind his ears. "Promise me you'll fight for another sixty."

Pietro placed his hands over Wendy's and pressed his forehead against hers. "If we still had a Neverland, I'd fight for six *hundred* with you. But I'll try for seventy, okay?"

They melted into a warm embrace and held it until the tree fibers slithered open again, revealing Captain Hook and the Lost Boys.

"Evening, scallywags." Hook smirked. "Feast your eyes on Zid's latest concoction. Watch carefully."

The pirate held his hooked arm in front of him and stomped his foot, sporting his own new pair of boots made entirely of brown leather. Pietro waited for something to happen, but Hook continued to stomp his foot, looking increasingly more frustrated.

"Zid told you to put the weight on your big toe," Nibs said. "Like this." He stomped his own foot, and Hook mimicked the boy.

An electric-blue spark crackled from the tip of his hook.

"Aha!" Hook cried. "That's it!" He stomped again and watched the sparks fly off his arm, cackling like a mad scientist in a lab. "An extra jolt for any rascal that tries to pick a bone with me tonight. That's a warning for *you*, Pan."

Pietro shook his head and smiled. He wasn't interested in antagonizing the pirate anymore. There were more important things to worry about. "Okay, Hook. Whatever you say."

"Good man."

"Does your suit do anything?" Nibs asked Pietro.

"Not especially. It's supposed to keep me lightweight and absorb light to protect me from those shadow things. Zack, Wendy, and I are all more susceptible to the shadow creatures than almost anybody else out there. We don't want them corrupting us. It's already happened to Zack before."

"Oh." Nibs shrugged and turned away, clearly unimpressed.

The tree peeled open again, and Enzo sprinted into the den, face red, hair coated in sweat, and lungs hard at work. He took one look around the room, his eyes rolled up in his head, and he collapsed against the wall, still breathing hard.

"Whoa, Kid!" Pietro cried. He rushed to Enzo's side, only to be gently brushed aside by Pino and Carla.

Pino rested a palm on Enzo's knee. "Son, what happened?"

Enzo gulped down a heavy breath. "Where did he go?"

"*Who*, sweetie?" Carla asked.

"There was a man," Enzo wheezed. "He wore a black robe like those people you showed me in the mirror." He paused, took another heavy breath, and the cadence of his speech slowed back to an easy rhythm. "He's been following me around. I saw him staring at me in Neverland and now in the Woodlands. I went after him, but he vanished."

"Man in black?" Wendy asked.

"Yes. Like, full-on Grim Reaper status. I couldn't even see his face."

Carla turned to Pino. "Who told us about a man who dressed like that? Recently?"

"Them." Pino gestured to the mirror depicting the dark army that surrounded Avoria's tower.

"No, but I feel like I've heard about a different man who wanted to *stop* Avoria."

"Alice met somebody," Pietro remembered. "Over by the bell tower. Somebody stopped her from intervening with an execution and helped her get into Wonderland to rescue Gretel. She was telling us after she broke us out of Florindale Prison."

Pino's eyes lit up. "Cherry. Also goes by Victor Frankenstein or Robin Hood. He told her he hoped we'd all be standing together for the final battle. I remember her story very vividly now."

"But why would this Cherry man follow our son around and not say a word to him? Why run away when Enzo tries to confront the man, if that's even him to begin with? I'm more inclined to say it was one of Avoria's people, and I don't like that they're following my son. This ends now. If I see *anybody* stalking my son, I promise I'm going to give them—"

"Your gloves, Mister Enzo." Zid returned through an opening in the tree, Zack close at his heels, and gave Enzo a handsome pair of brown leather gloves. "These will bind your knife only to you. If someone else should pick it up and try to use it against your will, it will return to you. Garon will provide the rest of your armor."

When Enzo tried on the gloves, Pietro saw them shrink a bit and conform to Enzo's hands like a second skin.

"How do they feel?" Zid asked.

"Like they're not even there." Enzo flexed his fingers a few times, making a fist and pounding it into his other hand. The dagger appeared in his grip. He slid it along the floor a couple times and tossed the blade away from him, only for it to come right back and snuggle into his fingers. "Thanks, Zid."

"Only the best for our Carver." The dwarf removed his helmet, tossed it to the ground with a hollow clank, and then surveyed the room. "Will there be anything else, warriors? What do you need from me?"

"Reassurance?" Enzo said half-heartedly.

"Got any snacks I can keep in my pocket?" Zack asked.

"How 'bout a little *courage*?" Pietro quipped in his best impression of the lion from *The Wizard of Oz*. This roused a fit of laughter from nearly everyone in the room, with the exceptions of Zid who stood there scratching his head and Hook who shrugged and grumbled about how courage was a valid response for Pietro and the answer wasn't funny at all.

Carla, the resident *The Wizard of Oz* lover, stood and gave Pietro a hug. She wiped tears of laughter on her shoulder when she walked back to her seat. After the laughter died to a lull, she gripped Pino's hand. "We can't stay behind while they fight. It doesn't feel right."

Pino nodded. "I was thinking the same thing." He frowned and gestured around him. "But who's going to keep an eye on all of this?"

"Maybe we don't need it," Carla suggested. "People go to war every day with nothing more than what's in their pockets. I've lived for forty years with no idea that a world like this even existed, Pino. And I *thrived*. What if we do something drastic? What if we destroy all these mirrors, we go forward, and we fight? What are these going to show us that we don't already know? We can't see inside the building. All we need to know is that we need to get past that army. We stand a better chance doing it together than watching everybody else. I favor might before magic, and the more I think about it, I don't trust these mirrors. What do *you* think?"

"I think I *want* you two to stay here," Enzo argued. "Out of harm's way."

Carla picked up Zid's helmet and rammed it against one of the mirrors. The glass dissolved like a seltzer pill and littered the floor. "And I want to protect my son and get revenge on the witch who stole me from him."

"Hey, easy on the helmet!" Zid held up a palm.

Pino took the helmet from his wife and smashed an even bigger mirror, eliciting a wince from the dwarf. "Sorry, great commander and son. Parents overrule this time. We're coming with you. We gave you life. We'll defend it to our last breath."

Enzo didn't protest this time. He bit his lip, jammed his hands into his pockets, and finally smiled. "I love you guys."

"Oh brother, I cannot listen to this. Bang my ears around to boot!" Zid rolled his eyes and snatched his helmet from Pino's arms. With a metallic click, Zid sealed the helmet over his head. On his way out of the tree, he grumbled, "Last call for armor."

THE NEW WORLD

The Order went underground shortly after Mulan and Rosana united their groups. Returning to the subways where Rosana basically lived for months had the ethereal feeling of a dream. Only this time, her mom was with her again, and there were many other people at her side. For about three days, they stayed in the tunnels a couple miles away from the Citadel. They trained. They rested. They looted abandoned shops on the ground level of New York and gathered food.

In those three days, Rosana witnessed the darkening of the skies, and she knew something had gone wrong. The dark skies had a particularly nasty effect on Liam's spirits, even though his vision didn't return until the third day. Rosana wondered if maybe he had been more attuned to the growing chill in the air, but he insisted harm had come to Snow White and he could feel it in his heart. Rosana and Mulan sat with him for hours at a time, insisting he hold onto hope for the Order's sake. He seemed to have aged ten years since Rosana met him, but nonetheless, he continued to train his people.

All the while, Rosana worried more with every hour that she didn't see Enzo. A part of her seethed at him for not communicating before he left the coronation. Where did he go? Was he even *in* the New World again, perhaps taken into the Citadel? Did he stay behind in the Old World and get himself hurt? If he was suffering somewhere, or worse, Rosana would hate herself for being angry with him, but unless he had scars on his body, she resolved to punch him squarely in the chest the next time she saw him.

"Rosana." Mulan's stern voice cut through Rosana's thoughts like a blade.

Rosana blinked hard, surprised to realize how far her attention had strayed, and her gaze snapped to the front of the room, where the woman warrior addressed the group.

"Stay with me." The compassion in Mulan's eyes suggested she understood everything Rosana was thinking. There was a time when Rosana found the woman nearly impossible to relate to. She had such an iron shell around her heart, always guarding her emotions and even her smile. Any time she even came close to laughing, her guard would fly up like one of those plastic shields on a nauseating roller coaster. Rosana would always see past it, but she could never break through. She supposed that soft look in Mulan's eyes was a step toward progress. It meant she was human.

Mulan folded her hands. "I don't have to tell you all how important this is. We're going out there tonight and taking out as much of that army as we can, all of this while battling weather, stress, time . . . our fears. Some of us will do battle with faces we recognize. Listen closely. If you find yourself looking into the eyes of one of Avoria's soldiers, you are looking into the eyes of the enemy, and you must not hesitate to incapacitate that individual. These are not the individuals you remember. They were corrupted after the Battle of the Thousand, and they are under the control of the Ivory Queen. If they are in a dark robe, *they intend to do you harm.*"

CHAPTER TWENTY-TWO

THE NEW WORLD:
NEW YORK CITY

When Enzo stepped through the portal back to the New World, the cold sliced at his skin. His breath unfurled before him in ghostly wisps and drifted high above to the iron-gray clouds overhead, every bit a part of something too big to fully see. He focused on the thousand-foot structure on the horizon, where all the fog converged. He imagined the tower inhaling the cold weather for a count of three, holding it, and then letting it all out with a voiceless *haaa*. The Citadel taunted him at the same time, daring him to attack.

Zack stood next to Enzo, arms folded and eyebrows in hard angles. "Well. Welcome home, bro. This is our world now."

"This isn't home," Enzo said. "This isn't even New York." The skyscrapers were there, stabbing the clouds. Beneath the glittering mounds of snow, Enzo made out glints of mustard yellow. The cabs were there. But this wasn't New York. New York bustled with life, lights, with good-natured adventure. Wherever he was standing, everything about it made him want to shrivel into a tiny ball of nothing.

"Kid." Pietro nudged Enzo and pointed to a dark mom-and-pop type shop by one of the buried taxis. "Isn't that where we had pizza together before we met Rosana?"

Enzo looked at the *Petrelli's* sign, and the nostalgia made his heart sore. Those were not easier days by any means. He'd been about a step away from becoming orphaned, completely in the dark about his family's lineage and what sort of danger threatened the world. Rosana had been nothing more than an idea—a wooden representation of a girl who couldn't possibly exist "any more than the guy on the oatmeal box." But there was something from those days that Enzo wanted to cling to. The ignorance, perhaps? Or maybe the ability to sit down and eat pizza, rolling his eyes at his goofy best friend as he drummed on a Parmesan shaker, pretending life was just a spontaneous road trip to be enjoyed from coast to coast? When was the last time any part of life had carried that levity? Maybe this was what aged people: realizing that no matter where one was in life, nothing would ever be as carefree as it once was.

"First thing I'm doing when this is over is finding a pizza place that's open," Pietro grumbled. "You in, guys?" He scooped Wendy and Zack into each arm and let out a broken laugh, followed by a light sniffle. "Man, it takes *everything* to joke right now. I hate this."

Enzo wrapped his arms around his parents, taking in what warmth they could offer in this weather. "I'd be up for a pizza," he muttered. When he realized by the hopeful smiles on everyone's faces that they had actually taken him seriously, he spoke with more volume. "Maybe I'll even get a little wild. Pineapples. Mushrooms. Jalapeños. And tell 'em to deep-fry it. I bet they'd do it."

"You're *ridiculous*, man." Zack shook his head, a look of disgust crinkling the corners of his eyes. "Of all the things you could say right now? Really? Leader?"

Enzo bit his lip. "Right. Sorry," he muttered. "Let's get—"

"And you didn't even think to top it with gelato?" Zack finished, his lips turning up in a smile. The group burst into laughter.

Enzo swatted his friend on the back and rolled his eyes. "Fine. You want deep-fried gelato pizza? Let's go earn it. Let's find our friends and storm that Citadel."

"But we don't know where they've gone to," his father pointed out. "We might use caution moving through these streets. They could be anywhere, but so could the shadows."

"Don't worry. I'll make it easier," Enzo assured. He bent down with eyes closed and put a knee in the snow. He drove his knife into the ground, his fingertips suddenly full with all the joy snow could provide on a normal day. In his heart, he heard children laughing, snowballs bursting, and reindeer prancing. He saw Christmas lights flickering, and the aroma of sugar cookies hugged his mind.

When Enzo opened his eyes, he held a small snow sculpture of a subway entrance, but he only looked at it for a total of two seconds before his gaze drifted to a dark shape nearly ten feet in front of him and staring without eyes.

The hooded man.

"Hey!" Enzo leapt to his feet. "That's him! Stop that man!" His legs whirred to action, and he dropped his snow figurine. The mini subway entrance burst into fine powder beneath his feet. "Stop!"

As he predicted, the man in black turned on his heel and ran in the opposite direction, almost straight for the Citadel. Something about the situation raised alarms in Enzo's mind. Almost as if the man *wanted* to be caught. Why wander right into the middle of the New York streets, coated in black cloth that stood out like a siren in the middle of the pearly snow?

He's baiting me, Enzo thought. *He's one of the army, and he's leading me straight to death's door. Straight to those dark things in front of the Citadel.* Regardless, Enzo continued pounding through the snow, determined to catch the stranger no matter what. The hooded man was a little faster, but his boots left deep, thick tracks and his long coat carved a shallow road out of the snow mounds with every step he took. The coat fanned out behind him, creating the illusion that the man had a dark pair of wings and glided close to the ground. One thing was certain: He wouldn't get away from Enzo again. The hooded man had nowhere to hide anymore.

"Come back here, you coward!" Zack called, leaping ahead of Enzo and skidding to the right as the stranger made a wild turn. Having Zack around—athletic and nimble—made Enzo's heart swell with gratitude. Zack pumped his arms as he ran, fire in his eyes that could have melted the snow in front of him.

Pietro, whose legs were the longest in the group, pushed past Enzo as well, drawing out a small dagger and clutching it in his fist. "Better hope I don't catch you!"

When Enzo thought about it, he'd never seen Pietro use a dagger before. He probably didn't want to catch up with the man either.

The stranger turned a corner and ducked into another street, where the hollow shell of a Starbucks forced a shot of reality into Enzo's heart. Not only was it strange to see the coffee shop closed, but Pietro didn't even look twice.

Zing!

An arrow whizzed in front of Enzo's nose. The tip came out at a straight angle, meaning somebody had fired at him from the ground level.

Somebody's close.

Enzo picked up the pace despite the fire in his lungs. He couldn't afford to look over his shoulder. If he didn't catch the man in black, the failure would haunt Enzo. He supposed catching the man would boost the group's morale. A small win, but it would be a win nonetheless. Losing him would drop morale, and drops in morale were costly.

The stranger turned another corner, and the group followed. That was when Enzo saw the broken building and, nestled in the rubble, the lifeless body of a dragon. The image made him dizzy. *Dragons in New York.*

To his horror, another arrow zipped by his ear, this time at a downward angle. He tilted his head back and caught a fleeting glimpse of another robed figure hanging from the fire exit of a ritzy hotel. One arm draped over the rung of the ladder, and the robed figure fired a second arrow when Enzo made eye contact. This one grazed his shoulder. He clapped his palm over the wound and kept running.

Behind Enzo, a blunderbuss popped, and the archer tumbled from the flagpole into a dumpster.

"Ha!" Enzo heard his mom cry. "Nobody harms my son!"

"Mom?" Enzo yelled without turning around.

"Keep going, sweetheart! I have you!"

Finally, the running man dipped into a subway entrance, and in his hurry to escape, his coat sleeve caught the end of the handrail. All it took was a moment's hesitation to unhook his sleeve, and Pietro grabbed the man's hood and pulled, revealing a head of thin gray hair.

"Stop," Pietro commanded, twisting the man's arm and pulling him into a chokehold. "Nowhere to run, man."

"Okay! Okay!" the man wheezed.

Pietro turned him around, and Enzo assessed the man. Looking at his face, he must have been at least Geppetto's age, but the man had the body of a warrior in his prime, thick chested, tall, and broad shouldered. Enzo's gaze immediately flew to the stranger's eyes, a strange combination of burnt orange and sea-foam green. His features were distantly familiar.

"I give up. You've caught me. Please do not hurt me. I'm on your side."

Enzo raised an eyebrow, lips scrunched to the side. "I don't believe you."

Zack jabbed a finger on the stranger's chest. "Prove it."

The stranger shrugged with some difficulty. "What do you want me to do?"

"Wait a minute." Enzo's father caught up to the group, gently pushed past Enzo, and looked the man up and down. "I was right. I've seen you before." Pino stroked his chin, and a spark of recognition shined in his eyes. With a nod, he said, "You've been over to my house a couple of times, when I was a young boy."

"When you were a *puppet*. In fact, I knew you even before *that*. And what a specimen you are, Pinocchio. Once, you were a block of oak. Now, you stand before me, real as any man I've ever seen." The stranger turned his head slightly and said to Pietro, "Kindly release me?"

"Nope."

The man sighed.

"I know who you are." Enzo remembered where he'd seen the man. Enzo dreamed of him in Neverland, walking alongside a young Geppetto. "You're about the same age as my grandfather. You knew my father before he even existed. You're . . . Master Cherry?"

"Yes."

Enzo's father wrinkled his brows at Enzo. "My dad told you that story?"

Enzo nodded and then turned back to the old man. "I want to know why you've been following me. If I tell Pietro to let go of you, will you give me your word that you won't run? Because now that we have you, we're going to find you over and over again."

"I should think The Carver and his army have a higher order of priorities," Master Cherry answered. "That being said, it was my wish to test your readiness for battle. I vowed that when you could finally catch up with me, I would deem you worthy of the answers you seek. And so, Enzo, I can give you my word. It is not my intention to flee from you again. Quite the opposite is true. It is my intention to aid you. It so happens that I need you."

Enzo narrowed his eyes into tiny slits. This man was an enigma if Enzo ever knew one. He looked at Pietro and nodded once. "Let him go."

"Are we sure about this?" Zack asked.

"Dad?" Enzo turned to his father, whose expression was rife with wonder.

His dad tilted his head. "Let's hear him out."

Pietro lifted the crook of his elbow off the stranger's neck and stepped back, looking relieved to put away his dagger.

Enzo wasted no time. He marched up to Cherry, chin held high. "How long have you been following me and why?"

Master Cherry popped his hood over his head again and took a step closer, stroking a chin that Enzo couldn't see. "I should confess that I have been watching you for quite some time now, quietly from afar. All of you. I've been observing your battle tactics . . . your interactions with each other and with your worlds. Forgive me for living in the shadows, but it is the nature of the life I have chosen. See, I've been studying all that Avoria has touched within her lifetime. Florindale, Wonderland, the New World, and everywhere in between. They bloom with data, precisely the kind I needed in order to understand how we must end this war. And for my research to yield the most accurate results, it was best if I didn't interfere."

Enzo couldn't believe what he was hearing. "If you *didn't interfere*?" he repeated. "You follow me from world to world, studying me like a lab rat while I almost died multiple times, and you thought it would be wrong to interfere? How much did you see? When the King of Hearts tried to kill me in Wonderland, were you there? When Hansel abducted Pietro in Hollywood, were you standing in the alley with us? How many horrible things did you witness without thinking to stop and *help us*? Huh?"

Cherry held up a hand, cutting off Enzo's words. "As you can see, you've done fine on your own. My interventions would have incinerated Father Time's butterflies, young man. You needed to end up at this point in space in this point in time. Should I have chosen to step in and battle the King of Hearts, for example, not only would I have failed, but it could have cost many other lives as well. I am not a warrior, Enzo. That prerogative belongs to the Order of the Bell, a faction in which you have settled quite nicely, I might add."

Enzo kneaded at his temples, overwhelmed at the realization that he'd been followed for longer than he realized. He felt like a pawn.

Cherry turned away and paced back and forth, leaving a deep trail in the snow. "I should confess that there have been minor occurrences when I let desperation get the best of me," he said. "I meddled with destiny when I appeared to Alice and sent her to the World Between. It is not an action of which I am proud, but it did yield the desired outcome after all. You are now safe. Young Gretel is safe. Alice and her daughter are safe." He turned around again, and his eyes glowed like fire. "Would you like to see them now?"

CHAPTER TWENTY-THREE

THE NEW WORLD:
SUBWAY TUNNELS

"Last thing you all need to know about swords," Mulan said, selecting a scabbard and spinning the handle in her palm a few times, "is that when somebody attacks you, the simplest calculation comes automatically. It's easy to hit your opponent's blade, and that's what you're going to try to do. You're going to try to hit metal on metal, and your opponent will see the opportunity to strike. Do not try to hit the enemy's sword. You must hit the enemy. Make the tougher calculation. Rosana, how's your arithmetic?"

Rosana looked up, completely unaware that Mulan was going to call on her for a demonstration. "Awful," she lied.

"Quick! Nine times seven!"

"Sixty-three!" Rosana cringed immediately after she answered.

"You're wonderful. Come spar with me."

Rosana sighed and stood while the rest of the Order chuckled. Specialized members were giving their final tips on combat strategies, and Mulan chose to turn her spiel into a full-length lesson.

"Wayde, come up with her," Mulan said. "You're going to shout out basic math problems for Rosana to solve while she attempts to land as many blows as she can and dodge my sword. Sword training is as much a mental game as it is a physical one. Got it?"

"Aye!" Wayde exclaimed.

"Sure, why not?" Rosana rolled her eyes. She grabbed a sword and faced the warrior.

"Ready?" Mulan asked. "On your guard!"

Rosana raised her sword and looked Mulan in the eyes. Then a shape moved behind her, and Rosana let the blade fall to the ground. "Excuse me." She broke into a run. "*Enzo!* I was so worried about you."

Enzo descended the subway steps with a group Rosana paid no attention to, and he immediately locked eyes with her. For a brief second, they were the only two people who ever existed. Rosana leapt into his embrace, cupped his face, and kissed him. In the background, she perceived Prince Liam's distant mumbling and Wayde claiming something about not knowing math anyway. When the kiss ended and Rosana pulled away, Enzo hugged her and she nearly melted.

"I was so worried," Rosana repeated.

Enzo clung tighter. "We're here," he said, his voice deep and low. "Together." He let go of Rosana and said, "I was a little afraid you would slap me right now."

"Oh, it crossed my mind. But we're not going to have normal lives, Enzo. Not for a while. We might as well get used to running."

Enzo hooked his fingers into Rosana's. "I missed you."

A throat cleared behind Rosana, and she spun around to face Hua Mulan again, surprised to see a smile on her face.

"Welcome back, Enzo and company."

Only now did Rosana assess the group that accompanied Enzo into the subway. The rest of the DiLegnos and all of the Volos were with him, but a strange figure in a black hood lingered behind them, his hands clasped behind his back. "Who's your, uh, friend?"

"Master Cherry," her mother breathed, standing up from the crowd and walking to the new group. "We meet again."

The man in black known as Master Cherry bowed his hooded

head. "And so we do. Lady Fortune is quite jovial tonight." He stepped forward and surveyed the group, who had gone quiet upon Master Cherry's arrival. Rosana had to admit he was rather intimidating. She didn't know many people—if any—who chose to walk around in a long black robe. He looked like the Grim Reaper without a scythe. "I've been eager to meet you *all*, my friends . . . to join you and share my gratitude for your endeavors. They call me Master Cherry. I imagine many of you are confused by my arrival."

Rosana tilted her head to the side, intrigued and eager to hear the man's story.

"All you need to understand is that I have completed my research," Cherry said. "Thanks to you, Alice, for returning my book to my hands, and to all of you for persevering in your fight against the queen. Now, as I have promised, Alice, I have come back to stand with you in the final battle. Unless you choose not to have me or to discard my research, in which case, I shall retreat back into the shadows and await our certain apocalypse, for I am aware that time runs thin." He put his hands up and then on his hips, surveying the group with an expectant look on his face. "What is your decision?"

Enzo massaged his temples and looked around the room at his friends. Nobody wore a clear expression of approval or disapproval. In fact, Rosana noted, most everyone's lips were flat, and their eyes expressed only uncertainty. Enzo leaned forward and wove his fingers together. "Master Cherry, with all due respect, sir, what exactly do you plan to do? You seem determined to help us, but how?"

"You pose intelligent queries." Cherry sat down, reached into his coat, and produced what had to be the oldest, most battered leather book Enzo had ever seen. Cherry slammed it in front of Enzo with a harsh thud. "My research."

Rosana took the book right away and peeled it open, flipping through the various tabs and pages that crackled when they turned. She walked the book around the room, trying to weave her brain around the words and diagrams Cherry had inked into the sheets. *Interrealm Travel. Core Soul Theory. Corporeal Resurrection.* She passed it to Enzo. "I don't understand *any* of this."

Cherry's gaze followed Enzo like moths follow a flame. "The last page," he said simply. "What most pertains to us now is the final page. My conclusion."

Enzo rifled through entire sections with his thumb, raising dust that had gathered between the pages over time. He turned away and coughed into his sleeve, waved the dust away, and then fixed his attention on the last page. His eyebrows immediately drew together, and he showed the page to Rosana. "Is that a heart?"

Rosana knew it was the wrong question. The valves, chambers, and little muscles had been inked so meticulously it might as well have been a photograph. Cherry had even labeled them in blood-red ink, which stamped its mirror image on the inner back cover of the book. The real questions Enzo should have asked were: *Why did you want me to see this heart? Why did you draw it?* In the silence, Enzo looked at Master Cherry, who didn't even go so far as to nod in return.

"What does it *mean?*"

"It's how we stop her," Cherry said. "You've labored under the assumption that Avoria is some sort of superhuman, but her heart is the source of her power and the cataclysmic event that will occur if she takes the final soul. Every time she's taken one, her heart has reacted in a peculiar way. I conjecture that it has formed a tough shell over the years, whereas the rest of her body has not reacted. The souls, therefore, are feeding her heart, and as such, the organ must be extracted. The answer, then, is simple. Stop her heart; stop the queen. She loses all power without it." Cherry tapped his fingertips together and assessed the group's reactions.

Rosana rubbed her forehead. In a way, the solution was much simpler than she'd been expecting. Of *course* Avoria couldn't live without a heart. Nobody could. On the other hand, how in the world were they supposed to get close enough to stop it?

"I have a question, Master Cherry," Enzo chimed in.

"Proceed."

"How do you know all this?"

Zack shrugged. "He's got a point. How were you able to study Avoria's heart all this time?"

"I had other test subjects," Cherry answered. "I recreated the exact conditions by which Avoria came to exist, and I tested them until I was sure of this conclusion."

"Wait," Hansel said. "*Recreated?* You mean—"

"Yes. I will not profess to having carried out the process with ease, but the concept itself is elementary. One only need extract the tusks of a Neverland lily tiger. Carve them until they take the shape of a human being. Imbue it with life and the venom of a snake, and watch what happens when the heart within absorbs the nucleus of a soul."

"*What?*" Enzo spat. He wasn't alone in his outburst.

She could see the dark puzzle coming together in her friends' minds. All the strands weaved together, and Rosana didn't like what she understood. She wished more than anything that she had misread Cherry's words.

Master Cherry nodded gravely. "You've made the connection. All this time, you've been dealing with my most dangerous experiment, a creation gone wrong. Do you see now why I've come to you? I've come back for redemption, to complete the circle. I must be the one to stop her, for I *created* her. I know that you intend to storm the Citadel tonight. If you would be so kind as to escort me to the top, I may be able to help you neutralize my monster." He paused and wove his fingertips together. "Yes, Avoria was carved from the ivory of a lily tiger. First, she was a table leg. I shaped it into a puppet later and gave her to a king. By fate, I found her again when she was queen and asked my help to bring down the giants. I never had the heart to tell her that she invited her maker—her *father*—into her own home."

CHAPTER TWENTY-FOUR

THE NEW WORLD: SUBWAY TUNNELS

Pino sat between his father and son, head cradled in his hands. Carla stood behind him, rubbing and patting his back, her touch like sunlight melting the goose bumps away from his body.

"She's not a real person," Pino said under his breath. "All this time, my family has been tortured by a dancing clump of ivory. She was said to be a good person before the snake bit her, but she wasn't even a person at all."

His father put a palm on Pino's knee. "Are *you* real, Pinocchio?"

Pino sat straight up and shook out the numbness in his wrists. "I'm . . . unnatural. I'm lucky wood. I'm not even sure what my heart looks like. I *feel* real. I wouldn't know how other humans feel because I've never been anyone else, but I *think* I'm about as human as I can be."

"You are, Dad," Enzo said. "You may not know how it feels to be anybody else, but nobody *feels* the way you do."

"Yes," Carla affirmed. She kissed the top of Pino's head, sending warmth rippling all the way through his toes. "You're more human than anyone I know. And I *would* know."

"You were not produced through natural matters," Geppetto said. "But you were created as an act of love. And that made you the magnificent person you've grown to be. I only wish I could have been a part of the transition, but how *proud* I am to know you've thrived. You have a beautiful wife. You have a brave, courageous boy. Your family is bonded, once again, by *love*, the very element that created you."

Pino met his father's gaze, and every sentiment poured through the brightness of his eyes. Pain snapped at Pino like a rubber band, a sharp sting that quickly subsided without a mark. He did wish he'd known his father better and felt horrible for having run away from a man with so much love for him that it pulled him into the depths of the Florindale mines and the dark pits of Wonderland. But Pino could never regret the decision that brought Carla and Enzo into his life. All Pino could do was move forward and resolve to spend more time with his father from this point forward.

"But Avoria," Enzo said. "She wasn't created as an act of love, was she?"

Pino's father bit his lip. "I don't suppose we can know for sure. I must confess I never knew my friend carved a living person in our lifetime. Pinocchio was the source of such envy when he came to life. I thought Cherry might never carve again. And indeed, I hardly ever *saw* him again." He sighed, his shoulders deflating, and he clapped a hand on Enzo's knee. "But those are matters of the past now. The most important question in this moment is what you'd like to do, my boy. Master Cherry would like to move in on the Citadel tonight and wants somebody to escort him to the top. Are you in favor of his plan?"

Enzo shrugged. "Mostly. I don't love the idea, but it makes sense. If Cherry created Avoria, he must also understand how to stop her. I just don't know if we're strong enough to make it to the top floor. We don't know what's in there. She fit a *dragon* in that building, and it destroyed part of New York City when she let it out. Are we really ready for this?"

"We're never going to be one hundred percent prepared," Pino said. "At some point, we have to settle for *ready enough* or lose to the clock. Do you trust yourself, Enzo?" He turned to his son, astounded at the man he was becoming. Enzo had grown a little taller in the time they'd spent together, and he'd learned quite a bit as well. *Is this really the boy who used to snap at everything I said?*

"I trust my friends," Enzo decided. "I trust *us*. We've spent so much time pushing through the unknown together that it's almost familiar. It's always a little scary, but somehow we all come through." They met each other's gazes, and Pino caught a full glimpse of the light that Carla called his firefly. "We'll come through again, right?"

Pino pulled his son into a hug. "Welcome to adulthood, son. Every day is the unknown." He paused and watched glimpses of his life flash through his memory. Kaa. Avoria. Bellamy's prison. The Cavern of Ombra. *You could run, you know,* he wanted to say. *You could forget you ever became a part of this and run like I did.* But out of a mixture of love, selfishness, and the knowledge that his son would never agree, Pino kept the thought to himself. Carla and his father joined the hug, and the DiLegnos fused into an electric bundle of warmth. "We'll come through."

The family stayed huddled like that for a long time, and Pino assumed by the silence throughout the hall that everybody else was sharing quiet time of their own together. He looked across the room and caught a wink from Pietro, who had both Zack and Wendy fast asleep with their heads in his lap. Pino nodded back and let his eyes slide shut. He tried not to think that this might be the last quiet moment they'd ever share together as a family. He wanted to seal this moment in a jar and keep it on a shelf to illuminate the room on stormy nights. He wanted to keep it in a jacket pocket, zipped to save for a frosty morning.

When Pino awoke sometime later, he and Carla were arm-in-arm while his father and Enzo sat against a wall, whispering and carving tiny figurines out of little bars of soap from a convenience store he raided with Rosana. Pino wasn't sure how much time had passed, because both his father and son looked quite rested and a bit cleaner as well.

Enzo used his knife to sever a loose thread in his boot. "Grandpa, I had another thought. About that story you told me in Wonderland? When you had that contest with Cherry all those years ago, and he carved that table leg . . . ?"

Pino's father nodded. "Yes. We had our falling out shortly thereafter. I never knew he kept working at that project long after the contest was finished. He was so upset when Pinocchio came to life. Now, I suppose we're going to battle with a puppet of Cherry's own making."

✳✳✳

"And so?"

"We've made our decision." Enzo took a deep breath, forcing himself to look the terrifying old man in the eyes. If Enzo could gaze into that fire and hold his own, he could say anything. "We're going to take you up on your offer. You're coming with us, and we're going to escort you to the top of the Citadel to confront Avoria."

Cherry bowed and clasped Enzo's hand. "I deem that a wise decision, Enzo. You have my gratitude."

Enzo jammed his hands into his pockets and nodded. Zack and Rosana flanked him at either side, their backs to the wall and their arms crossed.

"What do you need from us?" Rosana asked the old Carver. "If we're going in tonight, we need a plan. We expect that there will probably be some sort of danger on every floor, and we don't know how many floors there are. We're prepared to help you reach the top however we can, but if you need anything else"—she tucked a strand of hair behind her ear—"this is the time to let us know."

"Once we go inside," Zack said, "who knows when we'll come out again? *This* is kind of our final checkpoint."

"My thoughts exactly," Cherry agreed. "By Lady Fortune's grace, I require nothing that isn't already in this room. I only ask that you do your best to protect me, and each other. With that said, I would hope that your best warriors survive to journey up to the top with us. Surely, some will have to stay on the ground. Some will not live to enter the Citadel. You are prepared for this, yes?"

"Of course." Enzo restrained the urge to frown.

Cherry turned away and crossed his hands behind his back. "There is one thing that may be of use to us, if I have your permission to procure it."

Zack arched an eyebrow. "Yes?"

"Gretel is a special girl," Cherry explained. "Where she goes, moonflowers sprout from ashes. Statues begin to breathe. You know the effect she had on Prince William. I ask, then, for a small vial of her tears. Should any harm come to us in the tower, she may be our saving grace."

Rosana, who seemed to regard Gretel as a sort of little sister, twisted her lips to the side. "I don't know."

"Leave it up to Gretel," Zack suggested. "She's mature enough to decide if she wants to give up her tears. I don't think it's our right to decide one way or another."

"That's fair enough," Cherry said with a stiff bow. "Then these are my only conditions. When you're ready, Enzo, then I shall join you. I'm humbled you've given me the opportunity to rectify my mistakes. This event has been a long time coming. I believe a prosperous new age shall begin tonight. For all the trouble that's befallen you, I will labor to ensure that you three are properly installed where you belong, and that your existence is meaningful."

Enzo smiled, surprised that Cherry was capable of uttering any words of comfort. "Thanks," he said. "Then we'll forgive you for creating a monster."

Cherry lowered his head, bringing his hands to his lap. "You are kind. I'm afraid the damage runs deep, but perhaps with time, I will forgive myself as well."

The man was a walking paradox, a puzzle cut with impossible edges. Enzo didn't understand how a man could look ancient; possess the tall, thick, broad-shouldered figure of a college football player; and move with a sort of feline, calculated grace. Had all the experiments made him the way he was, an unnatural fusion of incompatible quirks? If one stripped away all the illusions in which Cherry shrouded himself, who was he at his core? Who was the Cherry that Geppetto had grown up with?

Seeing him with such regret, Enzo experienced a surge of empathy and compassion for the man. Enzo would never understand what Master Cherry had been through, but it was evident that beneath the cloak a troubled man looked to win redemption. Enzo had seen that in Hansel as well.

Enzo stood up, crossed the room, and laid a hand on Master Cherry's shoulder. "It's a brave thing you're doing. We respect you. We're here for you. The three of us will make sure that new age comes. It'll be a new start for all of us. We've earned it."

"Yes." Cherry sat straight up again and turned his head in Geppetto's direction. "I do believe we have."

Without another word, Enzo excused himself from the group and went to find Mulan. He found her doing a silent meditation by the fireplace, her legs crossed on the floor and her palms resting on her lap. Her eyes were shut, and her breaths were slow and even. Enzo watched her in awe, silently wishing he had the mental focus to sit still and breathe for more than three minutes at a time. Afraid of interrupting her, he spun on his heel and started to walk away, but a quiet voice cut through the air and stopped him.

"You broke your promise."

Enzo shut his eyes and leaned against the wall. Liam blended almost perfectly with the shadows of the tunnel, his arms folded and his gaze to the ground.

"After all we've endured, you failed the most important task. You came back without Snow."

"You *have* to know how hard I tried, Liam."

"I do." Liam stepped forward, grizzled and haunted beneath the eyes. He might as well have been wearing a mask. "I spoke with Pietro already. He was quick to defend you. Stayed with me for hours while I mourned."

Enzo grabbed Liam's shoulders. Liam raised his chin, and Enzo looked him in the eyes. "Then Pietro's nicer than I am. Know why? Because as sorry as I am—as terrible as I feel—I don't really have a lot of time for that right now. I'm going into the Citadel to get Snow back, and you're coming with me. Right?"

"Aye." Liam brushed his sleeve across his face, dampening his forearm. "I'm sorry you've had to see me like this."

Without another word, Enzo pulled Liam into a hug and didn't let go until the prince stopped crying.

Enzo worried that Liam's mood might have spread like a contagion, but throughout the night, most people stayed relatively calm, comforted by family and shelter in spite of the looming threats above the subway. While some people cried, others sang, slept, and strategized.

Mulan opted to meditate most of the night, after which she sprang to her feet and called the full group together.

It was a wonder to see, everybody finally standing together in one place.

"Are we here for dinner?" Chann asked. "I hunger."

Pietro reached into his pocket, unrolled a half-eaten bag of Cheeto Puffs, and then passed them to Chann.

Seeing the act, Mulan actually smiled, and then she cleared her throat. "We're here to call an unofficial meeting of the Order. Enzo, would you like to update your comrades?"

Enzo faced his friends, proud to see all of them together. They looked strong. They looked happy. Especially his parents.

"We're moving in on the Citadel tonight," he said. "Master Cherry has information that can help us stop Avoria. The priority is to protect him."

Silence rang through the air, but nobody protested. Nobody shed a tear or expressed fear in their eyes. The silence throbbed with resolve.

With Zack's help, Enzo stooped to the ground and lifted up a model of New York City he'd carved with Geppetto a few hours ago. It was about four feet long, and the Citadel stood in the center at about two feet tall. "This is where we are." Enzo pointed to one end of the board. "We need to attack on multiple sides. In waves. The plan is to chip away at the dark army until you see a gap big enough to get you into the tower. If you see your way in, go for it, but don't go in alone. Groups of three or more. Everyone understand?"

The group nodded and mumbled their understanding.

"Good. We'll all meet up in there somehow, but if you get in, don't wait. Keep moving. We're pretty sure Avoria will be at the top. It's her nature. She wants to look over the world like it's her own creation. But you can bet she'll be heavily guarded."

Mulan wove her fingertips together and continued. "Enzo, Master Cherry, and I will be a part of the group that goes in *last*, along with Liam and Geppetto. Does anybody wish to volunteer to be in the group that goes first?"

A thick knot congealed in Enzo's throat as every hand in the room shot into the air.

Mulan gestured to the group and put her hand on Enzo's back. "Divide them up, Enzo."

They were with him.

Everyone was with him.

CHAPTER TWENTY-FIVE

THE NEW WORLD: SUBWAY TUNNELS

Hansel had two major orders of business to accomplish before he died, and they weren't going to be easy. Like many difficult conversations, the first started with one word. "Enzo."

Enzo slipped a small dagger into a hidden side pocket in his boot. He looked up, cutting Hansel with his gaze.

Hansel wove his fingers together, rocking on the balls of his feet. "I'm not sure I've formally apologized to you. For everything."

"No, you haven't." Enzo spun his finger in a circle. "Turn around. You've got some loose straps in your armor."

Hansel turned and put his arms up. Enzo tightened the straps, jerking, twisting, and tinkering.

"Thanks for your help." Hansel winced when the leather pinched his shoulder blade. "I've grown a bit thinner recently."

"Not enough candy?" Enzo asked.

"Not enough warmth. Or sleep. Or comfort. Maybe after tonight all that will change."

As if on cue, Benjamin Baker walked by with a tray loaded with cream puffs, their steam coiling through the air with an intoxicating fruity aroma. "*Eat*," he commanded. "Both of you."

With no hesitation, Hansel and Enzo each scooped a cream puff into their palms. Hansel devoured his right away, feeling close to nirvana when the fluffy salted cream and hot lemon topping melted between his teeth. His tongue acted like a sponge, absorbing the dessert's warmth and spreading it all the way through his toes. *This is ambrosia.*

Enzo held his cream puff up to his face and studied it before he popped it into his mouth. Before he even started chewing, his face lit up like he'd received an electrifying kiss. He closed his eyes and chewed slowly. "How do you *do* this?"

Benjamin made a thumbs-up and carried the tray around the room. "I'm the Muffin Man. You don't need to know my secrets. You only need to know who I am."

Pietro cut across the tracks and grabbed two for himself. "Bless you, sweet prince."

Liam craned his neck. "Somebody called for me?"

"*Eat.*" Benjamin made a beeline for Liam and carried the steaming tray away.

Hansel swallowed, took a moment to savor the lingering taste, and then he cleared his throat. "Anyway," he said. "I haven't apologized to you yet."

"You don't have to," Enzo answered. "You're here. That counts for something. It counts for a lot, actually. You made a lot of bad things happen, but I *know* you're sorry. Your actions are enough. I don't need your words."

Hansel was surprised when tears coated the surface of his eyes. He still didn't feel he deserved the forgiveness. He turned away and massaged his eyelids, clearing his throat until he thought it was safe to look back at the boy again. "Might I at least say thank you?"

Enzo shrugged. "For what?"

"For letting me fight with you. For trusting me."

"Yeah. Sure thing," Enzo said. "Look, I've seen what Avoria's influence can do to the best of people. You don't know what happened in Wonderland. But deep down, you're good. You believe that, right?"

Hansel rubbed a hand over his stubble. "I know I'm good. Do you think Liam will ever see that? I've seen the way he looks at me. We haven't always—we've *never*—been the best of chums."

"Maybe we'll all get a fresh start soon."

After the handshake, Hansel went to look for Gretel, and he found her chasing a rat into one of the holes in the subway walls. He sat her down, took a knee, and rubbed the back of his neck while he tried to choose his words. *Listen, Gretel, if I don't come back . . . If I die out there . . .* Hansel took a deep breath. *No, I can't scare her like that.* "I don't want you fighting out there today," Hansel said. "You've been through more hell than all of us already."

"But I wanna help," Gretel said.

Hansel shook his head. "You've done so much already. I don't want Avoria near you again."

Merlin stepped forward and beckoned Gretel toward him. "Come, young one. I'll keep you safe." He flashed a full, warm smile at Hansel, melting any sensation that the magician still harbored resentment for him. "I've discussed this with Mulan. I won't be fighting today. Without my magic, I'm just a brittle old man who will slow you all down. I'll look after your sister until you come back. We'll guard the tunnels with Garon. It's important work. Right, Gretel?"

Hansel hugged his sister tight, kissed her on the forehead, and then shook Merlin's hand. "Thank you, Sir Merlin."

A low rumble whirred to life throughout the tunnels, followed by the flickering of burnt orange light. Hansel imagined a dragon roaring through the subway, but the mechanical clanks of gears, wheels, and screeching steel brought him back to reality.

Garon waddled into view, a black device in his palm as he launched into a final review of Mulan's battle plan. "And we're live." He shook the remote in the air. "I've rigged the subways into motion again. We can be sure Avoria's going to feel the movement underneath her, but she'll have to search every train on this damn island if she wants to. Every line will be live all night long, and all we need is *one*. Squadron One, your train will be here in seven minutes. You are to board, ride to the end of the line—approximately one mile past the Citadel—and disembark."

"Remember, seek high ground and attack the tower from behind," Mulan said. "Spare no arrow. Draw Avoria's hoods into the skyscrapers. In the meantime, Squadron Two and Three will move in from the side and start chipping away at the perimeter. Squadron Four"—she looked at Enzo—"will take the front gates and enter the Citadel after all other measures have been exhausted. We're in for a long night, everyone. Let's begin."

Nobody complained. It had already been a long twenty-five years. So much of the pain these people faced over the last two and half decades was the direct result of Hansel's actions, and he knew it. Had he never left his sister's side and spent the day gushing over Snow White when Violet sent his friends to Avoria's castle, the Ivory Queen might never have dragged Gretel into the mirror. Had he never meddled with the darkness in the Cavern of Ombra, Avoria might never have compelled him to abduct the seven prisoners she wanted, thus unleashing her into the New World and awakening her age of terror. Sure, he wasn't one of those silly kids playing in the mines anymore, but it was time his old friends knew he was more than the haunting shadow of his past.

When the train grinded to a halt in front of Hansel and his squad, he narrowed his eyes and made a fist. *I'm going to fix this.*

Tahlia Rose followed him into the train and took a seat next to him. "No turning back now, right?" The doors shut, and the train rumbled into motion. "What's coming will come."

Hansel looked out the window with a heavy heart. *Poor thing just lost her grandmother, and here she is. What thick skin she has.* He patted her back, crossed his arms, and faced forward.

Tahlia pulled at a blue strand of hair and studied it in front of her face. "You can't spend your whole life blaming yourself, you know. For whatever you did. Nobody will forgive you if you can't forgive yourself first."

Hansel raised an eyebrow. "You seem to be speaking from experience."

"I hurt a lot of people in Wonderland." Tahlia faced forward and rested her hands on her lap, closing her eye for some rest.

Hansel found that hard to believe. "I don't think you'd hurt a flea. I see through that mask. You act rough. You talk hard. But you're *soft*. You're like your grandmother. You wouldn't hurt anybody unless it was to defend yourself. We're both good people looking for redemption. So let's stick together out there, okay?"

Tahlia nodded back, not opening her eye.

The train rumbled onward for enough time to lull Hansel into a catnap, where no dreams came to him. His sleep flailed in a black abyss framed by the soundtrack of the train's squeaky wheels. The subway wasn't particularly comfy—in fact, the ever-present smell of mildew blocked Hansel from reaching a full slumber, but the motions were their own lullaby.

Unfortunately, the nap was short-lived. Cinderella tapped Hansel's shoulder from behind and made her way through the cart with five other soldiers, each fully alert and poised for action.

"Heads up," Cinderella said. "We've been spotted. The dark army had a group that boarded a train going in the opposite direction, heading our way. We crossed paths about a minute ago, and they disembarked. Be ready to fight."

Hansel stretched his arms, woke Tahlia, and then stood. Something was bound to unravel Mulan's battle plan sooner or later. Luckily, he learned to improvise long ago. "We'll be the distraction then."

Tahlia readied her bow. "It's an honor, right?"

The squadron spread out along the train and took cover behind different seats, poles, and by the doors. While the train had been bustling with comfortable chatter for most of the ride, all noise slowed to an eerie silence after Cinderella passed. Hansel surveyed the warriors around him, proud of the resolve and determination etched on their faces. This wasn't a group that would run away. He watched the signs pass in the tunnels and made a mental note of how far off they were from their destination. Luckily, they didn't have much farther to travel until it was time to get above ground.

Boom!

The subway lurched as something exploded near the front of the train, filling the tunnel with an orange glow, and the wheels slammed to a jerky halt. Tahlia bumped her head on the pole, and at the sound of her bone on metal, Hansel rushed to her side.

"I'm fine," Tahlia said quickly, holding her forehead. "It sounded worse than it felt."

Hansel gestured for Tahlia to stay down. He kept the upper half of his face to the window. Sure enough, about fifty soldiers in dark hoods marched through the tunnels. Broad silver mallets hung over most of their shoulders, while others bore tridents and lances. Some weapons even crackled with fire. Hansel ducked. "No bold moves, okay? You were made for long-distance fire. I'll cover you in this mob. Stay close."

Tahlia nocked an arrow and leaned back against the wall. "I appreciate that. But I'm giving this *everything*."

Crack!

Windows burst into crystal confetti all over the train, and the group exploded into battle. Dark-hooded figures thrust their gloved hands into the cart, and silver mallets swung in and out of the broken windows looking for victims. Hansel took the first opportunity to seize the head of a hammer and pull its wielder into the train. Tahlia fired an arrow into the opponent's chest, and he let go of the mallet right away. Hansel took its handle and prepared to swing.

"Nice shot," he grumbled to Tahlia, keeping watch out the window. Somewhere beyond the window, a white spark ignited. Hansel squinted and saw that the spark originated near a short blonde woman with her hood down, who held a thick long stick the color of copper. The white spark hovered around the stick, and when the woman made eye contact with Hansel, she grinned like a demon.

"Oh, no," Hansel said. "Someone out there's got dynamite. We need to get off the train. Everyone, *off* the train!" He pulled Tahlia to her feet as the dynamite sailed through the window and landed by his heel, its flame traveling down the dark fuse like a shooting star. While it fizzed and hissed, the dark soldiers took ten giant steps back and stood along the walls, throwing their hands over the part of their hoods where their ears should be.

"The doors won't open!" Cinderella exclaimed, pushing on the doors while the people around her searched for buttons and levers.

"Step back." Hansel brandished the silver hammer while Cinderella ordered everyone else to climb out the windows. A few of his comrades had managed to seize mallets as well, and they set to work on busting the rest of the windows and helping each other climb out of the train.

Thwack! Thwack! Thwack! Hansel hit the door with all his might, only for the hammer to bounce off without leaving a dent. He gritted his teeth and tried new poses to maximize his momentum, bending his knees and leaning into the swing, but the doors wouldn't open.

"We need to pry." Tahlia jammed an arrow into a crack between the door and its frame. She leaned into it and created a lever, managing to pry the door open about an inch.

When the crack grew big enough for Hansel to put a finger through, he thrust his hand through the door and pulled. For a few seconds, the door protested and his fingers screamed, reminding him of all the times he spent trying to pry a cursed mirror off his wall. Finally, a satisfying *crack* sounded, and the door flew all the way open. "Go!" he yelled. "Everyone off!"

Hansel exited after Tahlia, and the rest of the group started to follow. A good portion had already managed to make it off the train, and battle had ensued all over the subway tunnel. Cinderella was locked in combat with the woman who threw the dynamite stick, spilling other explosives all over the ground.

Boom!

The train exploded behind Hansel, engulfing him in warmth. He wrapped himself around Tahlia like a shield and dove to the ground. A chunk of metal swatted his back before he stood again and assessed the damage. The whole train had burst like a dead star, and as Hansel looked around the tunnel, a pang of sadness hit him when he realized that not everyone had made it off before the dynamite blew up. The group should have been bigger.

A group of five hoods swarmed on Tahlia, and Hansel knocked two of them out of the way. Tahlia and Hansel stood back to back and engaged the other three, kicking and elbowing and punching as hard and as fast as they could. It was a sick feeling, swinging the silver mallet around, and every time Hansel heard a bone crack, he forced himself to smile. He'd heard somewhere that smiles suppress the gag reflex. Tahlia's stomach seemed to be much stronger, for her expression remained flat and calm the whole time.

When they knocked out the five, Tahlia pocketed a stick of dynamite, and Hansel grabbed her arm.

"We should keep moving," he said. "Remember Enzo and Mulan's orders. If we find high ground now, we can give Enzo's group the advantage."

Tahlia gestured around the tunnel. "But what about—"

"Just have faith. They'll join us when they clear the tunnel. We won't be alone." Another stick rolled along the ground and stopped at his toe. He picked it up, buried it in his quiver, and headed for the steps. "Come on. Up we go."

CHAPTER TWENTY-SIX

THE NEW WORLD: NEW YORK STREETS

Have You Seen Alicia Trujillo?

Alicia looked at the torn remnants of the poster on the bulletin board while the rest of her squadron shuffled on ahead of her. Beneath her, the ground rumbled like a hungry beast, and somewhere in the distance, it sounded like bombs were exploding. She carried a sword, her mind set on attack until she confronted her own face on the missing poster.

It seemed like the photo on the poster had been taken forever ago, at a time when Alicia felt youthful and wouldn't have insisted on hiding from the camera. There came a time when she hated looking at photos of herself and started making goofy faces behind Rosana, who was a lot more confident in front of a camera despite her unwillingness to draw attention to herself. Alicia looked at the poster and tried to guess when the picture was taken. She felt like she'd aged ten years since then.

She peered in the window next to the bulletin board. The department store within was submerged in darkness, haunted by lonely mannequins and unfinished sales. A mirror hung in the window's display, and Alicia studied herself, comparing her reflection to her own missing poster. The reflection was a little less kind, more honest. It didn't hesitate to show her all the wear she'd been through and the subtle lines her adventures had carved under her eyes.

"Nobody believed me when it happened, you know."

Alicia closed her eyes and took a deep breath.

Rosana appeared behind her in the mirror image, taking off her hood and jamming her hands into the pockets. Her armor bulged underneath the hoodie. "I spent so much time trying to convince the police that what I saw was real . . . that you were abducted right before my eyes, and nobody believed me."

Alicia turned around and took her daughter's face in her hands. "You shouldn't have followed me, Rosana. I thought you were going with Enzo!"

"I'll catch up to him," Rosana assured. "But I couldn't bear the thought of us marching into battle without having this conversation. In case we don't make it. I wanted you to know that I missed you, and that when you would disappear for a while, I would look everywhere. But never once did I blame you."

A weight sank in Alicia's heart. "Rosana, you know I would take you all around the world if I could. One day I will. You deserve to see everything you want to see and more."

"I've already seen more than I ever asked for," Rosana said. "I just want to see *you* more."

Alicia hugged her daughter so tightly their embrace could have made a diamond out of coal. "When we finish this, I'll find another job. We'll finish your schooling. We'll travel the world, together. Or we'll stay at home together and live on the couch burning through our Netflix queue. Can you imagine? A piece of pie, a frosty glass of milk, a queue full of Channing Tatum movies. Just the two of us. That's my wish."

Rosana rested her head on her mom's shoulder. "Mine too."

They held the pose for a while, until Alicia looked ahead and realized she couldn't see her squadron anymore. Hook, the Hearts, and the Lost Boys moved ahead without her. She grabbed Rosana's shoulders and looked into her eyes. "Come with me?"

"Wait," Rosana said, her eyes wide with wonder. She pointed over Alicia's shoulder. "The mirror!"

Alicia whirled around and beheld a soft purple light beaming from inside the mirror's frame. She took a step back and shielded her daughter. "What's it doing?"

And then a periwinkle hand pushed through and seized the frame.

I'd know that hand anywhere.

Alicia kicked the department store window and climbed into the display, her heart racing against her ribcage. She seized the hand in the mirror and pulled, feeling as though she were playing tug-o-war with the glass. Alicia rocked back onto her heels.

Rosana ran over and pulled Alicia's shoulders. "Mom!"

The full arm emerged, and Alicia gritted her teeth. "Pull!"

Rosana tugged, exposing a shimmering sleeve and shoulder in the mirror's frame, and finally, a head of lavender hair. "Violet!"

"Oh, thank you, Lady Fortune!" Violet exclaimed. "Rosana and Alice! You may let go now. I'll climb the rest of the way. I had to be sure I was going through a *good* mirror, but I must confess I panicked a bit when you grabbed my hand. I thought you might have been Avoria!"

Alicia let out a relieved laugh and doubled over to catch her breath. "Miss Violet, we've been looking *everywhere* for you! We assumed you'd been killed! Where have you been?"

Violet climbed from the frame, and Alicia frowned when she realized that not only was the fairy missing her wings, but a hand as well. Her left arm ended in a stump.

"Don't fret, Alice," Violet said, dusting Alicia's knees off and ruffling her hair. "I can't have wings in this realm." The fairy pointed to her left arm. "This is how the New World decided to compensate for my missing wing. I'll make do. However, I should ask that you stand back."

"I'm so confused!" Rosana said. "Where have you been all this time?"

"You'll see." She faced the mirror, and in the reflection, Alicia could see Violet grinning. "I brought reinforcements."

Alicia wrinkled her brows. "Reinforcements? What kind of reinforcements?"

As if in response, the mirror turned purple again, and the head of an enormous cat poked out of the shimmering surface. It made eye contact with Rosana, and its bulbous eyes widened like saucers. "*Oh, boy! Rosana!* Am I ever glad to see you!"

The cat galloped out of the frame and pranced around the snow, and Alicia felt her heart lift up.

"Chester!" Rosana ran over to the feline and hugged its leg. In response, the cat bent down and licked Rosana's face with such force she fell on her back. Chester kept on licking her cheeks and pawing at her stomach, eliciting a full child-like laugh from her. "Stop! Chester, get off, that *tickles!*"

"I apologize if my disappearance alarmed everyone. It was my most cowardly move. I was in combat with my father's army, and I had to disappear. I've been watching progress from the other side, and in the meantime"—Violet beamed, her eyes sparkling with pride—"I've been recruiting. There's more where Chester came from."

A bulbous, multi-armed creature shimmied over the edge of the frame while an enormous bird squeezed through the top half one wing at a time. When the bird burst free, it spread its wings, tilted its head back, and let out a proud boisterous caw. A pair of bald men with football player builds clamored over the hairy multi-armed creature, seized it by the upper half of its body, and pulled it out to its freedom. At once, Alicia recognized Cat, the caterpillar she'd encountered in the World Between, though she'd been altered quite a bit by the appearance of black smoke and shadowy wisps. Cat's momentum pushed her into a roll, and she barreled through the snow until the wall brought her to a full stop. She shook the snow off her head and wriggled into a standing position. Making eye contact with Alicia, Cat bowed. "Greetings to you, dear Alice." She bared her teeth at the cat and snapped her fingers on every arm. "Chester! Stop licking the girl at once! You are *not* a dog!"

The two men brought out a set of pointed spears, clicked the blunt ends against the ground, and then snapped their heels together. "Tweedle Dee and Tweedle Dum reporting for duty, Miss Violet!"

Violet flashed Alicia a triumphant smile and gestured to the newcomers. "We've been rebuilding the realm of Wonder, dearest Alice. In return, the gang's all here to shine some light on *our* world. These are your comrades."

Rosana beamed from ear to ear and gave the Jub-Jub bird a friendly pat on the beak. The bird cooed like a pigeon, which was a feat to behold since it bore more resemblance to a pterodactyl. "I can't believe you brought Wonderland to us. This is incredible!"

"It was no easy task," Violet confessed, "but it was a necessary one. I should advise you all to stay away from this mirror, however. It will soon demand a trade for my departure. But for now, my friends"—she made a fist with her good hand—"we storm the Citadel!"

Violet burst into a sprint, and Alicia and the creatures of Wonderland followed.

✳✳✳

Pietro and Zack were a part of the third squadron, which would attack the Citadel from the right. Garon instructed the two to hang behind after the rest of the group left, and then he beckoned them to follow him into his crafting nook in the subway. When they got there, they found two white sheets covering bulky objects about Garon's height. He folded his hands in front of him and cleared his throat, giving Pietro and Zack a proud look.

"I've been working on something special for you two," Garon announced.

Pietro studied the white sheets and tried to make a guess about what they might be hiding. They looked like small mountains, with no perfect symmetry or distinguishing bulges that would give away their contents. "What'd you make us?"

"First," Garon said, "I'd like you two to raise your right hands."

Zack and Pietro exchanged funny looks, rolling their eyes and putting their palms in the air.

"Okayyy," Zack said.

"*I*," Garon said.

Zack and Pietro droned the word back to him.

"With more feeling!" Garon insisted. "This is a special gift. A desirable gift! You'll want to be excited about this one. One more time, now. *I*!"

"I!" Zack and Pietro repeated.

"Do so very solemnly swear . . ." Garon continued his spiel, waiting for the words to echo back to him after every pause. "To *maintain* and *love* this contraption . . . as if it were . . . my firstborn child . . . so help me Garon. Very good."

Before Garon could go on explaining, Pietro raised his hand higher and said, "But *Zack* is my firstborn child!"

"Precisely! Care for this beast as if it were Zack. This took time and love and resources one cannot simply find lying around anywhere." Garon jerked the sheets off his inventions with a wild flourish. As he yanked, he spun around, and the sheets ended up wrapping him in a thin cocoon. "Behold!"

Zack ran to one of the new inventions, his mouth wide open and his eyes wild. "*What?*"

"You know what this is, yes?" Garon asked.

Pietro scratched his head, a little too stunned to move closer. "Well, yeah. These are motorcycles, but why?"

"These aren't any old choppers, Pan. I fashioned these beauties with my bare hands, sparing no expense from either world. These are the first motorcycles ever to exist that have parts made from two different realms. As such, they will be formidable weapons against those dark things and the shadows. Stand behind me and observe."

Pietro put his hand on his forehead, still thoroughly in shock, but he obeyed Garon's orders and watched the dwarf sit on one of the bikes. It sank a few inches with a *whumph*, and Garon gripped the handlebars and aimed the front of the bike to the end of the hallway.

"I christened them the Shadow Riders. Seemed fitting for you." Garon pushed a button on the side of the left handle, and a beam of light blasted through the front of the bike. It illuminated the wall like a tiny sun, and despite the fact that they were behind the light source, Pietro and Zack both had to shield their eyes. "But I should name them the Shadow *Slayers*. None of those things have a hope of surviving when this beauty shines on them."

"*Wow*," Pietro said. "All this for us?"

"All this and more. Stand a little farther back, please." Garon pressed a button on the right handle, and a tiny cannon popped out between the handlebars with a springy *click*. After a second push, a missile the size of Pietro's thumb flew out of the new cannon, buried itself in the wall, and exploded. Dust and debris clouded the tunnel. "For your hooded friends."

Pietro coughed into his elbow and turned around. "You definitely just *broke* the tunnel."

"Oh, I'll fix it later." Garon waved an arm. "You enjoy your presents, I trust?"

Zack ran his fingers over the cushy rubber handles and warm leather seat. "I love this thing! But I don't have my license or anything. I'm not really supposed to drive."

"Where are the police?" Garon challenged. "Who's going to discipline you for driving without a license?"

"My mom."

Pietro winked. "She'll understand, Kid."

Zack laughed. "Thank you, Garon. I'll treat this thing like my firstborn child."

Garon nodded proudly. "When you're out there, keep one eye on the skies. Mulan called in a favor from Hollywood."

CHAPTER TWENTY-SEVEN

THE NEW WORLD:
BEHIND THE CITADEL

Hansel and Tahlia took the roundabout way to get to their vantage points in New York City, even knowing that doing so meant straying from Mulan's battle plan. As soon as they returned to street level, they hung an immediate right and looped around several blocks before circling back to the building Mulan wanted them to shoot from. Hansel knew the fact that Avoria's soldiers stormed into the subway meant she would also have warriors ready to go in other unexpected places. It would've been foolish to expect every single one of them to stay put by the Citadel. Some were likely under orders to prevent anyone else from getting that far.

Hansel ran scenarios in his head, lost in his own strategies when Tahlia shoved him to the side and a barrage of arrows rained on them from the fifth floor of Rockefeller Plaza.

"Down!" Tahlia ordered, pulling Hansel behind a frozen garbage can. She popped up with her own bow ready to fire, and she aimed for the windows. She concentrated for a second, swiveling the weapon from side to side before she scoffed and stamped her foot. "I need to get closer."

Hansel grabbed Tahlia's ankle before she could run away. "Hey!

Think about this. We can't waste time here. Five archers in the center aren't going to make a difference in the long run."

Tahlia's expression hardened, her lips a flat line. "They shot at us! I'm not going to let them get away with—"

"*Save* your arrows. If you run out, I cannot help you. The closer we get to that tower, the more we'll need them." Hansel released Tahlia's ankle and rolled into new cover behind an icy bush. "Let's go. We're not that far away."

Gritting her teeth, Tahlia slung her bow behind her back again and raised a finger at the archers in the windows. "If I still have my dynamite at the end of this, I'm coming back and blowing them into the sky."

"You do that."

Hansel ducked in another alley, leaving Tahlia a couple feet behind, and looked both ways for danger. Two hooded figures patrolled the sidewalk, moving back and forth with their hands in their pockets. They appeared bored, their heads tilted toward the ground and their feet shuffling aimlessly through the snow. Hansel made a series of hand motions at Tahlia, indicating that there were two enemies around the corner, and he put a finger to his lips. He pointed to his hammer and made two light swinging motions in the air.

He followed up a minute later, padding through the street as softly as possible and praying that the snow wouldn't crunch beneath him. The first hood spun around as Hansel approached, and with a gruff, masculine voice, the person underneath yelled, "Hey!"

Hansel conked the first person in the head, prompting the second to turn and fire an arrow into Hansel's shoulder. The entire movement unfolded in a blink, and biting pain rang through Hansel's shoulder like fire. As a reflex, his hand sprang open, and he dropped the silver mallet on the ground. With a girlish laugh, the hooded warrior unsheathed a dagger and raised it over her head. Hansel took a sliding step back, and a red-tipped arrow flew past him from behind and hit his opponent in the chest. He used his opportunity to pry the dagger out of her hands and plant his bootheel in her stomach. She collapsed next to her partner in a limp pile of cloth. Hansel grabbed her bow and quiver, and he tossed them to Tahlia, who trudged over to Hansel with a mound of snow in her hand.

"Hold still." Tahlia gripped the arrow protruding from Hansel's shoulder and gave him a sympathetic look. "One, two . . ." Without getting to three, Tahlia pulled the weapon out of his skin and slapped the handful of ice onto the wound. First it felt like a dog bite, and then numbness spread through the muscle. "Hold that there for a little bit."

Hansel frowned, his eyebrows in hard angles. "That really *hurt*."

Tahlia pointed at the soldiers. "At least you're not one of them."

Hansel looked down and used the toe of his boot to nudge one of the soldiers. "Make sure the other one's down."

While Tahlia shook the other one's shoulders, Hansel started to remove the robe from the first warrior. *We must be about the same size.*

Tahlia raised an eyebrow. "What are you doing?"

Once he fully removed the man's hood, he shook the snow out of it. The material weighed Hansel down and jolted his wound. He slung the robe around himself and absorbed instant warmth. Hansel threw the hood over his eyes, found two more blades in the inner pockets, and then he zipped up the front. He abandoned the hammer. "We're gonna be these guys for a while." He pointed to the other soldier one more time. "Put on her hood. We'll get through the streets more easily this way."

Tahlia's face lit up with understanding, and she wrestled the garment off Avoria's warrior, revealing a petite woman with curly auburn hair and milky-white skin. "Sorry, lady. You fought hard. I'm glad you at least have another layer on." When Tahlia threw the robe on, she wrinkled her nose for a second. "Who knows where these things have been? But what do you think? New wardrobe?" A chill scuttled down Hansel's spine when Tahlia twirled around. "At least they're somewhat comfortable, yes?"

Hansel rolled his eyes. "Let's just keep moving."

They pushed through the weather and did their best to imitate the slow, deliberate movements of Avoria's army. Hansel and Tahlia passed a couple more clusters of soldiers with little more than a quick glance and arrived at the base of the skyscraper that Mulan wanted him to watch from. From around the corner, Hansel could already see the Citadel sprawling with activity. Another one of his squadrons arrived already, and a pang of guilt welled up in his throat. He was supposed to be first. Did his detour cost any of his comrades some valuable time?

Tahlia and Hansel ducked into the building, a hollow shell of a national bank, and made a run for the nearest stairwell. "Tenth floor," Hansel instructed. "Don't stop until we get to the tenth floor."

The stairwell wound on for what seemed like an eternity. About halfway up, two more soldiers barred Tahlia and Hansel with a pair of spears. "Nobody told us we would have reinforcements coming! Who ordered you here?"

In response, Tahlia grabbed the soldiers, slammed their heads together, and shoved them down the stairs. Neither of them moved again.

Hansel scratched his head. "You frighten me."

"You should learn from me."

At last, they reached the tenth floor, a barren office space with a large rectangular window overlooking the ground below. With hearts in their throats and weapons in hand, Hansel and Tahlia crossed to the windows and beheld the battle below.

The view was all at once awe-inspiring, terrifying, and heartbreaking. For every man or woman fighting on their side, shadows swarmed the air and hooded warriors pushed back against them to protect Avoria's hive. Motionless bodies from both sides littered the ground, all coated in glistening white frost that turned a little bit pinker every minute.

"They should have *waited*!" Hansel growled.

"*We* should have *hurried*," Tahlia countered. "They didn't have extra time to wait."

Hansel took his bow in his hands. "Then let's buy some of that time back for them."

Tahlia followed suit and nocked an arrow.

Hansel squeezed one eye shut and drew an imaginary line down the center of the crowd. A pair of motorcycles mirrored his line of sight, shooting lights and tiny missiles in the snow. He blinked and squinted, trying to see who the riders might have been. Helmets covered their faces, but the lights and missiles cut through the shadows and hoods, so they appeared to be allies. "See where those two motorcycles rode in from?"

Tahlia nodded.

"Draw an imaginary line straight from the front motorcycle to the base of the Citadel. Shoot everything coming in on the right side of that line. Got it? I'll shoot everything on the left. Don't hit our friends."

"Got it." Tahlia let her first arrow fly. It sailed directly into the folds of a black hood, and its owner crumbled.

Hansel beamed with pride, nocked his own arrow, and fired.

✳ ✳ ✳

Rosana's heart smiled when the reinforcements from Wonderland arrived. Once Violet had explained herself, the group wasted no more time. Rosana climbed onto Chester's back and the two rode into battle together, each opting for invisibility as long as they could. Violet took to the skies on the back of the Jub-Jub bird, which Rosana was immensely grateful to have on her side. She was also in complete awe of Violet, boldly taking control of the bird with only one hand to hold onto its back.

As for Rosana's mom, her speed supplemented Tweedle Dee's and Tweedle Dum's battle skills. Neither of the twins moved particularly fast, but nobody could deny their brawn. The bones in their fists might as well have been made of iron, and their skin could've been stone. Rosana's mom could pack a punch of her own, but her strength shined in her wits and her agility. She ran into the battle with the twins flanking her, and Rosana watched the three of them become the ultimate fighting machine. Her mother sprinted and dodged through the mass of dark hoods, disorienting them and putting them in a dazed stupor before Tweedle Dee and Tweedle Dum introduced their spears and their fists.

What worried Rosana the most was Cat, the dark caterpillar, who seemed to be the least equipped for battle. It seemed to take considerable effort and time for her to wriggle even a few yards, let alone for her to stand. The structure of her body also didn't give her much of an edge to attack her enemies, who wasted no time identifying her vulnerability. She'd been inching her way toward the Citadel when a mass of black hoods converged around her and drew their mallets.

"Chester!" Rosana hissed, seeing the threat to the creature. "Let's move!"

Chester growled, leapt over a group of soldiers, and pounced in the middle of the circle of hoods. As he shielded the caterpillar with his massive body, his invisibility faded. "Hands off the caterpillar, bandersnatches!" He barked like a dog and whipped his tail in a half circle, knocking many of the soldiers onto their backs. "Leave her alone!"

The remaining soldiers jeered and hissed at Chester, raising their hammers and preparing to strike before Rosana removed her hood and took out her sword. When she reappeared on Chester's back, they leapt back in surprise and shifted their aim toward her.

Rosana pointed the blade in front of her and waved it back and forth. "I bet I'm a *lot* faster with this thing than you all are with those hammers. Care to test me?"

A flash of silver approached her from the left. Rosana raised her sword and blocked the hammer, though it was nowhere as easy as blocking another sword. The mallet crashed through the air with twice the momentum of the blade, and a throbbing pain shot from

Rosana's fingers through her shoulder. She cried out in pain, and as she recoiled, a second hammer swung at her from the right and knocked her off Chester's back. She landed on her side, pain gnawing on her shoulder bones.

Chester raised a giant paw and slashed at the soldier who struck Rosana, tearing open his robe and a bit of the skin on his chest. Mallets and arrows assaulted him from other angles, and he launched into a flurry of bites and scratches, refusing to leave Cat's side. Rosana pulled herself back to her knees, one hand on her forehead and the other clutching her sword. She didn't have much strength to stand on her own.

A storm of fireballs rained from the sky, annihilating a small group of black hoods. Rosana looked up and made brief eye contact with Violet on top of the Jub-Jub bird. While Rosana smiled at the woman, Violet mouthed something that looked a lot like *look out!*

Rosana turned her head to see a line of wraith-like shadows lunging for her. On instinct, she shut her eyes and threw her hands up over her face, knowing her reaction wouldn't serve any real protection from the darkness.

But when she opened her eyes, light filled them, and the shadows melted away like water turning to vapor. The sound of a motor roared toward her, and the next thing she knew, Pietro zoomed in front of her on a black motorcycle, helmet on his lap and eyes bright with childlike glee. He wheeled around, faced the crowd that assaulted Chester and Cat, and pressed a button on his handlebar. Missiles burst from the front of his vehicle and buried themselves in the black hoods.

Rosana blinked and rubbed her eyes. "Pietro?"

Pietro extended his hand and wrapped it around Rosana's wrist. "Jump on, Rosana. Grab onto me!" While she crawled onto the back of his seat, sheathed her sword, and leaned against his back, he shot a look at Chester and Cat. "You two good over here? You are a *very* large cat, by the way."

"Dog," Chester corrected, nodding his answer. "Thanks, pal!"

The ground lurched beneath Rosana as Pietro gunned the motorcycle and sped away from Chester. She wrapped her arms around his torso until she found her balance, suddenly feeling invincible. She pulled out her bow. "Thank you, Pietro."

"Don't thank me yet!" Pietro said. "Those things have been hounding me for hours. Zack and I split apart a while ago. The sound attracts too many shadows. We're quite a threat on this thing. So, I'm counting on you. This ride covers everything in front of us, but you've gotta protect our butts and our sides as much as you can. Can you do that?"

Rosana nodded. "I can do that."

Pietro found a safe spot to brake, removed his helmet, and then placed it over Rosana's head. The visor obscured the world in a bluish tint, but she was surprised it didn't take much of her peripheral vision away. "You're gonna need this."

When Pietro kicked his cycle into full speed, clumps of snow burst from under the tires and splattered a group of hoods behind them, knocking them on their backs.

Pietro rode toward the Citadel, swerving and spinning almost haphazardly to avoid the barrage of arrows and weapons that locked onto him from every angle. Every now and then, he'd ride away and disappear down a maze of alleys, looking for the best new angle to emerge and strike the army.

"*So* many hooded things," he complained, pausing in a snow-covered alleyway. "You see Enzo anywhere?"

"Nowhere," Rosana confessed. "Do you think he already made it inside somehow?"

"I don't think so," Pietro said. "Still too much in his way. Listen, though. At the first chance we get, we're booking it inside. Even if we don't think he's in there yet, we need to clear the way for him." He turned around and locked eyes with Rosana. "This whole thing started with you, me, and him. Let's make sure we stick it out 'til the end."

Rosana threw her hands up in a *duh* sort of move. "You think I expected it to be any other way?"

"I've always liked your attitude. Mental high five."

A black dot coasted through the sky and made a beeline for the Citadel. Rosana removed her helmet and squinted. "What's that thing up there? Is that a plane?"

Pietro looked up. "I can't tell. Hope it's on *our* side, though. It's flying too straight to be another one of those Jub-Jub things. By the way, that bird out there is *horrifying*. How did you even sleep in Wonderland knowing that thing was close by?"

"The bird was not the worst thing Wonderland had to offer. And that one *is* on our side." After a toss of her hair, Rosana fixed the helmet back on her head. "Should we get back out there?"

Pietro clicked on the beams. "You read my mind."

He gunned the motor and sped out of the alleyway, blasting through shadows and launching missiles into the dark army. Meanwhile, Rosana took care of the soldiers that attacked him from the side. Her sword made soft swishing sounds as she waved it from side to side and cut through falling snowflakes. Unfortunately, her simple sword and her arrows would do nothing against the shadows. Nearly five of them swarmed down in a spiral formation, cleaving through snowflakes.

Rosana sheathed her weapon and leaned onto Pietro's back. "Go faster!"

Pietro accelerated, though it jittered Rosana's nerves to think he could lose control if he drove too fast on the icy ground. "We need to try to get those things in front of us somehow," he said. "Keep your weapons down, and hang on to me. This is gonna get a little rocky."

Pietro jerked and swerved the bike a few times, making circles and ducking into alleys. While he maneuvered, Rosana caught sight of her friends. Her mother bolted and kicked her way through swarms of hoods, while Dum and Dee trudged behind her and snapped a pair of spears around. Hook and Nibs protected each other's backs and danced in circles. Wendy and Carla weren't too far away, standing back to back with what looked like blunderbusses in their hands while Pino brandished his famous knife and taunted one of the hoods. In a nearby building, a pair of hooded archers fired from a window high above the ground, and Rosana could have sworn their arrows made a deliberate beeline for a set of hoods that had approached Pino from behind. She wasn't sure if they intended to kill two of their own or if they were aiming for Mr. DiLegno.

"Pietro." Rosana's voice shook. "This isn't working. They're still above us. I think the shadows learned your pattern."

"Dammit!" Pietro pounded on his handlebar. She could almost see the gears whirring in his head. "Think, Pietro, think! Um. All right, help me look for an open door."

Rosana's heart dropped into her stomach. "Open door?"

"Open door," Pietro confirmed. "Any door. A bank. A movie theater. A mall. We're looking for low ceilings."

"What? No! I don't like this idea!"

"I don't either, but—"

Click!

A hot white light spilled from above, blasting Pietro and the path in front of him. He squeezed the brakes and grinded to a halt. Rosana threw an arm over her eyes, desperately trying to shut out the light. When she opened them again, Pietro was laughing and pointing at the sky.

The shadows were gone, blasted away by the hot light, and the source made Rosana's heart soar. A machine hovered above the tops of the skyscrapers, and she recognized it right away.

"There's our plane," Rosana said. "It's helping us fight the shadows!"

"You know that's not *any* plane, right?" Pietro smiled. "Garon told me Mulan called in a favor. Never thought I'd be so happy to see her jet again!"

CHAPTER TWENTY-EIGHT

THE NEW WORLD: NEAR THE CITADEL

Hansel ran out of arrows before Tahlia. His arms ached and his heart raced, and sweat beaded his entire body. He still didn't feel as though they'd made a dent in the dark army. Black cloaks continued to swarm like a cloud of smoke on the ground, and Hansel's own comrades seemed to be diminishing by the minute. He didn't see many people he recognized lying still on the ground, but the body count was enough to poke holes in his morale. When he fired his last arrow, he dropped his hands to his knees and crouched down to catch his breath.

"This is a massacre." His voice was deep and low.

"Don't you lose hope on me," Tahlia warned. "This is *not* the time. We can win this thing, but if you slump down and give up, that's one less chance we have." She reached into her quiver and tossed a few more arrows into Hansel's lap. "Stand up and help me."

Hansel pushed himself back off the wall and rolled the arrows in his hands. "How many do you have left?"

"Five."

"*Five?*" Hansel spat. "You jest?"

"I do not."

Hansel leaned out of his cover and counted the hoods swarming the ground. He gave up almost immediately. There were far more than five of them behind the Citadel. "All right. We fire the rest of them"—he let an arrow fly into the back of a hooded soldier on the ground—"and then we join our friends down there."

He felt good about his marksmanship and all the targets he'd managed to hit from his vantage point. He even felt ready to use fists and blades, but a different feeling overcame him when he and Tahlia emptied their supply. He sensed that by the time they used their last arrow, the dark army had seen through their disguises. When Tahlia curled her fingers by her chest, Hansel knew she had the same feeling.

"Something's changed," she said. "Look how the hoods are behaving now."

Sure enough, about forty percent of the hoods Hansel could see were all looking toward him. It jolted his nerves, watching all of their hooded heads converge on a single focal point. But it was even eerier to watch them all start moving as one and make a beeline for the very building he'd been shooting from.

Hansel rubbed his face, massaging his eyelids so hard little colored lights bloomed in his vision. "A thousand curses! They're not happy."

"They're coming up." She leaned forward, resting her forehead against the glass. "A bunch of them went inside and . . . no! Hansel, some of them are scaling the building! What do we do?"

Hansel hoped massaging his temples would knead the answer into his mind. He looked around the room for anything he could use to fight when the footsteps clunked up the stairwells. "I really don't know. If they're coming at us from both ways, we don't really have a way back down from here."

"Up?" Tahlia offered, her voice an octave higher.

Braaack!

A creature swooped around the corner of the Citadel, demanding Hansel's attention with its deafening screech. When he squinted, he could see Violet perched about the bird's neck, and she steered it in wide circles above the battlefield.

Instinctively, Hansel smiled.

"Up indeed." He squeezed Tahlia's shoulders and cast a fleeting glance toward the door. The hoods would be upon them any second. "Do you still have that dynamite?"

Tahlia's mouth fell open, and her eyes went round with surprise. She dug her hands into her inner pocket and turned away. "Why are you asking me this?"

"Trust me." Hansel used the butt of his dagger to knock away some of the remaining shards of glass sticking to the windowpane and then extended his hand to Tahlia. "Give it here, Tahlia. We don't have much time."

"Suicide? Is this your answer?"

"Just trust me! Please! Give me the dynamite!"

With a scowl and a shake of the head, Tahlia dug the crimson stick out of her pocket and shoved the weapon into Hansel's hand.

"Good." Hansel removed his hood and lit the tip of the dynamite fuse with a match he'd tucked into his bootstrap. The tip sparked into a sizzling white star, hissing its warning in Hansel's palm. "Now flag down that bird over there. Call for the rider. It's Violet. Get her attention."

Tahlia bit her lip. "You want me to attract the Jub-Jub? Are you crazy?"

"Do you wish to die?" Hansel pointed to the stick in his hand. "Make a wish, then." With a jerk of his arm, he lobbed the dynamite into the open door, where dark-hooded warriors had reached their floor on the stairwell. Hansel slammed the door behind him and leaned back, forcing his whole weight into the door. A few seconds later, the mob of hoods started pushing back against him from the other side. Hansel dug his heel into the ground and shut his eyes.

Tahlia leaned out the window and waved her arms over her head, making wild Xs and Vs as she screamed. "*Violet! Miss Violet! Help us!*"

Heavy thumps and kicks jolted the door and sent vibrations through Hansel's back as he joined in the yelling. "Violet!" *I really hope you hear me right now.* "Please!"

Braaack!

"It's circling around," Tahlia said. "I think she saw me! How much time do we have?"

Hansel gritted his teeth. He wasn't going to be able to hold the door shut much longer. "I give us about ninety seconds."

"Violet!" Tahlia called again. "Over here!"

There was a swoop and a flap that ruffled Hansel's hair and chilled his bones. He shut his eyes to blink out the cold air, and Violet's voice soothed his ears from afar. "I'm here!"

When he opened his eyes, Tahlia braced herself against the windowpane and took a giant leap out the window. His own heart jumped into his throat, but he managed to steady his nerves when the Jub-Jub bird ascended and leveled itself a few yards outside the open window, tinged in red fluid but firmly supporting Violet and Tahlia nonetheless.

Braaack!

Hansel had never been happier to see Violet, who nodded as soon as she made eye contact. Tahlia adjusted her balance on the bird's back and extended her hand. "Hansel! Jump! Hurry!"

Bam!

The door flew open behind Hansel and forced him to the ground. He caught himself with his fingertips, sprang back to his feet, and bolted for the window.

"Run!" Tahlia screamed.

Hansel mustered one look over his shoulder on his way across the room and immediately wished he hadn't. There must have been close to a hundred hoods piling into the room, and they were after blood. They chased him like a rogue wave in a black sea, even managing to seize his robe and tug on it from behind. Hansel grabbed the dagger from the inner pocket, slipped out of the garment, and sprinted.

When he reached the edge of the window, a cold, thick hand closed around his foot. He had forgotten there were also hoods scaling the building. He looked over the ledge, confronted a red-haired man with a build like a football player, and toppled as the climber yanked on Hansel's ankle. He slipped, went over the side, and caught the ledge, dangling over the ground and clinging to the windowpane for dear life.

"No!" Violet cried. In the window's reflection, Violet veered the bird around so it faced the building, and with a retch, the Jub-Jub coughed up a massive ball of fire and hurled it into Hansel's attacker. The hood let go of Hansel's ankle and plummeted, hitting the ground below as a burnt crisp. Violet steered the bird a little closer. "Grab Tahlia's hand."

The muscles in Hansel's arms trembled around his bones, but with some effort, he lifted a hand. When he looked up, a silver mallet arced over the shoulder of one of the hoods in the room he'd fallen from, carving a deliberate beeline for Hansel's fingers.

Once Hansel braced himself for pain, Tahlia reached over and wrapped her fingers around his hand, prying him off the ledge and heaving him onto the feathered body of the bird.

"You . . ." Tahlia breathed, "are *heavy*."

Before Hansel had a chance to respond, the dynamite exploded with a thunderous boom, and a rolling cloud of orange flame swallowed the building.

CHAPTER
TWENTY-NINE

THE NEW WORLD:
HOTEL LOBBY

Enzo sat in the hotel atrium with his squadron, his chin in his hands. At a million miles a minute, his mind whirled to the soundtrack of blades ringing, arrows whizzing, guttural screams, and the occasional ground-shattering boom. He wanted nothing more than to go outside and join the fight, but Mulan refused to let him move. She sat by the window curtain, watching and updating the group every time the tide seemed to change. *"It's not looking great."* *"An enormous bird just entered the field! I think that's Violet!"* *"There goes another one of our own."* *"Great shot, Chann!"*

Geppetto, Liam, and Master Cherry hung onto every word with minimal reaction. Nobody had changed position since the battle began. But now Liam paced back and forth, biting his lower lip while his eyebrows remained in scrunched, hard, broken lines.

Geppetto sat with his elbows on his knees, mindlessly whittling a block of wood into a haphazard pile of splinters at his feet.

Occasionally, Master Cherry, who sat on the other side of the room from Geppetto, would make conversation with the elder Carver.

Any other day, Enzo would have been fascinated to listen in on the chatter between the old men. According to Geppetto, they were once the best of friends. He even compared their friendship to the bond Enzo shared with Zack. But the brotherhood between Cherry and Geppetto also courted rivalry that eventually led to a sort of falling out. There had been so much time, history, and unspoken emotion between the two, and Enzo wondered how in the world two friends would manage to pick up on the other side of that gap of time. But he was so distracted by his own worry and anxiety that he heard little more between the two than cryptic bits and pieces.

"Where were *you* all this time?" Geppetto asked.

"Around."

And the conversation would end as quickly as it began. Later on, Cherry would pick up again with, "Made any other, uh, interesting things since we last met?"

Geppetto gestured to the splinters on the ground. "Even a pile of splinters can be interesting."

Enzo kneaded at his temples. What was going on? When would Mulan finally let them leave? Who was still alive? What would they find inside the tower?

Clearly, Liam had many of the same thoughts. At one point, he stopped pacing, folded his hands behind his back, and cleared his throat. "Master, with all due respect, this is *hell*. When are we pressing onward?"

"Any minute now. Sit down and save your energy."

"What are we *waiting* for?" Enzo groaned. "What difference does it make if we leave now or if we leave in five minutes? You think Avoria's army will really be that much smaller in five minutes?"

"One less enemy is one more opportunity to get inside the Citadel," Mulan said simply. "I promise we'll leave soon. I'm waiting for a particular signal."

"And what might that be?"

Mulan responded by saying nothing.

Enzo stood and kicked over his chair. "You know, you could at least fill me in on your plans! I am in a *nightmare* sitting here waiting and wondering what's happening to my parents out there, or Rosana, or my friends. At least have the decency to answer my question! *What are we waiting* for?"

Suddenly, the low-pitched moan of a jet plane roared somewhere overhead, and Mulan scrambled into action, grabbing her materials. "*That's* what I was waiting for. I called in my pilot to help us out, and Avoria's army is nice and distracted by the new threat. We have about five minutes to take advantage of their vulnerability."

Braaack!

Boom!

Enzo's blood went cold. "Something really big just exploded." He ran to the window and peeled back the curtain. Flames engulfed a nearby building, and Enzo couldn't believe what he saw flying away from the fire. The Jub-Jub bird carried three different people on its back and veered down to the ground. Just above, Mulan's jet circled the Citadel, a bright light beaming down from the bottom. "Your jet's not out there dropping bombs or anything, is it? Because our people are out there too!"

"Relax," Mulan pleaded. "Ricky isn't dropping bombs. He upgraded the jet to fire missiles, each with a miniscule and calculated blast radius. We will not be hurting our own people."

Even with Mulan's reassurance, Enzo's head still spun. "Can we go now?"

"Grab your stuff."

"Finally," Enzo breathed. He threw his belongings together and ran through a mental checklist. He had his knife. He had all his armor on. He had a bow. And he had enough anger and fear to fill his body with a river of adrenaline. He'd been angry for a long time, ever since his father first vanished from their home. Along the way, Enzo knew he'd acquired what he needed. Confidence. Independence. Belief. And the knowledge beyond a shadow of a doubt that he had a wealth of friends and family worth fighting for.

Liam took a few practice swings with his sword and started for the door. "I'm leaving."

"Master Cherry, are you ready?" Mulan asked.

"I am as ready as I will ever be. How I have longed to correct our course."

Geppetto placed his palm on the old man's back. "And so we shall, my old friend."

The two men faced each other. "So we shall."

With that, Liam threw the door open, and icy winds blasted Enzo, washing away every lingering sense of warmth and safety. When the group charged outside, the cold sliced at his fingers and flooded his nostrils. But Enzo got used to it quickly, because he soon had a much more pressing worry. Seven hooded soldiers charged into view, and two more leapt onto the ground from somewhere above Enzo's head.

One of them immediately lowered her hood, revealing a dark-haired woman with bushy eyebrows. "The Carver boy is here!" she sneered. "We're going to gut your friends, Carver boy!"

Enzo sighed. "So much for a distraction."

Liam, Geppetto, and Mulan snapped together in a circle around Enzo and Cherry.

"Let *us* handle them," Liam said.

"Stop coddling me." Enzo ducked under Liam's arms, pushed forward, and then tackled the dark-haired woman with all his might. "You won't touch my friends! Not today, or ever!"

The woman hit the ground, crying out in pain, and then seized Enzo's throat. Her fingernails were like daggers in his neck, and the air in Enzo's lungs begged for release. "You never tackle a woman, you insolent little brat! Try that on Avoria, and I promise you'll be dead before you hit the ground! I oughta finish the job for her!"

"Let him go!"

Whoosh!

An arrow buried itself in the back of the woman's hand, and she let go with a high-pitched shriek. Enzo took his opportunity to spring to his feet, but the woman hooked her legs around his ankle and pulled him back down. He kicked at her chest and clawed at the snow to crawl away from her, only to find himself at the feet of a balding man with large, muscular calves.

The man looked down on Enzo and grinned. "Silly boy. You don't need to kiss *my* boots, but I appreciate you getting on your knees." He raised his foot above Enzo's skull. Luckily, adrenaline kicked in and Enzo managed to seize the man's foot. With an upward thrust, Enzo threw the soldier's momentum behind him, knocking him completely off balance. "Whoa!"

"Up, chum!" Liam skidded past Enzo and heaved him up to his feet. "Go!"

Enzo was surprised to find all but one of the ten hoods incapacitated on the ground. The tenth was running away from the group, from the Citadel, and from the entire hellish scene. For a minute, Enzo considered firing an arrow at the runaway but decided against it. *I might regret this later,* Enzo thought. But he wanted to give the soldier the benefit of the doubt. *Maybe they're genuinely afraid and ready to start a new life. Maybe they don't want to be a part of Avoria's army anymore.*

A second later, an arrow sailed through the air, and the runaway fell face down. Mulan hooked her bow around her back and aimed a finger at Enzo. "I repeat: If they're in one of those black hoods, they intend to do you harm. Do not leave them that chance."

Enzo swallowed his guilt and ran after Mulan and the group. Up ahead, the swarm of black blossomed into view. While it had shrunk considerably since the start of the battle, it still wasn't nearly small enough for Enzo and his friends to have any hope of getting into the Citadel.

Unfortunately, from what Enzo could see, his own army dwindled as quickly as Avoria's. As he ran, he had his eyes fixed on the dwarves, each swinging their pickaxes and swords this way and that, when the Jub-Jub bird plummeted from the sky. The fall raised a cloud of snowy mist around the bird's body, and when the cloud faded away, it was clear something killed the Jub-Jub. Its feathers were soaked in red, its wing hung crooked, and it lay stone still. Its eyes turned dark, the remaining life eclipsed by shadow. A pang of sadness burrowed in Enzo's heart, and then he thought of the riders. Two people got off the bird's back and ran toward the building.

A few seconds later, Enzo ran past the lifeless body of one of the Lost Boys. *No,* he thought. *We got them involved in this. They didn't have to be a part of it. They could have been so happy. We could've fixed it! Neverland could've still been here.*

"Don't look at them." Geppetto gave Enzo's elbow a gentle tug. "First we finish. Then we grieve. *Capisci?*"

Enzo wiped a tear from his eye and followed his grandfather. "I understand."

But as they continued to run for the Citadel, Enzo simply couldn't help it. Every time he passed a fallen warrior on the ground, his gaze wandered, numbness trickling through his bones. He didn't recognize many of the people, but guilt trampled on his heart. *Why didn't I know you better? Why couldn't I have helped you fight?*

Along the way, a gauntlet of soldiers leapt in Enzo's way and attacked, sometimes individually, and sometimes in groups of two to five.

When the shadows came, Liam drew his blade and threw arcs of powerful light in the creatures' way, tearing them into black mist one by one.

Most of Avoria's army still had their attention turned to the sky. Many were attempting to pelt Mulan's jet with snowballs, rocks, and arrows. None of their projectiles even came close to reaching the plane, which was one of the few comforts Enzo took from his surroundings. No matter what the army did, they could do little to dismantle a jet.

However, a high number of hoods still had no interest in the jet, and many of them chose to surround the front door of the Citadel while their comrades fought on.

"What are we going to do about *them*?" Enzo asked. "Five of us versus about fifty of them."

Mulan ducked behind a frozen taxi. "I confess I had higher hopes that more of them would have been distracted by the plane," she said. "There are still far too many of them guarding the door. I'm not sure I want to risk facing them head-on."

"It looks like suicide," Liam added.

"Your friends have been facing that for hours by now," Cherry said matter-of-factly. "We owe them the same effort."

"*Aspetta.*" Geppetto held up a palm and turned to Enzo. "Grandson. Tell me once more how you called the serpent from the water."

Enzo wrinkled his brows. "But what does that have to do with—"

"Please," Geppetto interrupted. "It's important."

"I'm with Enzo," Mulan said. "This is hardly the time for stories."

Geppetto lowered his chin and stared at Mulan over his glasses. It was the kind of look that would've scared Enzo into cleaning his room if he'd been on the receiving end as a kid.

"Well," Enzo said, "I lowered my knife into the water, and I focused on what the ocean told me. It was really the same as carving any block of wood, only a lot more exhausting. It knocked me out for a while when I finished."

Geppetto pressed his lips together and turned away, staring up at the world with his hands on his hips. After a minute, he turned back and said, "Then so be it."

"Sir!" Liam cried. "What are you saying?"

"I'm saying I mean to use all this damn snow to our advantage. Avoria wanted it to be an obstacle. I'm going to throw it right back at her army." He tilted his head toward the Citadel. "All at once."

"No!" Enzo skidded across a patch of black ice and grabbed Geppetto's shoulders. "Think about what you're saying. I *really* don't want you to do this. I told you it knocked me out when I used the water. I was unconscious for days. If you do this, well . . ." Enzo rubbed his forehead. "I worry about your strength. You're healthy for your age, Grandpa, but—"

"But nothing! *Niente!*" Geppetto squirmed out of Enzo's grip. "You all know it's our best chance. I'll do this one time. We'll call something out of the ice. We'll let it mow over the hoods guarding that door. And then you all can go inside and finish this." He rubbed his chin, and a faraway look gleamed in his eyes. The group fell silent as he stared out at the Citadel.

"You *know* it's our best chance," Geppetto repeated.

"Let me," Enzo repeated. "No offense, but I'm stronger. I already know what the effects feel like. Then *you* all can go inside and—"

"While you lie unconscious on the Ivory Queen's doorstep?" Geppetto barked. "I don't think so. I'm in this to protect *you*, Enzo."

Mulan hung her head. Enzo could see her chewing on her cheek. She knew Geppetto had a point, and Enzo knew it too. But that didn't mean he had to like it.

Master Cherry stalked over to Geppetto and faced him with arms crossed. "Old friend," Cherry said. "Might I talk you out of this? We were reunited only recently. I had rather hoped we'd have more time to talk about what we've missed over the years and what is yet to come. I hope to see you again sooner rather than later."

Geppetto clasped his friend's hand and gave it a brotherly shake. "Don't lose hope, Antonio. Perhaps I shall wake in an hour and arrive in time to stop you from doing something *asinino*. Like the old days."

Enzo swallowed the knot in his throat, and when Master Cherry stepped aside, Enzo jammed a finger in Geppetto's chest. "If I lose you—"

"Enzo," Geppetto said, his voice soft but his tone firm. "I love you, okay? But I've made up my mind about this." With no further warning, Geppetto pulled Enzo into a tight hug that could've crushed bones. "Finding you is one of the best things that ever happened to me. *Sinceramente*. You filled my heart with youth I never knew I could possess again. You brought my son and me back together. The fight is much grander than I knew, but *you* taught me I had much more to fight for than I ever understood. The only thing left for me to say is *grazie mille*. Thank you. That, and please stand back."

Enzo took a minute before he obeyed Geppetto's request. Enzo wasn't ready to let go quite yet, knowing that it could likely be the last time. When Mulan wrapped her fingers over his shoulder, the tears cut a line down his cheek. He forced himself to step back and into the empty space between Mulan and Liam. They caught Enzo between their shoulders, and each wrapped an arm around him.

Geppetto took out his knife and tossed it up in the air three times. The blade spun like a pinwheel with every toss, and Geppetto caught it cleanly by the handle each time, grinning at his own trick. After he caught it the third time, he gave the group one final nod. "When it's done," he said to Enzo, "this blade is yours."

Master Cherry turned around and lowered his chin into his fist, while Enzo nodded back at his grandfather.

Geppetto pawed at the snow with his heel, took a knee, and then drew a smiley face inside his own footprint. Finally, he squeezed his knife and closed his eyes.

With that, The Carver plunged the dagger into the snow, and five seconds later, the ground lurched beneath Enzo's feet. He followed Mulan behind the frozen taxi and gripped onto the sideview mirror to help steady his balance.

Grawr!

A mountainous shape exploded from the ground, and the head of a polar bear appeared beneath Geppetto's knife handle. The snowbeast must have been fifty feet tall, rising like a tidal wave. Geppetto stood on top of it with his feet spread apart, looking a bit like a surfer trying to find his balance.

No way, Enzo said, staring at the polar bear as it lunged its front paws in the air and let out a thunderous roar that sprayed mouthfuls of snow into the air.

Geppetto pried his knife out of the snow and pointed the blade at the Citadel. "Hello, beastie. *Attacca!*"

With that, Geppetto's polar bear raced through New York City with all the speed and force of a tsunami, mowing over the guards at the gates of the Citadel and leaving the rest of the scene—and the old man—obscured in a thick veil of icy white mist.

CHAPTER THIRTY

THE NEW WORLD: NEW YORK STREETS

Enzo made a run for the Citadel as soon as the polar bear disappeared. He wasn't sure if it exploded when it hit the building, melted back into the ground, or simply disintegrated and lost momentum as it moved. All he knew was that a thick white cloud obscured the building, and he needed to know what happened to his grandfather.

"Enzo, wait!" Mulan cried. "We don't know how many of them are left! It's not safe yet!"

"I don't care!" Enzo's legs moved on autopilot. He sprinted as fast as the snow would let him, feeling as though he were running into an uncertain future. He couldn't even see Mulan's jet in the air anymore.

Please, please, let my friends be okay. Let Geppetto be okay. Enzo listened for the sounds of a struggle, or any indication of life within the cloud. Only the crunch of snow met his ears, along with his own breaths bursting from his lungs.

Liam caught up to Enzo and kept pace beside him. "Stars, Enzo," Liam said. "Your grandfather is a courageous man."

"Yeah," Enzo breathed.

Enzo ran into the haze and waited for his eyes to adjust. He did a full turn and realized he didn't even know where the Citadel stood anymore. The snow enveloped him.

"*Geppetto!*" he called. "Grandpa!"

His voice echoed back at him, making him feel utterly alone. If Liam, Mulan, and Cherry weren't standing right behind, Enzo would've sworn he was the only person left in the world. He cupped his mouth and yelled again. "*Geppetto!*"

"Kid!"

Enzo's heart simultaneously soared and split when Pietro called out in the distance.

"Kid, where are you?"

Enzo followed the sound of Pietro's voice, occasionally stumbling over mounds of snow or solid objects. Corpses? He didn't dare look down. "Pietro!"

"Enzo! I'm over here!"

Enzo ran about ten steps to the left and collided with a solid body. Only then did the fog lift and unveil the aftermath of Geppetto's actions.

Pietro caught Enzo in a brisk hug, a bit of blood smeared above one eye. Rosana pushed Pietro aside and threw her arms around Enzo, tears drying in a frosty path along her cheek. Behind her, Hansel and Tahlia waded through a crowd of unconscious hoods, raiding their robes and picking weapons and supplies out of their inner pockets.

The Citadel doors stood only a few yards away from Enzo's feet, towering five stories in a gleaming mound of marble. They were completely unguarded, surrounded only by snow and fallen soldiers.

Amongst the sea of black, Enzo's grandfather lay peacefully on his side, his eyes closed and his knees curled up to his chest.

Enzo took one look and ran to Geppetto's side. "Grandpa! *Grandpa!*"

"Kid, don't do this yourself," Pietro pleaded.

Enzo ignored his friend and knelt next to Geppetto, shaking the old man's shoulder. "Geppetto. Grandpa. Wake up. You cleared the way for us. The soldiers are gone. Wake up now, please."

Rosana turned away and buried her face in Pietro's chest. "Please, no . . ."

"Grandpa!" Enzo shook harder, but the old man remained locked in sleep, a peaceful smile carved permanently into his face. Enzo already knew his efforts were fruitless. "Grandpa! Dammit, wake up!"

"Enzo, stop," Pietro whispered. "You can't bring him back from this."

"No!" Enzo argued. "He passed out! It happened to me, too, remember? He'll wake up!"

"I know you loved the man, but we can't do this right now. We probably have two minutes at most before trouble comes back."

Mulan descended on Enzo and wrapped her arms around his shoulders from behind. "He's right, you know. Your grandfather just carved us the gift of time. We'd be wrong to waste it. We'll honor him by finishing the job," she whispered. "I'm sorry, Enzo. So very sorry."

Enzo buried his head in his knees and counted to five in his head. *This will all be over soon,* he thought, looking back up. Tinker Bell floated above in slow circles, her dust hovering in the air like angel tears as Violet, Hansel, the Volos, and Enzo's parents rushed to Geppetto's side. *It'll be over and we can bury my grandfather and I'll go back home with my parents.* He wiped a tear from his eye and stood slowly, grasping Mulan's hand while he rose. "We can't leave his body here."

"I'm staying here with him," Enzo's father said under his breath. He plucked the knife out of Geppetto's grip and passed it to Enzo. The handle—the legacy—sank in Enzo's hand, anchored to his pain. "Take care of it while you're in there, my son. Your mother and I will be right here when you come back out. You will come back, right? I can't lose you too. More than anything, I wish I could take your place right now."

"No." Enzo pulled his father into a tight hug, but his embrace was stiff and mechanical. He was wincing. *He's going stiff again,* Enzo thought. His father was never meant for this world. "Dad, I'm going to be fine, okay?" Enzo hugged his mom, too, memorizing her natural warmth—her cherry cobbler scent.

Wendy took Enzo's hands in her own. "Zack and I will be securing the doors for you. There are more hoods out here, behind the building, in the towers, and all over New York. We promise they won't follow you in. But you'll keep an eye on my husband?"

Pietro swooped in and kissed his wife. "Don't you worry. Enzo and I look out for each other."

Enzo finally managed a smile. "I promise, Wendy."

"Waste no more time at Avoria's doorstep, dears." Violet swooped in and embraced Enzo. She made her rounds to Rosana, Pietro, Liam, Mulan, and finally, Master Cherry. "We'll be out here fighting for you. Until we see you again in this life or the next, the light will be with you *all*." She took a knee and smoothed Geppetto's hair. "As will he."

CHAPTER
THIRTY-ONE

THE NEW WORLD:
THE CITADEL

Enzo entered the Citadel through a tiny opening within the big door, his knife drawn at his side while the hinges creaked open.

He expected resistance right away. More hoods. Shadows. Fire. Avoria herself. But in the end, a simple hallway greeted him and led to a second door, this one round and made of wood with a shining silver doorknob.

The outermost door closed with a thud, sealing the outside world away from Enzo along with Mulan, Rosana, Liam, Hansel, Tahlia, Pietro, Master Cherry, and finally Wayde, who snuck into the group as Violet bade them good luck.

"I was with you in your first journey to the Old World, Mister Enzo," Wayde insisted. "I wish to accompany you for this one. If I may."

Enzo's heart soared at the dwarf's offer. He had most of his original group together, save for the cowardly Mr. Bellamy and his brave daughter, who chose to lend her efforts outside. When the inner door closed, Enzo put his hands on his hips and studied his group. All of his original people had come such a long way since he met them. "This is it," he whispered. "We're inside. I'm going to open this next door now."

"Let me," Hansel commanded, pushing his way to the front. "I'm the most expendable."

"But—"

Before Enzo could fully protest, Hansel pulled the door open, and Enzo faced the inside of the Citadel.

Marble. More marble than he'd ever seen.

The ceiling stretched to the heavens. Convex translucent pillars held it together, each one jutting out at strange angles and giving off an odd frosty light as if it were an ice sculpture. The same material supported the walls as well, including the fireplace in which a dark-blue flame consumed logs of oakwood.

But Enzo's gaze snapped to the sheer amount of people. There must have been thousands, leaving little breathing room after Wayde shut the door. Strangest of all, none of these people were hooded or cloaked. They looked like everyday people Enzo would have seen on the street, and that reminded Enzo of something Avoria said when she spoke to him in Wonderland.

"She wanted this to be a public event," he whispered to Rosana. "She wanted everyone to be here when she declared herself Queen. These people must have been here the whole time we've been in New York. Probably on some other floor drinking her nasty shadow Kool-Aid."

"And all this time we thought New York was evacuated," Rosana said. "This is awful."

"But this can't be *all* of New York," Enzo said. "There's a lot of people here, but this can't be everybody."

"Maybe they're on another floor, or . . . let's not think about the *or*."

Enzo's gaze swiveled upward to a large balcony, on which one-hooded figure stood with a goblet in his hand. The crowd shifted its attention to him after an excited chatter, and when Enzo looked up, the hooded man raised his goblet and addressed the crowd. *That's the man from the movie theater!* Enzo realized. *The one who threatened me. Avoria called him the general.*

"Welcome, loved ones, to tonight's festivities. And how spectacular they will be. You have come to witness the ascension of a queen! But you will see something much more memorable before the night is through. For you see, Avoria has *challengers* in the building with us tonight."

The general paused and soaked in the excited murmurs and shocked gasps throughout the room. Enzo closed his eyes and let a defeated breath escape his lungs. *Trouble already.*

The general lowered his hood, revealing an elderly man with angled eyes and a pointed chin. "One of them is my own daughter."

Out of the corner of his mouth, Liam muttered, "Do not react," and Enzo noticed Mulan had balled her hands into fists, her jaw muscles stiff with tension.

"It is confounding that any one man or woman can assume to win a duel against our fearless leader, Avoria, but if you look to the doors, a boy has come with a *fellowship* behind him. I ask you, do they stand a chance against the illustrious queen?"

"*No, no, no!*" the crowd jeered.

Enzo's eyes widened. *She's already controlling them*, he thought. *They're puppets on her strings.* They were rooting for a madwoman. If she collected the eighth soul tonight, she would have the whole *world* doing her bidding.

"Never," the general answered. "That is correct. However, Queen Avoria wishes to ensure that you're sufficiently entertained. Thus, I propose a vote! Let your voices be heard! All in favor of letting the fellowship proceed to the top floor and their ultimate demise?"

The knots weaved together in Enzo's shoulders.

"*Yes, yes, yes!*" the crowd answered and then immediately snapped back to silent attention.

"I believe that's a majority." The general fixed his gaze on Enzo. "We will let you through, boy, but make no mistake: there are no playgrounds on these floors. There are no restarts. There is only the rest of your life and what follows beyond."

"I'm not afraid," Enzo blurted, his voice echoing through the hall and causing all the attendees to turn their heads. He hated the looks on their faces, staring like hungry hyenas. Mentally, he shut out the crowd's gazes and focused on the general. "I'm not. The scariest thing I can think of is losing the ones I love to a tyrant. You stand up there and you ask people to vote like Avoria's world is gonna be a democracy. They won't even be able to think for themselves. I've seen what it looks like when she gets in somebody's head like that. There are people with me tonight who have *lived* through it. So tell Avoria to do her worst. I'm still coming for her."

A gravelly lurch rumbled through the walls, and the fireplace slid up along the wall on the other side of the room, revealing a silver door with an ovaloid symbol etched into its center. When he squinted a bit, Enzo realized the symbol resembled the mirror he destroyed in Florindale once upon a time. It even shimmered the same way.

"Then proceed, Carver," the general commanded. A set of humongous panels popped out of the walls on opposite sides of the room, each reminding Enzo of an IMAX screen. "We'll be down here watching your progress and toasting your wounds. *A drink for all!*" The general snapped his gloved fingers in the air, and goblets appeared all over the room. He raised his high above his head. "Let us make the first one now. Long live Her Illustrious Majesty, Avoria, The Ivory Queen!"

"Long live the queen!" the crowd echoed. The stranger and the spectators tipped the contents of their goblets into their mouths, and the general tossed his onto the ground below with an obnoxious *clang!*

Enzo hooked his arm around Rosana's elbow and pressed a palm against Pietro's back. "Come on," Enzo muttered. "We don't need to listen to him anymore."

"You sure you're up for this, Kid?" Pietro asked. "You can turn around. Whatever you say, you know I'm with you."

"I know you are." Enzo sounded much calmer than he felt. With every step he took through the jeering crowd, his heartbeat escalated and his mouth dried up like a desert. He almost wanted to grab somebody's goblet and dump its contents into his throat.

As if he'd read Enzo's mind, Wayde handed him a leather flask brimming with water. "Drink, Mister Enzo," he whispered. "It's one of Garon's inventions coated with elements from our old mine. It never runs out of water. There's plenty for all of us."

"Thank you," Enzo whispered. He unscrewed the cap and splashed the icy cold water over his tongue while he walked. With every sip, he felt the flask grow lighter, but when he took it away from his mouth, its original weight returned. He passed it back to Wayde. "If we get out of this, tell Garon to make me one of these for my birthday."

"When we get out of this, this one's yours."

Rosana slid her forearm down to Enzo's wrist and locked her fingers around his, slowing his heart as if she'd touched a special nerve. With his friends behind him, Enzo approached the silver door.

"Is there a knob?" Liam asked.

Enzo shook his head. "Nothing."

"Make a wish," Pietro suggested.

"Avoria wouldn't build things that way. Not with our wishes." Enzo stroked his chin and then pushed on the door, shoving and leaning on the balls of his feet.

"Try your fears," Cherry commanded. "Focus on your nightmares. Name the evil that haunts your dreams. That's what Avoria feeds on: your terror, not your heart's desires."

Enzo swallowed hard. "I hate that you're probably right," he said. "Let's try it."

He shut his eyes and let his fears project on the inside of his eyelids. Visions of black widows scuttled through his brain, leaving a tickle on his shoulder.

"Dig deep," Cherry advised. "Explore the darkest chambers of your heart. Make it count for something. Only then can we confront our greatest threat!"

Enzo squeezed his eyelids tighter. Dark walls pressed against his mind, confining him into an imaginary iron box. Cold shadows swooped in and circled him, taunting and jeering and poking at his thoughts.

A tight squeeze rippled through Enzo's palm and nearly electrified his arm. His eyes snapped open, and he found Rosana scrunching her face into a portrait of fear, a sharp breath falling out of her mouth.

"Rosana," Enzo whispered. "I'm still here. I'm still with you."

She steadied her breath while Enzo sifted through his thoughts. The dark spaces and shadows weren't what he expected to think of first, but the image nagged at him and he found himself asking why. *Why didn't I think of Avoria first?*

But he knew the answer.

Enzo approached the door and stared into the mirror symbol. The door wavered like he'd disturbed a body of water, and his own reflection appeared in the center of the mirror etching. His own face surprised him. He'd matured a bit since the last time he looked at his reflection. Thin stubble painted his jaw, which had hardened and taken on a more defined, chiseled shape. More surprisingly, nobody stood behind him. Only an empty ballroom.

Panic gripped Enzo's heart and he turned around, relieved to find his friends still there.

"What is it, Kid?" Pietro asked.

Enzo rubbed his face and massaged his eyelids. "Did you see that, too? Did you see what I saw?"

"You mean the wolf?" Tahlia asked, her face ghost white.

"I saw something different," Pietro said. "But it's okay. It's a mirror. It's here to screw with our minds. As long as we have our guard up, we're gonna be fine. We go in there ready for anything, and we take away Avoria's power to surprise us."

"Your optimism is commendable," Master Cherry said.

Enzo looked back at the door. He was still alone in the mirror's image. But a few seconds after, the door disappeared entirely, and a white marble hallway appeared lit by blue-flamed torches. On the other side, a pair of elevator doors awaited him.

"Let's go." Enzo stepped through the threshold.

"*May the darkness be with you, Carver,*" the man on the balcony boomed, provoking the ballroom guests into a fit of laughs and jeers before the fireplace thundered back onto the ground and sealed Enzo's group inside the marble hallway.

"Who was that?" Enzo asked.

"That is my father," Mulan said, her voice rough and cold. "Any other questions?"

Enzo wasn't sure how to respond. His heart broke for Mulan. He tried to imagine seeing his own father in league with Avoria. The thought refused to register. "I'm so sorry, Mulan."

"Forget it," she answered, each syllable a staccato. "Let's get in the elevator and go." She hadn't even finished her sentence when she pushed through the group and charged down the hall, each footstep echoing like thunder on the marble floor.

"Wait," Enzo said, "let me lead on, please. We don't know what's ahead."

"The Ivory Queen is ahead," Mulan answered without looking back. She jammed a white button that turned gold in the wall as soon as she took her finger off, and the silvery-blue doors slid apart to reveal an elevator decorated with mirrors of various shapes and sizes.

"*Welcome to the Citadel!*" a warm female voice greeted. "*Please enter.*"

Mulan stepped inside first, followed by Enzo. The rest of the group piled in after.

"Is it me, or does the elevator sound really happy to see us?" Pietro asked.

"*I'm pleased to see you, Pietro Volo.*" The doors smacked together, and the elevator gave a violent lurch. Enzo tightened his hold on Rosana's hand and pulled her closer. "*Which floor would you like?*"

The trouble with the question: there wasn't a single button in the elevator.

Just how high is this building? Enzo thought.

"Take us to the top," Rosana commanded, speaking to the ceiling. "Please."

"My pleasure, Rosana."

Enzo flinched. In a building with a queen who wanted to rule the world, it unsettled him to get into an elevator and have it speak to him with such warm, polite tones. The image didn't fit together. He would have preferred it if the elevator berated him and spoke in daggers.

The platform lurched again and began a slow, rocky ascent, every inch rumbling like gravel on wood.

But after a small eternity, the elevator bumped, and the voice announced, *"Arrived. Thank you for riding with me! Please come back in the next life."*

The doors sprung open, and frigid air screamed into the elevator. Enzo immediately shut his eyes and wrapped his arm around Rosana's hip. The group tightened together for warmth. Once Enzo's body adjusted to the icy breeze, he opened his eyes and stared ahead.

A collective panic rolled through the group, but Enzo was proud of how well everybody managed to control the new fear that gripped them. A few of them gasped, most of them stayed quiet, but everybody's bodies stiffened.

The doors had opened to a concrete platform nearly a hundred stories over New York City. Enzo stepped outside and studied his surroundings. Little button cars stayed still on the ground, and about a football field away, straight ahead, another elevator stood at the top of a building painted in a *Stargle Magazine* billboard of Avoria's bejeweled face.

Between the two buildings, a tightrope hung in the air, razor thin so that Enzo didn't even perceive it until he noticed the black line that cleaved Avoria's face in half. He bent down and plucked the wire like a guitar string. It made a nice tight *twang*, but it wasn't enough to reel in his nerves. He looked at his friends, and they all seemed to understand what needed to happen.

"Well," Pietro said, "it's been fun, Kid. Time to turn around and go back." He spun on his heel and took a single step before the elevator doors clapped shut in his face and disappeared in a shimmering vapor. "Uh-oh."

Tahlia peered over the edge of the platform and swallowed. "What is this?"

Master Cherry assessed the group, his hood swiveling from person to person until it fixed on Pietro. "This is a manifestation of one of your fears. We cannot proceed until it has been conquered."

Pietro rubbed his hands together and blew into them, a thin fog rising into the air. "This is what haunts me, friends. Peter Pan's not so fearless after all when he can't fly." He peeked at the ground and took a step back, kneading a palm on his forehead. "Welcome to my nightmare."

CHAPTER THIRTY-TWO

THE CITADEL

"We are *not* crossing New York City on a tightrope," Tahlia asserted, voicing everything Pietro had repeated in his mind for the past minute and a half.

"What choice do we have?" he snapped back. "None. You see another way over there? Our elevator's gone. We stay up here and freeze, or we take the death rope across the sky. *Man*, I wish I could fly right now!"

"Pietro," Enzo said, using the same tone Wendy would've used with Zack after an outburst. "Calm down. We're gonna find a way over there. Someone look for a stairwell. We'll take the long way. Down, over, and up."

"I cannot recommend that," Master Cherry cut in. "This is meant to be a challenge of nerves. Avoria would not allow any other way across except to take the high road. I suggest we get started."

Pietro crossed his arms behind his head and walked in tight circles. "This isn't happening. This is *not* happening."

"This is happening," Rosana said softly. She took Pietro by the shoulders, digging the pads of her thumbs into his collarbone. "You're gonna be okay, Pietro. Promise."

Pietro patted Rosana's hand. "You are made of steel." He glared at Avoria's enormous painted face and made a gesture he was glad Wendy didn't see. "I hate you, lady."

"She knows." Rosana closed Pietro's hand and lowered it to his side. "Look back at me now. Listen." She clapped Pietro's face between her palms. "Focus, okay? Follow our lead. We're not gonna let you fall. Now, who here has a rope?"

"Got it." Hansel reached into his pack, produced a thick snake of sandy brown rope, and then tossed the coil to Rosana. She looped it around her arm and turned to Enzo.

"Enzo, can I borrow your—" She stopped short and let out a terrible scream.

Pietro cut his gaze over to where she had been looking, and his stomach dropped when he found Mulan padding across the tightrope, already about fifteen feet away from where she started. She moved with cat-like grace, one foot in front of the other, arms spread and flat as a board, and her head remained aligned with the rope, never shifting. Pietro could've placed an apple on her head, and her steps wouldn't have disturbed a single hair.

"*Shh*," Liam hissed. "Stars, you don't want to startle her!"

Rosana clutched her chest, and Pietro covered his mouth with a fist. *Don't hurl, Pietro. Keep it together.*

"I know," Rosana breathed. "I just wasn't ready to see anybody start yet."

"Kinda losing faith here," Pietro groaned.

"No, no, I believe in you!" Rosana sighed and her shoulders sank.

"She'll be quite all right. I've seen her do the impossible." Pride illuminated Liam's eyes. "That's my master."

"She's meditating, isn't she?" Enzo asked. "I saw her doing that earlier."

Liam nodded. "When she gets like that, you couldn't pull her out with a hook. Let her be."

"Okay." Rosana cleared her throat and asked Enzo in the most forcibly calm voice, "Enzo, may I please borrow your knife?"

Enzo unsheathed his dagger and handed it over. Rosana proceeded to unwind the rope into strands the length of her armspan. She cleaved the material and tossed it at her feet in messy coils.

"Start grabbing, people," she commanded. "Wrap them around each leg, and tie them around your waist. Leave some room for another knot on the end."

"Harnesses?" Wayde guessed.

"Yep."

Wayde nodded. "We used these to descend into mineshafts in the good ol' days. I see what you're getting at."

"Can you help tie the knots?" Rosana asked.

"Of course." Wayde picked up a rope and helped Hansel weave it around his waist, looping one end into an intricate knot. "Are you next, Mister Hansel?"

Hansel blew a long breath between his lips and cracked his knuckles. "Let me get this over with."

Wayde snaked the other end of the rope around the wire, leaving enough room for the loop to move freely about the tightrope. He yanked on it a few times, and the knot held strong. Pietro wasn't convinced the idea was foolproof, but he would feel a bit more secure in a makeshift harness than on a free walk across a razor-thin wire.

Hansel tugged on both ends of the rope. After a satisfied nod, he approached the edge of the building.

"Should you lose your balance, you'll merely take a sit," Wayde explained. "Then, you can pull yourself across. How's the strength in your arms?"

"Quite a bit stronger than my stomach." Without another word, Hansel took the first step onto the tightrope.

Tahlia offered to go next.

"Nerves of steel, Kid," Pietro said, fixing his own harness around his waist.

Mulan and Hansel both reached the other side, and they reacted so differently it was hard to believe they'd finished the same task. Hansel collapsed onto his back, arms and legs spread like a starfish. Even from the other side of the tightrope, Pietro could see Hansel's chest rising and falling like a buoy on stormy waters. Mulan, on the other hand, stood stone still with her fingers weaved together at her waist and her expression calm as ever.

One by one, the group members crossed, and Pietro tried to study their techniques. Would it be better to roll along heel to toe with arms wide open like Hua Mulan? Would Tahlia's sideways shuffle work better? Liam lost his balance first, and Pietro thought his heart might burst through his chest. The prince sank a good three feet, cried out in fear, and a collective sigh of relief rolled through the group when the rope caught him by the waist. He hung in an awkward half-sitting position, and he spun in midair a few times before he proceeded.

"Stars, this is a hellishly uncomfortable position!" he called out.

"It's not supposed to be comfortable!" Mulan called back. "It's supposed to keep you *alive!*"

He pulled himself across the wire inch by inch until Hansel and Mulan were able to hoist him onto their roof and unhook his makeshift harness.

Master Cherry crossed next, looking like a ghost the way he glided across the wire with relative ease. His cloak fanned out behind him like angel wings, and his hood convulsed in the wind. But his body stayed upright and centered, leaving Pietro behind with Enzo, Rosana, and Wayde.

Enzo swallowed hard and shook out his wrists and ankles. "I'm next," he said. "Wayde, hook me up, please."

Pietro bit the inside of his cheek. "Kid, I really wish you didn't have to—"

"Nope. It's too late." Enzo held up a palm. "Happy thoughts only from here on out. One way or another, we *have* to get to the top floor.

There's no other choice."

Pietro couldn't help but feel a swell of admiration for the kid who once stormed off in the middle of a Renaissance fair, refusing to believe where he came from. Pietro always harbored a deep familial sort of love for the boy, but there were times when it took a special level of effort not to bop him in the jaw. Somewhere on the crazy road they'd traveled, that boy grew into a paragon of young men. He was brave. He was confident. And he wouldn't stop for *anyone*. Hurricane Enzo was a force to be reckoned with.

Once Enzo finished hooking up his harness, Rosana stood on her tiptoes and kissed him. "Be careful. I'll be right behind you."

"I know you will." Enzo stepped onto the wire, looked over his shoulder, and added, "Hey. I love you, you know."

Rosana flushed pink, blinked out of sight for a split second, and then appeared right in front of Enzo's face and kissed him again. "I love you, too. Let's go."

"I made you two happen," Pietro said. "Only saying."

"Sure, yeah you did, Pietro." Enzo rolled his eyes, faced forward, and then started his walk.

His crossing took the longest, but he managed to stay upright and finish without losing his balance. As promised, Rosana followed, padding across with admirable speed and grace. She disappeared three times, likely having trouble controlling her nerves, but the harness followed and scooted along the wire so Pietro could keep an eye on her progress.

Well, the good news is none of us died. Yet. But when Pietro caught a glance at the billboard, he could have sworn Avoria smirked at him, her lips squirming over the window they'd been painted over.

Rosana reached the other side, hugged Enzo, and the group cheered Pietro on. "Come on, Pietro! It's your turn!"

Wayde bowed at Pietro. "I'll be right behind you, sir! Then we can proceed to the next floor!"

"Let's get it over with," Pietro grumbled, knowing he couldn't stall anymore. He put up his hands to let Wayde hook the rope around the wire. Once secured, Pietro tapped a hesitant toe against the wire as if testing the temperature of a pool and then quickly jerked his foot back.

Wayde gave Pietro a gentle nod. "One foot in front of the other. Same as walking."

"This is not the same!" Pietro hissed, leaving no spaces between the words. "Shush for a minute. Let me concentrate."

This is for Wendy. This is for Zack. They would do this for you. They would do anything for you, and you would do the same. That's what love is. Pietro shut his eyes and put the ball of his foot on the wire, leaning into the step until his full weight rested on one leg. He opened his eyes again.

Help.

Pietro took the next step.

With both feet on the wire, he breathed in and spread his arms. His heart pounded in his temples. *It's like flying. That's all I'm doing right now. Just don't look down.*

The wire stayed as tight as he would've hoped, hardly jittering at all beneath his toes, but it was like trying to walk on the edge of a ruler. His feet wobbled this way and that, and by the time he had taken five steps across, Pietro's ankles throbbed. It was worse than ice-skating, and he *hated* ice-skating. People weren't meant to stack their joints on razor blades like that.

An itch tickled Pietro's nostrils.

Oh, no. "Guys!" he called. "I have to sneeze!"

"Don't do it!" Enzo warned. "Don't sneeze! Purple elephant!"

Pietro plugged his nose and took another step. He opened his mouth and took in strobe-like breaths, his lungs filling up like balloons.

No, no, no, no, n—

He sneezed. It came out dry—more of a thunderous cough than anything else—but it shook Pietro's bones enough to disturb his balance. His feet shifted and he threw his arms back to his side, doing a wild surfer sort of pose in the hopes of collecting his equilibrium again. Luckily, he found it. His feet didn't leave the wire, but he was sure his heart would leave his chest.

"I saw my whole life in front of me," he said.

"Keep going!" Rosana cried.

Pietro watched his feet and kept moving, finding it a little bit easier to balance with each step despite the dull burn trickling through his muscles.

Wayde called out from behind, "I'm coming on, Mister Pietro! Keep going!"

When Wayde took the first step, a dull hum vibrated through the rope and buzzed through the soles of Pietro's shoes.

With the next step Pietro took, a thin shadow blanketed the land.

Pietro looked up. A storm cloud stared him down, daring him to take another step.

The wisps and vapors converged and swirled with the speed of a rushing wave on the beach, and panic gripped Pietro's lungs.

"Pietro, Wayde," Enzo called out, "I don't mean to rush you guys, but there is a thundercloud above you. You might want to hurry."

Thick gusts of wind riffled through Pietro's hair and tickled his goatee. A tiny speck of dust pierced his eye and he brought his palms in, grinding at his eyelids to quell the burn. That was when his feet spilled off the wire.

"*Whoa!*"

The three-foot fall was the scariest of his life. His stomach took a while to catch up with the rest of his body, and the rope bit into his thighs like flames. He clutched the bit of rope that bound him to the wire, amazed that it managed to support his weight. The material only had about an inch of girth. One inch separated Pietro from certain bloody death on the New York pavement.

"I'm okay!" he cried out. "I'm alive, kinda!"

The wire shook again, and Wayde cried out. He had lost his balance, too.

"Pull yourself across!" Hansel shouted. "You're more than halfway! Hurry!"

Pietro reached up and gripped the tightrope. He pulled himself a few inches. The burn spread from his leg muscles to his forearms.

Boom! Thunder cleaved the air, and a white light flashed.

Lightning fell from the sky and zapped the tightrope on the starting end. The bolt sawed the rope in half immediately, and Pietro fell through space. He gripped the tightrope for dear life, the smell of burnt wire drifting through the air and the shock burning his palms. He screamed.

This is nothing like flying.

Blissfully, the rope supported him, swooping him diagonally as it approached the building. He felt like Tarzan swinging on a vine, but the swinging wouldn't last long. The rope could only go one way, and once he hit the building, he would be in a world of pain.

"*Pietro!*" Enzo screamed from above. "*Pietro!*"

His friends' screams mixed with the cries of the wind, and Pietro could have sworn the Avoria billboard laughed at him. In fact, he swung straight toward her mouth as if he were her next meal. Luckily, her lips were painted on a window.

Pietro kicked out, aiming for the window and bracing himself for a crash.

It came all too soon.

His feet hit the glass, and it burst into a jagged, imperfect puzzle stained in red. Pietro squeezed his eyes shut and tucked his chin into his chest, feeling tiny bits of glass bite into his arms and legs. His heels scraped carpet, grinding him to a halt, and he finished his ride of terror with a messy somersault that ground the glass into his knees.

Pietro opened his eyes to find himself in an empty apartment bedroom, thrown into the shadows by the looming storm cloud outside. Lightning flashed again. Pietro stood and threw what was left of the rope outside the window. Not a second later did a horrifying thought come to him.

Wayde.

Pietro stuck his head out the window. "Wayde!" he screamed. "*Wayde!*"

"Pietro!"

He looked up and saw Rosana leaning over the edge of the building. "Rosana!" Pietro called. "Where's Wayde?"

"I don't know!" Rosana answered. "Can you find a way up here?"

Not sure whether to feel panicked, relieved, pained, or exhausted, Pietro gripped the windowpane and collected his breath.

Pietro mastered his fear of heights, but the trial claimed a life.

He picked some of the glass out of his forearms and rubbed his forehead, trying his best not to cry. "Yeah," he said. "You all wait there for me, okay? I'll try to find a way up."

After he took one more look around the room and another dizzying glance below, Pietro shook his head and started for the door, hoping he'd find an elevator or a stairwell somewhere. *You owe me that much, at least, Avoria. You owe us big.*

CHAPTER
THIRTY-THREE

THE CITADEL

By the time Pietro emerged on the roof, Hansel's heart had frozen over.

There was no sign of Wayde. One minute he was on the tightrope, and after the lightning hit, he wasn't anymore. The group spent a small eternity peering over the edge of the roof, hoping to find him clinging to a window ledge or a balcony. Hansel called his name multiple times, each time infusing his throat with a little more pain.

"He's gone," Mulan said, a note of hurt in her voice. "We're down one man."

"No," Rosana said, a sob choking her. "We can't be. We can't lose Wayde. He was loyal and kind and wonderful and . . ." Her lip quivered, and she buried her face in Enzo's shoulder.

Hansel cleared his throat and rubbed the tender skin below his eyes. "We'll honor him. When we sort all of this out, we'll have a memorial for the fallen. For Wayde the Fearless."

"In the meantime, might I suggest we continue?" Master Cherry gestured to the door beside them. "The climb awaits us, and if we should remain here, we will surely be caught in the storm."

The group silently agreed, wiped their eyes, and Enzo pressed the glowing white button to call the elevator.

But when the doors opened, they didn't find an elevator at all but a winding, vast set of ivory stairs that only led upward. Each step seemed to float in midair, unsupported by walls. Dark space hovered around the steps as far as the eye could see.

Hansel took the first step, relieved that it held his weight and didn't wobble or waver in space. Solid footing would always be welcome after the agonizing tightrope trial. From now on, he would take every step as though his feet were kissing the earth.

He looked up, and his head spun. The stairs spiraled above for what looked like miles, forming perfect concentric circles above him. "We have quite a climb ahead."

Hansel didn't know how long they climbed or how many steps they'd actually taken, but it didn't take long for his legs to become hot iron, protesting with every twitch of the knee. Fire coursed through his thighs. Vertigo gnawed at his vision. How many circles had he made? How high up had he climbed?

At one point, Tahlia tripped, smacking her elbows on a step and nearly rolling off into the darkness. Liam caught her and helped her to her feet, and they all walked a little slower after that.

The next door was a goldish red etched with a perfect circle in its center. Swirls bloomed from the middle like a pinwheel, and a long rod protruded from the bottom. Hansel knew he'd seen that symbol before, but the memory was fuzzy in his mind, like peering through fog.

He pushed the door open and greeted the warm, sweet scent of hot brown sugar caramelizing in a pan. Butter popped and sizzled in his ears. Cool mist drifted from an open freezer.

I've been in this kitchen before.

Fear gripped Hansel's spine, freezing his nerves and all the little tendons in his body.

"Something smells fantastic," Pietro remarked.

"*Don't,*" Hansel warned. "Don't sniff. Don't eat. Don't touch a thing."

Pietro clutched his stomach and frowned. "Why not? Not even like a gumdrop?"

"No." But Hansel's own stomach gnawed at itself when he looked around the room. Someone had stacked frosted cakes into a sugary mountain on a nearby table. Lemon bars glowed beside them, sprinkled with powdered sugar. Cookies, donuts, pastries, and little blocks of fudge taunted him from colored tins and bits of cellophane. There were even frosty cold glasses overflowing with bubbling drinks, smooth scoops of ice cream, and paper straws with red stripes. And by the rough texture and warm aroma of the walls, Hansel knew they were made entirely of graham crackers and gingerbread. Ivory-white icing held the corners together.

Tahlia narrowed her eyes at Hansel. "This is *your* nightmare, isn't it?" Without waiting for him to answer, she continued. "I always heard rumors about this house. My grandma and I didn't live too far away from it. They said the owner was crazy and that she would lure kids from the Woodlands in with candy. I've had friends who never came out."

Hansel looked down, surprised to see that he had been digging his nails into his palms. "Sometimes I wish I hadn't either." He flinched, got his bow ready, and pushed through the kitchen. "Weapons out."

"On your guards," Mulan commanded.

Wood scraped on wood and metal scraped on metal as arrows and blades came out. When the metallic ring died away, the sizzling pan shrouded all other sounds in the room. Its once pleasant sweet aroma gradually soured, and a thick sheet of smoke spread through the room. The caramel burned. Hansel pulled his shirt up to his nose and padded into the living room, a dense forest of furniture compiled with tangled strands of licorice. A sugar cube television blared a grainy image in the corner of the room, crooning a jolly tune through a muffled layer of static.

Where are you? Hansel thought. *Where's the witch? Come out, hag. I dare you.*

Behind him, a thick sponge of pumpkin bread and gumdrop windows swung outward and hit the outside wall with a hollow thud.

Hansel spun around and fired an arrow out the edible door, but he never saw where it went. The thunderstorm carried onto this floor, soaking what looked like a convincing rendering of the Woodlands. Gray water drenched the world outside, and crickets and toads chirped and groaned in the night.

Hansel heaved a sigh of relief, burying his fingers in his hair. *The storm opened the door.*

Enzo took a step outside and held out his arms, letting the rain slap against his palms. "Should we maybe go outside? See if there's another door out here?"

Hansel pushed ahead and nocked another arrow. "Let me lead. I know the Woodlands best."

Tahlia caught up and wrapped her cold fingers around Hansel's elbow. "Me, too," she said. "I'll lead with you."

Hansel stared into the girl's dark eyes. They were a storm of their own, yet a tiny spark revealed a young girl beneath the surface. Hansel hoped that light would never go out. He nodded once. "But don't get ahead of me."

The group huddled together and pushed through the storm as quickly as they could, every step either squishing a pocket of mud or snapping a wet twig. Hansel swept his bow from side to side, Tahlia covering another angle. Every movement in the trees provoked him to take aim, only to discover that the shadow had been a squirrel or a snake wriggling in the rain.

"How is it that we're indoors right now?" Enzo asked. "We're inside a building, who knows how many stories in the air, and we're being rained on."

Nobody answered.

The trees rustled again, and Hansel pointed his bow in their direction only to find another squirrel scampering up the trunk. He shook his head. Perhaps he was being too jumpy. The gingerbread house, the storm, and the Citadel had boiled his nerves. He lowered his bow.

And then the squirrel fell dead from the tree, hit the ground with a thud, and Hansel watched the animal drift sideways into the forest as if being pushed by a gust of wind.

"Who shot it?" Pietro cried.

"Nobody!" Hansel said.

"But where did it go?"

"Wind."

"Wind doesn't *do* that," Master Cherry mused. "Something killed that animal and dragged it away."

"You're imagining things. Keep mov—"

The tree trunk snapped in half with a sick, thunderous crack, and the top half came careening down toward the group.

"Scatter!" Liam shouted.

Hansel grabbed Tahlia's sleeve and threw her out of the tree's path, making a diving leap for the ground. His elbows sunk in a grimy puddle of mud, leaves, and rocks, and part of the falling tree hammered into his anklebone. He winced and shook the water off his bow. After he centered his vision, the next tree snapped a little closer to the root, and a ten-foot oak tumbled down and narrowly missed his ear.

"What's happening?" Rosana cried.

Tahlia scrambled to her feet, her expression a portrait of wide-eyed fear and desperation. She knelt and squeezed Hansel's hand, dragging him into a standing position. "We need to run. I know what this is! It's . . ."

"Chameleon wolf," Mulan finished. "We're in *your* nightmare, aren't we?"

"What the *hell* is a chameleon wolf?" Hansel spat.

"I helped her grandmother kill one long ago," Mulan said. "Claws. Appetite." Another tree fell, and a terrible guttural growl rumbled through the air. "Camouflage."

That's hardly fair at all.

Tahlia swiveled her bow wildly, pointing it at haphazard angles and shooting arrows in random intervals. Her breaths were uneven and frantic. "Where *is* it? *Where are you, demon?*"

"Don't provoke it!" Cherry ordered. "Remember the rules. We *must* confront the wolf. But you must be calm. You must be still, quiet, and tranquil. Compose yourself."

Hansel let his eyes drift shut and focused on his breath. *In. Out. In. Out. In.*

Whumph!

Something smacked his chest with an upward force that sent him careening through the air and over the mangled tree trunks. When he opened his eyes, the most terrible monster materialized on the ground below, a behemoth of gray-brown fur, bright yellow eyes, bloodstained teeth, and impossible musculature. It must have been over seven feet tall and stood on hind legs, its slender tail sweeping back and forth like a pendulum.

The chameleon wolf drew a breath, lunged toward Tahlia with a piercing roar, and then Liam charged toward it from the side, brandishing his blade.

Hansel's back hit the ground, and needle-sharp pain darkened his nerves.

"Hansel!" Rosana ran over to him and then grabbed his hand. "Can you stand?"

Dark spots and drops of rain blurred Hansel's vision. "I can try."

The Woodlands became a tangle of arrows, blades, teeth, and claws. The chameleon wolf was an impossible fighter, blinking out of sight after every other step and pouncing from places nobody saw it hiding. It was a wraith, a sorcerer, and a feral monster all in one. Liam and Mulan stood back to back, arms extended and swords drawn, and Pietro and Enzo followed suit with their daggers.

"Kid, don't you do anything stupid. Don't leave my side."

"*You* don't do anything stupid," Enzo said.

Tahlia fired arrows into trees until Master Cherry finally glided after her and snatched the bow from her hands.

"You waste your arrows, foolish girl!" he snapped. "Stand still."

Rosana patted Hansel's shoulder, pulled her cloak over her head, and then vanished. The sound of splashing puddles trailed away from him, and then he lost track of her path.

"Rosana!" he hissed, pushing on the ground until he could get to his feet. He stumbled and spun a few times, his head pounding and throbbing.

The next thing he saw was Tahlia Rose flying through the air and colliding with a tree trunk. Almost immediately after, a sickening howl bloodied the air, and both Rosana and the chameleon wolf appeared in a narrow beam of moonlight. Rosana had the creature's severed tail in her hands, and she straddled the wolf's back, attempting to strangle it with its own tail.

The wolf writhed and bucked beneath her, making every attempt to throw her from its shoulders. Her head jerked back and forth, but she gritted her teeth and pulled harder. "Come on, Kujo!" she snarled. "Go down!"

Hansel nocked an arrow, determined to seize his opportunity to shoot the wolf while he could see it, but it tossed about so violently he wasn't sure he could risk the shot without the possibility of harming Rosana instead.

Liam and Mulan sprang out of their back-to-back formation and prepared to cleave the monster through its chest, but with impossible reflexes, the wolf spun around and attempted to use Rosana as a shield. Both warriors lowered their blades, and the next thing Hansel knew, Enzo leapt onto the scene and struck the wolf in the jaw. Pietro stomped on the bloody stub where its tail used to be and jammed his dagger into the creature's ribcage. Unfortunately, the wolf seemed entirely unfazed. It howled and thrashed, appearing angrier than ever, but no assault weakened its energy.

Hansel had the crippling realization that Tahlia hadn't moved since the wolf threw her. She lay limp and brittle against the tree, the most painful image to behold. Hansel thought of that tiny pinprick of light he'd seen when she insisted on leading the way with him . . . the little spark of childhood that reminded him of his sister. In some ways, she reminded him of the days when life was easy and carefree, when he could play with young Peter Pan and Alice and visit the girl in the meadows any day he wanted. In other ways, she modeled adulthood, and Hansel admired the woman she was quickly becoming.

Tahlia needed to reach her full potential.

Tahlia needed to cling to that single spark of childhood.

Tahlia needed to survive her nightmare. For Gretel.

Hansel staggered through the rain, making a beeline for the unconscious girl. *Wake up, Tahlia,* he said. *I'm going to save you. I'm going to help you out of here.* He waded over broken branches and tree trunks, shaking rainwater out of his hair as he trudged along. The sounds of battle and struggle wove through his ears, but he had a single purpose in mind. Maybe this was his time for redemption. After all the trouble he'd caused, he could be there for Tahlia.

Hansel knelt by Tahlia's side and touched her shoulder. "Tahlia," he grunted, every syllable a concentrated effort on his tongue. "Tahlia. Wake up."

The girl didn't move.

"Tahlia, help me out here! Wake up and get back to your feet!" He gave her a little shake, and her head tilted toward her shoulder. "Come on!"

You are sweet, an icy voice whispered to his mind. *You see your sister in this dying soul. You cling to familial bonds in times of terror. Will blood ties be enough to save you from your fate, huntsman?*

Hansel whirled around and confronted his fear: a graying woman with burnt, charred skin, eyes milky with cataracts, and a toothless grin. With a gnarled hand, the candy witch grabbed Hansel by the collar, and all his muscles went limp. He barely had the strength to move his eyeballs, and he was forced to watch the hag's face contort into a furry, sharp-toothed, yellow-eyed beast.

"Tahlia," he wheezed. He squeezed his eyes shut. "Wake up. *Run.*"

CHAPTER THIRTY-FOUR

THE CITADEL

By the time they finally wore down the chameleon wolf and put it to sleep, no amount of rain could've washed away the exhaustion in Enzo's body. His muscles and tendons and bones were on fire. His mind was numb. He lay sprawled on the ground with Rosana, their fingers loosely wrapped together and their lungs nearly empty.

"Let's never go looking for one of those," he heaved.

Rosana shook her head, her hair a messy tangle. She tossed the wolf's tail far behind her. "I won't argue."

Enzo sat up, rested his elbow on a sore knee, and looked at Mulan. "How did you spend every day doing things like this?"

"Same way I'm doing it right now." Mulan dipped her sword in a rain puddle and flicked the water and blood over her shoulder. "When you have no choice, you *make* it happen."

Enzo didn't believe that at all. *She's been a badass since birth,* he guessed. Then again, how much of this moment was influenced by choice? Enzo didn't get to choose having Pinocchio for a father or Peter Pan for a neighbor. He didn't get to choose Hansel breaking into New World homes and abducting families, or the showdown in Wonderland. Enzo didn't get to choose the Ivory Queen building her dominion in New York City.

He looked at Rosana and wondered when he chose her.

They met on top of the Empire State Building. Most people who could say the same would probably speak of what a romantic location it was, but Rosana and Enzo would always think of the danger. Did he choose to meet her? If his father hadn't carved a small figurine of the Empire State Building long ago, would Enzo be sitting next to her?

She looked back at him and flashed a tired smile, barely a curve in her lips.

I do *choose you*, he thought.

Pietro nudged the dead chameleon wolf with his toe. "You think we can cook this thing?"

Liam wrinkled his nose and turned his head.

"That's a no, huh?" Pietro stroked his chin. "Is that because you've tried it, or is that because you don't like the idea of it?" He studied the wolf and rocked back and forth on his heels. "You know, if we do it right, it might come out a little bit like beef jerky."

"I don't recommend it," Mulan said.

"I recommend we move on and look for the door." Rosana looked around and counted the members of the group, mouthing the numbers to herself. "Wait. Where's Hansel?" She moved her finger about and recounted. "We're missing *two* people."

Enzo stood and counted for himself. "Tahlia," he said. "Hansel and Tahlia. Anybody see them?"

"Don't call out their names," Cherry advised. "We don't want to attract any more unwanted guests."

Enzo rubbed his eyelids, moved his hands into his hair, and clawed at his scalp. The stress boiled his blood. "We *can't* lose another person in here! Three people are too much. It's only gonna get more dangerous the higher we go. Why would Hansel and Tahlia wander off?"

"Come on." Rosana wrapped her arm around Enzo's shoulder. "Let's look for them. Maybe they had to empty their bladders or something."

"What do we do about *that* thing, though?" Pietro nudged the dead chameleon wolf again.

"Leave it," Mulan commanded, grabbing her sword to follow Enzo. "We don't have time for burials or bonfires."

Pietro jogged a few steps to catch up with Mulan. "I just think about how sometimes you kill a bumblebee and then like fifty-six other bees show up like they're looking for revenge. Do you think wolves follow the same code of vengeance as bees do?"

Mulan responded with a side-eye. "You are hysterical."

"I'm *concerned*. Excuse me for trying to be proactive and C.O.B."

Liam scrunched his eyebrows. "*Cob?*"

"*Cover our butts*, Liam," Rosana explained.

"But all of us are wearing . . ." Liam paused and then nodded in understanding. "Huh. Clever."

"You ought to know that the chameleon wolf is an endangered species, Mr. Pan," Master Cherry said. "There are thought to be less than five remaining in Florindale. I estimate four now, exclusively male. And there certainly has not been any evidence that they abide by a *code of vengeance*."

Pietro stabbed Master Cherry with a glare. "Don't do science on me, old man. We've both lived through enough to accept that there are things in this world you can't explain with science."

"All phenomena are quantifiable. All things can be described, predicted, and ultimately controlled. Your New World *depends* on science. Florindale foolishly exhausts its endeavors on magic alone. When you have lived as I live, you might understand why both worlds are susceptible to destruction. Neither accepts the laws of the other. Science and magic can coexist in a perfect union, you know. One explains the population of the chameleon wolf. The other protects us lesser beings when the chameleon wolf rises above man on the food chain. It is our failsafe, restoring the balance when nature goes awry."

"Which one helps us defeat Avoria?" Enzo asked.

"We'll know when we've done so."

Enzo knew it was useless to keep digging. He believed Master Cherry's intentions to be pure, but Enzo didn't fully understand the strange man's thoughts. Enzo knew from the silence that everybody around him was too tired and cranky to wrap their minds around Cherry's words. If worse came to worst in the end, Enzo would face Avoria alone the way he intended. He didn't *need* Master Cherry. Master Cherry needed the group, and perhaps a healthy dose of social skills.

And maybe we need a map. And an umbrella. And a bed and a roof.

After what seemed like hours of walking in the dark, Enzo slumped down against a tree and wrapped his arms around his knees.

"Hey," Rosana said, kneeling and tapping Enzo's foot with the heel of her hand. "Come on, Enzo. We don't have time for breaks, remember?"

Enzo bowed his head so his nose touched his knees. "I'm just exhausted, Rosana." His voice came out in a parched, weak croak. "We've been walking forever. This rain won't go away, we can't find our friends, we can't find our door, and I'm starting to think we're going in circles. This is actual hell. I'm losing hope."

"*Don't.*" Rosana snapped. "Come on, you can take anything. Look at me."

Feeling like his neck was made of lead, Enzo sniffled, raised his head, and met Rosana's gaze. Both their faces were soaked, neither from just the rainwater. Rosana's hair framed her cheeks in wet, sticky clumps, and her eyelashes fanned into asymmetrical stars. She looked beautiful. She reached out and gently took hold of Enzo's chin, and the next thing he knew, their lips were together. It was a quick, simple kiss, but it jolted Enzo's spirit to life.

"I love you, Enzo. There's nobody else I would rather be fighting with right now." She grabbed his hand, her palms a beacon of warmth. "You've come a long way since I met you. Listen. You and Pietro drove a truck into my life when I needed a home the most. In that hotel, that truck, Prince Liam's Renaissance jail, Mulan's jet, or even the shadows of Wonderland, I learned something. I could be under a different roof—or no roof—every single night, and I'll feel at home if you're there, because you're strong. You're brave. You're *you*, and the *you* I know does not give up. So stand up and help me *think*." Rosana helped Enzo to his feet.

Enzo's joints still protested, but Rosana's touch made everything more tolerable. When he sat upright again, he hugged her.

Rosana peeled a thick strand of hair from her face and smiled. "Okay. Here's what we know for sure: We are inside a building. We may be in the Woodlands, but objectively, we're in a finite space. There has to be a wall somewhere."

"But by that logic, there must also be a ceiling," Mulan pointed out. "And that's not true. We know it's not true because it's raining all over us."

As if to reinforce the point, Pietro picked up a smooth stone the shape of a pancake and tossed it high over his head. Everyone watched it spin and soar into the air, slicing through raindrops with little effect on the world around it until it surpassed the height of the tallest tree.

Thunk.

Enzo's jaw dropped as the rock came back down. *Did I really hear that?* He looked at Rosana, and the same perplexed expression peppered her face. That was all the confirmation he needed.

Splash.

"That rock hit something up there. I heard it."

"But it couldn't have . . ." Mulan shook her head, but her eyebrows conveyed her doubt.

"Do it again." Liam picked up a rock of his own, and both he and Pietro launched their stones over their heads at the same time.

Tha-thunk!

Liam stepped out of the way to avoid getting hit by his own stone. "They came back down from the same spot. There's a ceiling there."

"It's raining from the ceiling," Enzo breathed.

"What does that mean?" Pietro asked. "What do we do now? First I was overwhelmed by the size of the Woodlands, but now that we've established we're in a box? I'm starting to get a little claustrophobic."

"We have to break out of one box and into the next," Rosana said simply.

A contemplative silence descended on the group, and Enzo became aware of all the gazes converging on him. He understood immediately what everyone wanted. He took his knife out of his pocket and looked up. "You want me to climb the tree and carve the sky open."

"It makes sense," Liam said. "We can't find a door, so a Carver makes one for us. Who better than you?"

"But we need to find Hansel and Tahlia," Enzo said. "We can't leave without them."

"Enzo, I hate to disagree with you, but we should proceed," Mulan said. "It's for the best."

"How can you say that?" Enzo shook his head. "What if that were Liam? You'd want to go back and look. I would too."

"Always," Mulan answered, "but even if that were *you*, Enzo, I would still say that our priority is to reach the top of this tower, and we were bound to reach it with some casualties along the way. We will lose time and energy if we go looking for two people who—forgive me—are likely dead at this time."

"*No.*" Enzo jammed his knife into the tree trunk and then crossed his arms, making sure to look every member of his group in the eyes as he spoke. "*This* is the plan. I will carve through the roof, but you all need to look for Tahlia and Hansel. If you haven't found them before I'm done, then fine, we keep moving, but if none of you are even gonna try, then turn around and leave. I'm dead serious. I may be guilty of giving up on myself sometimes, but you are *not* welcome to come with me if you're going to give up and abandon a friend. If you would try to justify that, I might as well fight alone." He paused for a deep breath that calmed his emotions a bit, and then he lowered his voice. "Are you all still with me?"

Mulan's gaze flitted to the ground, and her lips quavered once. She clasped her hands at her waist, bowed to Enzo, and then hugged him. "Forgive me. I let my judgment falter for a bit. We will continue searching while you climb the tree." She turned around and addressed their friends. "Won't we, everybody?"

The group sounded in confident accordance. *Yes! Of course!*

Enzo beamed. "Okay. Come back when you see a crack in the sky. And be careful."

Liam led the group away from the tree, with Rosana being the last to leave. Before she walked away, she squeezed Enzo's hand and said, "Have I mentioned how much I love assertive Enzo? That was kinda studly of you."

Warmth filled Enzo's cheeks. "Shucks, ma'am."

Rosana rolled her eyes. "We'll be back. Be careful."

After Rosana turned around, Enzo picked up another rock and flung it high above his head, listening for the *thunk* and making a mental note of where it would change direction to come back down. He did this twice more until he was confident about where the ceiling was, and then he started to climb the tree next to him. It towered high enough to get him to the invisible barrier, but he hoped it would support his weight when it tapered to a thin point toward the top. There would only be one way to know for sure.

Enzo had climbed a few trees in his life—all shortly after he grew out of the preschool notion that only monkeys were allowed to climb trees—but he never tried to climb one in the rain, and most weren't even half the height of the trunk he scaled now. Most also had more branches than this one, which stood frustratingly bare. He found his footing on little knots and knobs, and he discovered that he could get great leverage by plunging the knife into the tree at a downward angle. The dagger seemed to know that it needed to support his weight, and it refused to slip out of the trunk until Enzo wanted it to. The rain complicated matters by making the handle slippery, and Enzo knew his fingers were going to be red by the time he reached the top.

It's like gym class, he told himself. *Only my life and all my friends' existence depend on finishing the rock wall.* Zack would have excelled at this task. Enzo hoped everything was going well on the ground floor outside the Citadel. *Please let everybody be alive. Please let them live.*

Enzo stopped in a humid layer dense with the perspiration of sticky leaves and rough branches slick with rainwater. He felt a great swell of relief to be able to step more freely, reach for solid branches, and have more to hold onto, but he couldn't think about the height he'd ascended. Here, he had no harness, only gravity. So it was a beautiful moment when he climbed to the next branch, hoisted himself up, and conked his head on nothing at all.

Thunk!

"Ouch!" Enzo pressed on his scalp with one hand, the other wrapped firmly around a branch for support. He rubbed his head, looked up, and then extended his arm above his head.

No way.

His hand hit a barrier, producing soft pink indentations in his fingers, but there was nothing to see above him. Enzo swept his fingers back and forth along the invisible ceiling. The sensation was like scraping a showerhead. Rainwater built up and trickled down his fingers.

Enzo knocked on the sky. He hoped for an easy hollow thud, but he might as well have pounded on marble. Regardless, he took his knife and jammed it upward until the blade disappeared in the invisible substance.

A sliver of warm light trickled through the slit he made.

"Please make us a way out of here," Enzo whispered, and then he began to cut. *Up, down, up, down.* The stream of light grew longer, and strangely, rain stopped falling from the crack where Enzo opened the sky. The water poured *around* it now.

When Enzo had carved a line as long as his arm, he switched

direction and made a perpendicular cut, but as his knife sank in again, a haunting scream cut through the air. Fear took over, and Enzo almost dropped the blade. "*Rosana!*"

Several more cries sounded from Pietro, Liam, Cherry, and most horrifying, from Mulan, who Enzo believed to be a woman without fear. But all of them were clearly terrified, and so was Enzo when the sounds split the air: a mix of guttural growls, the hard snapping of teeth, and the low, longing cries of several wolves. Judging by the different tones, Enzo guessed there had to be at least three beasts howling at once.

Rosana peeled into view, sprinting like her life depended on it, and scrambled into the tree. Her red cloak hung at her shoulders in shredded tatters.

Pietro, Mulan, Liam, and Cherry followed, clawing into nearby trees, and the chameleon wolves followed. Cherry had been wrong about one thing: There must have been far more than five left in existence, because seven careened into view, some sprinting on two legs and some galloping on four.

"*Rosana!*" Enzo screamed. "Hurry! Watch out!"

The wolves snapped their teeth at the bases of the trees while Enzo's friends climbed like maniacs.

"Keep *carving*!" Rosana cried back.

His heart in a panic, Enzo shoved his blade back into the invisible ceiling and sawed as fast as he could. He intended to cut out a square big enough for all of them to climb through, but in his frantic rush, his outline turned into a cross between a triangle and a half circle.

Below, the sound of a tear ripped through the air, and Pietro let out a scream like Enzo had never heard before. He was afraid to look down. He bit his lip until he almost drew blood, and he cut even harder and faster. The muscles in his forearm started to burn, and a vein protruded from the back of his hand. Thunder almost shook him out of the tree, and Enzo started to hope lightning wasn't an issue on this floor of the castle.

A wolf cried out in pain, several started barking, and Mulan yelled, "Close your eyes and keep climbing! Open your senses!"

At that same moment, Enzo finished tracing the path in the invisible ceiling, and everything inside of his tracing fell away and conked one of the chameleon wolves in the head.

A column of white light spilled into the Woodlands from the floor above, but not a minute later, a thin layer of smoke blanketed Enzo's vision. Dark, dense, and wispy, the smoke drifted up from somewhere below. He looked down into a swirling sea of gray, unable to see his own foot, and almost cried out when a wet hand closed around his ankle.

"Enzo, it's me," Rosana coughed. "I'm sorry. I didn't mean to grab you. Hurry and go through the ceiling! I'm right behind you."

"We're right there," Enzo answered. "Let's go." He covered his nose with his shirt, grabbed a chunk of the ceiling, and then pulled himself up. The burn in his forearms spread to his shoulders, chest, and back, rounding out all the pain in his body. His legs still throbbed from the climb and the tightrope. He wondered how he could possibly endure any more floors of hell and still have energy left to face Avoria.

The smoke curled through the hole Enzo made, staying at eye level with him so as to obscure his vision when he ascended into the next story. The cool, smooth touch of the ground told him that the surface was made of marble, and thankfully, no rain had descended on his new terrain. He lay on his stomach, poked his head into the hole, and extended a hand. Rosana wrapped her fingers around his palm a few seconds later, and he tugged her through.

Below, wolves were still snarling and growling, but Enzo didn't hear much from his friends, and he didn't perceive any shapes.

"My cloak," Rosana breathed. "It's ruined. I can't use it anymore."

Enzo's heart twisted inside his chest, not because the cloak's destruction rendered her unable to disappear again, but because the cloak had once been a hoodie her mother handed down to Rosana. In a way, it tied her family together.

"Are you okay?" Enzo asked.

"They were everywhere, Enzo. Cherry was wrong about the wolves. We got chased by so many of them. Mulan kept dropping these smoke beans to throw them off our trail. Only the beans put us in the dark as well, and our noses aren't nearly as powerful."

"And Hansel? Tahlia?" Enzo was afraid to ask the question, but he needed to know.

"Nowhere," Rosana choked.

Enzo had the crippling thought that if he hadn't been insistent on sending his friends to find Hansel and Tahlia, the chameleon wolves might not have attacked. They all could have been safe if they'd proceeded together. Enzo might have doomed them all.

Master Cherry crawled through the hole next, fully hooded and gasping for breath. He didn't say a word.

Liam scrambled in, pulled Mulan after him, and peered into the hole.

By Enzo's count, only Pietro remained.

"*Pietro!*" Enzo called, desperately squinting and blinking to make out any sort of shape in the dark cloud.

For a long minute, all was deafeningly quiet. Enzo's ears rung. He wished he could hear the chameleon wolves howling and snarling. He wished he could hear Pietro making any noise whatsoever.

Bam!

Pietro slammed his hand through the hole, and Liam grabbed his friend immediately.

"*Help me,*" Pietro sputtered.

"Pietro!" Enzo took Pietro's other hand and pulled.

Little by little, the smoke cleared away, lifting the veil off the carbon copy of the Woodlands and everything around Enzo. When Pietro came through the hole, all seemed well until Enzo got a good look at his friend's leg, rough with missing patches of skin and soaked in a layer of blood. Pietro collapsed on the ground and extended his gored calf for Enzo to see.

"One of them mauled me," Pietro croaked. "It burns something fierce, man. I think my blood is on fire."

Enzo blew a long breath through his lips and took a good look at his surroundings: a short corridor of white marble and more blue-flamed torches, all culminating in a crimson metal door about fifteen feet tall and etched with gold swirls. *Too easy,* he thought. He bit his lip and grabbed Pietro's shoulder. "How do we help?"

"For one thing." Mulan stood, yanked a torch out of the wall, and tossed the flame into the dark hole. The wolves whined, and Enzo tried to put a mental block over the nightmarish sound. "Burn those monsters."

Rosana removed the tatters of her cloak and broke it into further shreds, tears welling in her eyes. "I'll bandage you, Pietro. No, I can't believe any of this . . ."

"The tears!" Enzo said. He turned to Master Cherry and held out a hand. "I think now's the time, Master Cherry. Pietro needs the healing. Did you get Gretel's tears?"

Master Cherry took a sweeping step back and folded his arms. "Are you certain we'll not need them in a time to come? We still have much ground to cover. An increase in danger and injury is, frankly, inevitable. Do you truly wish to waste an elixir on a flesh wound?"

Enzo buried his fingers in his hair. When he pulled away, a few dark strands fell out.

"This man is *hurt!*" Liam roared louder than Enzo had ever heard before. "He needs healing!"

"No, no," Pietro said, a bit of a gruff bite in his voice. He aimed a finger at Enzo. "Kid, I can deal. Rosana can bind me up. We're not wasting precious resources on my—"

"Your possible infection?" Enzo turned back to Cherry. "Do those things carry disease?"

"Why ask him?" Liam muttered. "He didn't even know how many

chameleon wolves still lived in the Woodlands."

"My research was not flawed," Cherry insisted. "This Citadel is a funhouse."

"So much for your science, then," Mulan said. "Facts aren't going to save us anymore. They did less than nothing for Tahlia and Hansel."

"*Stop!*" Rosana screamed, pausing in the middle of her work on Pietro's leg. "Stop it, stop it, *stop—fighting!* I'm not gonna listen to this anymore! We're supposed to be on the same side. Who cares about the number of wolves in the Woodlands or why we got attacked? We're losing people. Let's stop fighting and have some freaking common sense already!"

In the silence that followed, Enzo nodded at his girlfriend and grinned. He folded his arms and looked around the room. "Yeah! What she said!"

Enzo and Rosana worked together to finish wrapping Pietro's leg, and then they helped him to his feet. He winced and sucked in a lot of air through clenched teeth, but he insisted he was ready to keep going.

Pietro the warrior, Enzo thought.

He approached the red door and touched the cool metal, wondering what could possibly lie beyond. He pushed it open.

A man cloaked in black stood at the end of a bright marble hallway that ended with an elevator door. Behind the cloaked man, three people—a distraught Madame Esme, a weakened Jacob Isaac Holmes, and a blonde woman Enzo had never seen before—jangled a set of chains along the wall.

Behind them, an elevator door popped open, revealing a woman with fiery red hair.

When Avoria stepped out, the cloaked man reached behind his back, faced Enzo, and pulled two twin swords from their sheaths.

CHAPTER THIRTY-FIVE

THE CITADEL

When Enzo saw the red door, he knew by the cold gleam in Mulan's eyes that the group had ascended into her nightmare and out of Tahlia Rose's. He'd been dreading this moment almost more than he dreaded his own nightmare. Hua Mulan—the woman warrior! What could she possibly be afraid of?

"When I was a little girl, long before I ever arrived in the Old World, my family lived in a palace barred by a crimson door," Mulan spoke. "I'll never forget the cool reflection of iron and gold, how my father used to punish my wrongdoings by making me polish it until I could see her reflection. I only had to do this three times before I learned never to disrespect my elders."

Enzo thought of the general and the terrifying encounter in the New York theater—that impossible grasp and the way he hoisted Enzo in the air like a broken toy. "Mulan," he whispered. "Are you . . . afraid of your father?"

Mulan didn't answer, and she didn't add a single word when the red door opened and revealed the general on the other side.

Behind the general, the elevator door slid open, and the Ivory Queen stepped out.

"Avoria!" Enzo breathed.

"Silence." Avoria snapped her fingers, and paralysis spread through Enzo's veins, locking his muscles into place with a heavy sense of numbness. His gaze froze on the center of the room, where the general unsheathed his swords and then crossed them at his chest.

Shhhing!

Avoria clasped her hands at her waist and walked across the room with her lips in a half-smile. Nobody else moved or spoke. The queen stopped in front of Enzo and said, "Your turn is just around the corner, Carver. I promise we'll do our dance, but right now"—she turned away—"you can watch the festivities."

She circled the group, occasionally sweeping her palm across someone's shoulder or tapping their chin as she passed. She addressed Liam next, who stood frozen in a state of wide-eyed horror. She tapped him on the shoulder, and to Enzo's surprise, the prince took a step back. Avoria caught him and squeezed his cheeks between her fingernails. "I'm letting *you* move up, handsome. Your wife awaits you. I shall let you say goodbye before the final confrontation. Consider this my *final* act of mercy."

"Consider those your final words!" Liam drew his sword and slashed.

Avoria slid and arched her back, a rare look of surprise rounding her eyes. "*Fool!*"

Get her, Liam! Enzo willed his body to move, frustrated by the numbness spreading through his joints. *I can fight this! Liam, you can get her!*

The prince was a machine, twisting and thrusting and hacking his way across the floor, but to no avail. For every move Liam made, Avoria was two steps ahead, dodging him with calculated grace while the general observed with monk-like calmness.

Before Liam could fight his way across the floor, Avoria rammed her palm into his chest, uppercut him in the jaw, and seized the handle of his sword.

No! Tension built in every inch of Enzo's body. He felt as though he might burst like a rubber band.

Avoria smirked at the prince, and with one swift move, she kicked Liam in the chest.

The general waved his hand to the side, and Liam lost his grip on the blade, skidded across the room, and crashed into the elevator. The doors boomed shut behind him, and he disappeared.

Enzo wanted nothing more than to dig his thumbs into the queen's eye sockets for the way she treated people. *Release me for one second,* he thought. *That's all I need. I'll give you the fight of your life.*

Avoria rounded on Mulan and flashed a wicked grin. "Welcome to your nightmare, Warrior Princess. Are you enjoying your stay at my Citadel?" Avoria laughed through her nose. "I presume you're comfortable with your arrangements. This is going to be your *favorite* part."

The general removed the hood from his head. His eyes were sunken in, the whites a sickly shade of pink.

"Your father is a failure," Avoria declared. "I gave him a simple task. I asked him to make Esmeralda spill her secrets."

On the other side of the room, Esmeralda lifted her head. Evidently the prisoners weren't paralyzed, but the chains kept them immobile. *Poor Madame Esme. And Jacob!* Enzo guessed the third prisoner was Belladonna, who Jacob had intended to rescue.

"And you know what? He couldn't do it," Avoria continued. "It wasn't enough to administer threats. It wasn't enough to be merciful. It wasn't enough to kill the bell ringer."

Enzo's heart burst into twenty pieces inside his chest. *Quasimodo.* A hot tear slid down his face. He was powerless to stop it. *All he wanted was a peaceful life.*

Avoria smirked. "So, now, the general is going to kill the thing he loves the most—you. The only information he managed to discern is that *you* are not the final soul I am looking for. How very fortunate, because *you* make me sickest of all." She nodded once and snapped her fingers at Mulan's father. "Whenever you're ready, General."

The pieces of Enzo's heart pulsed in every nerve of his body as Mulan's father stepped forward and bowed to her. "Daughter," he said, "What I am about to do will bring great everlasting pain and sorrow. For that, my heart is sore. I am sorry for everything."

He raised his swords and centered them in front of Mulan's heart.

She wouldn't even get to close her eyes.

Don't do this! Enzo screamed in his mind.

The general raised and lowered the swords two more times as if aiming a pool stick at a cue ball. A dark expression crossed his face, exposing his teeth and angling his brows, and with a harsh cry, he turned on his heel and hurled one of the blades at the far side of the room.

Clang!

Jacob Isaac Holmes's chains fell free, and the Beast sprang to life. The general turned the other blade to Avoria's throat while Jacob scrambled to free Esmeralda and Belladonna. Enzo's heart knitted itself back together again, but it had no time to slow, for Avoria screamed and lunged for the general with a feral rage.

"You dare defy me, you insolent, incompetent heathen?"

Sensation and movement surged back into Enzo's body, and he propelled himself forward to attack the queen, who must have lost focus in her rage. Chaos unspooled from his friends.

Jacob snapped Belladonna's chains, kissed her, and then thrust a paw behind him. "Go! Take Esme and head for the ground! I'll be right behind you!"

Another man ran out from behind one of the columns and grabbed Esme's hand, filling Enzo's heart with a burst of warmth.

"*You didn't kill the bell ringer?*" Avoria screamed. "*I gave you one job!*"

Enzo reached into his bootstrap, plucked out a knife, and threw it. A second later, it reappeared in his hand.

Pietro unsheathed his own dagger and ran, limping the whole way.

Rosana shifted her gaze to Master Cherry, who remained eerily still as if assessing the situation.

"Now!" she screamed at him.

Before anyone could reach Avoria, a blade sunk into the general's heart. The color spilled from his cheeks and he dropped to his knees, his dark robes soaked with liquid.

Enzo gritted his teeth, his heart breaking for Mulan. He gripped the dagger and lunged for Avoria.

And then the mad queen screamed, and the walls and floor exploded around them, revealing a dark sky that pulled the group into its abyss. Avoria smiled one more time and burst toward the stars like a rocket. Enzo floated in a pool of black and watched Mulan's tears stream down her face while her father's body faded into the dead stars. That was when he understood: Mulan was never afraid of her father. She was afraid of what war might do to her family, and Enzo couldn't help but wonder if it would tear his own apart next.

No, he thought. *Avoria is never going to tear us apart.* "If you can hear me, Avoria," he shouted, "you'll never tear us apart! We're coming for you!"

As he focused on the brightest star in the sky, he made peace with the fact that he was shouting into the void—into dark matter. Nobody was ever going to hear him.

We just might die out here.

CHAPTER THIRTY-SIX

THE CITADEL

Enzo used to wonder what it would be like to walk on the moon, to skip with such levity and float in a vacuum. Space had always fascinated him, and he knew Rosana agreed. She'd once told him how she made a list of places she wanted to travel to, and it started with Saturn.

But Enzo knew it also terrified Rosana to think about space, about losing gravity and floating in a place where she would feel tiny and insignificant. So when the Citadel walls disintegrated and revealed the curvature of the Earth beneath their feet, his heart dropped into his stomach.

Rosana screamed.

"Rosana! Rosana!" Enzo thrust his arm out and seized Rosana's hand. He forced his breathing back to a steady pace. *We're still in the building somehow. We're in a closed, finite space. It's all an illusion. That's how we can still breathe.*

They held each other by three fingers until Enzo pulled her into his embrace. "Don't let go of me, okay?"

Rosana caught her breath and buried her head in Enzo's shoulder.

Pietro floated by as if he were swimming and caught Rosana by the sleeve. "Guys," he said, "what is this?"

"Our final test, I presume," Master Cherry boomed, tumbling

by until Pietro pulled him in. "The queen threw her panic switch, preparing for her last stand. I don't have to remind you to be wary."

Mulan dug her fingers into Enzo's collar, her expression blank and unseeing. Enzo's heart burst for the woman. All five of them had been through hell. They confronted the queen herself. Mulan confronted death and lost her father. That she could hang on to Enzo at all was a testament to her strength and fierce will.

The five hung on to each other and spun for a while until Enzo said, "Should we be trying to move anywhere? I don't want us to float forever. Where do we go from here?"

"Wherever Lady Fortune wills us to go," Cherry answered. "We cannot control the current of the stars."

"But what if we're stuck out here forever?" Rosana asked.

"Avoria will draw us back in," Cherry assured. "Yes, of that much I'm sure. In the meantime, do not let go. We must not drift apart."

Rosana let out a small sob, and Enzo tightened his embrace.

"Hey," he said. "We're okay. We've got each other. We're okay."

"I know." Rosana stifled a quaver in her voice. "I just started thinking about how Liam's probably all alone out here somewhere. And that's horrifying to imagine."

Enzo imagined other faces probably plagued her mind at the same time. He didn't want to make her speak their names, but Cornelius Redding and Matthew Hadinger were probably dead for all Enzo knew. No man could survive tumbling in space without food and water for months without end, and there was even less of a chance when those two men were determined to kill each other. Sometimes Rosana had talked about them, and her voice always shook. Matt had been one of the kindest people they'd met on their journey, and the whole time, he carried the secret of having betrayed Rosana's mom, framing her for murder to keep her closer to the chest at a time when all she wanted was to go home. Enzo suspected there was more to the story they might have learned if Matt didn't fall out of their lives that day. One day, maybe Rosana's mother would open up, but until then, Rosana promised Enzo that she'd focus on what she learned from her own time in Wonderland: Nobody would ever lie to her again.

"We're okay," Enzo whispered again. *And Liam?* Enzo refused to speculate. Bad news would've been too much to handle. Good news would've been too much to hope for.

The group stayed quiet for a while, letting the vacuum of space carry them about, but Pietro broke the silence when Rosana had nearly drifted to sleep in Enzo's arms.

"You know how they tell us to wish upon a star? They make songs about it and everything." Pietro looked around and sighed, a soft spark of contentment in his eyes. "This would be the time to do that, you know. They can hear us out here. Isn't it funny? For flying so close to death, I'm overwhelmed by the *beauty* of it all." He yawned and rubbed his jaw, prompting Enzo to pull him in and grip his wrist. He didn't want his friend to fall asleep and drift away. "Make a wish."

They floated for what felt like days, hand-in-hand in a pocket of infinite space and time. In those moments, time replayed in little flashes, moving scene by scene in Enzo's mind, from the first wooden figurine his father ever made him—a Dalmatian with ears that actually moved—to the agonizing time in the Citadel. Every day, both fantastical and mundane, floated into Enzo's mind against a backdrop of stars, splashed around a bit, and gently drifted away. He noticed his memories were much brighter when they introduced a new person. The first time he spent the night at Zack and Pietro's house. The night he met Rosana in New York. His first flight with Liam and Mulan. The day Geppetto sparred with Enzo in Wonderland.

By the time Enzo's memories wound back to the present, something shifted in his surroundings. The group, previously huddled together in a tight ball, spread into a star shape, and the sensation of like-charged magnets buzzed through his arms, begging him to let go of Rosana.

"You feel that?" Enzo asked.

Rosana's eyes widened. Moons and asteroids and tiny planets circled around them, and she dug her nails into Enzo's wrist. "We're moving faster."

"Something's trying to pull us apart!"

The pull strengthened, untying Enzo's shoe and leaving the laces dangling over the edges. He felt like he was about to lose his footwear on a carnival ride, only there was no safety system in place. There were no seatbelts, straps, buckles, or clicking mechanisms. There was only Rosana's hand.

Mulan's hands shook, her knuckles red and throbbing. She squinted in concentration.

"Enzo," she wheezed. "Take my sword."

"You mean to let go?" Cherry inquired.

Enzo felt like a brick had been shoved into his chest when Mulan nodded.

"We will be separated one way or another," Mulan said. "I want Enzo to go protected. Enzo. Rosana. Pietro. Please find Liam and save us. It's been a wonderful adventure. I *enjoyed* myself with you."

Rosana's lip quavered. "What if . . . ?"

Enzo knew she didn't finish her question because there were too many possibilities. What if letting go killed Mulan? What if they never met again? *What if, what if, what if?*

"Take the sword," Mulan commanded. "Hurry!"

Enzo didn't want to take his hand off Rosana, fearing that he would lose her. Mulan's sword protruded from a loop in her belt, the bright metal tip staring him in the face. "Rosana," he said. "Grab my elbow, okay? I'm going to let go of you for five seconds. Just five."

When Rosana closed her hand around Enzo's elbow, he reached for the sword, prepared to grasp the handle, and—

Whoosh!

The pull of space ripped Mulan away before Enzo could grab the weapon, and she sailed away, tumbling and twirling until she became a bright speck of dust in the universe, and then she was nothing.

"*Nooo!*" Enzo cried. "No!"

"Enzo." A soft voice cut through Enzo's grief and commanded his attention. He turned and felt Pietro close both of his hands around Enzo's collar, a vivid expression of fear in his wide eyes. "Enzo," Pietro said, "I think I have to let go, too, buddy. I'm having a *lot* of trouble hanging on right now!"

Enzo locked eyes with his friend. "Don't you dare let go."

"Kid."

Enzo hated Pietro's tone.

"Thank you for being a part of my family."

"Don't you dare let go," Enzo repeated. His voice went hoarse and rough, like he'd swallowed a patch of sandpaper. "I won't let you."

"Pietro," Rosana whispered.

"It's been one hell of an adventure," Pietro continued. "The grandest. Remember what I told you at McDonalds after we left home?"

"Dammit, Pietro—"

"I couldn't be prouder to have been a part of this with you. You're gonna save the whole damn world right now, and I'm not gonna be next to you, but I'm always gonna be with you, okay? Tell me you understand. Tell me you believe that."

"Stop—"

"I'm not asking you to say goodbye, Kid. You're gonna win, and we'll meet again. I've never believed anything stronger." Pietro swallowed, and pools filled his eyes. "Do you believe?"

Enzo bit his lip. His eyes stung with the salt of his tears. "I believe," he choked. "I believe, Pietro."

"Good man," Pietro answered. And with that, he let go of Enzo's shirt, and the pull of outer space ripped The Flying Man away.

Enzo didn't let his eyes move for a long time. His gaze stayed frozen on one place, a hollow spot in the middle of the dark sky, while tears drifted out of his eyes and congealed into crystal orbs floating around him. He'd almost forgotten that he and Rosana weren't alone until Master Cherry wrapped his thick arms around the two and pulled them into the warmth of his robe.

"Don't you worry," Cherry whispered as they tumbled deeper into the darkness. "I will stay with you both. I will stay with you both until the deed is done."

I don't care about the deed anymore, Enzo thought. He closed his eyes and pressed his forehead to Rosana's. They clung to each other for warmth and love and all the words they didn't need to say, and they stayed like this for a long time. Holding her, a warm glimmer of tranquility swelled within him, because between them, at least one of them had a pulse and a heartbeat.

And then a cold voice cut through space and shocked his heart into overdrive.

"*You've arrived,*" the voice breathed. It swallowed the stars, the darkness, and every fiber of the universe. "*You've completed your journey, Carver. You will wake in the next life, in a world more glorious than you could ever have imagined.*"

Enzo opened his eyes, and an icy-white shape appeared in space, pulling him like a magnet. First, it appeared as a speck. Then, it grew to the size of a meteor. But then the meteor sprouted a face and a cascade of red hair and a gold, pointed crown.

Avoria sat on her throne, Enzo, Cherry, and Rosana accelerating toward the queen. They sped through space faster and faster and faster until *snap!* The Ivory Queen clicked her fingers and the weight of Earth's gravity careened onto Enzo's stomach and his back hit something cold and solid. Light sliced through his eyeballs. He wanted to throw his hands over them, but he hadn't adjusted to the weight of gravity again. The weight of a car pressed him to the ground, slick like marble again. A roof stood over him again, from which two enormous rubies dangled like chandeliers. In one of them, Snow White slept.

Enzo wiggled his fingers and scooted them along the floor, relieved when they found the warm palm of Rosana's hand. Neither of them had the energy to squeeze.

"Welcome to the top floor, darlings." Avoria's voice echoed in his ears. "I cannot tell you how long I've waited for this day."

SOMEWHERE IN THE CITADEL

She dreamed of wolves in every corner of her dreary mind.

Every gust of wind and every breath was a growl.

Every touch was a fiery scratch or a bite that cut to the bone.

They surrounded Tahlia at every angle, and she pleaded for consciousness or the ability to wake up and run. If she couldn't have that, she wished for death.

The world twisted with snarls, growls, and lonely howls, each a bit more territorial than the last. There was definitely more than one creature nearby, and they each wanted blood. The breath of fire permeated the air. It would all be over soon.

Grandma, Grandma, I wish you were here. I need you right here.

She clung to the memory of hot chocolate and strawberries, of crepes and honey, of her grandmother's minty scent . . . of warmth and hugs and stories by the fireplace.

And then something clung to *her*, penetrating her dreams.

Claws grazed her shoulders. Heat breathed down her neck. Fur and the hint of scaly skin wrapped around her wrists.

"Back away, heathens. This one's *mine*." The ashy voice nearly made Tahlia shiver.

She heard a scratch on leathery skin, a series of crunches that curled her stomach, and the pained cry of an animal in pain.

"I have the huntsman," a dreamy voice announced. "Madame Esme cannot tell if he breathes."

"We'll confirm on the ground." A scaly pair of arms scooped Tahlia from the ground. "Belladonna, you and Quasimodo take the girl."

"Jacob! Where are you going?"

"Back up. They need me up there. The Order hasn't finished its fight yet. Get Hansel and Tahlia back to the ground."

CHAPTER
THIRTY-SEVEN

THE CITADEL:
TOP FLOOR

The clicking of heels on marble echoed in Enzo's ears like a clock on a microphone, ticking in slow motion and counting down to his death.

Tock.

Tock.

Tock.

Each step echoed louder than the last. With every breath, Enzo relived a moment of loss from his past year. Hansel abducting his father. Zack succumbing to the shadows in Wonderland. Losing Wayde, Hansel, Tahlia, Mulan, Liam, and Pietro in the Citadel. Each one of their faces burned bright in Enzo's mind, and when he exhaled, he expelled fear from his lungs.

"Welcome," Avoria droned. "I was getting lonely at the top. It's quite a breathtaking view, but what is a queen to do with a beautiful window and no throne to sit on? Have you come to bring it to me?" She stepped into Enzo's view, towering over him with her hands crossed on her belly.

Enzo rolled his eyes. "You ran from me. You're afraid."

"Afraid." Avoria swiveled her head, and her lips spread into a full grin. "Afraid of the little Carver boy and the girl who thought she could live unseen? Speaking of which, how did that work out for you, Rosana? I see you quite plainly now. Your loyalty to this boy is foolish at best, but there's something to be admired about your gumption. And you've even brought *Victor*. He's looking a little frayed, I must say. Poor fool."

Enzo had forgotten about the man lying beside him, arms and legs sprawled at his sides. Master Cherry didn't answer.

"I've been assessing your nightmares," Avoria continued. "Such simple fears. Heights. Chameleon wolves. A lack of gravity. You must wonder whose nightmare you're in now, Carver. Tell me, what did you see in the mirror tonight?"

"Not you." Enzo breathed, the strength oozing back into his fingers and toes. "I've never been afraid of you. I actually feel a little *bad* for you. If somebody had loved you—"

"I was *loved!*" Avoria screamed, the subsequent silence producing a harsh ring in Enzo's eardrums. "I was loved," she repeated more softly.

"Bellamy?" Rosana spoke. "Was there ever any love between you two? Or was your marriage strictly political? Did you *always* terrify him? Because he took that fear to the grave."

"I was loved," Avoria said once more. "Until *he* took it all from me."

Avoria's most recent sentence chilled Enzo to the bone. A deep undertone in her voice made it sound as though there were *two* people speaking.

"And now I'm taking it back," Avoria continued. "I'm taking back control and claiming my new world, so say your goodbyes, *Carver!*"

"*No!*" Enzo snapped back. Fighting the pull of gravity and growing used to his own weight again, he sprang to his feet and whipped his knife out at his side. He and Avoria stood inches apart, so close that her scent overwhelmed him, like a burnt rose soaked in vanilla. He watched her eyes dance with the glare of white marble and her rose-red lips twist into a dark smile. Every movement fueled his fire. "*Forget* it.

There's *no way* you're taking my soul!"

Without wasting a breath, Avoria twisted her arm upward, summoned a long sword into her hands, and spun around. She thrust her momentum into her arm while she turned, and Enzo ducked in time for the blade to whip over his head.

"Enzo!" Rosana pulled herself up and rushed to his side, standing there only a second before she threw herself in front of him and spread her arms apart. "You can't have him!"

Enzo gripped his girlfriend's shoulder. "Move, Rosana!"

"Misguided children," Avoria snarled. "Son of Pinocchio, your tainted soul means less than nothing to me. It's not him I want, little girl."

Enzo felt like he'd been hit in the chest with an enormous snowball, flushing his body with cold pain from the inside out.

Avoria smirked, and she uttered the truth Enzo had not been prepared to hear, even if it was burrowed in the back of his mind for quite some time. "It's *you*, Daughter of Alice."

A half-second later, Rosana wasn't in front of him anymore. Only a vast pocket of air separated Enzo from Avoria. "*No!*"

Enzo flicked his gaze to the enormous gem overhead, not willing to accept what he knew he would see: Rosana's sleeping body suspended in midair.

Instead, the sleeping pod hung empty, and Avoria's lips curled into a sneer.

"*What?*" she breathed. "Where are you, Daughter of Alice? Where is she?" Avoria took one sweeping step forward, closing the gap between her and Enzo with a flick of her arm. She picked Enzo up by his neck, fingernails scraping the tender skin of his throat. She brought his face up to hers. "Where did you put her, Son of Pinocchio?"

Enzo swallowed with some difficulty and choked, "I didn't touch . . . don't . . . know."

A smooth, soft sensation brushed the back of Enzo's hand, and something squeezed his palm. At once, he understood.

She learned to vanish without the cloak.

A beam of pride opened in Enzo's heart and spread warmth through his veins. *Rosana, you surprise me every day.* His expression remained flat as he locked eyes with Avoria.

"Reveal her!" she insisted. "Give her up to the dark before I take you both!"

Enzo thrust his foot up and kicked Avoria in the stomach, causing her to release him and cry out in anger. While she recovered, he raised his knife and aimed for Avoria's chest.

Avoria countered immediately and shoved her sword against his, pushing with enough force that he tumbled onto his back. "You will die, Carver! Alone and helpless!" She raised her arms, and a dark cloud appeared above her head. Her eyes whitened, and the cloud spread so that it covered the entire ceiling. Once it had knitted itself into a full dark cottony web, a thick volley of snow began to fall, covering the marble floor in a glossy film of powder. Avoria kicked off her shoes and spoke with a bite, "You think you can hide from me, Daughter of Alice, but I'll find you in the snow!"

Enzo gritted his teeth and stood again. *Come on, Master Cherry, help me!* Enzo thought. *This was your idea!*

As Enzo thought about his mission, faces and words bounced in and out of his mind.

Believing is only part of the deal. You have to act. People are counting on you, Enzo. A lot of people. He hadn't known Rosana for long when she told him that, but he suspected that was probably when he started to like her. She forced him to be better. She believed in him. So did Snow, Geppetto, Liam, and even Violet. They made Enzo believe.

Enzo looked down at his knife. The blade had grown. In his hands, he held a fully-fledged sword with an ivory handle, cool to the touch.

Turning the blunt edge to the side, Enzo broke into a run. He wasn't properly equipped to run in the snow, so he nearly lost his footing a few times, but he rode into his slips and owned the momentum. Avoria raised her sword to counter, and Enzo angled his blade accordingly. The two sticks of metal clashed with a deafening ring, and for the first time, Enzo could see the fatigue in Avoria's eyes. The lids sagged. The brows wilted. The whites were filled with a milky, translucent shade of pink.

"Getting tired?" Enzo taunted.

"Feeling alone?" Avoria snarled back.

Enzo shook his head. "No. Never."

In the corner of the room, the softest crunching sound nibbled at the air, barely audible but noticeable enough to cause both Enzo and Avoria to turn their heads. A pocket of snow shifted, packed together, and congealed, revealing a lone footprint in the ice.

Enzo's heart sank.

Avoria smirked. "Come out, come out, little red hood girl!"

She waved in the direction of the footprint, and from behind Enzo, a rogue snowball sailed through the air and over his shoulder, smacking Avoria in the head and bursting into little white flakes that her blood-red hair quickly absorbed. She whirled around, and fire danced in her eyes.

In an instant, the snow shifted, careening sideways and doubling in volume. Enzo threw one hand over his eyes to shield them from the makeshift blizzard, and with the other arm, he blocked an attack from Avoria. She attempted to cleave him as she glided across the room looking for an indication of where Rosana hid.

"You're not going to find her!" Enzo declared. "She's too clever for you. She can spend ages under your nose, and you'll never even *smell* her."

Avoria attacked again.

Cling! Clang! Clack! Enzo parried, counterattacked, and whacked the Ivory Queen in the shoulder, opening a thin wound. Avoria danced away and resumed her hunt.

"Come back here!" Enzo ordered. "Come back and face me! Do I scare you or something? Don't you want the world to see how high and mighty you are? Fight me, you *coward*!" He swung again, and the blade sank below Avoria's armpit. He thought he should have been satisfied by the sensation of putting blade to bone. Instead, it surprised him. He froze, his heart hammering his ribcage. "Fight *back!*"

Avoria screamed, a haunting wail of pain laced with anger, and the snow doubled yet again. The flakes became a barrage of thin ice crystals pummeling his back, and numbness bit at his fingers. He yanked on his sword handle, removing the tip from Avoria's skin, and then he locked his gaze on the center of her back.

Enzo made a mental calculation of where her heart should be.

A shape appeared in the center of the room, an air phantom outlined by a thin veil of snow. It sprinted toward Avoria, leaving a trail of footprints along the way, and then Avoria's hand shot out and met the invisible shape where its neck might have been.

Rosana appeared, pale and frigid in Avoria's grip, and the Ivory Queen lifted the girl in the air.

"I've found you."

Time expanded. The next three seconds bloomed in a pocket of eternity.

Rosana's gaze flicked over to Enzo. Her eyes had never looked greener or more beautiful. Her smile never looked warmer.

Oh god no, Enzo thought, his heart thundering even in his kneecaps. "Rosana!" He sprang into a feral, wild leap, the tip of his sword making a shimmering beeline for Avoria's back.

"Enzo," Rosana whispered. "Love you."

The sword tip pierced Avoria's dress and then a thin layer of skin, exposing a rivulet of crimson liquid that screamed its existence against the white of the snow, and—

Boom.

Thunder. The floor shook. Enzo lost both his balance and his grip.

And Rosana disappeared in a blink. This time, it wasn't an act of her volition. She appeared less than a second later in the snow-capped ruby suspended in the air, and Avoria began to glow.

A sunny luminescence burst from Avoria's skin, throwing Enzo off her back like the repelling force of a magnet.

Enzo hit the ground with his face beneath the floating gem, forced to watch both Rosana's and Snow's shrink, shrivel, and blacken at an alarming rate. As the gems' sizes diminished, Enzo's spirits faded as well. All the light that once kept him fighting transferred to Avoria, who grew brighter by the second until the rubies were the size of an apple.

Rosana.

The last snowflake fell from the ceiling, and the clouds cleared away. The snowflake landed on Enzo's palm, and his finger twitched. He thought that might have been the last of his energy and will to live, snuffed out in the twitch of a finger. His joints went cold and numb, and his gaze rested on no point in particular.

The rubies became black gems the size of Enzo's thumb, and then they dropped from the sky and into Enzo's palm.

Rosana.

Enzo wanted to scream, to curse Avoria's name and make sure the world heard his grief. But he didn't possess the strength to work his lungs anymore. Even his inner voice could only whisper.

I failed.

I failed to keep my promise to Liam.

I failed Rosana.

But I won't fail the world. I'm not finished yet.

Enzo used his fists to push himself onto his knees, too numb to say a single word as he brandished his grandfather's knife. His own knife—and the sword it had become—was nowhere to be seen. He thought his gloves were supposed to call it back to him, but there were rips in the palms and frayed strings at the fingertips. He narrowed his eyes at Avoria and wiped the blood off his lip. As Avoria turned to confront him, he stabbed Geppetto's knife into the marble floor.

His energy poured from the knife like water from a hose. His joints grew sore, and from the ground, seven patches of marble bubbled like water. Then, ten-foot stone replicas of his mother, Pietro, Rosana, Zack, Wendy, Alice, and Snow White climbed out of the floor and charged the Ivory Queen. In the drowsy haze that sapped Enzo's clarity, the seven stone warriors looked like gods and goddesses straight from Olympus, and even Avoria screamed in terror when they thundered toward her.

Avoria conjured a sword and made sporadic chips at the attacking monuments, dodging and running between hacks. Enzo wanted nothing more than to stand and go after her, but his bones were like peanut butter. His neck felt heavy, and his eyelids drooped . . .

"Drink."

A single drop of liquid touched Enzo's lips, and the energy filled his body like a waterfall. He looked up to see Master Cherry cork a vial, make a fist, and say, "Let's finish her."

They moved together, and by the time they reached her, Avoria whittled the seven statues to broken bits of marble all over the floor, though the struggle left her in bad shape. Her hair clumped in sweaty tangles, her skin sagged beneath her eyes, and blood ran down her lip.

Dagger in hand, Enzo ran and made a calculated leap toward the Ivory Queen.

Avoria whipped around, thrust out her foot, and kicked Enzo to the floor, the impact a fire in his bones. With another spin, she threw Master Cherry into the wall.

Avoria clicked across the hall and stood over Enzo, her luminous face looking like it had been chiseled from clay, her eyes black sockets filled with malice. "You and the Order put up a good fight, Carver. Generations have attempted to thwart me, and only you have come close enough to disturb my sleep. Never let it be said that I do not *commend* you." She smirked, her red hair a storm of fire billowing behind her. "But Lady Fortune smiles upon *me*, Son of Pinocchio. You lose."

A black shadow moved behind Avoria, and it took Enzo a second to realize Master Cherry was back on his feet and approaching the Ivory Queen from behind.

Help me, Enzo pleaded silently. *Save us, Master Cherry. Finish this.*

Avoria raised a knee and drove her heel into Enzo's chest. Pain exploded through his nerves.

"That's quite enough from you, Avoria." Master Cherry stretched out his arm and Avoria went stiff, her back straight as a board and her expression hollow. "You've fought most admirably, but your time is at its end." The scientist jerked his arm back as if pulling an invisible thread, and Enzo watched in horror as a bone-white substance in the shape of a heart rocketed out of Avoria's back. There was no blood or any other indication of gore, but the heart pumped and pulsed as though it were nature-made. It flew into Cherry's open palm, and he closed his fingers around the pumping valves.

Enzo froze. *It's over,* he thought. *Is it really over?*

As if to answer, a ghostly cackling sound poured from the heart. An icy, airy laugh filled the air with darkness, and the heart pounded faster in Cherry's fingers.

Crush it, Enzo thought. He stretched his hand out and croaked, "Master Cherry! Destroy it!"

Master Cherry held the heart up to his face, tilting and turning and studying it as though he were inspecting an apple for bruises.

Avoria hung frozen in a sort of trance until Master Cherry gave a careless wave of his free hand, and the Ivory Queen collapsed in a broken, bloodless heap on the ground, a messy tangle of ivory limbs. She didn't even look human anymore but, instead, had taken on the glossy complexion of a life-sized doll.

The war appeared to be over. Countless people had waited for this day, and yet something in Master Cherry's expression put a dam on Enzo's elation and relief. The casual upturn of Cherry's lips. The dark mirrors in his eyes. Something wasn't right.

"Master Cherry," Enzo said, his voice a little more solid. "Destroy the heart! Or give it to me."

Master Cherry didn't react.

"Can you at least help me up?" Enzo continued. "*Master Cherry.*"

"What is this strange feeling?" Master Cherry breathed. "This . . . power?"

Enzo's mind reeled. "Don't let it corrupt you! Break it!"

"Oh, I face no danger of corruption, Son of Pinocchio. In fact, I'm feeling more myself than ever before." Master Cherry stalked over to Enzo and placed a booted heel on his chest, right where Avoria had stomped on him only moments before. The nerves were still tender, pulsing where the man pressed his weight. "I've never felt power quite like this before!"

Enzo had fought this war with one assumption: Queen Avoria was the ultimate evil. Staring up at the pulsing white organ in Master Cherry's hand, Enzo lost touch with every fact he had been sure of since the day he left home. Was the sky really blue? Did one plus two equal three?

With his free hand, Master Cherry removed his hood, his orange irises gleaming. "How I longed to correct the course I set us on for so many years. But now!" He held the heart over his head like a trophy. "Now I see the darkness for its beauty! I've never felt anything quite like this before. Only a fool would waste this vessel. I, Antonio Vinci, Avoria's creator, will finish what my beautiful puppet could not accomplish on her own."

Enzo reached beside him and took Avoria's hand. Warmth still coursed through her fingers, but there was no movement. He looked at Cherry, still struggling to twist his mind around the man's words and actions. "What have you done? What is this?"

"This is victory!" Cherry declared. "This is the beginning of our glorious future. It is time for the world to accept me as the Master Carver."

CHAPTER THIRTY-EIGHT

THE CITADEL:
TOP FLOOR

Enzo blinked, hardly daring to believe the old man's actions. "What are you talking about? Give me the heart, Master Cherry!"

Master Cherry grinned, tossing the heart up and down. "Your grandfather was an ambitionless man. Lazy. Tired. He had all the talent in the world, and he wasted it daydreaming about the day he'd welcome a son into his home. After Geppetto embarrassed me and stole my glory by fashioning himself a living boy when all I had was a *table leg*, I set out to build my own puppet, never knowing what she would become one day." Cherry tossed the heart into the air and caught it again. "Of course, I needed some help. Miss Esmeralda has been so gracious to predict the future and steer my fate in the right direction, without either of us knowing the impact she had. She found the family that raised Avoria into royalty. And how I missed her! She never knew her connection to me, even when she hired me to help her stop the giants. At that time, all I wanted was to be a good father."

Enzo's mind reeled. "Then how did you let it all go wrong?"

"Kaa was supposed to cure her of her ailments, but little did I know I had set up the conditions that would bring her to her full potential. And since that day, I watched her from the sidelines, the underground, learning her weaknesses and fears, occasionally crossing paths with the Order of the Bell and wondering how I might stop her. I wore many faces . . . masquerading as Robin Hood for years, as Dr. Frankenstein, any face that would get me closer to shutting her down.

"But now I see the real genius of my work! With just the right alchemy, I took a puppet and made her the most powerful woman in all the worlds. The ultimate servant to collect souls for me. The souls of the young and pure and gifted. The souls that would knit together and make *this* for me. Who knew darkness could be stitched together from a few pounds of ivory, the shadows of Wonderland, and a drop of snake venom?" Cherry held the heart high above his head. "*This* is going to make an empire, a world where people know Antonio Vinci, the Master Carver."

Enzo looked back at Avoria's lifeless body, suddenly overcome with pity for the woman. "She could've been good if you hadn't messed with magic you didn't understand! All this pain and destruction the worlds have seen . . . you started it, and you didn't even know it! You broke her!"

"She didn't even have a *soul*," Cherry argued. "She was a well-constructed shell incapable of feeling a thing. A mere projection, unlike your father, created from living, breathing oak."

"Was Zack a shell?" Enzo asked. "After you started taking my family and friends and their souls, were they shells? They feel as much as anybody else. All you took from them was the ability to fly, or carve the future, or whatever it is that they didn't even need in the first place. Avoria could have been good. Happy. Free. And yet you separated families. You ruined lives. You drove her husband to imprison people out of fear. You drove princes and kings to murder!" His mind spun. "Who could respect you after all this?"

"After I created a heart? The heart of an empire?" Cherry sneered. "Boy, after all your travels, you've still seen less than nothing. This is the single greatest breakthrough in the worlds of art *and* in science. This is the heart of our *future*. Who won't remember my name?"

"If you were really that great, you wouldn't have needed to go through all this trouble," Enzo argued.

"The trouble is the beauty of the art," Cherry answered. "Who else could pull strings this masterfully? Certainly not the great Geppetto, may Lady Fortune rest his soul. His own son's soul is trapped in *this* heart, all the more extraordinary for the memories and hardships locked inside it. For you see, a heart cannot *truly* exist without the pain and suffering you all experienced. If I had simply carved away at a block of ivory and trapped eight souls inside it with no *embellishments*, then that wouldn't be a heart at all. It would be nothing but a sad, hollow shell, like my dear sweet Avoria here." Cherry reached down and patted the Ivory Queen's head. "I really am going to miss her, for what it's worth. But now I see the worlds for what they really are! These worlds are my stages, and you are an inconsequential marionette. You can leave now and wait for the fireworks to start, little Carver boy. I'm sorry you couldn't save your family, but like your grandfather, you were destined to fail." Cherry turned on his heel and walked away, heading toward the pedestal in the front of the room.

"Don't you talk about my grandfather ever again!" Enzo snapped. "How dare you breathe his name when he had nothing but love for you!"

A set of footsteps pounded into the room and Liam and Mulan rushed to Enzo's side, filling him with a temporary moment of relief.

"Enzo!" Mulan cried. "We're here! We're here beside you!" She clutched her knees and caught her breath. "Rosana was right. No matter what illusions fall on this place, it's finite. We'll always find our way back to you in here. They can't keep us from you."

Liam knelt beside the queen and felt her neck for a pulse. "Is it done?"

"Not quite," Enzo said coldly. He raised an arm and pointed at the cloaked man in the front of the room, whose hands rested comfortably at his waist with a serene, calm expression on his face. "It's *him*. Master Cherry let the heart corrupt him."

Cherry laughed. "The heart is returning to its true owner. And now

I suppose the Order of the Bell means to apprehend me?"

Enzo curled his fingers into a pair of fists. "Drop it, Master Cherry! You'll break this whole world."

"Hmm." The old man laughed. "Contrariwise, I'm creating this world. I always found it rather dull. Really, boy. Weren't you bored before Avoria graced you with her presence?"

"Snake. We *will* stop you!" Liam declared. "For our friends and our loved ones and our children's children, we will always stop you!"

"You would seek to hinder the advancement of civilization," Cherry said. "You would stand in the way of art and science to preserve your own self-righteous values."

"We would stand for what's right for *all*," Mulan corrected, "and we would have justice for the lives you ruined for your own gain."

"So you choose to rebel against the world's greatest puppet master." Cherry frowned at the heart in his hand and gave the group a knowing smirk. "Good luck with that."

A deafening, feral cry shook the Citadel, and Jacob Isaac Holmes dropped from the ceiling, knocking Master Cherry onto his elbows. The ivory heart skidded out of his hands and rolled toward the window, springing the rest of the room into chaos.

"*Grab that heart!*" Enzo sprinted down the hall, hot on his friends' heels.

Meanwhile, Cherry raised an arm, and Jacob soared off the madman's back, flying upside down to the opposite side of the room and colliding with the door. With a subtle jerk of the wrist, Cherry brought the heart back into his right hand. In his left, a tall ivory staff appeared. He used the end as leverage to pry himself back to his feet, and with a mighty swing, he struck Enzo and Liam back onto the floor. Stars and ugly black spots danced in front of Enzo as the pain shot through his back.

Cherry turned around and walked to the window. With a soft push, he let it swing open. A frigid wind drifted into the Citadel, fanning

Cherry's cloak out in a sort of funnel behind him and raising little white bumps all over Enzo's skin. Television screens descended from the ceiling, some offering views of the crowd on the first floor—which had stepped outside—and the others projecting their new ruler's face.

"People of the New World!" Master Cherry announced. "You've been invited here tonight to celebrate your new leader. I regret to announce to you all that Queen Avoria has fallen. She was slain only minutes ago by a boy who would seek to bar your entrance to the future. But fear not! I, Antonio Vinci, have risen to take her place and usher you into a new era where all is perfect and wonderful. New World Prime will see you all be happier, healthier, and worry free. You needn't swear your loyalty to me. I already know you'll act according to your heart's desires." Cherry held the heart out in front of him with one hand. The staff disappeared from his other hand, and a tiny crystal vial appeared in its place. A painting of a moonflower adorned one side of the vial.

Gretel's tears. Enzo's blood boiled beneath his skin.

Cherry uncorked the vial with his teeth and spat the cork over his shoulder. "Let me be the first to welcome you to New World Prime. And may you all live happily . . . ever . . ." He tipped the vial's contents over the heart, and a single drop of clear liquid splashed the organ with a steamy sizzle. "*After.*"

The Citadel rumbled like an earthquake from the core, and then everything went dark.

CHAPTER
THIRTY-NINE

THE WORLD BEYOND

When Enzo woke up again, he was all alone.

He recognized the checkered pattern of the ground, though the tile no longer sparkled or flashed with every step. Time and war had corroded it with blood and footprints.

This is Wondertown!

Enzo looked up. The floating island hung high above the city, but wisps of fog and thick sheaths of cobweb masked the cliffs. Where the crystal waterfall used to flow, drops of black oil and green slime trickled down the side of the dry ground, threatening to spill onto the castle below.

The crackle and grind of wheels on dirt filled the air, and Enzo watched in horror as a chariot lolled down the street, pulled by three people he recognized. The first was Matthew Hadinger, shirtless and starved and no longer wearing his trademark cap. His gaunt face twisted into a pained squint as he trudged down the street, the soles of his boots flapping and exposing a blackened heel with every step. Beside him, Rosana and her mother pulled their own sets of reins hooked around their shoulders.

"*Rosana!*" Enzo screamed. He broke into a run and threw himself in front of the carriage, spreading his arms apart to expose himself to the drivers: Cornelius Redding and a beautiful blonde woman Enzo could only guess had once been the Queen of Hearts. "Stop!"

To Enzo's horror, Rosana, Alicia, and Matt didn't acknowledge the command. They simply continued to pull, gazes to the ground and tears staining their chins.

"I said *hurry up!*" Cornelius took a whip and lashed it on Matt's bare back, causing the old King of Spades to clench his teeth and wince.

"Let them go!" Enzo ordered. "Rosana, stop. You don't have to do this. Rosana! Look at me!" He reached out and touched her shoulders, but she had no reaction. He tapped Alicia and then Matt. Nobody acknowledged Enzo.

No, he thought. *I've failed everyone. This is our new reality. This is our new world.*

Rosana.

She was a slave now. She existed to cater to the King and Queen of Hearts.

A tear slid down Enzo's cheek, and a sob choked him from within. He wiped the tear away and followed the carriage down the road, stepping in front every now and then to take Rosana's hand or brush her cheek. "I'm so sorry, Rosana. This isn't the ending you were meant to have. Alice. Matt. I'm so sorry."

The castle doors swung open, and the carriage moved to the entrance. Enzo followed the coach all the way into the building, but when the doors closed behind him, the carriage vanished.

What?

Enzo did a full turn, and when he faced forward again, the scene changed. He wasn't standing inside the castle of Wondertown anymore. He stood in the Woodlands of Florindale.

These Woodlands, however, had a different feel than the Woodlands Enzo had grown accustomed to. There wasn't a patch of green to be found. Dark, thorny vines snaked along the ground and embraced dead trees. Spiders of assorted sizes scuttled through the air, twisting and writhing on their webs.

"Hello, chum."

Enzo turned and faced a crumbling cottage that appeared in his path, where a familiar body stood in the doorway in raggedy clothes. Enzo embraced the man immediately. "Liam! You can see me?"

"Of course I *see* you." Liam pulled away and wrinkled his brows. "I hardly know who *you* are though. How might you know me?"

The glimmer of hope in Enzo's chest faded away. *Of course. It would have been stupid to think things were in order here.* "We were friends in another world." *More like another life.* "Prince Liam, I'm Enzo."

Liam shook Enzo's hand and chuckled. "Prince? That's kind of you, chum, but I'm more of a pauper. Stars, you look ravished! Can I help you with something? I'm afraid I don't have much to give, but if it's food you need, I know a lovely lady who makes divine apple pies."

Enzo gently kicked a rock at his feet. "You wouldn't be talking about Snow White, would you?"

Liam flinched, putting a finger to his lips. "*Stars* no! Never her. Mister Enzo, please don't invoke her name again. I'm talking about Helga, the woman with the candy house. People are rapid to pass judgment on her, but I'd sooner eat from her kitchen than from that evil queen's any day."

"But . . ." *You married her.* Enzo swallowed his words, suspecting they would do more harm than good. "Look, uh, Liam, I'm just trying to find my way around here. Is there any chance you can show me out of these woods?"

"Couldn't say." Liam picked a spider off his shoulder and flicked it onto the ground. "All my life, I've never been out of here myself. For all I know, these woods go on forever."

"Really? Aren't you interested in finding out what else is out there?"

"I've always wondered. But the queen will have my head if I put one toe out of bounds."

"*Who goes there?*" a harsh female voice called. "Who intrudes on my Woodlands without my permission?"

Enzo turned his head to see the strangest sight: Snow White marching into the woods in an iron-gray spiderweb dress. She wielded a jagged staff with a crystal orb on top of it, and a small group flanked her at either side. Violet's wings were black and crackling with red lines of fire. Hansel's hair had grown out, and a bushy beard concealed the lower half of his face. He squeezed the handle of a musket in his fingers while on Snow's other side. Mulan sauntered along, tapping the head of a wooden hammer against her palm. Merlin hovered behind her, cocooned in a dark aura that turned his eyes red.

"You need to go," Liam insisted, "before they spot you. The Master Carver has required the Order of the Bell to kill intruders on sight. That means *you*."

Enzo's feet felt like they were made of lead. He couldn't stand seeing his old friends like this. He wanted to call out to them and sort things out—make them remember who they were meant to be.

But he didn't have to say a word.

"There!" Merlin cried. The group halted and fixed their gazes on Enzo. "You, boy! Stop! You are trespassing and violating The Carver's decree!"

"This is not good," Liam whispered.

Enzo put his hands up. "Merlin! Snow, everyone. It's me. I'm Enzo."

In response, Hansel raised his musket.

"*Run!*" Liam seized Enzo's collar, and the two sprinted through the dark with the Order of the Bell on their heels. "This way, my friend! Don't fall behind!"

Bullets tapped the ground by Enzo's heels. Dark pulses of energy stung his back. Mulan cackled like a hyena. He pumped his legs as fast as they would let him until he wove his way out of the Woodlands and confronted open land.

"Where do we go?" Enzo asked. "There's nowhere to hide!"

Liam pointed to a small hill where patches of grass had withered to a dead shade of brown. "There's a mineshaft around that hill. I don't know your mission, but I will hold the Order back for you. Light be with you, sir!"

Enzo had no time to protest when the shots thundered and Liam crumbled to the ground. Enzo booked it for the hill, swiveled around the corner, and then dove into the mineshaft without looking twice.

Darkness and the cold air sliced at Enzo's face until gravity shifted and he tumbled in midair and reversed direction. He fell *up*, and the mineshaft disintegrated into dust all around him. He zoomed through bright, open sky, watching Florindale Square recede into little matchbox houses below him. With another midair twist, Enzo found himself shifting into an upright, standing position again, and his feet touched the hard stone ground of Clocher de Pierre.

A hundred stories below, the houses and pubs and buildings began to transform like Lego structures, growing taller, wider, and more complex, adding smokestacks, gears, levers, pulleys, and nuts and bolts galore. Tiny cottages became dirty skyscrapers with busted windows. The bells above Enzo's head became bits and pieces of a broken airplane, fused into a shapeless blob of metal. That was when the smoke assaulted Enzo's nostrils. He looked down to see flames engulfing the base of the tower, and before he knew it, he fell again. He squeezed his eyes shut and plummeted into the hot, orange bed of fire, only it didn't burn him. It chilled him. It intercepted him and framed every inch of his body.

Enzo opened his eyes. He was under water.

Crocodiles circled in a clockwise fashion while an aquamantula pulsed around above him. Below, Master Cherry appeared as a merman with a dark tail and a silver trident. Rising almost to Enzo's toes, Master Cherry sneered.

"Welcome to your new world, Carver," Cherry said, bubbles exploding from his mouth with every word.

Enzo kicked and his heel connected with Cherry's forehead.

Without wasting a second, Enzo swam upward and seized one of the sea spider's legs. The aquamantula jerked and rocketed to the surface of the water in time for the crocodiles to converge and bump heads in the center of their circle.

When Enzo broke the surface, he met the shores of Neverland, which was thoroughly corroded and covered in ashes. He let go of the aquamantula and clawed at the ash until he was able to stand on the ground again. Then he sprinted into the dark rainforest, throwing his gaze over his shoulder every few steps to see if Master Cherry emerged from the water. As far as Enzo could tell, Cherry never came up.

Enzo stopped and panted for a minute, desperate to catch his breath again. "I'm in a nightmare," he breathed. "A living nightmare."

"Nightmare?"

The shadow of a boy descended from the dark treetops and landed softly on the ground. His body followed and touched down next to his silhouette. The child and his shadow mirrored each other, hands on hips with daggers at the ready.

Enzo gasped. There was something familiar about this kid's eyes, hair, and even that pose he was doing with his wooden sword. "Pietro."

"Who's Pietro?" the boy scoffed. "I'm Peter Pan. Who are *you?*"

"I'm . . ." Enzo swallowed and shook his head. "Just a visitor. Hey, Peter, do you happen to know a boy named Zack? Or a girl named Wendy?"

The shadow scratched its chin while Peter paced back and forth with his arms folded. "Hmm. I know your Wendy. Never heard of a Zack before, though."

Enzo's heart sank. In this world, Zack didn't even exist anymore. Peter Pan had never grown up.

"Wendy's mad at me," Peter continued. "She thinks I'm bad in fluents and called me a big stupid. Do you think I'm a big stupid?"

Enzo took a knee and beckoned the boy to come closer. Young Pietro took a step forward, and his shadow followed. "I think someday, you can become one of the best, bravest, most wonderful men this world will ever see. And Wendy is going to grow old with you, and the two of you are going to love every minute of each other's company. But you're going to love your son even more." Enzo chuckled under his breath. "Does any of this make sense to you, Peter?"

Peter shook his head. "No."

"Good," Enzo decided. "You'll figure it all out, though. I promise."

Peter tapped his chin for a minute. Enzo could see the gears whirring in the boy's head, bringing his eyes into a squint. Peter leaned forward and whispered, "I'm in a nightmare, too."

Enzo's eyes widened. "You are?"

"Yes," Peter whispered back. "I keep hearing a heartbeat. It's coming from the island. I'm afraid to go look for it because it might come from a monster. And I'm here all alone, so I can't kill the monsters by myself."

An alarm blared in Enzo's mind. *A heartbeat.* "Where did you last hear the heartbeat, Peter?" he asked. "It's crucial that you try to remember. Can you think really hard for me?"

But Peter didn't have to think. As soon as Enzo finished speaking, the pulse sounded from deep within the rainforest. Like a bass drum. Like bootheels on a hardwood floor. *Buh-boom. Buh-boom. Buh-boom.*

Peter aimed a finger into the darkness. "There."

Enzo swallowed a lump in his throat and reached for his carving knife. "Stay here."

He set off deeper into the rainforest, and Peter's shadow followed, leaping from tree to tree like a spider monkey.

Avoria's heart is the key to finishing all of this, Enzo thought. *All my friends' souls are trapped in there, but I can set them free. It's what Carvers do.*

When Enzo didn't think his legs would carry him anymore, a wooden trunk appeared in a beautiful clearing kissed by the sun. Flowers circled a spring of crystal waters, and the chest bobbed up and down in the center. Enzo had no doubt that what he needed lay inside that trunk. Beneath the bronze lock, he could hear the wood pulsing.

He reached over the flowers and fished the trunk out of the water. The chest was heavier than he expected, but it also sounded quite hollow. Enzo could hear a single object rolling around in the confines.

Enzo stabbed the lock, opened the trunk, and sure enough, the glossy-white heart pulsed in front of him, beats growing louder and more frantic since the organ was exposed. He put out his hand and prepared to grab the infernal entity, but then the ground stretched in front of him and the heart receded deeper into the forest as if on the world's fastest conveyor belt.

"No!" Enzo shouted. "No!" *I was so close!*

A cabin sprang up from the ground between Enzo and the heart, and the scent of cherry cobbler drifted in smoky wisps from its open window. But it wasn't *any* cherry cobbler.

Mom's cherry cobbler.

Enzo pushed the cabin door open, afraid of what he'd find.

"Mom?" he called. "Dad?"

The tarty smell disappeared, and a faint groan sounded from behind a closed door in the room.

"Dad?"

Enzo rushed to the door and pushed it open to find himself in his father's bedroom in their Virginia home. He lay stiff on the bed, straight, and he had turned entirely to wood, his veins replaced with the lines and rings of an oak tree.

"Dad!" Enzo cried. "Dad, I'm here. Can you hear me?"

"*Uhn . . . I . . . luf . . . you.*"

Enzo ran to the bed and fell to his knees, unsure of how much more his heart could take. He grabbed his father's wooden hand, breathing in the scents of cedar and oak, and closed the smooth fingers over his own. "Dad," he choked. "I love you, too, Dad. So much." Enzo kissed his father's hand. "I'm not going to let anyone take you this time, okay? However this ends, I'm here with you."

He sat like that for a few minutes, quietly crying and cursing his new hell. Did *anything* turn out right in the end? Did any of his journey make a difference for the better?

A shadow fell across his father's bed, and Enzo looked up to see Lord Bellamy standing on the other side, hands clasped behind his back.

"Hello, boy."

Enzo tilted his head. *Bellamy?* "What are you doing here?"

"You already know," Bellamy answered. "You remember what happens next. Somebody has to take your father away from you."

Of course.

"No," Enzo snapped. "Nobody's taking my father anywhere. Nobody's touching my family ever again."

"And you'll fight for them?" Bellamy asked.

"Always." Enzo dove across the bed and seized Bellamy's coat, plunging fingers into every pocket until finding a long dart with a red tip. *Just what I was looking for.* Enzo rolled it in his palm and took one last look at his father. "I'll see you again soon, Dad," he said. Enzo stabbed the dart into the side of his own neck.

The walls vanished. The house disappeared. The ground between Enzo and the heart snapped back together like a spring, and the whole time, the trees burst and shredded themselves infinitely into dust. The forest ground hardened into a marble floor, and a roof appeared hundreds of feet above Enzo's head.

He'd returned to the Citadel with the ivory heart.

Master Cherry stood there, too, and four hands clutched the pulsing organ.

His eyes were black sockets, and his lips were in a flat, pale line across his face.

"So your dive into loneliness wasn't enough to kill you," he mused. "Well then, I suppose I must end you myself."

Enzo had never punched another living soul until this moment, when the walls spun and contorted around him. He took one hand off the heart and struck the madman across the jaw.

A satisfying crack sounded in Cherry's bones, and then he jammed his bootheel into Enzo's stomach. "*Down*, wretched boy!"

Despite the blunt, hot pain that exploded through Enzo's nerves, he kept a firm hold on the heart and stayed upright. "I will *never* back down."

Cherry kicked again, and this time Enzo couldn't maintain his grip. He slipped and hit the ground headfirst while Cherry towered above him. "You *weak*, pathetic—"

Enzo jammed his knife straight down into the toe of Master Cherry's boot, eliciting a guttural scream from the man's throat. When Cherry swung his other foot out, Enzo removed his knife and log-rolled away until he could pull himself back to his feet. Then he wiped the blood from his blade and pointed its tip at his enemy.

"Stay back," he warned. "There are worse places I can stab you."

Master Cherry limped across the room, a cold-blooded scowl painted on his lips. "You stupid boy," he growled. "I know better than to accept your empty threat. You're far too nice for your own good, Enzo. Arrogant, perhaps. Bull-headed, yes. But you wouldn't dream of harming one of your elders. Least of all with a tiny blade! Come now. Accept your fate. Yield!"

A shadow stirred behind Master Cherry's back, and Enzo stepped forward and swiped the knife in front of him as a sort of warning. "I swear I'll do it."

"Ha!" Cherry laughed, waved his arm, and an invisible force knocked Enzo back on his side. Stars danced in his vision. "It's already done, boy! Look around you! Look at all the graves your comrades will have to dig in the snow. Look at the glorious new world I've created, which Geppetto will never get to see. And in case you missed it, stupid boy, you're alone. I've won."

Enzo swallowed and tasted blood. He wiped his forehead, climbed back to his knees, white-hot anger brewing in his veins.

"Why waste your energy?" Cherry asked. "I am powerful. You are *weak*." He waved his arm again, and Enzo slid back several feet as if carried by a gust of wind.

Enzo plunged his knife into the ground and held on with both hands. *Get up*, he told himself. He gritted his teeth. "*You're* weak," he said. "You're just an old man blinded by the dark. That blindness? That arrogance? That's what's gonna be the end of you."

"By your hand? Oh, poor me!" Master Cherry dropped his jaw in a look of mock defeat. "The great and powerful Master Cherry, thwarted by a teenage boy and his pocket knife. He's going to be the end of me!"

"No, he isn't," a male voice sounded behind Master Cherry. "*We* are."

With that, the tip of a blade burst through the front of Cherry's chest, crimson and thin.

He stared down at it in fascination, and Enzo froze.

After a long pause, the puppet master wheezed, "Long live The Carver."

Cherry fell to his knees, revealing Liam—the prince, not the pauper—standing tall behind the old man, and then his skull smacked the ground. Liam removed his sword from Cherry's back, wiped the blood off, and then collapsed beside the fallen enemy.

CHAPTER FORTY

THE CITADEL: TOP FLOOR

There was no noise for a very long time.

Cherry didn't move.

Neither did Liam.

Enzo could hardly dare to believe the battle was over, but the man in the black coat didn't breathe anymore. The life drifted out of him like air from a balloon until he was nothing more than a statue. Enzo made sure of it with a few nudges, using the toe of his boot to poke at Master Cherry's chest. When Enzo turned away, every step he took sounded like thunder in the hall. Finally, he slumped down next to Avoria and mopped his forehead with the back of his hand.

He rested his hand on the woman's shoulder.

"For everything he put you through," he said, "I'm sorry. There must've been more within you somewhere." Enzo closed Avoria's eyes with two fingers and rested her hands across her chest.

"It's done, chum."

Enzo jumped when he heard Liam's voice. The prince stirred and sat upright, palms against his eyelids and knees bent in front of him.

"It is done. All of it. Cherry. Avoria." Enzo buried his forehead in his knees. "The world as I knew it."

Liam stumbled to his feet and pressed a palm against Enzo's back.

He might as well have pressed a button that released a reservoir of tears, and before Enzo could stop himself, he was sobbing uncontrollably on the prince's shoulder.

For Rosana.

For Pietro and Wendy and Zack.

For the friends he'd made across the worlds, only to lose them to Cherry's hellish war.

He wept for his parents.

For Geppetto.

For himself.

"It's all right," Liam whispered. "It's quite all right."

As much as Enzo appreciated the kindness, he knew things were *never* going to be all right again. Nothing was ever going to be the same, or even remotely okay. Liam was all Enzo had left, and the worst part of all was that Liam would never be the same. He killed another man. He also lost the love of his life after all they'd been through to hold onto each other. Enzo could hardly imagine the prince as the same man he'd met in Maryland. It would have been better if he were the pauper—the Liam in Cherry's world who forgot who he was.

It would've been for the best, because Enzo's curse was entirely different. He would remember every detail and more for the rest of his life. Every face would remain carved into his consciousness within arm's reach. Every kiss with Rosana would hang forever on his lips, forever tasted but never shared again. Every word, every step, every life he encountered would linger like a ghost in the forefront of his memory, and nothing that would happen from this point on would be worth remembering.

Enzo didn't have the will or the strength to move.

"Somebody has to write it all down," he said with a sniffle. "Someone needs to make sure their stories are told. That our friends are remembered."

Liam tilted his head. Redness coated his eyes.

"People need to know about Snow White's kindness and goodness and Pietro's youth and Mulan's bravery. Hansel's redemption. My parents' spirits." Every name Enzo spoke was a knife to his soul. "Somebody needs to make sure they're never forgotten."

The two men sat in silence for a while. Every few minutes, a shiver would run through Enzo's bones and he would pull his knees against his chest, hoping if he curled into a tight enough ball, he might disappear altogether. There was nowhere else to go except to stop existing . . . to go away in a swift cut to black, like the end of some primetime TV serial that would never get renewed. As for Master Cherry—Antonio Vinci, Victor Frankenstein, Robin Hood, or *whatever* his real name truly was—his corrupted final vision would air forever, long after his body decayed. Enzo wondered if Cherry really *would* deteriorate after all the strange magic and science experiments he performed. Would he rot the same as everyone else, or would he crumble into ashes and billow away like some phantom in the wind?

Or would he lie forever? A broken puppet on his own stage?

Enzo's mind spiraled so deeply into the terror that he jumped when Liam spoke in the softest tone Enzo had heard in days.

"You think one should preserve our friends' memories? Carve their stories into the world?" Liam whispered. He raised his arm, pointing over Enzo's shoulder. "Maybe it can be you."

Enzo blinked the tears out of his eyes and forced himself to turn around and follow Liam's line of sight. When the tears cleared away and the blur in Enzo's vision subsided, he froze.

The window was still open, cold wind spilling in from the hells beyond, but a single bright object stood out against the dark sky.

A fairy.

The golden fairy.

Tinker Bell drifted peacefully through the window, her pace serene and leisurely as if she had gone out for a casual flight. In her tiny hands, she carried Avoria's ivory heart.

No way.

"Sorry to arrive late," Tinker Bell said, her breaths forced and heavy. She flitted over to Enzo, and her feet touched his lap. She offered Enzo the heart, a calm expression on her face. "I flew *miles* to catch this for you."

Enzo resisted the urge to hug the fairy, afraid that he might crush her in his arms. "You caught it?"

Tinker Bell nodded. "It seemed important. Like the universe required me to save it. I think it's because when I hear it beating, I hear somebody I should know. Or maybe somebody I *do* know, from another life or another world. It's like remembering somebody I never met, and I miss them." She looked down at her tiny feet and sighed. Her breath ruffled her bangs. "You can take it, Enzo. I won't let it corrupt you. Remember, there's fairy dust in your bones. The light lives in you. I'm sorry. I'm not making much sense, am I?"

Enzo picked up the heart and held it up to his ear. Somehow, he thought he could detect *multiple* heartbeats. Some were calm and warm, the kind he'd want to listen to when he was falling asleep. Another was charged with energy and light, not frantic, but very much alive and full of adventure. One sounded hollow, like wood, but Enzo had never heard one more comforting.

"Tink," he said, "you always made all the sense in the world to me."

Beside him, Liam scratched his head. He cocked his thumb at Tinker Bell and squinted at Enzo. "You can understand the little fairy bells?"

Enzo nodded. "Every bit."

"What does she tell you?"

"It's not what she tells me, Liam." Enzo tapped the ivory heart and smiled. "It's what *this* tells me." He held it up to his other ear. Every pulse harbored a memory. A spirit. Every beat told a story. "I know you're all in there," he whispered.

Enzo took the knife from his pocket and carved. His fingers moved without thought, as simply as though he were tying his shoes. The material buzzed gently in his fingers, and the blade plunged into it as easily as though it were pizza dough.

He carved until his knuckles went a little sore, and the events of the past year seeped into Enzo's muscles. It wasn't a burdensome pain that weakened him, but a gentle pain that reminded him he was still alive. That he had fought up to the last possible minute. That he had people worth fighting for. His body would remember everything he went through to bring them back. As Enzo thought about that, a tear slid down his cheek and splattered the ivory, which started to take a curious shape.

He carved until rays of sunlight burst from the valves, warming his hands like a cup of tea. *Enzo*, the light whispered. *It's going to be okay.*

The light spilled from the heart like water, and then it filled the air, washing away the walls, floor, and ceiling of the Citadel until Enzo sat in a sea of liquid gold and swirling lights. There were eight tiny balls of luminescence circling him—each a different size and color—before they all zipped away in different directions and left Enzo on his own.

Though his hands were still moving, Enzo had the strange urge to shut his eyes and sleep. Perhaps the warmth relaxed him. Maybe it was the pent-up fatigue and the fact that he hadn't sat down in what seemed like ages. Maybe in a strange way, he felt a glimmer of peace that he couldn't explain.

Enzo turned his head, and in the midst of all the light, he made out a single figure staring back at him with kind brown eyes. Her red hair flowed down to her shoulders like honey, and she wore a white dress that nearly blinded him. Once upon a time, Enzo would have been terrified to look at her directly. But as she stepped toward him with the grace of a swan, he couldn't look away.

"Enzo," the woman said, her voice barely above a whisper. "You wonderful boy. Or perhaps I should call you a *young man*. How the fountain of youth moves so much more like a river these days. And in you, Enzo, the rivers are mighty."

Enzo blinked, resisting the urge to scoot away from her. *"Avoria?"* he whispered.

Avoria laughed, a warm, welcoming sound Enzo never expected to come from her body. "I am the soul of Avoria as she was meant to exist—as I *did* exist before everything went wrong. It takes the heart of a child to believe in impossible things and fantastic worlds beyond the forest of your own mind. In that respect, you've grown a little younger since you left home. But it takes the courage of a man to step outside his door and fight the darkness once the child sees the light. In that way, you've become a paragon of men. You are no puppet, Enzo. You are as real as they come. You are an *event*, always in motion." She sighed. "On some level, I was always there, buried deep within all those layers of darkness Master Cherry put there, trying to claw my way back to light. And it broke my heart to be at war with a soul like you. I can only be grateful now that you've set me free to go somewhere beyond, somewhere the shadows cannot touch me. As for Florindale, and your world? I can only hope the light stays."

"The light?"

Avoria put her hand over her chest and concentrated for a second. After a few seconds, she nodded. "Yes. To recognize and share the light is the most basic power of a Carver and his vision, or a girl who moves unseen to find her mother, or a boy who only wants to fly like a hummingbird. You, Enzo, set free the light so many other people simply tried to snuff out of me so many years ago. And with it, you freed the light of our worlds. In a short moment, I will leave you, and that light should restore *most* of this world back to the state in which it was meant to be. That is not to say that you won't have some work to do, some wounds to bind. But you are a Carver. The past is in your carvings. The future is in your hands."

Tinker Bell flitted back to Enzo and rested on his shoulder.

He swallowed a knot in his throat. "And my friends? What will happen to them? The ones who were lost?"

"They'll be with you, Son of Pinocchio. Everywhere you go from this day forward, the Order of the Bell—not to mention, your *loved ones*—will be with you in every breath you take, in this world or the next or the one between."

Enzo took a strobe-like breath, his respiration interrupted by a silent sob he couldn't control. A tear came out of his eye. *They really aren't coming back. I was so sure.* He forced a half-smile. "Yeah. I know," he said glumly. He tapped his chest with the tip of his thumb. "They'll be right here, huh? That's what you mean."

"That does hold true." Avoria clasped her hands together. "Finish the fight, Enzo. Whenever you're ready, there's only one thing left to do."

Tinker Bell hopped off Enzo's shoulder and showered the room with dust, blanketing everything in sight. And with a final smile, Avoria disappeared for the last time.

CHAPTER
FORTY-ONE

NEW YORK CITY

When the dust cleared away, Enzo stood in the middle of the New York streets, hoping all would be restored to normal. He wanted the frantic foot traffic, the taxis, the coffee stands and pizza parlors. He wanted his family, Rosana, and the Volos beside him.

But Enzo's gaze went immediately to the Citadel, still looming in front of him and shrouded in shadow and ice. Bits and pieces had broken off from odd corners and left plumes of smoke in their absence. The ground around it had cleared—not one dark hooded figure or evil shadow was to be seen—but his friends and family were nowhere to be found either. Enzo turned in a full circle. He might as well have been the last person on the planet. Even the wind had abandoned him, along with all the sensation in his body. Despite his injuries, there was no pain. Despite the snow all around him, he wasn't cold. *It's just me and the Citadel now.*

Enzo thought of Avoria's words. *That is not to say that you won't have some work to do, some wounds to bind. But you are a Carver. The past is in your carvings. The future is in your hands.*

I know how to get everyone back.

With all the remaining strength in his body, Enzo trudged through the snow and made his way to the broken castle in front of him. As he moved past the iron gates, he cut through the bars as though they were butter. When he reached the spot where Geppetto took his final breath, Enzo planted his feet and stared up at the top of the building. *My world can't exist while this thing's still here. I'll bring it down on top of me if I have to.*

He sank to his knees and let the knife hover over the ground.

"The world I know is made of beautiful things," he said, fully aware nobody would ever hear him. "Pietro taught me that it's full of light and adventure, that it's meant to be enjoyed at all ages. Liam taught me that it's full of opportunities to be brave, to grow, to find yourself even if you've been lost for a while. Rosana . . . Rosana. More than anybody else, you taught me about magic. You weren't even from Florindale, and you showed me that it's everywhere. It's in the subways, in the stars, in your reflection, and it's . . . it's in the way I feel about you. Mom, Dad, Geppetto . . . you showed me that the world is full of love. I love you guys."

The ground beneath Enzo rumbled a bit, almost as if it had heard him. The world was full of beautiful souls waiting to be set free. The amount of energy it would cost to release it would probably kill him, but Enzo was ready. Dying to save the world would be infinitely better than living in a world where Rosana, Pietro, and Zack didn't exist.

"Guys," Enzo whispered, "this is for you." He raised the knife and brought it down.

After some lurches and rumbles from the ground, a crevasse opened by the tip of the blade and rocketed toward the Citadel, cracking the castle in half and spilling ashy debris around Enzo. As the Citadel began to fall, a weak smile spread across Enzo's face. *I did it,* he thought. *I saved the world.*

Then the street rushed up to meet him.

✳✳✳

"Well, Enzo, here we are. Sure is a beautiful thing, isn't it?"

Enzo blinked.

I'm alive?

The last thing he remembered was being sure he was going to die as the Citadel crumbled in front of him. It had all been so vivid, and yet here he stood on the Empire State Building in a black shirt, faded jeans, and a tattered pair of Converse.

Beside him, Pietro rested his elbows on the rails of the top floor, staring at the New York skyline. It looked almost as Enzo remembered it from his first time visiting—no massive citadels, no dragons—but some of the buildings had the hollow, unfinished look Enzo had seen only moments before. On the other hand, many others looked taller, brighter, and sturdier than Enzo remembered. "Bit nippy, huh?" Pietro pointed into the horizon. A star blazed over the Brooklyn Bridge and faded into the darkness. "There! You gonna make a wish?"

"Pietro?" Enzo asked.

"What? Should we go find your parents? Maybe grab a bite? See if we can find that pretty girl your father modeled his carving after?"

Enzo stood for a moment with his fingers to his temples, turning in a full circle. "Is all of this real? You saw everything that happened, right? I didn't dream all of that?"

Pietro scrunched his eyebrows as if Enzo had asked a difficult math question.

"Pietro?"

Pietro bit his lip and scratched his scalp. "You're asking if I saw the full-on war in the middle of New York and the crazy hooded man possessed by an ivory puppet?" He leaned in and whispered, "Kid, I *lived* that with you. Come on."

Enzo breathed a sigh of relief.

"But, you know, maybe don't ask anybody outside our little circle.

Some people have tiny, fragile little minds, no imagination, and terrible memory. Mention everything we've been through, and it might break them. Also, you might have *Stargle Magazine* all over you again."

Enzo shuddered and then recovered with a smile. "I'm glad you're back, Pietro."

"I'm glad I'm back, too. I missed me." Pietro smirked and threw an arm around Enzo's shoulder. "You too, I suppose."

The two men leaned over the railing, a cool breeze licking at their cheeks. A tapestry of white stars spattered the sky, and another meteor shot over the bridge.

"Do you think everyone else made it out of the Citadel?" Enzo asked. "Jacob and his girlfriend? Madame Esme?"

"I have a pretty good feeling. Esme's a tough lady. I think I only interacted with her once when I was a boy, but I sure would never want to mess with her. It's a dangerous thing, messing with the light. You'd think a scientist of all people would know he'd get burned." Pietro looked up, a meteor's reflection blazing in his eyes. "Nobody ever learns the easy way, do they?"

Enzo considered Pietro's words. What a strange life they had come to live. "Where's everybody else?"

"They're around," Pietro said. "You'll be happy to know Snow's okay. She's with Liam on the ferry to Liberty Island right now. Quasimodo's touring St. Patrick's Cathedral with a handful of others. Wendy and Zack are waiting for us with your parents at Petrelli's. Hope you were serious about that deep-fried gelato pizza."

"You *would* be the one to hold me to that," Enzo chuckled.

"What would you do without me?" Pietro shrugged. "Or how about *her*?" Pietro pointed across the rooftop, and Enzo followed the path of Pietro's finger until it led to a girl who rested her elbows on the balcony rails and stared off into the New York night. She wore a tattered, faded, well-loved crimson hoodie, and she rubbed the sleeves and pulled its drawstrings as though she were breaking it in for the first time.

In an instant, Enzo's heart came unspooled, pounding like a hummingbird's wings. With his eyes misty and bright, he looked back to Pietro. "No way. She's back?"

"Yep. And I think it might be a long time before you decide *not* to believe anything I tell you." With a wink, Pietro swatted Enzo's shoulder and turned to walk away. "Go get her, Kid. I need to find my lady and my moose. I swear that kid gets taller every minute."

Enzo hooked a finger into Pietro's sleeve and tugged. "Wait!"

"What?"

"What's gonna happen now?" Enzo asked. "Where do we go?"

"With our luck, Enzo, I really don't know. You'd think with no evil puppet queens around—for now—we should get to choose." He leaned on the coin-operated binocular station, frosted by cold air, and looked at the sky. "But wherever it is, whatever it's meant to be, I think we're gonna be all right."

Enzo stood still for a minute, hands rooted in his pockets. "My dad can't stay here." He let the realization sink in, a soft pain in his stomach. "And I don't know if I can stay *there*."

Drumming on his thighs, Pietro said, "Looks like you have some choices to make. That's the scariest thing about growing up. You learn as you go though, and you are never alone. You've got plenty of love, Kid. You have a shooting star, a flying man, a loving family, and a girl in a red hood." Pietro smiled. "Gonna go talk to her? I can play wingman again."

"I'd rather you didn't."

Pietro laughed harder than Enzo had heard in a long time. "Go on, then." Only then did Enzo realize Pietro's feet were a few inches off the ground, and his shadow was giving Enzo two thumbs up. "See you at the bottom."

Enzo smoothed a wrinkle in his jeans and made a beeline for the girl in the red hood. As he walked, he wished upon a star.

THE OLD WORLD

Six sat at the table.

Two drank beer, one ate a pie, and one explained the contents of a letter he found pinned to the thickest tree in the Woodlands. He folded up the tattered parchment and tucked it into his vest as he addressed the rest of the group.

"She refused to leave Wonderland to those dark creatures," Liam said. "She went back knowing the mirrors always require a trade. Somebody comes out; somebody goes in. Better her than any of those shadow things."

Zid scratched his head and took a swig of ale. "So she's gone to rebuild the World Between. That may be the last we ever see of Miss Violet."

"Doubtful," Merlin said. "She always finds her way when she wants something. And who's to say she doesn't want a new life entirely? She watched her father succumb to darkness. She grew up in the shadow of a puppet stepmother, and she's clearly exhausted. Wonderland can give her a fresh start, once they've restored proper order."

Mulan fidgeted with a gold bangle she hadn't worn in a while. Her wrists had grown thinner in all of the adventure of the past few years, so the bracelet slipped around until she took it off and set it in front of her. "I guess this means you're in charge of the Order," she said to Merlin. "Yesterday I watched Hook steal a ship and sail away. I didn't have the heart to stop him. And I don't think Jacob intends to stay here."

Merlin chewed on his cheek. "And you?"

"I resign." She bowed. "I will always fight the battles that need to be fought. I will always do the right thing. When I'm needed, I will step up the way my father did. Until then . . . I choose a quiet life."

"So I see." Merlin casually twirled a flame suspended above his palm. "This is the New Age of the Old World."

"Maybe we'll have a period of peace," Zid said. "We've earned that much, right?"

Liam removed the letter from his vest one more time and reread the last few lines.

If only eternal peace existed on either side of our doors. But so long as there is jealousy, anger, and hate, we must always be on guard and be ready to defend our light.

I won't be coming back to Florindale, Liam. After all, my own blindness and ignorance steered us down the path to destruction. I know I'm leaving the world in great hands as long as you live. I won't impose a single decision on you—not even the requirement to maintain the crown—but my one wish is that you will find somebody to document all we have endured and fought for. That your children will walk in brighter light.

As Florindale rebuilds, I will be working on the other side of the mirror to brighten the ruins of Wonderland. It seems a fitting task for me. I don't fully understand my own genes. I'm not even certain Dominick Bellamy was my father. But something in my blood requires me to meddle wherever I go. Maybe I'll finally meddle for a good cause this time.

Finally, don't hide from mirrors, Liam. They mean you no harm, so long as you recognize the man who looks back at you and take care of him every day. I wonder—had Avoria done the same, would I be writing this letter today?

Please give my best to your wife, your people, the Order, and ultimately to the son of Pinocchio. He's carved a much brighter path for us than I ever could have.

May the light be with you,

V

"You know," Snow said, "it sounds rather nice. I think I'd like for us to have a fresh start of our own. Somewhere far from the evil queens and the poisoned apples and mad scientists." She patted her belly. "Somewhere all the future warriors of Florindale can be safe."

Liam eyed his wife's satin-gloved hands resting lovingly on her tummy with her fingers tapping a delicate rhythm, and tears sprang to his eyes. He scooted in and put his palm over her hand.

"How long have you known?" he choked.

"Not long," Snow whispered. "I think it's going to be a boy, though."

Mulan did something Liam had never seen from his old master before. She clapped her hands together and let out a sound between a cry and a laugh, eyes wide with joy.

"Stars." Liam rubbed his face.

Snow squeezed his hand. "I'd like to name him Enzo. If you don't mind."

Garon raised his goblet. "Ho ho! Excellent!"

"That's going to be a fiercely popular name in this age," Merlin chimed in, chin resting on his fist. "My warmest congratulations."

"Enzo." Smiling through his tears, Liam sniffled and then planted a kiss on his wife's cheek. "Yes. We'll go wherever you want to go! You say the word. I'm with you to the very end."

"But the crown!" Zid pointed out. "Who would rule if you left?"

Snow White laced her fingers into Liam's and squeezed. "I'm sure we could think of a few deserving people."

FLORINDALE SQUARE – ONE YEAR LATER

The owner of the new bakery in Florindale Square gave his shop a simple name: Hansel and Gretel. The siblings weren't alone, however. Hansel managed most of the business. Gretel managed most of the baking. But Benjamin Baker graced them with his presence every now and then, concocting his impossible muffins and inventing new types of tarts. As for Tahlia, she didn't work for Hansel, but she supported him unwaveringly and proved to be an amazing networker, garnering over two hundred visitors on the day the shop opened. Hansel also managed to convince Nibs to stay and work with them as well, while the rest of the Lost Boys headed straight back to Neverland in the hopes that they would find it whole again. Hansel didn't hear their conversation with Pietro before they took off. He only saw their interaction through the window. There had been tears and a small tantrum from one of the boys, but after Pietro took a knee and held the kid's hand for a while, they exchanged a solid embrace, and the kids took to the skies shortly thereafter.

Nobody saw much of Peter and his family, or Enzo and his parents, or even Liam and Snow, for that matter. They all popped into Florindale Square once in a blue moon, but they never stayed long.

Alice, on the other hand, had been a complete mystery until the day Hansel opened his shop, when she strolled in and asked for one of everything. She stayed for hours that day, but she only ate one of her gingerbread cookies. The rest, she explained, were for her daughter.

"How is she?" Hansel asked.

"She's well," Alice said. "I think it's a little hard for her living a few states away from Enzo and Zack, but they'll be able to see each other more often soon. She'll be getting her license next week, and then they have some road trip planned. Look out New York." She made a playful expression of fright by rounding her eyes and twisting her mouth to the side.

Gretel hopped up onto the table and asked, "Do you think they'll ever come back?"

"They talk about it sometimes. They've all kind of decided they want to finish school first. But they wonder how everybody's doing here. I tell them things I hear sometimes, that Hook sailed far away, Violet disappeared, and things don't really feel the same without Augustine or Geppetto. But they'll be happy to know that life went on. One way or another, it always does." She wrapped a strand of hair around her finger and stared out the window. After a moment, she said, "Is that Liam?"

Hansel followed Alicia's line of sight, where a man and a woman— clad in casual New World jeans and hoodies—pushed a stroller through the square where the bell tower used to stand. The woman bit into a caramel-covered apple on a stick; the man ate what looked like a fried macaroni and cheese triangle. The couple stopped, made eye contact with Hansel, and waved.

They held eye contact for a while, and the sight warmed Hansel from his ears to his toes. *Good for you two*, he thought. *Good for you.* He nodded back at them, smiled at Alicia, and returned to his pastries.

SIX YEARS LATER

The Carver stood by his father, his mother, his wife, and a handful of his closest friends. Enzo's knuckles ached a little—he'd been nurturing the gargoyle with his old paring knife for days now—but the labor was worth it when he climbed Clocher de Pierre to admire the view of Florindale Square.

Pietro squeezed in and threw his arms around Rosana's and Enzo's shoulders. "Would you get a look at that view? Astonishing. Amazing. Awesome. *All* the *A* words. Who would ever question the beauty?"

"Hmm, I dunno, Pops," Zack said. "I think no matter where you are, you have to get out and live a little. Might get a little old staring at the city every single day."

Pietro turned around and waved a palm over his face. "I was talking about *us*. The view of *us*. Attractive. Astounding."

He raised his eyebrow at Wendy, who took a paintbrush to the Florindale mural on the far side of the wall. She smeared it around to put the finishing touches on the trees of the Woodlands.

"*Alluring?*"

"*Annoying*," Wendy answered. "Fly home, lovebird. You have some writing to do."

"I'm almost done," Pietro said. "Although you may have to refresh my memory on some little details, because I want to make sure I get all of this right: the fun, the danger, the love . . . When did you two get married again? Lovebirds?"

Rosana put her hands on her hips, a playful scowl on her face. "Uh, yesterday. You were there, remember?"

"Oh, that's right!" Pieto exclaimed. "And remind me, *who* was the loyal and handsome best man to the royal groom?"

"That'd be me!" Zack raised his hand. "His best friend since birth!"

Pietro frowned.

Enzo laughed until a dull pain radiated in his sides. "We love you, Pietro."

"But not enough to make me your best man. Hmph. Whatev. It's okay, *Your Majesty.*"

"I told you not to call me that," Enzo said. "Speaking of which, did Liam and his family already leave?"

"This morning," Zack confirmed. "But he left you some photos he took at the ceremony, and some he brought of the family. He wants you to go visit them again, and he loves how the tower's coming together."

Alice put down her brush, and she blew on the painting of the Jub-Jub bird. "I think we did a good job with this. Sturdier and taller than ever. Violet would be proud, you know."

Enzo crossed his hands behind his back and walked along the mural, tracing the layout of the Old World with his gaze. He could think of a lot of people who he wished would have seen the world as it existed today . . . as the world would come to exist and change and improve over time. Enzo rubbed his finger over the fallen names etched into a brass plate on the wall. Augustine Rose. Finn and Wayde. Hua Jiahao. Sadly, the list was much longer than any list of casualties should have to be, with several trailing behind Mulan's father, but Enzo hoped their new memorial would be one step in honoring their memory. Pietro's books would be another. Enzo himself had also been working on a series of figurines to place around Clocher de Pierre. They would go in a glass case his mother made, and Rosana had been working diligently on a series of blurbs and images to include in the memorials.

Enzo didn't think it would ever be enough, but it would be a start. And maybe, if he and Rosana played their cards right and the people of the worlds were willing to listen, maybe another memorial wouldn't be required for the rest of his lifetime.

"You look like you could use a wish." Rosana approached Enzo from behind. "I'm gonna head down with my mom and the others and admire the view from below. When we get back home, we'll do a birthday cake?"

Enzo had almost forgotten he would turn twenty-two tomorrow. He moved a strand of hair out of Rosana's face and kissed her. "Sure. I'll be down in a bit, okay? Try not to disappear."

"We'll be around, Kid," Pietro said. "I can still call you that, right? It's not treason or anything?"

With a chuckle, Enzo waved Pietro away. "Go down with your family, Pietro. I'll see you soon."

Instead of flying away like Enzo expected, Pietro pulled Enzo into a tight hug and held it for a minute. The embrace bound Enzo's arms to his sides so he couldn't move them to return the hug. He stood passively with a goofy smile on his face and waited for Pietro to let go.

"I'm so proud of you." When he loosened his grip, Enzo hugged him back. Pietro stepped away and did a pair of finger guns at Enzo. "And we need another road trip soon! You, me, Zack, Rosana, and whoever! You know I've seen all of *this* already"—Pietro waved his hand out between the columns and gestured to the ground below—"but I've still never been to the Wizarding World of Harry Potter. Wendy thinks I'll be disappointed because we've seen—you know—Old World magic already, but I've been dying to try a Butterbeer."

Enzo gripped his old friend's shoulder and nodded. "Another road trip? You're on, Pietro." Leaning forward, Enzo whispered, "Also, tomorrow we're going to vote on putting a Starbucks in Florindale Square. For you."

Pietro beamed and turned on his heel. "All the power you could have, and you put the most important things to a vote." Before he bolted into the air, he pointed at Enzo with both index fingers and said, "Long live The Carver."

One by one, his friends headed back into town until Enzo was left standing with his parents at either side. Without a word, they sat cross-legged on the edge of the tower and stared into the sunset, fingers woven under their chins.

Enzo broke the silence as the sky turned a bright shade of fuchsia. "I wanna show you something." He scooted over and pried a loose brick out of the floor. Up to this point, it had been a secret only between Rosana and himself. The brick slid out with a little work and some help from his knife, revealing a wooden box about two feet long. Enzo dug it out, blew the dust from the edges, and then handed it to his father. "Wanna open it?"

His father scrunched his eyebrows. "It's not a cursed mirror or anything, is it?"

Enzo shook the box. It rattled like a jigsaw puzzle. "Not this one."

His father accepted the pack and slid open the compartment on the side, revealing a collection of figurines in varying conditions. His lips parted in a wide smile. "You told me you'd lost these!"

Enzo picked out the tallest figurine—a wooden rendering of the Empire State Building—and spun it between his fingers. "I had to get them back. Even the ones you made me as a kid. They're too important. These are the people, the places, and the events that will stay with me for the rest of my life. These are my story." He wrapped his arms around his parents. "They're our story. It's because of these figurines that I knew I was never alone."

"When I was little, I had a box like this filled with toys and figures and collectibles. I held onto it like I hold onto my family." His mom took the box in her arms and sifted through the artwork, taking the figurines one at a time and holding them up to the sunset. "I used to invent stories about those toys and take them outside with me to play every day. They meant the world to me. And now you have our story here in this tower. Is this our old house?" She picked up a tiny model of the house they once lived in, right outside Richmond, Virginia.

Enzo nodded. He hoped Jacob and Belladonna were happy there.

Enzo's mom set the box down and sighed. "I've been thinking. There's one name missing from that plaque over there." She pointed to the bronze plate in the wall. "I can't help but think you have a bigger plan to memorialize the eldest Carver of the family?"

A bittersweet feeling welled in Enzo's heart as he remembered Geppetto and everything he stood for. "Well, you know where the gargoyles used to go? There's space to add some figures on this tower. I thought we'd add a statue or two. Would you want to do that, Dad?"

His dad lowered his head and tapped his fingers on his lap. "I think he would appreciate that. He might say he's not worthy of all the space or something goofy, but I think we can be the judge of that." A tear fell out of his eye and onto his sleeve. He brushed his cheeks and smiled at his son. "*Thank you* for bringing us all back together, my boy. It may have been a short time, but it made all the difference." With another glance toward the sunset and the town, he nodded, "I think we did good, son. We did real good."

Enzo leaned back and dug a chunk of wood out of his pocket. He rolled the tiny piece of timber around in his palm and passed it to his dad. "Do you think maybe you can make me another figurine sometime?"

"You want to add another one to that box?" Enzo's father smiled. "After all this time? You're not too old for *stupid toys?*"

"They're more than toys. They're stories. *Our* stories. And I can't wait to see what you come up with next."

"Do you think maybe we should do one together?"

Enzo pulled out his knife and held it up to the sun, tossing rays of beige, scarlet, and splashes of azure on the town below. "Yeah," The Carver said. "Let's make one together."

THE END

ACKNOWLEDGEMENTS

Before I thank any one person, I really need to thank the Twitterverse, because strangely enough, this all started with a hashtag—#PitMad! Where would I be without the goofy little number sign that brought Blaze Publishing and me together? Love you, number sign!

If writing a novel is a roller coaster, then a trilogy is the entire theme park, complete with all the bells and fireworks, the exhilarating highs and exhausting lows, the routine maintenance after dark, the annoying maintenance that shuts down the ride in the middle of the day, and the pizza! It's been the project of a lifetime—certainly not the only or the last of its kind, but one on which I'll look back fondly. I'll remember the encouragement from the Scribophile community, the late nights I followed with early mornings, the laughs, the sweat . . . yes, we do sweat. Writing is P90X for the brain.

Above all, I'll remember all the support I had along the way. I can't say it any better than I've already said in the previous novels, but I do have a few more people to mention:

Katie, Jenna, David, Alexia, and Michael: thank you for what you brought to my author circle—and to my Comicon experiences! Long live the dragons!

Fellow Blazers: it's so fun to stand beside you and learn from you, and occasionally take goofy selfies with you in the rare moments we can get together. I couldn't be more proud of you.

Heather: it's important that you be acknowledged for helping me fit three novels into a schedule that otherwise would not be compatible with my lifestyle. Thank you for not only tolerating and being flexible with this endeavor, but for actively supporting it! Bear Down!

Alas, we've come to the crossroads, and it's every bit as wistful and bittersweet as I imagined. It's time for me to let Enzo, Rosana, Liam, and Pietro wander off the confines of these pages. That's not to say that this is goodbye. As long as there are shooting stars, I'm sure our paths will cross again. Until then, Enzo and his friends will be just fine.

There are so many worlds in my head, and I can't wait to see more of them. But as the first one I visited, Florindale will always remain close to my heart, and I have every intention of returning to see who else—and what else—we might find under the bell tower. I hope you'll come back with me one day. After all, Florindale's a huge place, and there are many stories to be told.

About the Author

When Jacob Devlin was four years old, he would lounge around in Batman pajamas and make semi-autobiographical picture books about an adventurous python named Jake the Snake. Eventually, he traded his favorite blue crayon for a black pen, and he never put it down. When not reading or writing, Jacob loves practicing his Italian, watching stand-up comedy, going deaf at rock concerts, and geeking out at comic book conventions. He does most of these things in southern Arizona.

https://authorjakedevlin.com/

Character Glossary

THE OLD WORLD (FAIRY TALE REALM)

Queen Avoria of Florindale – the once-benevolent queen who went dark after an incident involving a serpent engineered to steal the souls of giants. Avoria is building an empire in the New World to exhume absolute rule, but needs to find eight core souls to complete it. At the start of THE HUMMINGBIRD, she has six souls and an army of five-hundred to protect her from Enzo and the Order.

Violet – the morally gray fairy guardian of the Old World. Trains and recruits the Order of the Bell.

Dr. Victor Frankenstein/Master Cherry – an old friend of Geppetto whose experiments corrupted Queen Avoria. He has since gone into hiding, occasionally stepping out of the shadows to offer aid to the Order.

Geppetto – Crescenzo's grandfather. A gifted Carver who taught Crescenzo to harness his abilities.

Snow White – the seventh of eight core souls Avoria needs to ascend to power.

Prince William Chandler Arrington (Liam) – Snow's husband. Responsible for the murder of King Dominick Bellamy in *The Unseen*. One of Crescenzo's trusted allies.

Hansel – a good-natured commoner who has finally been reunited with his sister Gretel. Seeking redemption after Queen Avoria used him as a pawn in THE CARVER.

Gretel – Hansel's sister. Escaped from Wonderland with Enzo after nearly twenty-five years under Avoria's captivity. Her tears have mysterious properties, such as the ability to make moonflowers grow.

Tahlia Rose – Augustine's granddaughter. Escaped from Wonderland with Enzo.

Garon – leader of the seven miners.

Finn – one of the seven miners. The cleanest of the seven. Murdered at the gallows by Dominick Bellamy.

Jinn – one of the seven miners. The dirtiest of the seven.

Wayde – one of the seven miners. Has a bit of a nervous tic. Accompanied Enzo to the Old World.

Zid – one of the seven miners. Is a known dragon enthusiast.

Chann – one of the seven miners. Food connoisseur.

Bo – one of the seven miners. A bit of a jock; loves physical activity.

Cinderella – a warrior who escaped from Wonderland with Enzo and the group.

Jack Frost – a warrior who escaped from Wonderland with Enzo and the group.

Benjamin Baker – a warrior who escaped from Wonderland with Enzo and the group.

Hua Mulan – Liam's tutor. A fierce warrior who once defied Avoria and survived. Helps train the Order.

Merlin – famed magician of Florindale.

Augustine Rose – resident of the Woodlands. A fierce hunter with an aptitude for guns and bows.

Jacob Isaac Holmes – a cursed man who has taken on a beastly form, granting him brute strength.

James Hook – a known pirate lord with a bit of a temper and a hook for a hand. Sent by Violet to recruit the Lost Boys for the Order.

Quasimodo – the bell ringer. Watches for danger and communicates with Violet to assemble the Order.

THE NEW WORLD (THE WORLD WE KNOW)

Crescenzo DiLegno (Enzo) – 15. The son of Pinocchio and a Carver in training. Recently defeated the King of Hearts and escaped from Wonderland. He has finally been reunited with his parents in Florindale. Intends to save his home from Queen Avoria's reign.

Rosana Trujillo – 15. The daughter of Alice. Grew up in New York City and has finally reunited with her mother. Her red hoodie/cloak renders her invisible when she desires. Currently dating Enzo and training with the Order after their bold escape from Wonderland.

Zack Volo – 15. The son of Peter Pan. Enzo's childhood best friend and neighbor. One of Avoria's core souls. He has accompanied his parents to Neverland and means to help Crescenzo save their home.

Alicia Trujillo (Alice) – Rosana's mother. Former resident of the Old World, but she became jaded by childhood and tired of being misunderstood. One of the eight core souls abducted by Avoria. Training with the Order.

Pino DiLegno (Pinocchio) – Crescenzo's father. Former resident of the Old World, but he had become jaded by childhood and tired of being told what to do. One of the eight core souls abducted by Avoria.

A gifted Carver who is training with the Order.

Pietro Volo (Peter Pan) – Zack's father. Crescenzo's neighbor and mentor. Former resident of the Old

World, but he had become jaded by childhood and tired of not being taken seriously. One of the eight core souls abducted by Avoria. Currently en route to Neverland with Captain Hook.

Wendy Darling-Volo – Zack's mother. Former resident of the Old World, but she decided to accompany

Peter Pan to the New World on a "grand adventure": adulthood. One of the core souls abducted by Avoria. Currently en route to Neverland with Captain Hook.

Carla DiLegno – Crescenzo's mother. The first to be abducted in Avoria's plan to steal the core souls and ascend to power. Currently training with the Order.

Madame Esme – a mysterious fortune-teller in Avoria's captivity.

Made in the USA
Middletown, DE
20 January 2022